Mary L⸺ was born in Belfast and, after forty happy years ⸺ now lives in the north-east of England. She is mai⸺ ith three sons.

Visit M⸺y's website at www.marylarkin.co.uk

Praise for Mary Larkin

PAINFUL DECISIONS

Mary Larkin

SPHERE

First published in Great Britain in 2007 by Sphere
This paperback edition published in 2008 by Sphere

A CIP catalogue record for this book
is available from the British Library.

ISBN 978-0-7515-3986-8

Typeset in Sabon by Palimpsest Book Production Limited,
Grangemouth, Stirlingshire
Printed and bound in Great Britain by
Clays Ltd, St Ives plc

Sphere
An imprint of
Little, Brown Book Group
100 Victoria Embankment
London EC4Y 0DY

An Hachette Livre UK Company
www.hachettelivre.co.uk

www.littlebrown.co.uk

I dedicate this book to my husband, Con, for his constant support.

Acknowledgements

I would like to express my sincere gratitude to my editor, Nancy Webber, for her input and keeping me on the straight and narrow when I was inclined to slip up.

Grateful thanks to my son, Con, who was always at hand to help me with any computer problems.

Author's Note

The geographical areas portrayed in *Painful Decisions* actually exist, and historical events referred to in the course of the story are, to the best of my knowledge, authentic.

However, I wish to emphasise that the story is fictional; all characters are fictitious and any resemblance to real persons, living or dead, is purely coincidental.

1

'You're late!' Cathie Morgan hissed angrily.

Louise McGuigan had passed through the foyer of the Clonard picture house and was walking along the corridor where the queue was forming. They were standing three deep, and before her eyes got accustomed to the dim light she would have passed her two friends without realising if a hand had not reached out and grabbed her arm, pulling her into the queue.

'I know, I know.' Louise leaned close and whispered in her friend's ear. 'Me ma and da were having a bit of a barney again and I didn't want to leave the house until I was sure she was all right.'

Louise never ever said a wrong word regarding her father, but Cathie Morgan had heard it rumoured that in the past he had had a reputation for his violent outbursts. Of course there was an excuse for him. He had been in action at the Somme. Her expression softened somewhat. 'It's just that this crowd isn't going to be very happy at you jumping the queue,' she warned. 'So prepare yourself. Just ignore them and let on you're not wise or something.'

Jean Madden, the third member of the group, giggled and whispered, 'That shouldn't be too hard,' earning herself a baleful look from Louise for her dry wit.

As if on cue murmured grumbles started up behind them. 'Hey, you, there's a queue on, as if you didn't know,' one disgruntled girl complained loudly, and her whine was taken up by some others, making Louise writhe with embarrassment.

'I'll go to the end of the queue, Cathie, and you and Jean can try to keep me a seat between you. OK?'

'Pay no attention to them, Louise. Pretend you don't know who they're talking about,' Cathie advised. 'They'll soon get fed up and find something else to grouse about, so they will.'

Louise shuffled about in discomfort for some moments as the sarky remarks continued to be directed at her. At last she could bear it no longer. 'I can't stand any more of this barracking, Cathie. I think I'd better go to the end of the queue before it gets any worse.'

To their surprise, help was at hand. 'Ach, leave the wee girl alone, for heaven's sake.' The words came from a lad who lived in the same street as Louise. Conor O'Rourke had a soft spot for Louise McGuigan, although he kept it well hidden. Now he defended her gallantly. 'After all, it's only one seat,' he said reasonably.

'As long as you're willing to stand if there's a shortage,' someone further back retorted.

Raising his head Conor peered over the heads of the others and eyed the offender, a pert-faced brunette. 'If you don't get a seat, love, and I do, I promise you can have mine.'

'Huh! Chance would be a fine thing.'

'You mark my words.' Conor licked his finger and stroked the air. 'I'm a man of my word, so I am.'

Liking what she saw, the brunette laughed and retorted, 'I'll hold you to it, mind. Who knows, I might even consent to sitting on your knee.'

A delighted grin spread across Conor's face and he laughed gleefully. 'You're welcome to do that if you've a mind to.'

The good-hearted banter eased the built-up tension and subdued the others somewhat, and the loud grumbling faded away into more hushed individual private conversations. Louise smiled and catching Conor's eye gratefully mouthed 'Thank you' at him for coming to her rescue. He held her eye and gave her a broad smile in return. Hot colour suffused her face and a warm feeling filled her body. Out of the corner of her eye she saw Cathie give Jean a knowing nudge and was annoyed at herself for blushing. They would have some fun teasing her later.

'Oh, stop it,' she muttered.

'Stop what?' Cathie was all wide-eyed innocence.

The crowd from the matinee started to file out and a woman who had been scanning the faces in the queue as she passed by stopped beside Louise and took hold of her arm. 'I've been looking out for you, young lady, so I have. You're Johnnie McGuigan's sister, aren't you?'

The woman was vaguely familiar but Louise couldn't put a name to the face. Eyeing her warily, she gave a brief nod of confirmation.

'Can I have a word . . . in private?'

The queue started to shuffle slowly towards the ticket kiosk and Louise shook her head. 'I can't stop now. We're getting in and I don't want to lose my place in the queue.' She tried in vain to shrug herself free from the woman's strong grasp.

Sadie Gilmore's grip tightened like a vice on her arm. She had no intention of letting go. 'This won't take a minute,' she assured her, and tugged at her arm until, with an annoyed tut-tut, Louise shoved her ticket money into a bemused Cathie's hand and allowed herself to be edged out to the foyer.

Thrusting her face close to the mystified girl, Sadie whispered, 'Tell your brother that my Mary has a bun in the oven, and I want to know what he intends doing about it. Will you do that for me?'

Louise knew now who the woman was. She was the mother of Mary Gilmore, Johnnie's ex-girlfriend. She shuffled with embarrassment as the implication of the words sank in and nodded wordlessly. Imagine sending a message like that through her. How could she say a thing like that to her brother? Why hadn't this woman confronted Johnnie himself?

Sadie Gilmore watched Louise closely and, as if reading her thoughts, said, 'In case you're wondering why I'm asking you to relay my message . . . it's because he's avoiding me, so he is, and my Mary's crying her eyes out every night. Tell him if he doesn't come and see me . . . I'll land round at your parents' house. I mean that, so don't you forget to tell him.'

Cathie's voice reached them in a plaintive wail. 'Come on, Louise! Get a move on, for heaven's sake. I've got your ticket.'

Pulling her arm free, Louise hurried to join her friends. Sadie's voice followed her, loud and clear. 'Remember what will happen if you don't tell him.'

An angry toss of the head was all the answer Louise deigned to give her.

Jean, the quiet one, was nevertheless intrigued enough to ask, 'Who was that?'

'I'm not sure,' Louise lied. 'But she asked me to pass on a message to our Johnnie.'

4

Guessing that Louise was being evasive Jean mused, 'She's a tough-looking auld biddy, that one. I wouldn't want to trample on her toes if I could help it.'

'Me neither,' Louise agreed and changed the subject. 'Let's make sure we get a good seat.' Pushing all thoughts of the plight of Mary Gilmore from her mind, she gripped Jean's arm and followed an impatient Cathie into the cinema just as the lights dimmed.

'See what happens when you dally? We can't see a bloomin' thing. We'll be lucky if we find three seats together now,' Cathie grumbled.

Determined not to let Sadie Gilmore spoil her evening out, Louise blanked the threat from her mind, and as her eyes adjusted to the dim lighting she concentrated on her quest to find three empty seats. After all, it was Johnnie's concern, not hers. He was the one who would have to face their da's wrath. Louise shivered at the very thought of what that might involve.

In the near darkness they groped their way to the front of the stalls, which was a glorified name for the rear section of the Clonard picture house. In reality it was just a short distance back from the pit, from which it was separated by a wide aisle and a waist-high wooden partition running across the width of the seating area, and then a single step up to the stalls. Still, having upholstered seats all over, even in the pit, the Clonard was more comfortable and therefore more popular than the Diamond and Arcadian picture houses, whose seating arrangements consisted of long wooden benches in the pit and a small balcony with cushioned seats.

Spying three empty seats together in the centre section, Louise urged her friends, 'Up this row. Quickly, before someone gets in from the other end.'

At last they were seated, chatting idly and, with eyes

now accustomed to the gloom, covertly viewing the local talent until the lights dimmed further and the curtains parted; the musical accompaniment started and there was the usual derisive cheer from the patrons. In spite of herself, during the film Louise found uninvited thoughts of her brother drifting in and out of her mind. Her da would do his nut when he heard that Johnnie had got a girl in trouble. The shame of it would send Tommy McGuigan berserk. As for her ma, she would be heartbroken. She doted on her elder son. Although she was blind to them, he had his faults, just like any other young man of his age, but she thought he could do no wrong.

So did her da for that matter, ever since that night nearly three years ago when Johnnie had just turned sixteen and their da had returned from the pub, drunk as usual. In a rage because his wife hadn't waited up for him, he had swiped all her cherished ornaments off the mantelpiece, breaking two china figurines, her most precious possessions, in the process. Awakened by the crash, Johnnie had bounded from his bedroom and taken the stairs into the hall in two leaps, followed by a worried Louise and their younger brother Harry and sister Peggy. A quick glance round the room took in the wanton destruction. Grabbing his father by the neck, Johnnie had dragged him bodily across the kitchen and thrust him up against the wall. 'There'll be no more of this bloody nonsense in our house! Do you hear me? And if you touch me ma ever again I'll give you such a hiding you won't be able to show your face outside for a week.' He shook the bewildered man roughly. 'Do you understand what I'm saying?'

Louise and Harry stood open-mouthed in awe at the bravery of their big brother and young Peggy started to weep fretfully. This was the first time anybody had dared

6

stand up to their father. They were all frightened stiff of him. They waited with bated breath to see how he would react, expecting the worst.

Tommy McGuigan had looked blearily through a drunken haze at his elder son. 'Huh! You and what army?' Amazed at Johnnie's audacity, he lifted a fist in retaliation. Then, feeling the strength of the arms that had him practically lifted off the floor and pinned against the wall, he had second thoughts. 'All right! All right. Simmer down. No need to get the hump up.'

Johnnie's grip on him slackened, and he pushed him roughly aside. 'What are you talking about, anyway?' his father demanded. 'Your ma's not even here. I haven't laid as much as a finger on her, so I haven't.'

'No, but that would have been your next move, wouldn't it? Remember . . . I'm not a kid any more, Da. I know you and your auld tricks. You touch me ma ever again and you'll answer to me.' Turning to leave the kitchen, followed by his bemused sisters and brother, Johnnie gestured at the broken ornaments on the floor and threw over his shoulder, 'Give the pub and horses a miss for a while and buy her some new ones. You can afford it.' It disgusted him that his father, who had come back from the Somme with a medal for gallantry, and whose job in the tram depot had been held open for him while he was with the army, could gamble and drink away most of his wages each week. Other men would gladly have given their right arms for the opportunity granted to him, and all he could do was waste his money on drink and horses. It infuriated Johnnie that his ma should have to go out to work in the mill, but she had no choice because of the way her husband squandered his wages.

Long after his family had climbed the stairs, Tommy

McGuigan gazed resentfully at the doorway. 'How dare that wee upstart,' he muttered through clenched teeth. 'By God, he'd better watch himself or he'll feel the weight of my hand.' Then a reluctant smile of admiration creased his face. This elder son of his was going to be a chip off the old block. He had to admire him for his gumption. He'd also have to be very careful, in future, how he treated his wife. He was ashamed of himself where Nora was concerned, and he knew that she tolerated his brutality because she blamed it on the awful things he had experienced fighting the Germans on the front line, but deep down in his heart he knew that the Guinness and the Bushmills were the deciding factors.

Awoken by all the commotion, his wife tentatively opened the wee room door, and peered nervously into the kitchen. Seeing her he motioned her to wait. 'Stay where you are. I had an accident. There's broken glass on the floor.' She couldn't believe her eyes when he knelt and started picking up pieces of broken china and placing them on an old newspaper. Wonders would never cease.

After the show in the Clonard the three friends dandered up the Falls Road and stood at the junction where it met Grosvenor Road. Seemingly they were discussing the film but in reality they were eyeing up the lads who passed by before going their separate ways home, Louise up Springfield Road to Springview Street, Cathie and Jean in the opposite direction down Grosvenor Road to Sorella Street where they both lived.

'Don't look now but Conor O'Rourke is coming up the road. Do you know something?' Cathie gave her friend a sly dig in the ribs. 'I think he's got a crush on you, Louise.'

Louise blushed. 'Oh, don't be daft.'

'What do you think, Jean?' Cathie looked at her for confirmation.

'I'd be inclined to agree with you.' Jean raised her voice and hailed Conor. 'Hi there, Conor. Did you enjoy the film?'

Glad of the excuse to stop, Conor grinned at them and nodded. 'I always enjoy a good comedy. He introduced his mate to the girls. 'This is my friend, Joe McAvoy.'

Louise did the honours for the girls. 'You already know my name, Conor, but for Joe's benefit, I'm Louise McGuigan and this is Cathie Morgan and Jean Madden.'

'Pleased to meet you, girls.' Conor gave his friend a nudge.

Obviously embarrassed, Joe muttered, 'Hello, girls.'

'Oh, by the way,' Louise said, 'thanks for standing up for me earlier, Conor. It was very kind of you.'

'It was my pleasure, Louise.'

He smiled into her eyes and Cathie and Jean went into a huddle, giggling hysterically, bringing a questioning lift of the eyebrow from Conor. Embarrassed, Louise made excuses for them. 'Ignore them, they're not right in the head. They're only let out once a week.'

The craic was good. Joe was a little reserved but Louise was surprised at how friendly and outgoing Conor really was. She had always looked on him as being a bit of a snob, if anything. It certainly took him all his time to acknowledge her whenever they chanced to pass in the street. Not that she had expected him to be friendly towards her. Hadn't Mrs O'Rourke made it quite clear to her neighbours and anyone else who would listen that none of the neighbourhood girls would be good enough for her Conor? She had earned herself a reputation as a snotty old bitch and, as a result, was ostracised by some of her neighbours. A clever, studious boy, Conor had won a scholarship to St Malachy's College and she had big plans for him. If he passed his exams this year he would be going to Queen's University to study criminal law. Louise had to admit that the woman was right. With his dark good looks and brains Conor should do well for himself. A common mill girl was unlikely to feature in any of his future plans.

After a lot of happy banter about nothing in particular, Louise remembered the message she had to deliver to her brother and sighed inwardly at the task ahead of her. If she hurried home now she might just catch Johnnie when he came in from his night out.

'Oh, look, it's getting on. I'll have to run. I'll see you two girls tomorrow.' She smiled at Joe. 'It was nice meeting you, Joe. See you around. And I bid you all good night.'

'I'll walk up the road with you, Louise, since we live in the same street.' Conor's gaze swung between the other two girls. 'Where do you live?' he inquired.

Cathie nodded down the Grosvenor Road. 'Down there. But don't you worry about us. We'll be all right. We'll probably run into you again some time. OK?'

'Joe goes in that direction too.' Conor turned to his friend. 'You'll see the girls get home safely, Joe, won't you?'

Joe looked so embarrassed that Cathie said, 'Never mind, Joe. We don't need an escort. We're big girls, you know. We always see ourselves home and nothing bad has happened to us yet. If you're in a hurry, you go on. Jean and I will dander down at our leisure.'

Put on the spot, and with a baleful glare at his friend, Joe said, 'No, I'll be happy to walk you down the road. I live in McDonald Street. Good night, Louise. See you tomorrow night, Conor.'

Louise and Conor crossed the Falls Road in silence, Louise momentarily oblivious of his presence as she tried to figure out just how she would break the news to her brother. It was all so embarrassing. Anything to do with sex was taboo in their home, but obviously not so outside, as far as her brother was concerned. How else had Mary Gilmore gotten herself in the family way? Was Louise supposed to pretend that she didn't know how that came about? How could her brother have been so bloody stupid!

'A penny for them?'

Louise stopped in her tracks and swung round to face him. 'Oh, Conor, I'm so sorry. I didn't mean to be rude.'

'You've obviously got a lot on your mind . . . was it something that woman said to you when we were in the queue at the pictures?'

Marvelling at his powers of perception, she nodded.

'Want to talk about it?' he invited. 'A problem shared . . . ?'

'No. It's just . . . well, I've been asked to deliver a message to my brother and I don't know quite how to put it to him. To be truthful, I'm annoyed that I was asked to deliver it in the first place. It's really none of my business and it'll be awfully embarrassing for me.'

'Well then, don't. Tell whoever asked you to do their own dirty work.'

She smiled wryly. 'I'm afraid it's not as easy as that.' They continued walking and turned into Springview Street. He lived at the Springfield Road end and she lived at the far end near Waterford Street, so she bade him good night.

'I'll walk you to your door,' he insisted.

'Thanks, but I'd rather you didn't. You see, I hope to catch our Johnnie before he gets into the house. What I have to tell him will' – she grimaced with distaste – 'I

11

imagine come as a big shock, to say the least, and I don't know whether he'll want me ma and da to know anything about it.'

Still trailing along beside her, Conor whistled through his teeth. 'As bad as that, eh?'

She nodded and admitted, with an exaggerated sigh, 'Worse!'

After a final farewell, she made to move off, but his hand on her arm detained her and he said hesitantly, 'Would you fancy going out with me some night?'

Louise was taken by surprise, and her eyes widened slightly. Conor was quick to notice and backed down. 'It's all right. It was just a thought. I shouldn't have been so presumptuous,' he apologised.

'Don't be so touchy. I'd love to go out with you. It's just . . .' She shrugged, and floundered for an excuse. 'It's just that it was a bit of a shock, that's all. When do you want to go out with me, then?' She certainly was surprised, but she was pleased as well. Her haste to catch her brother momentarily forgotten, she waited patiently for his answer.

'How's about Saturday night?'

'At the corner of the street.' She nodded back towards Springfield Road. 'At seven o'clock?'

'That's great!'

'See you then. Good night, Conor.' She grinned broadly at him.

'Good night. And thanks, Louise.' He smiled as he watched her trim figure hurry up the street ahead of him, until he reached his own door. She really was a pretty sight. Roll on Saturday night.

Louise hung about for ten minutes outside the house, but there was no sign of Johnnie. He was cutting it fine.

12

Silly taking chances where the curfew was concerned. It was a way of life now, having to be indoors before half past ten, and many a one had been shot for being on the streets after the witching hour. She gave up her vigil, and was just stepping into the hall when both her brothers turned the corner from Waterford Street.

'Hi, sis. We're all arriving home together for a change,' Harry greeted her.

'I'm not just getting home. You two are taking chances – I'm sure it's after half ten. I've been hanging around here for ages to have a quiet word with our Johnnie.'

'Me?' Johnnie exclaimed, obviously surprised.

'Yes, you.'

Harry lingered and, bestowing a look of annoyance on him, Louise added, 'Alone. If you wouldn't mind.'

'Oh, don't mind me,' Harry said huffily. 'I don't want to hear any of your sordid little secrets.'

Giving his brother a gentle push into the small hall, Johnnie promised, 'I'll tell you all about it later, Harry. Be a good lad and put the teapot on.'

'Hah! I'm sure you will,' Harry grumbled, but went into the house.

When the vestibule door closed on him, Johnnie turned and raised a questioning brow at his sister. 'Well . . . what's the big secret that's kept you hanging about outside to tell me? Wouldn't you have been more comfortable waiting indoors?'

She grimaced and gazed down at her feet. 'It's too embarrassing, so it is.'

Johnnie stood in silence for some moments, a puzzled frown furrowing his brow, and then his eyes widened in astonishment. 'Ah, dear God, Louise, you haven't gone and got yourself in trouble, have you?'

She looked at him in bewilderment before the penny

13

dropped. 'Why, you cheeky bugger. You'd be the last person I'd confide in if I were in *that* sort of trouble. You, who can't even look after yourself,' she said accusingly.

'And just what's that supposed to mean?'

'I'll tell you what it means,' she said aggressively, but suddenly found herself swamped with embarrassment and paused to find the right words.

Completely bemused by his sister's attitude, Johnnie growled, 'For heaven's sake, if you've got something to say, get on with it! It's cold standing out here, in case you haven't noticed.'

Really peeved now, Louise didn't bother trying to soften the blow. Thrusting her face towards his, she ground out, 'Mary Gilmore has a bun in the oven, so she has. What are you going to do about it?' It sounded so crude coming from her lips that she grimaced.

She could see that her brother was shocked to the core. 'Mary? Did she tell you that?'

'No, but her mother did. And she says to tell you that if you don't come to see her soon, she'll come round here and have a word with Ma and Da. So there!' She brushed roughly past him to reach the door. 'Believe me, I wouldn't want to be in your shoes if she sticks to her promise. She's a right auld battleaxe, that one.'

A motion of his hand stayed her. 'Hold on a minute. When did all this happen?'

'Tonight. When I was queueing up to get into the Clonard, she was coming out of the first house and collared me.'

'What? Did she just say it . . . you know . . . out in front of everybody?'

'No. She had the decency to take me to one side.' She gave a slight laugh at the memory. 'Manhandled would be a better word for it. Not that I thought so at the time,

14

mind you. In fact I thought she had a cheek hustling me out of the queue to tell me your sordid secrets. I can tell you, I was mortified. She said you were avoiding her.'

'I didn't even know Mary was expecting, that's the God's honest truth, Louise, so why would I avoid her? Eh?'

'How would I know? Furthermore, I don't want to know anything more about it. Tell Mrs Gilmore your excuses and see how she takes it. Just leave me out of it.'

She pushed open the vestibule door but he pulled it shut again. 'Don't you breathe a word of this in front of me ma and da,' he warned. 'Do you hear me? I'll sort it out in my own way. I don't know what Mrs Gilmore's going on about. It was Mary who finished with me. And that was a good few weeks ago.'

'Huh! I wish I'd never heard tell of it. Me da will be mad. And you won't be the only one to suffer. You know what he's like when he gets started. He'll take it out on all of us so he will,' she said, going into the house.

The McGuigans lived in one of the many rows of terrace houses built at the beginning of the century to encourage people disillusioned with working on the land, and lured by the promises of good wages and housing to seek work in the mills that were sprouting up all over Belfast. A kitchen, a small back room and a tiny scullery made up the lower floor, with two bedrooms upstairs. They considered themselves lucky to have an outside lavatory of their own. In other streets some families had to share.

Their parents slept in the small back room off the kitchen and Louise and her younger sister Peggy shared the front room upstairs. The two boys shared the rear bedroom, overlooking the back yard. Louise crossed the

15

linoleum-covered kitchen floor to say good night to her mother.

'Your ma's asleep,' her father, dozing in the armchair by the dying embers in the grate, roused himself enough to say.

Slanting her eyes at him suspiciously, Louise said, 'I'll just check for myself, if you don't mind.'

There was no answer to her tap on the door.

Her da was now upright in his chair, craning forward. 'See? I told you she was asleep. You'd better not wake her, girl, or you know what you'll get.'

His insistence started warning bells ringing in Louise's head. Hadn't she been loath to leave her mother earlier this evening? Hadn't she sensed that her da was after money for booze? Money her mother couldn't afford to give him. Still, he'd got it from somewhere, because he was obviously under the influence now. Had he used physical force on her mother to get the cash from her?

Without more ado she opened the door and went into the small room. A double bed took up almost the entire space, with just enough room along one side for a small chest of drawers and a bedside table. A hand signalled in agitation from the bed, indicating that she should close the door. More worried now, Louise left the door open just enough to let some light from the gas mantle filter through from the kitchen, and approached the shrouded form on the bed.

'Ma, are you all right?' She reached for the box of matches to light the candle on the bedside table.

'Yes, I'm all right. Don't you dare waste that candle, girl. Do you think we're made of money? Get yourself upstairs to bed and let me get some sleep.'

Louise peered closer, but in the dim light she could see nothing untoward. A pale face gazed defiantly back

16

at her, leading her to believe her mother had something to hide.

'Ma . . .'

Nora McGuigan gripped her daughter's hand and, pulling her closer, whispered grimly, 'Mind your own business. Do you hear me?'

Really concerned now, Louise whispered back, 'Did he hit you? Tell me, Ma, did me da hurt you?'

'No, he didn't! Listen, Louise, I don't want any bother. Tell Johnnie I'm all right. Please, love, go on up to bed.'

In two minds about what to do, Louise dithered.

Glad of the reprieve, Nora whispered, 'Please, love, bear with me. We'll talk about it in the morning.'

'Promise?'

'I promise.'

Louise had to be satisfied with this answer. Kissing her mother softly on the cheek she whispered, 'Good night, Ma. God bless. See you in the morning.'

Johnnie was waiting in the kitchen doorway, alert and watchful. 'Is me ma all right then?' he asked as his sister silently made to move past him into the hall to go upstairs. He blocked her way. 'Well, is she?'

With a baleful glance in the direction of her father, who was straining forward to try to catch what was being said, she kept her voice low, and confessed, 'I'm not sure, but she doesn't want any bother. We'll just have to wait and see what she's like in the morning. OK?'

Johnnie's lips tightened into a thin straight line but he reluctantly agreed. 'Whatever you say.'

Harry came from the scullery and placed a mug of tea on the table close to his father's chair. 'There you are, Da. Maybe that'll sober you up a bit.'

'I'm not drunk,' he growled.

'Of course you're not. Just a wee bit tipsy, eh?' Harry

17

said derisively and turned to his sister. 'Would you like a cup, sis?'

'No, thanks. I'm off to bed now.'

'What about me ma? Do you think she'd like one?'

'She's almost asleep and doesn't want to be disturbed.'

'Well then, good night.'

'Good night, everybody.' Louise brushed past Johnnie and slowly climbed the stairs. She quietly opened the front bedroom door and tiptoed stealthily into the room, careful not to waken Peggy who appeared to be in a good, sound sleep. Louise wished she was more like her. Most nights Peggy would be asleep practically before her head hit the pillow. As she undressed in the gloom and slid into bed beside the slight form of her sister, Louise knew there would be little sleep for her this night. Too many disturbing thoughts were already invading her mind. Pulling the patchwork quilt up to her chin she silently recited her night prayers, at last falling asleep with thoughts of Conor O'Rourke foremost in her mind.

Next morning as Louise had a quick wash at the big brown sink in the scullery she heard the rumble of her father's voice in the room next door and the sound of her mother's quiet reply. She couldn't hear what was being said but imagined her father was warning her mother to keep her mouth shut regarding the previous night.

A little later, her mother joined her in the scullery to stir the porridge she had risen earlier to prepare and left to simmer on a low light on the stove. Louise studied her covertly; no sign of any bruising. Just dark shadows under her eyes through lack of sleep. With a defiant look Nora McGuigan once again held her face up for her daughter's scrutiny.

'Go on! Take a good look.'

18

Distressed, Louise examined her mother, looking for signs of physical violence, her eyes taking in the fact that her mother had her neck covered. Pulling down the high collar to show an unmarked neck, Nora taunted, 'Well? Are you satisfied, or would you like me to strip off? I told you I was all right, didn't I? I wish you'd leave well enough alone.'

Chancing her arm, Louise retorted, 'Then why was me da warning you to keep your mouth shut, just now?' She could tell by the look of alarm that flared briefly in her mother's eyes that she had hit the nail on the head.

Immediately Nora was on the defensive. 'You mind your own business. You hear me? I don't want any interference from you or your brothers. I can fight my own battles, so I can.'

As she turned away Louise gripped her arm to detain her and Nora could not suppress a sharp intake of breath between her compressed lips.

Gentle now, Louise rolled up her mother's sleeve. The exposed vivid purple bruising brought tears to her eyes. 'Ah, Ma. Why does he do this to you? Has he no conscience at all? Why don't you throw him out of the house? We'll all stand by you, you know.'

Pulling free from her daughter's painful grip, Nora hurriedly tugged the sleeve down and explained, 'You've got to understand. It was the war that changed him. He came back from the Somme a different man, but he did come back, thank God. And for that we must be grateful. Thousands didn't make it home at all.'

'For heaven's sake, Ma, catch yourself on! It's years since he came back from the front. He's not trying to get over it. He's playing on your sympathy, so he is, only you can't see it. He's just a selfish auld bugger who won't face up to life and blames you for all his troubles.'

19

'And why not? I'm his wife, after all. And we made a solemn vow in front of God, for better or worse, in case you didn't know.'

'Ma!' Louise was aghast. 'How can you stand there and say that? You may be his wife but you're not his slave! Or punchbag. Or chopping block, and don't you forget it. If our Johnnie knew . . .'

'You leave our Johnnie out of this. Do you hear me? I'm not like you. I can understand what drives your da to it. You don't know the nightmares he still has about that terrible war. The awful time he spent in the trenches, ankle deep in mud, and the bodies of his dead comrades lying all around him. And you're wrong, he might never get over the horror of it. I don't think anyone who was out there ever would. He deserves our sympathy, so he does, not our contempt.'

Louise had heard her father cry out in fear many a time during the night as the demons got hold of him, but she blamed the drink for keeping those memories alive. 'Ma, I know all that, but it's the drink that keeps it going. I bet you it's pink elephants he sees in his nightmares now. If our Johnnie knew he still tortures you there would be wigs on the green and me da would really have something to give him bad dreams.'

'God forbid that Johnnie should ever find out. Murder would surely be done.' Nora was unable to hide the pride she felt in her elder son. She gripped her daughter's arm. 'And what good would that do? Eh? Johnnie must never know. Promise me you won't tell him. Now that he's doing so well in McFadden's shop, I don't want to spoil things for him. Mr McFadden's not a young man any more. With a bit of luck he'll retire soon, and with him having no sons and Hannah being a bit backward like she is, he just might leave

Johnnie in charge of the business. Maybe even, in time, offer him a partnership.'

Louise felt like weeping. She thought of the bombshell about to be dropped when Johnnie confessed that he had to marry Mary Gilmore. What else could he do? Still, that was Johnnie's problem and surely Mr McFadden wouldn't hold it against him? Meanwhile, her da shouldn't get away scot free with hurting her ma. 'Me da's a sly auld git, so he is, marking you where it won't show,' she said bitterly.

'Please, Louise, let it go.' Unwittingly, Nora expelled a long sigh of defeat.

Louise was quick to notice and wailed, 'Oh, Ma. I don't know what to do for the best. He can't keep on beating you and getting away with it. He just can't. It's not fair! I can't just stand by and do nothing about it. You've enough to put up with. He deserves a good hiding himself and maybe then he'll know what it feels like. It might just bring him to his senses to get a dose of his own medicine for a change. It would certainly make him think twice before lifting his hand to you again.'

Losing patience, her mother whispered furiously, 'It's none of your business, so keep your nose out of my affairs. I'll handle it in my own way, so I will.'

Lips trembling, Louise watched her mother tidy the plait she wound round her head to keep the hair back off her face. Nora had beautiful hair, pale ash blonde with a natural curl, but her children rarely saw it loose. Her husband never took her out anywhere. Finished at the small mirror on the wall near the door, Nora tied the belt containing the necessary tools for spinning securely round her slim waist, grabbed her shawl and made to leave the house. Louise cried in alarm, 'Ma, have you had any breakfast yet?'

'I had a little porridge earlier on,' Nora lied. 'I don't

want anything else, thank you.' And without more ado she hurried out of the door.

Louise was annoyed with herself. All she had achieved was to make her mother go to work on an empty stomach. 'Poor Ma. Poor, poor Ma,' she wailed. Was there no end to Nora's troubles?

Tommy McGuigan was on shift work and this week he was on from two to ten. In these circumstances he usually slept late and Louise was surprised when she left the scullery to see him up so early. From his seat by the fireside he watched covertly as Louise ate a bowl of porridge. Had Nora told her daughter anything, he wondered?

Aware of his sly glances, Louise cried, 'Me ma's away to work without any breakfast, thanks to you.'

'Thanks to me?' he growled low in his throat, his face a picture of mock innocence. 'What have I done now?'

Nodding her head in frustration, Louise insisted, 'Yes! You're the cause of it. She's afraid of me telling our Johnnie that you're still hurting her, and that's what drove her out of the house without any breakfast.'

With a furtive look towards the ceiling in case his sons heard them in their bedroom, Tommy muttered fiercely, 'Keep your voice down, girl. What makes you think I hurt your mother? What's she been saying?'

'Not a lot. More fool her. She should bring it all out into the open. And I don't *think* you hurt her. I *know*! I saw the state of her arms. She must be in agony. How she'll be able to do any work, especially on an empty stomach, God only knows. She has a terrible day ahead of her, so she has. Not that you care a damn. So long as nobody finds out what a cruel auld bugger you are, you'll keep on taking your rotten temper out on her.'

Hearing movement upstairs and knowing Johnnie

would be the next one down, Tommy leaned closer and said threateningly, 'You watch your language, girl. And don't you dare say one word, or so help me I'll make sure you suffer for it.'

'Huh! I should worry? Don't you kid yourself, I'm different from me ma. I might wear a skirt but I'm not afraid of you.'

'Just you watch your tongue. Your mother won't thank you for interfering.' His face was twisted in anger. The vestibule door opened and at once her father's face took on an amazing transformation. It was immediately wreathed in smiles as if he had just shared a joke with his daughter. 'Good morning, Johnnie. Sleep well, son?'

Johnnie looked from one to the other, saw his sister's tight-lipped angry expression and his father's affable smile, and was at once suspicious. 'What's going on?' His glance took in the empty scullery. 'Where's Ma?'

'She had to go in to work early today.'

Tommy held his daughter's eye, daring her to contradict him. When she remained silent, Johnnie went into the scullery and helped himself to some porridge.

His father's voice followed him. 'Is that Harry fella up yet?'

'It's a bit early for him, Da. Now that he's starting in Kennedy's next week he may as well take a lie-in while he can.'

'How he ever managed to get started in Kennedy's bakery, I'll never know.'

'Because he's no dozer, that's how! You sicken me, Da. You know that? You've no confidence in any of us. You'd think we're a bunch of halfwits the way you go on.'

Not to be silenced, Tommy turned his attention on his younger daughter. 'What about Peggy? Eh? Can't you get her started in the mill, Louise?'

'There's no jobs going at the minute. Besides, Peggy's too delicate to work in the mill. She wouldn't last a week.'

'Too delicate? Is she now? And what other work do you think she's likely to get? She's not exactly the brightest spark in this family,' Tommy growled.

'Give her a chance. She's just left school, for heaven's sake.'

'The sooner she earns some money the better.'

Louise rose to her feet. Leaning over, she planted her hands flat on the table near her father and glared across at him. 'Better for who . . . you? So that you can get more money from me poor ma to gamble and drink away? You'd be the only one better off,' she cried derisively.

Rising threateningly to his feet, Tommy towered over her. 'I'm warning you, girl. You'd better watch that tongue of yours, or it'll be the death of you.'

Louise opened her mouth to retaliate but a slight shake of the head from Johnnie in the background caused her to close it again. Thinking he had cowed her, Tommy grunted with satisfaction and shuffled his way through the scullery and out to the yard.

Louise rounded furiously on her brother. 'Why did you stop me? Now he thinks I'm afraid of him, too.'

'It's not worth while getting into an argument with him. It doesn't accomplish anything. You know that, Louise. You know he rants on and on until he gets the last word in. Besides, with a bit of luck I'll get Peggy started in the shop. Just at the weekends, mind you, but she'll earn a bit and it'll keep me da off her back. Now that he's out of the way, tell me, is me ma really all right?'

Louise considered her options. Should she tell Johnnie

about her mother's bruises? With a sigh she decided against it. It would cause too much aggravation and her mother would probably suffer all the more because of it.

'I think so.'

'A plain yes or no will do,' he said. 'Was she marked?'

'No.' The lie stuck in her throat and Johnnie straightened warily in his chair. Before he could question her further, she added hastily, 'At least I couldn't see any marks on her face.' That was stretching the truth a bit, she knew, but she didn't know what else to do for the best.

'Well then, let's not jump to conclusions. Let's give me da the benefit of the doubt, eh? It's a long time since he's left any marks on her.'

Thinking of the hidden bruises on her mother's arms, and imagining how she had managed to hoodwink them all with her silence, Louise wondered just how long this torment had been going on, and what else her mother was keeping from them. Here they were all thinking everything in the garden was rosy and all along her da was continuing to brutalise their mother in such a way that no one was any the wiser, as he carefully covered his tracks. Still, if her mother was willing to suffer in silence, who was Louise to blow the whistle?

To lighten the atmosphere she stuck her tongue out in a cheeky manner, and as Johnnie pretended to lunge at her she grabbed her coat and dashed from the house and walked briskly down the street. The mill horn was blaring its early warning to stragglers as she hurried along Springfield Road. She had five minutes to get to the Blackstaff and make a start on her looms in the weaving shop.

* * *

25

Nora trudged slowly up Springfield Road. Having missed out on her breakfast, she was early for a change. Early and hungry and very depressed. The smell of freshly baked bread coming from Hughes's bakery on the opposite side of the road made her mouth water and her belly rumble all the more. It also brought a faint smile to her lips as she thought of her younger son starting work next week in the new bakery that had recently opened over on Beechmount. J. B. Kennedy was extending his empire and some time ago had purchased the land that had at one time been used as playing fields. The new bakery that duly arose on the green site would bring much needed jobs to the district. Harry had successfully sailed through his interview and was required to start work there next Monday. His job would be attending the horses that pulled the bread carts around the town. He loved horses. Although born and reared in the city he had no fear whatsoever of animals and was excited at the prospect of feeding and grooming his charges.

Nora was glad that neither of her sons had to work in the mill and the extra money that would soon be coming in should make a big difference to her financial status. However, she wished her children would keep their noses out of her private affairs at home. Heaven knows she had enough on her plate, without them setting their da off every time they opened their mouths.

In the early years of their marriage, Tommy and she were fortunate enough to get the rented house in Springview Street. Then, when Tommy, through a family friend, had managed to get a job out of the mill and in the tram depot, they had thought they were set for life. What wonderful plans they had made. They were going to save hard for a deposit on a house with a garden for

Johnnie and Louise to play in. To Nora's reckoning, they would need about twenty pounds deposit for the kind of house she aspired to and the rent would be high as well. An awful lot of money, but they were determined to give it their best shot. Two years and two more children later their savings had dwindled and Nora's dreams were put on hold. But Tommy and she were still very much in love and she had high hopes for their future. They would just take a little longer to achieve than she had at first anticipated.

Four children in as many years had taken their toll on Nora and she was exhausted and at her wits' end, staving off Tommy's advances every time he got close to her until he finally accused her of having another man on the sly. Of course this was a lot of nonsense as he well knew. How in God's name would she ever find the time to see anyone, let alone have an affair! Bravely she defied him, vowing that there would be no more children. Four was enough for any woman to rear these days, she told Tommy, adding that at this rate they would never be able to afford a house with a garden.

He disagreed with her, pointing to the many couples who had eight or more children and were able to keep a roof over their heads. Nora was quick to retort, 'And just look at the conditions they're living in. They're existing from one day to the next. Besides, I don't want to keep someone else's roof over my head. They'll never be in a position to buy a house, let alone one with a garden. Some of them can hardly afford to pay the rent, for heaven's sake. I want a house of my own.'

'Garden! Why are you always harping on about gardens? What's wrong with Dunville Park, eh? The kids love playing there with their friends.'

'I want a garden for my kids to play in safely, and

that's that! And I don't want any more arguments about it.'

And in spite of his pleas, Nora was not to be swayed. It was her body, she reminded him. She was the one who carried the babies for nine stressful months and suffered the pains of labour, not he, so there would be no more children.

Unknown to him, she went to see her doctor, who was very understanding. He agreed that four children was plenty to look after, especially in the present climate. She sat in his comfortable surgery and listened intently to his every word as he explained to her how the female hormones worked, and when she was most unlikely to conceive, which he referred to as the safe period. The days when she would be most fertile and lovemaking should be avoided at all costs he called the danger period.

To say that Tommy was angry when she told him that they could only make love at certain times of the month would be the understatement of the year. He was practically foaming at the mouth, and horrified at the very idea of her daring to discuss their marital relations with another man. He had threatened to bring the parish priest round to see her. She stood in the middle of the kitchen, jaw fixed, facing him arms akimbo, and, just as angry as he, retaliated by saying that he could bring the Pope himself if he had a mind to, but it wouldn't make the slightest bit of difference whatsoever. She wouldn't be swayed. Or bullied for that matter.

However, as Nora had well known, Tommy was too proud a man to discuss his private affairs – especially those of a sexual nature – with the parish priest or anyone else. But she might as well have shouted at the wall for all the good her threats had done. He stubbornly declined to wait for those safe days, demanding his conjugal rights as and when he felt like it, and Nora suffered his brutality in silence, afraid the children might hear as she strived to avoid his unwanted attentions. For five long years, she waited in trepidation each month for her period to appear and sighed with relief when each month she was granted a reprieve. Could he possibly be sterile? Their marriage became an unhappy and bitter alliance. Somehow she managed yet another year without conceiving, but not without a fight. There was constant bad feeling and bickering between them, and in frustration Tommy turned to the bottle to console himself.

With the threat of civil war and the news that thousands of UVF men had marched to Balmoral in a show of strength against home rule in Ireland, shock waves were sent through the outnumbered Catholic communities. Rumours of guns being delivered from Dublin to a hall on the Falls Road were rife, and young men were observed marching up and down that thoroughfare each weekend, preparing to defend their districts. Civil war, however, was averted when Britain declared war on Germany and the UVF and Irish volunteers joined up to go to war for their country and fight a common enemy.

Each weekend Tommy trained with the other young men of the district in case of civil war, and when Britain finally declared war on Germany he was one of the first in the district to volunteer to fight for his country, saying he would be better off fighting the bloody Jerries than living in a house without love. Nora, with the children gathered around clinging to her skirt, stood at the Springfield Road junction and watched with other families as the local volunteers climbed on board lorries on the first step of their journey to France. As she proudly waved him off, Nora was also ashamed at how relieved she was at his departure. She did shed a few tears but they were mostly tears of guilt.

With the war, prosperity came to Belfast. Harland & Wolff was working flat out building ships, and the mills and engineering works were fully employed producing linen, ropes, weapons, ammunition and other commodities that were essential to the war effort. Employment and the ability to earn a good living brought hope to those left behind.

As the days passed into weeks and the weeks into months, Nora lived in dread as she watched the red bicycles of the telegram boys come and go, and saw blinds being drawn as wives and mothers received official word that their loved ones had been killed or were missing in action. The grief and sorrow was awful to behold and as she comforted friends and neighbours she was sure her turn wasn't far off. How would she deal with it? She blamed herself that Tommy had rushed to join up. It would be her fault if he died in action. She could only pray that he would be delivered safely back to her, although it didn't look very likely from all she read in the newspapers.

The war raged on relentlessly and when Germany at last was defeated, Tommy was one of the fortunate ones who survived, although not unscathed. He had been away almost three years before he eventually returned home, lame from a shrapnel wound to his leg. Nora thanked God for delivering him back to her and promised all sorts of good deeds in return for His mercy. She had been so proud of her Tommy, showing the medal he had received for bravery to everybody who would stop and listen. She must have bored people out of their minds with her twittering on about his war heroics.

Whilst he was away his wages had arrived regularly each month and her mother looked after the kids while she worked part time as a doffer in the Blackstaff Mill. In her eagerness to do well she happily worked barefoot in appalling conditions and eventually reached the status of spinner, saving all her wages so that when Tommy came home they would have some money put away to start them off on a new life. The future looked bright indeed.

Eventually Tommy arrived back in Belfast. He was a patient in the Royal Victoria Hospital for some weeks having treatment and therapy for his leg wound and Nora visited him daily, until at last he was released and able to return home on crutches. The kids were jubilant and showered him with hugs and kisses to show how much they had missed him. Neighbours popped in all day long to wish him a speedy recovery and it was late that night before husband and wife were alone.

Bursting with pride, Nora showed her husband the savings book indicating how much she had tucked away in the Post Office. The plans she had in mind for their future gushed from her lips until Tommy's silence brought her ramblings to a halt.

'Is something wrong?' she asked apprehensively.

'I'm only home, woman. What makes you think I'm in any condition to start making plans for the future?'

She was immediately contrite. 'Oh! . . . I'm sorry, love. I just got carried away there, but aren't you glad I managed to save so much money?'

'You can't take all the credit. It was me risking my life fighting the bloody Germans that enabled you to save so much,' he reminded her curtly. 'So don't you go claiming all the glory for yourself.'

Feeling deflated when he showed no gratitude or enthusiasm for her endeavours, she retaliated. 'I'm not claiming

31

any glory. But don't you forget either that I also worked damned hard for everything I earned. I scrimped and did without any wee treats all these years to put us in a position to buy a house.' She leaned towards him entreatingly. 'And we can, Tommy, we can buy a house. Johnnie has been promised an apprenticeship in Harland & Wolff when he turns fourteen next year and me ma will look after the others so I'll be able to work full time. This is our chance to do well for the kids. We'll have good money coming in.'

'Is that all you can think of, woman? Money? What about showing me a bit of affection, eh? Haven't you missed me at all?'

She gulped deep in her throat. This was what she dreaded; it was the danger period. Was all her hard work to be in vain because her husband couldn't control himself for a few days? Were all her efforts to be jeopardised? She opened her mouth to tell him it was the wrong time of month, but the look in his eyes stopped her. He held out his hand and slowly she moved towards him. It would be pointless to argue with him now; he wouldn't want to know. Sitting on the settee beside him she let him draw her close. She would just have to take her chances.

As it turned out, she needn't have worried about getting pregnant. Tommy was unable to perform. Of course he blamed her for not jumping on him the minute he got into the house and showing him that she loved him, and how much she had missed him. She wasn't miffed when he left her alone for some time after that; she understood that he was afraid of failing again, putting another dent in his ego.

He wasn't long in finding an outlet for his frustration.

The devil's brew, alcohol! As soon as he was able to hobble about unaided, he was off to the pub every evening. Nora watched helplessly as he went through their savings like a hot knife through butter. Squandered all her hard-earned money in the pub, buying drink for a lot of hanger-ons, with strangers patting him on the back and telling him what a brave fellow he was.

Also, a thing he had never done before, he took to betting on the horses. She hated his selfishness, and in an endeavour to bring him to his senses she threatened to take the children and leave him, but the threats fell on deaf ears. While he was admired by all and sundry for his courage during the war, and for his generosity in the pub, he wallowed in all the new-found glory and refused to listen to Nora's pleas to take things easy and save their money. Everybody thought he was a wonderful man. And why not, since he was standing them all free drinks?

Behind closed doors it was a very different kettle of fish. The kind, caring, generous man she had married who had left to fight in France was no more. In his place was a tyrant who cowed his wife and terrified his children; a man who arrived home from the pub half drunk, demanding his rights, and when she refused would cruelly beat her to show that he meant business and wasn't going to stand any of her old nonsense. Her mother sensed what was going on and urged her to leave him, offering to take her and the children in until she found somewhere else to live, but pride stopped her from letting anybody know just how bad things were at home. She couldn't bear to be pitied, and slowly but surely her love for Tommy died.

Bitterness at Tommy's cruelty and disregard for her feelings kept her from giving in to his sadistic demand to have more children. Because that's all it amounted to: the desire to break her, force her to bow to his will, in fact make her his slave. She was sure that he was contented with his four children but was determined to show her that he was boss in this house and she would do as he bid. But at what cost! She was determined there would be no more children. She had enough on her plate as it was. So although through necessity they shared a bed, they drifted ever further apart.

2

Life dragged on and Nora realised that her ambition of owning a house with a garden, and giving her children a better lifestyle than she had known, was not to be. She devoted all her time to providing as much as she could, while she could, not that that was a great deal. There were several more obstacles to hamper her endeavours. When the war ended in November 1918 animosity between Catholics and Protestants flared up again. During the war those Catholic men who had not enlisted had obtained jobs that they would not have stood a chance of getting beforehand, and they had no intention of giving them up easily just because the war was over. By sweat and toil they had in their own way worked hard to serve the Empire and they meant to stay put.

Since being elected as Britain's Prime Minister in 1916, when Herbert Asquith resigned, David Lloyd George had done a lot to raise the standard of living in Ireland. During the war, wages for manual labour had risen, but now skilled workers were looking for increases to keep the pay differential between them and unskilled workers. When the Engineering & Shipbuilding Trades Federation negotiated a national working week of forty-seven hours, the shipyard workers were incensed. They wanted a forty-four hour week. By an overwhelming majority they voted in favour of an all-out strike and on 25 January 1919 the shipyard workers downed tools. It became known as the 44 Hour Strike. The shipyard men were joined by the gas and electricity workers, and consequently the city was quite literally brought to a standstill. The trams could not run, cinemas were closed and thousands of mill workers were put out of their jobs. The Belfast Ropeworks closed down as did the big engineering works. Those shops that would not close their doors quickly changed their minds when their windows were smashed. The strikers were confident that the authorities would listen to them and they would win a shorter working week.

To add to the misery, by the end of the first week bread – the mainstay of the poorer people – had become very scarce, as flour failed to get through to the bakeries. Nora's family had taken it in turn to queue outside Hughes's Bakery on the off chance the bakery would manage to get some flour, and bread become available.

Then, in spite of fierce opposition from the Ulster Unionist leaders whom the striking workers had voted into power at the last election, British troops were brought in. On 14 February soldiers manned the machinery in the gas works and the electricity station and soon the factories were working again. The trams were set in motion and slowly but surely the city came back to life. The shipyards and engineering works remained idle for a further few days; then, embittered and resentful against the authorities, the men grudgingly returned to work. The strike had been a waste of time and money.

*　　*　　*

The south of Ireland was also having its problems at that time, which certainly didn't make things any easier. The north learned that guerrilla warfare had broken out between the Irish Republican Army and the security forces, and in the early months of 1920 the IRA extended their activities into rural Ulster.

However, it wasn't until July that riots erupted on the Falls Road. On the Twelfth, the day when Orangemen celebrated their victory at the Battle of the Boyne – where the forces of William of Orange defeated James II's army in 1690 – Sir Edward Carson delivered a highly inflammatory speech at Finaghy. In it he expressed his fear that the loyalists of Ulster were in danger from Sinn Fein. He said that, since the government showed no sign of defending them, Protestant men of Ulster must protect their own interests by whatever means they had at their disposal.

On the first full day back after the Twelfth holidays, Protestant workers were called to a meeting at lunchtime. Speakers recalled Carson's advice that loyalists must take action themselves if help from the government wasn't forthcoming. The call to drive out all *disloyal* workers was supported with great enthusiasm. After the meeting Catholic workers were attacked and driven out of the Harland & Wolff shipyard.

There were outbursts of violence all over the north, but it was on 21 July, the day the Catholic men were driven out of the shipyard, that all hell broke loose. The district around the Falls and Springfield roads was in an uproar when, in the middle of the afternoon, the men straggled home battered and bruised, their clothes in tatters on their backs, some soaked to the skin where they had been thrown or jumped into the Musgrave Channel in an endeavour to escape their attackers. Nora could still see it all in her mind's eye, the state of her son and her neighbours, blood pouring from their wounds and many of them needing hospital treatment. It was something she would never forget as long as she lived.

In frustration the men held meetings to decide what recourse they had. Someone suggested they retaliate by waylaying the trams that transported Protestant workers to Mackie's Foundry here in the heart of Catholic Springfield Road, their very own neighbourhood. The idea was enthusiastically latched on to and crowds gathered near Dunville Park and along the wall that housed the asylum on the far side of Grosvenor Road, lying in wait for the tram carrying the workers to Mackie's. When it slowed to a crawl over the crossing at the Grosvenor–Springfield junction, stones were thrown, smashing the windows of the tram, and men swarmed aboard, some armed with heavy sticks. Others disconnected the trolley from the overhead wires, making sure the tram remained stationary. The workers inside were trapped and, in fear for their lives, fought fiercely back.

Leaving Louise in charge of the two younger children and warning her to stay indoors no matter what, Nora had joined anxious neighbours at the corner of the street and watched the awful scene unfolding before their eyes. The situation would have become much worse but for the intervention of the local police. They soon arrived in numbers from the nearby barracks and warned the women to take their children and return to their homes and stay there or suffer the consequences. She was grateful that Tommy, one of the lucky ones who still had a job to go to, was safely at work, but terrified that Johnnie, who had been one of the apprentices thrown out of the yard, would be caught up in the affray. To her relief she could see no sign of him but that wasn't very reassuring as the crowd was a swaying mass of fighting men and it was difficult to distinguish all the faces. Those that she did catch a glimpse of were covered in blood and barely recognisable, but she thought that she would surely recognise her own son if he was one of the fighting mob.

The police drew their batons and charged the crowd. The local men took to their heels down the Falls Road, closely pursued by some of the constables. Anticipating that their quarry would backtrack up Waterford Street into the neighbouring side streets where some of them lived and others would surely take refuge, other constables raced down Malcomson Street and Springview Street to cut them off. The rioters found themselves sandwiched between two groups of baton-wielding policemen.

Things would have got really ugly but for the arrival of the local parish priest, Father Convery, from St Paul's Church, who happened to be visiting a sick parishioner at the time. A small man, he took up a stand in the middle of Malcomson Street and defied the police. Facing the constables charging towards him with batons drawn, he brandished his blackthorn walking stick in the air and demanded that the sergeant recall his men. In the face of such bravery the sergeant did so and his men reluctantly backed off without further injury on either side. An uneasy peace settled on the district for the rest of the day.

However, that was far from the end of it. More like the beginning, as it turned out, because it was the start of tit-for-tat shootings and bombings. The few Catholics who worked in Mackie's Foundry were attacked at work and some ended up in the nearby Royal. All were too frightened to return to their jobs.

Homes in the Clonard district were set alight, and women, some with babies clutched to their breasts while they tugged young children along the street, sought refuge elsewhere with family and friends whilst fathers and sons attempted to defend their homes. Nora had given refuge to some of these women and children until safe accommodation could be found for them. It was the start of a terrible period, when each new day brought further tragedies, including the murders of innocent men. Even some women were shot standing outside their own houses, and families were burned out of their homes.

To those involved, it appeared that the Falls and Springfield districts seemed to suffer the worst of the troubles. More and more people lost their jobs, and without money to feed their families they fought desperately to defend themselves. To try to curb the outbursts of rioting and shooting, a curfew was imposed from dusk to dawn. It was still in force, and people had learned to plan their lives around it. Nora had fretted many a time when Johnnie was a few minutes late getting home, and she was thankful that the others were too young to be out late at night. Anyone venturing on to the streets during the curfew hours did so at the risk of being shot. This was no idle threat, and indeed some men and women who dared defy the order were fatally wounded.

The local picture houses shut their doors after the first showing and pubs were forced to close early. This didn't cause too many problems, as most families could ill afford to eat, let alone spend money on such luxuries. There seemed to be no end to the troubles and families didn't know where their next bite was coming from. Tommy McGuigan had managed to keep his job at the tram depot, and although Johnnie had been thrown out of the shipyard he was lucky enough to get a job in Mr McFadden's grocery shop, so the McGuigans were better off than most folk around them.

Because of the troubles, Harry had been unable to find any kind of work since leaving school, so it was a godsend when J. B. Kennedy had chosen to open new bakery premises at Beechmount, and he had managed to get a job there. Of course, the way Tommy McGuigan got on, one would think that his son hadn't tried to find employment. As for poor Louise, when she left school the only avenue open to her had been the mill. Indeed they were lucky that the Blackstaff Mill, situated where it was in the heart of St Paul's parish, still needed to employ Catholic workers.

Just looking back on those terrible times brought bitter resentment and misery to Nora's heart. How they would have survived without help from the south, where their fellow countrymen offered refuge and sent financial aid and food parcels, she didn't know. The American White Cross, asked for help by the bishop, sent thousands of dollars each month. The money kept families from having to go into the workhouse, and was later used to build new houses for the homeless. It seemed strange, while all this was happening around them, that those who were brave enough to venture into the city centre reported that life appeared to be going on as normal.

Going through the gates of the Blackstaff Mill, Nora shook her head to rid it of the unpleasant memories of that awful era and made her way up the yard towards the spinning room.

Close on her heels, Bill McCartney, delighted at the opportunity to talk to her, lengthened his stride and fell into step beside her with a cheery greeting. 'Good morning, Nora.'

Putting on a brave face she shot him a swift smile and said softly, 'And a good morning to you, Bill.'

'You're in early, aren't you?'

She smiled wryly. 'Aye, couldn't sleep. I must have a guilty conscience or something.'

He noted the dark shadows under her eyes and the sad droop of her sensuous lips. 'That I don't believe. You were always a good woman, through and through. I know that from experience, remember.' He moved closer. 'Are you all right, Nora?' he asked softly.

She drew back, startled at his concern. 'Yes. Yes, I'm fine. Just a bit of a headache, Bill, that's all.'

They made their way into the spinning room. It was empty, and, leaning towards her, he said earnestly, 'If you ever want someone to confide in, Nora, remember I'm here. I'll always be here for you. Just say the word.'

Her heart started pounding at the nearness of him and this declaration of his loyalty. She was dismayed but excited that he could still affect her like this after all the years apart. Their friendship had started when he had been sent home wounded, during the early stages of the war, and declared unfit to go back to the front. When he had eventually returned to work in the mill he had been very good to Nora, sometimes taking her and the kids to the pictures on a Saturday afternoon, or on a good evening for walks over Daisy Hill, where they sat and talked while the kids played football and rounders with their friends in the late sunshine. Sometimes on a Sunday they dandered into the countryside and strolled up O'Neill's loney to the foot of Black Mountain.

When he could afford to, he treated them to a tram ride to the end of the line at Chichester Park. Nora especially enjoyed these outings. They made a point of getting seats at the open end of the top deck of the tram and a whole new world opened up to her enthralled gaze as they passed the beautiful houses that were being built along each side of the Antrim Road, while Bill spent his time drinking in the beauty of the young woman seated beside him.

Watching the families in the houses that were already occupied, as they tended their gardens in the warm sunshine, she was consumed with envy, and was more than ever determined to one day buy a house with a garden for the children to play in. Not that she was daft enough to think that they would ever be able to afford one as grand as these, no, but new houses were also being built further up the Falls Road. Beautiful detached and semi-detached homes. Bill, at her request, had accompanied her to view the new houses at St James's Park. Still too grand for her, she conceded, but there were other less expensive ones with gardens being built and it was one of those she aspired to.

Only once had Bill done anything out of character, only the one time, but that was enough to spoil everything good there was between them. Maybe it was just as well he had made his move to show her he cared. It made her aware just how attracted she was to him and how dangerous the relationship could become, and God alone knew where that would lead. It was enough to bring an end to their happy outings.

That wonderful summer day was etched in her memory and would be for all time. Often, over the following years when she was down in the dumps and Tommy was being more infuriating than usual, she would relive the emotions that Bill had aroused in her that day, revelling in the sure belief that he had felt the same. It had filled her with longings that she felt free to dream about, thinking that her desires were harmless because she would never see him again.

It had been a beautiful summer's day. The distant sky

43

above the rooftops was the palest of blues with only a few gossamer clouds crawling slowly across its surface, the sun a blazing fiery ball casting hot rays down on them. On these occasions Bill always brought a haversack packed with bottles of fizzy drinks and buns for the kids and sandwiches for Nora and himself, and a rug for them to sit on. He forbade Nora to bring anything, saying it was his special treat and a pleasure into the bargain, and she was happy to fall in with his wishes, enjoying being spoilt and cosseted by this kind man.

Completely at ease with each other, side by side they had walked slowly up Springfield Road to the mountain loney, making desultory conversation. Louise and Peggy were running excitedly ahead, impatient to reach the spot where the water tumbled down Black Mountain, pausing now and then for the adults to catch up with them, chattering and laughing away all the while. Johnnie and Harry rarely accompanied them on Sundays except when the treat was a tram ride. Johnnie considered himself too old to go walking with his mother, and Harry always followed his brother's lead. They usually played football in Dunville Park or Daisy Hill, going to their grannie's in Oakman Street for their tea or if they needed anything urgently.

On arrival at the foot of Black Mountain, Bill, as usual, found a sheltered spot near the small waterfall that tumbled down the mountainside, crystal clear and icy cold. Louise and Peggy liked to play there, delighting in paddling and splashing in one of the many shallow rock pools. The girls loved coming here and soon became absorbed in a fantasy world of their own.

Nora, completely at ease with Bill, had stretched trustingly out on the grassy bank, relishing the warmth of the sun on her limbs, the softness of the rug under her body. She little dreamed that her outings with Bill were about to be threatened.

Her eyes closed in the bright sunlight; enjoying the soft breeze ruffling the wispy curls of hair about her face, she gave herself up to the sheer pleasure of being alive. Bill watched her for some moments as the breeze gently lifted the fine blonde curls back from her smooth brow. She really was beautiful. Perfect skin and big violet eyes, the lashes now a golden arc which fanned out thick and bright against tanned cheeks. Today she was even lovelier than usual with her blonde hair loose about her shoulders. The temptation to kiss her was strong, but for some minutes he managed to curb his desire by just enjoying the sight of her; thinking how beautiful she looked lying there unaware of his adoring scrutiny.

The two young girls were wholly engrossed, splashing about in the water and paying no attention whatsoever to the adults. In their sheltered nook no one could see them, and at last, against his better judgement, he gave in to the overpowering desire that gripped him and leaned over to brush her full sensuous mouth with his lips. Her own unconsciously parted and she sighed with pleasure before becoming aware of what was happening. Startled, she opened her eyes quickly and made to sit up in alarm. His hands pinned her gently down by the shoulders and he whispered softly, 'Don't fight it, Nora. You must know I care an awful lot for you.'

Even so she had struggled against his restraining hold, whispering urgently, 'The girls . . .'

'The girls aren't the least bit interested in us.' He raised his head a fraction. 'I can see them but they can only see the top of my head.' His hands gently pressed her back down on the rug. 'Don't panic. Just lie there and relax.'

Mesmerised, she watched as his lips came closer until

45

at last they claimed hers again. They were soft and moist and the kiss went on and on, sending sensual excitement quivering through her warm body, exciting him all the more as she let him caress her breast. She silently urged him on, enjoying the feel of his hands on her body. Suddenly a squeal from one of the girls brought her to her senses. Pushing him roughly away she gaped at him in dismay before struggling to her feet. Pausing briefly, drawing slow deep breaths into her lungs to control the emotions that gripped her, she hurriedly smoothed her hair with her hands, and threw him an apprehensive glance before going to investigate what the screaming was all about.

It was just a small dispute between the girls about whose turn it was to pour water over some wild flowers. Was it God's intervention to bring her to her senses, Nora wondered? When she had placated her daughters she returned to where Bill sat, but avoided joining him on the rug, sitting instead on a small boulder in full view of her children. She was surprised and annoyed at herself. How could she let another man kiss her like that and her husband away fighting for his country? What kind of woman was she? Not only had she allowed him the privilege, but she had eagerly returned the passion. She couldn't believe that she had been so stupid! Her lips still tingled from the pressure of his, and she could still feel the heat from the touch of his hand on her breast and she yearned for more. Oh, yes, she yearned for more; much more. Her whole body ached with longing.

Then shame hit her like a slap on the face. Dear God, how could she have been so reckless? Oh, she was well aware that other women in her position were playing the field while their men were overseas. Hadn't she over-heard them in the mill, boasting of their conquests? But

46

she had never been that way inclined; it had never occurred to her that she might be tempted to do the very thing she despised them for. Not virtuous Nora McGuigan. Oh, no, not she.

One girl in particular was going to have a hell of a job explaining away an unwanted pregnancy, if her man returned from the front. But Nora was ashamed and surprised at her own wanton behaviour. She honestly hadn't thought of Bill in that way. She had regarded him purely as a very good and cherished friend. Hadn't felt in the least bit sexually attracted towards him. Had laughed at the foolishness of married women getting caught up in relationships with other men. How could they be bothered, she wondered? Actually, she had thought them irresponsible for taking a chance like that. Was one man not enough for them?

Now she was no different from those young women she had criticised. She herself was behaving like a common tart. Her only excuse was that she was hungry for love and the feel of his lips on hers had set nerve ends tingling with all kinds of desires. Well, wasn't that exactly what drove the other women to chance their arm outside marriage? Weren't they missing their husbands and *that* side of their marriages? She was also sure that Bill would be a kind, considerate lover and worried that, if given the chance, he would pursue it further, and she might be tempted to let him. It was a risk she couldn't afford to take in her vulnerable state. What if she became pregnant? Tommy would kill her! There was no doubt in her mind about that. In her innocence, she never even considered the possibility that Bill, unlike her husband, would make sure that she didn't conceive.

Bill sighed in resignation as he watched the conflicting emotions flitting across her face. He realised that it would be futile to try to persuade her further, so he kept up a running conversation from a safe distance to let her know he would behave himself.

She listened to his banter, but, in spite of his obvious concern, worry kept her quiet the rest of the afternoon. Why did he have to go and spoil everything, she lamented inwardly. She wanted his friendship more than anything else in the world; needed his companionship. It was what kept her sane, and now she would have to stop seeing him. Put an end to a lovely, innocent affair. How could she take any risks when poor Tommy was away fighting for his country – maybe even at this very moment lying mortally wounded in some mud-filled trench somewhere in France.

Bill wasn't surprised that that was the end of their outings. He berated himself for being so rash; he should have been more patient, given her more time to become dependent on him; let her get used to the idea that he was attracted to her. He sensed that she felt an underlying attraction towards him, perhaps not admitted to, but there none the less. He should have nurtured it, let them come together in her own good time. But on that warm, sultry day her beauty and nearness had proved irresistible and he had been unable to restrain himself.

For a long time he wouldn't take no for an answer. Had plagued her with promises that he would respect her every wish, keep his distance if only she would let him take her and the kids out again. Remembering the feel of his lips and the longing for his touch she remained steadfast in her resolve not to take any more chances where he was concerned. It wasn't him she was afraid of, it was herself. The following months were lonely and there were times when she almost reneged, but fear of the consequences, should they ever get carried away and

Tommy find out, made her determined to keep Bill at arm's length.

Shortly afterwards Bill left the Blackstaff and later she heard that he was living in Newry. That was the last she had seen or heard of him for years until two months ago when he had returned to Belfast and got his old job back in the mill. Their paths did cross from time to time in the course of their work, but Nora tried, when her machine needed attention, to get one of the other maintenance fitters to repair it. Thus she had managed to keep Bill at bay even though she didn't know whether or not he was married, or indeed still remotely interested in her.

Now here he was, the man she had so often dreamed and fantasised about, gazing down at her and she couldn't drag her eyes away from the longing in his. Her heart was thumping within her breast like some great trapped bird and she thought that he must surely hear it. She swallowed deeply, striving to contain her emotions, but in vain: her eyes said it all. Excited by the look in them Bill carefully lowered his face toward hers, ready to draw back if she showed any sign of rejection. The blood raced through his veins like an electric current as he watched her lips part in anticipation. He drew her into the nearby storeroom and locked the door behind them. Throwing all caution to the winds he drew her into his arms and she willingly gave herself up to his passionate demands.

After what seemed like ages, the sound of the spinning room door opening caused alarm bells to ring out a warning to them. With a grasp of anguish Nora pushed him off her and scrambled to her feet straightening her clothes, while Bill unlocked the door and peered out before giving her the all clear signal. Nora literally flew out of the door and down the length of the spinning room in blind panic.

With a sigh Bill watched her out of sight. Nora McGuigan was the reason he had never married. She held his heart in her hands. He had tried to forget her, but he had never come close to the way he felt about her with anyone else. With a baleful glare at the two unsuspecting young doffers who had unwittingly curtailed his moment of pleasure, he slowly followed in Nora's wake. He must make a point of seeing her. Find out if he stood any chance with her. He had heard rumours that her marriage was far from a bed of roses, so who knew? He might very well be in with a chance, now that her children had grown up and could fend for themselves.

Nora stood in the toilets shaking like a leaf as she examined herself in the grimy mirror. Her cheeks were beetroot red. Glad that she was alone, she gulped great deep breaths into her lungs and fought for composure. Only then did it dawn on her that it was her danger period. How could she have been so stupid as to let this happen? She was used to her husband's fumbling attempts, fairly certain by now that he must be infertile because of his traumatic experience during the war. But Bill McCartney was a different kettle of fish. 'Dear God, what was I thinking of, doing that? I can only bring grief to this kind man, and disgrace on my family if I get pregnant.' She didn't realise that she was praying aloud until a cubicle door opened and a workmate eyed her in concern.

'Excuse me, Nora, did you say something there?'

She flashed the girl a nervous smile. 'Just talking to myself as usual, Bessie. They'll be sending for the men in white coats one of these days if I'm not careful.' She backed out of the room leaving the girl gazing after her in bewilderment.

* * *

Living so handy to the mill, instead of bringing sandwiches with them, Nora and Louise went back to the house to join Peggy for lunch each day. Today they went home as usual, but Peggy was at her grannie's. Harry was usually out at this time, and the house appeared to be empty.

Louise bustled into the kitchen in front of her mother. 'You sit down, Ma, and I'll put the teapot on. I'm sure you're starving, love.'

A perplexed frown furrowed Nora's brow as she checked the wee room and the scullery. They were both empty. 'I wonder where your da is?'

'Maybe he went off to work early,' Louise answered hopefully. She filled the kettle and put it on the gas ring.

'Huh! More likely he's nipped out to the bookie's.'

The flush of the toilet cistern in the back yard made them grin at each other. 'Imagine us not thinking of something as common as that where me da's concerned.' Louise stifled a giggle as the back door opened.

Tommy stopped at the sink in the scullery to wash his hands before entering the kitchen. 'What are you two eejits grinning at?' he asked, looking suspiciously from one to the other.

'Nothing. Nothing important, Da.' Louise cut some cheese and put it between two thick slices of bread she had buttered. She threw a reproachful look at her father before addressing Nora. 'Here, Ma, get this into you. The tea will be ready in a minute. You must be starving. Thanks to him, you left without any breakfast this morning.'

'Don't you give me any of them dirty looks, girl. Do you hear me? It was you who drove your ma out on an empty belly, not me.'

Nora gave her daughter a warning glance. 'Louise, sit

51

down and eat your own lunch, please, or we'll be late back to work.'

'I'm coming.' Louise delayed to pour two cups of tea, then joined her mother at the table.

'What about me? Don't I get anything?'

Nora frowned. 'You've usually had your lunch by now.'

'I wouldn't've said no to a mug of tea, though, if you'd had the decency to ask. And what about my sandwiches for work, eh? Have you made any up?'

Nora rose wearily to her feet. She had hardly slept the previous night and really did feel exhausted. Her arms ached and she stifled a moan. 'I'll make them now,' she said resignedly.

Louise was on her feet in a flash. 'You will not! He's been here all morning. He's not a cripple. Let him make his own.' Louise gently pushed her mother back down on the chair and defiantly faced her father.

Tommy moved threateningly towards her. 'Just who the hell do you think you're talking about? Eh? Who's *he*?'

Feeling brave, Louise said primly, 'Sorry for any misunderstanding, Father dear. I thought you'd realise I was talking about you since you're the only man here.' She nodded her head and held his eye. 'I'll put it a bit more clearly, shall I? So there's no misunderstanding. I said you're not handicapped. You're quite capable of making your own sarnies.'

She had pushed her father just that wee bit too far. His open hand caught her on the left cheek and the sting of it made her yelp with pain and stagger back against the table.

'Don't you ever speak to me like that again, ye wee hussy. Do you hear me? You'll show me some respect while you're under my roof or you'll get more of that and worse.'

Clutching her stinging cheek and defying tears that threatened, Louise cried, 'I'll speak to you whatever way I like. I'm not afraid of you. You're nothing but a big bully. Only bullies lift their hands to defenceless girls.'

His arm rose again but Nora moved quickly between them, pushing her daughter out of harm's way. 'Leave her alone, Tommy,' she warned him. 'I'll make your bloody sandwiches.' Her chin jutted out as she gave him an ultimatum. 'In future you're going to have to pull your weight in this house. Is that clear?'

'What do you mean?' he snarled. 'I bring in more money than anyone else. I deserve to be waited on.'

'I'm not denying you earn more money than the rest of us, but you drink and gamble most of it, and I'm sick of bowing and scraping to your wishes and pretending I'm happy because I don't want the neighbours to pity me.' Out of breath, Nora stopped short. There, it was out of the bag at last. Pride! The reason she was forever making excuses for him.

It was a close thing who was the more surprised. Louise stood in stupefied amazement, unable to believe what she was hearing. She felt like jumping up and down and cheering. At last her mother was standing up on her back legs. Tommy's mouth dropped open and he had difficulty closing it, as he spluttered for words of retaliation.

Surprised at her husband's silence and her own audacity, Nora continued more confidently, 'As from now on, I'm a changed woman. Things will be different around this house. You can start now by making your own bloody sandwiches. There's enough cheese left in the cupboard if you want any. Come on, Louise. Time we were getting back to work or we'll be locked out.'

53

Relieved that her husband made no effort to stop her, she pulled her shawl round her shoulders and grabbing what remained of her sandwich nodded for Louise to do likewise. Outside the house Louise slipped her hand under her mother's arm and squeezed it close to her side. 'I can't believe you just stood up to him, Ma. I'm so proud of you. Oh, I could just hug you.' And she did exactly that.

'I should have done it years ago. I've let him get away with murder.' Nora gently touched the livid mark on her daughter's cheek. 'Today he overstepped the mark and I wasn't going to sit there and take it any longer. I had to do something. Is it very sore, love?'

'It was worth it, Ma, to see you standing up to him like that. You were brilliant.'

Suddenly all the bravado that had galvanised Nora at the sight of Tommy hitting their daughter evaporated and she wailed, 'I'll not get away with it, you know. He'll get his own back on me. Just you wait and see.'

'We'll look after you, Ma. I'll tell Johnnie and he'll warn him off.'

Nora stopped dead in her tracks and pulled Louise round to face her. 'Listen to me, love. That's the worst possible thing you could do. You mustn't let Johnnie know. If he interferes, your da will put him out of the house and then what will we do? Eh?'

'We'll all go with him.'

'Talk sense, for goodness' sake. Where would we go?'

As deflated as her mother now, Louise muttered, 'We'd find somewhere. What about Grannie Logan? Can we not stay over in Oakman Street with her until we get a place of our own?'

'No we can't. There isn't enough room. Besides, your grannie's got enough troubles of her own without us adding to them.' They had reached the Blackstaff and Nora said, 'Let me think about it, love. Perhaps I'll be able to come up with something.'

'I'll wait for you at the front gates tonight and we'll go home together.'

'OK. See you then.'

Nora's arms ached as she strove to keep the spindles turning smoothly. It was just her bad luck that Mr Dobson, the manager, chose today of all days to make a tour of the spinning room. He didn't do it very often, generally leaving the running of the shop floor to the foreman. But now and again he took a walk round the mill to keep them all on their toes.

It was disapproved of to let your spindles overload with thread and normally Nora had no bother changing them at the right moment, but just as Mr Dobson drew level with Nora's machines a thread snapped and a spindle spun out of control. With her painful arms she had difficulty stretching to spin it off. It was unlike her, and she was aware that Mr Dobson was watching, a frown on his face. Throwing him an apologetic smile she managed to ignore the pain and, replacing the bobbin, spun it into action. With a slight smile in return the manager passed on. He was well aware that Nora was one of his better spinners.

Today it hurt each time she had to stretch her arms. It was her own fault. She knew her husband would get money out of her, one way or another. She should have let him have it when he first asked, then he wouldn't have gripped her so hard and shaken her until she told him where the money was hidden, and her arms wouldn't be in this awful condition now. Still, didn't she know that once he had drunk enough porter and whiskey he would come home tipsy and demand his conjugal rights?

She sighed in defeat; she couldn't win. It was the wrong time of the month for that, so she would have got a bruising anyhow as she fought him off. Things couldn't go on the way they were.

He was imbibing more and more and she couldn't afford to fork out her hard-earned cash for him to squander. She supposed in her own way she must still love him, but he was ruining everything that was good between them, as he continued to abuse her. She deserved better. Bill McCartney's face rose before her mind's eye and she amended her former thought. *Did* she still love Tommy? Even after all this time, Bill was obviously still interested in her, whereas on the other hand her husband was letting the drink and the horses ruin their marriage, and all that once had held them together.

With an angry tut-tut she chased after another bobbin. This would never do! If she wasn't more careful she could lose her job and then what would she do? She'd just have to stop her thoughts distracting her from her work. Suddenly she sensed someone watching her. Bill stood some feet away, his gaze intent, until she turned and looked at him. Her face flushed with hot colour. My God, what did he think he was doing, standing there staring for everyone to see?

Coming closer he said softly, 'I just wanted to make sure you're OK.'

'Of course I'm OK. Why shouldn't I be? You'd better go, Bill, Mr Dobson's on the prowl.'

She turned her attention back to her work. He came closer and put a hand on her arm, only to quickly release it when she winced in pain. Taking her by the hand he gently rolled her sleeve up. 'Who on earth did that?' he gasped in dismay, as if he didn't know. Her arm was a mass of deep purple blotches.

'It's none of your business!' Another spindle ran free and she cried, 'Look, you'll be losing me my job if you don't take yourself off.' He watched helplessly as she rewound the spindle and sent it twirling again. 'Go away, please!'

'Only if you agree to meet me some night. I only want to talk to you.' Seeing she was weakening, he urged her, 'Please, I promise to behave myself.'

Her hands spread wide. 'I don't know if I can manage it.'

Overjoyed, he said, 'Your husband works shifts, doesn't he?'

Her eyes went round with surprise. 'How do you know that?'

He tapped the side of his nose with a finger. 'You'd be surprised what I know. Is he on lates this week?'

Apprehensive, she nodded. 'Yes, but I'm not going to meet you.'

'You don't have to. I'll come to your house.'

Shocked at his audacity, she said warningly, 'You'd better not.'

'Then meet me somewhere.'

She chased another bobbin and repeated crossly, 'Go away.'

'I'll wait for you outside tonight.' With these words he turned on his heel and before she could argue sauntered off down the spinning room, hands in pockets, whistling away.

She gazed after him in anger. Well, tough, she thought, so will Louise.

With trepidation Nora left the mill that evening. She wasn't surprised to see Bill in conversation with her daughter.

'Hi, Ma. What do you think? Bill recognised me after all this time.'

'Oh did he indeed?' she answered drily. 'How wonderful.'

'I've seen her about. She's the picture of you, so she is.'

Nora kept on walking. 'Good night, Bill. See you tomorrow.'

Not put off by her abruptness, he said, 'That's a promise.' Then doffing his cap in their direction he strode off.

Louise immediately voiced what was on her mind. 'Do you think me da will have stayed off work today, Ma?'

'I don't know, Louise. I'll not be surprised if he's still in the house when we get home. He'll be thinking how hard he was done by. If he's still there, he'll have worked himself into a right state by now. We'll have to be very careful what we say, so don't you go aggravating him.' She was only half paying attention to her daughter. Bill McCartney had implied that he would see her tomorrow. She hoped he wouldn't; she had enough on her plate at the moment without further complications. She shivered at the thought of what her husband's reaction would be to her lunchtime ultimatum.

Louise was quick to console her. 'Don't worry yourself, Ma. Johnnie will be home by now and me da won't dare touch us while he's about.'

Nora laughed inwardly. There was no one better at harbouring a grudge than Tommy McGuigan. That was something she had learned from experience, and Johnnie had told her he would probably be late home tonight, as he had a bit of business to attend to. Her heart sank when she saw the flicker of the mantle gleaming behind the net curtains. It could only be Tommy at home. Peggy was babysitting for one of the neighbours and would have made herself a bite to eat and gone on up to the house. Harry was going to the first show in the Clonard picture house and he'd have grabbed something to eat as well, so he could be off early to get a good seat.

Sensing her mother's concern, Louise gently brushed past her and opened the vestibule door a crack, peering cautiously round it. Harry was setting the table and paused, a mug in his hand, head thrust forward to see who was creeping in. Flashing her mother a reassuring glance over her shoulder, Louise pushed the door wide. A quick scrutiny of the kitchen and scullery showed no sign of her father.

Harry gave her a huge smile. 'I thought I'd give you all a surprise. I've started the tea. I'm making sausage and beans if that's all right with you, Ma?'

'It certainly is, son.'

'You gave us a bit of a shock there. We thought you'd be away to the pictures by now,' said Louise.

Harry grimaced at her. 'Am I not allowed to change my mind?'

'Didn't know you were capable of such an effort. Did your date let you down?' she teased him.

Pretending to take offence, he said, 'You all think I'm thick, don't you? Not capable of changing my mind. As for my date . . . you know fine well I'm not interested in girls.' He grinned and admitted, 'Well, at least not the girls who are interested in me.'

Nora gave him a quick hug. 'Of course we don't think you're thick, son. And you've time enough bothering with girls. They're nothing but trouble. We just half expected your father to be here when we got in.'

Harry frowned. 'Excuse me if I'm wrong, but isn't he supposed to be on the evening shift this week?'

'Oh, he is, but he wasn't feeling too well at lunchtime and we thought he might have taken the day off.' Nora shrugged off her shawl and removed her belt of tools. 'Thanks for making the tea, love.'

Johnnie walked down Peel Street, his thoughts running wild. He dreaded facing Mrs Gilmore, knowing only too well that she would be on the warpath, and with good reason. Mary was only seventeen years old! Dear God, far too young to be tied down with a baby. He couldn't understand why Mary hadn't come to him when she discovered she was pregnant. For the past two nights he had tried to waylay her, but in vain. He had hung about the corner of the street watching her front door. There had been no sign of her in the shop when he had passed. So where was she? As far as he could see, Mary hadn't left or entered the house. He came to the conclusion that she must be off work. Perhaps she was ill. He was aware that some women suffered morning sickness when they were pregnant, which could be reason enough why she wasn't at work. She wouldn't want her workmate to find out she was pregnant – that would give her something to gossip about!

He hesitated, debating whether he should wait and during his lunch hour next day visit the greengrocer's at the corner of Milliken Street where she worked. No; if she was at work she wouldn't like that. Her workmate probably knew that she had broken off with him and would hover around all ears. No need to go public just yet. It wouldn't be a very nice thing to do, putting her on the spot. He needed to speak to her in private. Find out just what she was playing at. He should go on down now to her house and have a word with her, get it over with one way or the other.

He had to face the wrath of her parents on their home ground, because he didn't want Mrs Gilmore to carry out her threat and come to his house. His mother would be devastated with shame and God alone knew what his father would do. The very thought of his reaction filled Johnnie with dread, not for himself, but for the rest of the family. As Louise had so wisely pointed out, he wasn't the only one who would suffer for his sins. His da would vent his spleen on the whole family. No, until they had settled what was to be done this was between the Gilmores and himself.

To his relief it was Mary who answered his knock. One startled look at him and she quickly left the kitchen, hastily pulling the door to behind her. Big brown eyes wide with alarm, she hissed, 'What are you doing here?'

Bewildered by her attitude, he growled, 'Your mother wants to see me. As if you didn't know.' His voice dripped with scorn.

'Ma? Why does she want to see you?'

He eyed her closely. What was she playing at? 'Something about a bun in the oven?' he inquired sarcastically.

Her hand shot up to cover her mouth in agitation. 'Oh my God, she hasn't been to your house, has she?'

He nodded. 'Well, not actually to the house, but she sent me a message. Through our Louise of all people. So just what are you up to, Mary Gilmore? Why didn't you tell me yourself?'

The vestibule door was pulled open and Sadie Gilmore feigned surprise at seeing Johnnie. 'Oh! Hello, Johnnie. I hoped it might be you,' she said with a knowing smile. She turned a baleful look on her daughter. 'What are you keeping him standing out here for? Come in, son. Come inside.'

She moved back and Johnnie had no option but to step reluctantly into the kitchen followed by a distraught Mary. Mike Gilmore looked up from the newspaper he was reading by the fireside and threw him a friendly greeting. 'Hi, Johnnie. How are you?'

'Hello, Mr Gilmore. I'm fine, thanks.'

'Sit down! Make yourself at home, son,' Sadie enthused, as if delighted to see him. Which, on second thoughts, he decided she probably was, since she hoped he would resolve all her immediate problems.

He had only been in this house once before and he hadn't felt very welcome then. Indeed, far from it. It was a couple of years ago during the troubles and he had been unemployed at the time, having been put out of the shipyard. Mrs Gilmore had given the distinct impression that she didn't think he was good enough for her only daughter. Indeed, Mary had broken off with him shortly afterwards and they had only renewed their friendship six months ago. He was the same lad as he had always been, but now he had a job and good prospects for the future. He was still a local lad from Springview Street and here she was welcoming him with open arms. He had no intention of making things easy for Sadie Gilmore, even if he should feel obliged to make an honest woman of her daughter. There would be no pretence where Sadie was concerned: he didn't like her and that was that!

He remained standing near the door, prepared for a quick exit if necessary, and said politely, 'No thank you, Mrs Gilmore, I won't be staying long.' He turned to where Mary hovered close by. 'Can I have a word with you in private, Mary?'

Before her mother could suggest otherwise, Mary moved quickly to the foot of the stairs and lifted her coat from the banister. 'Let's go for a walk. I won't be too long, Ma.'

Sadie's voice, all sugary sweet, bringing the bile to his throat at her fickleness, sailed after them. 'See and bring him back for a cup of tea, won't you, Mary?'

'No bloody chance,' Johnnie muttered under his breath. Without another word, he followed Mary from the house and up the street. She was practically running and he was forced to grab her elbow to slow her down.

'Hold on, Mary. Why the big rush?'

She stopped abruptly and faced him, hot colour in her cheeks. 'Listen, Johnnie, I want you to believe me when I say I didn't know anything about me ma talking to your Louise. I can't believe she'd do a thing like that!' Her head drooped low, so that her chin was almost touching her chest as she muttered, 'Poor Louise. I'm mortified so I am at the very idea of it. How she must hate me. What must she be thinking of me, allowing that to happen? How on earth will I ever face her again?'

She was so distraught, he found himself believing her and sought to offer consolation. 'Hold on. Don't worry about it. Louise will soon get over it – she's the least of your worries. What I don't understand is, why didn't you tell me? You should have come to me before you told your ma, Mary. Even if you want nothing more to do with me, we could have faced her together and at least sorted something out. You didn't need to be on your own.'

'Oh, Johnnie!' She turned from him in despair. 'Just why do you think I didn't come to you?'

He was disconcerted. 'Surely you weren't afraid to tell me!'

Her head bowed again and there was shame in every inch of her posture. 'I was too ashamed! I know your parents have big plans for you. When Mr McFadden retires I'm sure you'll take over the running of that shop. And if you play your cards right he'll probably offer you a partnership one day. You don't want to be tied down at eighteen with the likes of me and a child. Your parents will hate my guts. In normal circumstances, if we had taken our time and had a bit of a courtship, you know, saved up to get married, they might eventually have accepted me as a daughter-in-law. But the awful shame of a shotgun wedding?' Her head swung in despair. 'They'll never accept me now. Never in this wide world.'

Johnnie knew only too well that she spoke the truth. His parents would be so disappointed in him. Still, it takes two, and she shouldn't have been afraid to tell him that she was pregnant. Now he gently chided her. 'And just what did you intend doing about it, eh? In this close community we were bound to bump into each other some time or other. Did you think that once you started to show I wouldn't realise it was mine? Surely you didn't think I'd abandon you?'

Tears filled her eyes. 'I don't know. I haven't figured out what I'm going to do.' She gave a harsh laugh. 'You know, believe it or not, I told me ma it wasn't yours but she didn't believe me. Now I know why she's being so calm about it. She thinks she can force you into marrying me.'

'She doesn't have to force me. I was willing to risk it; to face the consequences if we were caught, so I'll do just that if you'll have me, Mary. I loved you. I thought you loved me or this would never have happened.' And in spite of her giving him the brush-off and the misery it had caused him, he realised he still cared deeply for her.

She gently touched his face. 'I know you'd never shirk

your responsibilities, Johnnie.' She started to walk again, slowly this time, and he fell into step beside her.

He was confused. Not a word of whether she still cared for him or wanted to marry him. He shook his head slowly in confusion. 'I must be thick or else I've missed something,' he confessed. 'I don't understand. Please explain why you broke off with me. I thought it was because you fancied some other guy.'

'Johnnie, please understand. When I discovered I was pregnant I was horrified. I didn't want to have a baby. Can you blame me? I'll be a mother before I'm eighteen. I knew you felt the same. Marriage was the furthest thing from your mind. That's why I stopped going out with you. I didn't want you to feel trapped into something you didn't want.'

Drawing her into the doorway of a shop near the corner of Peel Street, Johnnie took her gently in his arms and cupping her face in his hands wiped at her tears with his thumbs. 'The gentleman's always supposed to have a hanky to give to the damsel in times of distress, but I'm afraid I haven't got one. Shall I let you use my cuff?' he jested, hoping to lighten the moment.

To his dismay she cried even harder, great sobs from deep within her, tearing at his heartstrings.

'Hush, Mary. Don't worry, we'll get married as soon as we can. That is . . . if you'll have me?'

'No! I don't want your name dragged through the mud. Can't you see? That's why I tried to hide my condition when I stopped seeing you. I thought that the longer I went without anyone knowing, people would be less likely to say it was yours. I intended making up a cock and bull story about someone I met at the Gig and went out with for a while before he cleared off and left me in the lurch. But I was sick every morning and I couldn't hide it.

Although I tried to deny it, me ma knew right away what was wrong with me. She dragged me along to Dr Murphy's surgery. And I mean that quite literally – she pushed and shoved me up that Falls Road, calling me every bad name under the sun. Everybody was gaping at me. I was mortified.' She shuddered at the memory of the humiliation and wiped at her eyes with the heel of her hand. 'When Dr Murphy said I was three months gone, she took a swing at me. I thought she was going to kill me there and then. I'll never forget it. It was so embarrassing.'

Johnnie was horrified as he imagined her plight. Hell roast Sadie Gilmore, disgracing her own daughter like that in front of all and sundry. What kind of woman was she? 'She didn't!' he growled. 'The rotten auld cow.'

'Oh, she did. I'm telling you the truth. If the doctor hadn't intervened I don't know what would've happened. I'd probably have ended up in the Royal. He came round his desk like a shot and pulled her off me. He gave her a right ticking off, so he did, and warned her to be careful how she treated me in future or he would make sure she suffered the consequences. He's a lovely man, so he is. Kindness itself.'

'You poor girl. What about your da? Did he say anything?'

'He doesn't know yet. He thinks I'm upset because me and you had a lover's tiff. If only that were the case. He's very fond of you, you know. Even when me ma thought you weren't good enough for me he spoke up for you. Said what a fine upstanding young man you were.' She laughed harshly. 'That was a gag, wasn't it? Me not good enough for you! Me ma's certainly changed her tune! Me da tried to console me by saying it would all blow over and we'd be friends again. I bet he was delighted to see you tonight, God help him. He'll think everything's back to normal.' She glanced aside in dismay, nipping at her lips to stop the sobs. 'He's going to be so disappointed in me. I've let everybody down. Look, I'll have to get back now and face the music. Tell Louise I'm very sorry, will you? Me ma shouldn't have gone to her.'

'What about your Liam?' Johnnie felt apprehensive. Liam was her older brother and a bit of a hothead. He was very fond of his sister and Johnnie was surprised he hadn't made it his business to seek him out.

'He doesn't know either, but when he finds out I'll swear it isn't yours. If he threatens you . . . you let me know and I'll deal with him.'

'I can look after myself.'

'Not if Liam has a couple of his mates with him. He won't fight fair, you know. What a mess. Just watch your back, Johnnie.' She turned to retrace her steps, but although she waved him away he insisted on accompanying her back home.

'They have to know, Mary, so the sooner the better. Don't worry about me. Do you want me to come in with you now and confess I'm the father?'

She drew back, alarmed. 'No, I want you to give this some serious thought. I don't want you to feel that you're obliged to marry me. To be truthful, I didn't really think it could happen. I mean, we never went the whole way, did we? I thought we were safe. The nuns at St Vincent's were right. They warned us that the only safe way is to say no! I wish now that I'd heeded them.'

He gripped her arms. 'I don't have to give it a second thought. I want to marry you. I love you.'

She stopped before they arrived at her door and smiled nervously at him. 'I *insist* you give it some thought.' He bent to kiss her but his lips landed on her cheek as she abruptly turned her head away. 'You'd better go now before me ma gets wind of us out here and collars you again. And, Johnnie? Thanks for being so understanding. But for God's sake don't feel obliged to marry me.'

He looked at her pale woebegone face and felt like weeping. 'I wish this hadn't happened, Mary. Not because I don't want to marry you, but because you obviously don't feel the same way. Meet me Saturday night, at the corner, at seven and we'll discuss it further. OK?'

She nodded, but it was a defeated gesture and she left him with an abrupt good night. As he made for home his heart was full of misgiving. If only he'd been more careful, shown her more respect, they wouldn't be in this predicament now. He squirmed as he pictured his parents' reaction when he told them. All hell would be let loose. Thank God his da was on the late shift today. When he got home, he'd break the news to his mother and see how she reacted.

Nora came from the scullery, a questioning look on her face, when Johnnie came through the vestibule door. 'I thought you said you'd be home late tonight.'

'I did, Ma. But my wee bit of business didn't take as long as I expected. Anything left to eat?'

'Sit down, son, and I'll rustle up something. Would you believe it? Our Harry made the tea tonight. Wasn't that kind of him? We just had sausage and beans but I enjoyed having it made and handed to me. Would you like me to boil a couple of eggs?'

'That would be lovely, Ma.'

Johnnie sat at the table and, feeling Louise's inquisitive gaze, lifted an old newspaper and buried his head in it.

'Are you looking for anything in particular in that paper?'

'Mind your own business!'

'It might be a bit easier to read if you held it the right way up.'

Johnnie glanced at the paper and with an exasperated snort folded it and threw it to one side.

'Have you been to see Mary then?'

Louise's voice was quiet but still he shushed her. 'Keep your voice down and keep your nose out of my business.'

'Here you are, son.' Nora bustled from the scullery and placed a plate of buttered bread and two boiled eggs in front of him. 'I'll just pour your tea. I made a fresh brew.'

Leaning towards Louise where she sat in their da's chair, Johnnie said softly, 'Could you make yourself scarce, sis? I want to have a private chat with Ma.'

Without a word Louise rose to her feet and headed for the door. She guessed he was about to break the bad news and she certainly didn't want to be around to witness her mother's shock and dismay when he dropped his bombshell. Johnnie listened until her footsteps crossed the bedroom floor upstairs, and when Nora set his mug of tea on the table he said, 'Sit down, Ma. I've something to tell you.'

She sat down slowly and eyed him closely. 'Are you all right?' With a slight shake of the head she answered her own question. 'No, of course you're not! You look awful. What is it, son?'

Not knowing where to begin he sat head bowed, left arm resting on the table, gazing blindly at his plate. With his free hand he reached unconsciously for his tea.

She covered his hand with her own, and patted it. Apprehensive now, she said, 'It's bad news, isn't it?'

A nod was his answer and she immediately thought

of Mr McFadden. Had he sacked Johnnie? Surely not. Johnnie was too good a worker to be dismissed without any kind of warning.

'Tell me what it is, son. What's so bad that it's knocked all the stuffing out of you?'

He twisted his hand round and gripped hers in a hard clasp. 'I'm sorry, Ma. So sorry.' His eyes brimmed with tears. He knew how disappointed she would be.

Alarmed now, Nora cried, 'For God's sake tell me. What's happened?'

'Mary Gilmore's pregnant.'

Her face dropped with shock and she jerked her hand free and slumped down in the chair. She swayed and he put out an arm to save her from toppling over but she pushed it away and with a great effort, pressing her palms on the table for support, she pushed herself unsteadily to her feet.

'Ma . . . I'm sorry.'

'Huh! Too late for that. Is it yours?'

'Of course it is.'

'I was under the impression that you finished with her some time ago.'

'No.' He looked sheepish. 'I may have led you to believe that, but it was her who finished with me.'

'Did she say why she was breaking it off? I mean, did she meet someone else?'

His voice was guarded. Hadn't he himself thought that Mary had fancied another man? 'Not that I know of.'

'I see.' Nora's lips pursed as she became lost in thought. 'And now she's back saying she's expecting your child. Do you believe her? It all sounds very suspicious to me.'

He was on his feet facing her defiantly. 'Of course I believe her!' Then he paused, because suddenly he wasn't so sure. After all, Mary hadn't come to him. It was her mother who had approached Louise. Why? Why hadn't Mary come to him? 'It's my child!' he repeated, not knowing whom he was trying to convince. Suddenly he was uneasy. He didn't feel so certain now and it came across in his voice. Could there possibly be someone else involved? No! Mary wouldn't do that to him. Still, the doubt niggled at him. Was that the reason she hadn't come to him?

Sensing his uncertainty, Nora leaned towards him and voiced her misgivings. 'If I were you, son, I'd make sure it was mine. You don't want to rear someone else's child, now do you? How far gone is she?'

He wanted to tell her that it was none of her business, but contented himself with, 'About three months.'

'And when did you two fall out?'

'Oh . . .' He shook his head, confused. This was something he hadn't thought about. He trusted Mary; hadn't been doing any arithmetic. 'I'm not sure . . . four, maybe five weeks ago. Listen, Ma, Mary wouldn't pull the wool over my eyes. She's not like that. I trust her.'

'Well then, why did she wait so long to tell you? Eh, son? I'd look into it further if I were you,' Nora insisted, although it wasn't in her nature to sully a girl's character. After all, Mary would probably end up as her daughter-in-law, and least said soonest mended. But she wanted him to be sure he wasn't being taken for a fool. She wished she could tell him it didn't matter, that these things happened and it would all work out, but she was too numb; couldn't think straight. She'd had such great hopes for him. So had Tommy. Her face blanched at the thought of her husband's reaction. What would he do? She hoped she was having a bad dream and would soon wake up. But no, it kept on.

'No, Ma. I tell you, Mary isn't like that. She wasn't going to tell me at all. She was going to pretend it was

71

someone else's but she was sick every morning and her ma put two and two together and sent me a message by our Louise.'

Nora's eyes went wide with shock and her mouth went into a round silent Oh! To think she was trying to find excuses for this wretched girl and Sadie Gilmore had approached her Louise. She lost it completely. Rearing to her full height she bellowed, 'Are you telling me that Sadie Gilmore told our Louise that Mary was pregnant?'

He leaned back in the chair, taken aback at her wrath, and nodded apprehensively up towards the ceiling. 'Hush. Louise will hear you.'

'Well, she already knows, doesn't she! Thanks to Sadie Gilmore. How dare that woman speak to my daughter about something like that? She had no bloody right. She was completely out of order, that one!'

'Ah, come on, Ma, be reasonable. She had to get a message to me somehow.'

'No she hadn't!' Nora strove to get a grip on her temper. 'It was up to Mary to tell you,' she muttered.

'I told you, Mary was trying to protect me. She knew you'd be disappointed. She's devastated by all this.'

'And so she should be! She's right, son – I am very disappointed. And that's putting it mildly. You'll never know how much.' Nora headed for the wee bedroom. 'Ah, sweet Jesus, just wait till your da hears about this. There'll be murder done, so there will.' She shut the door none too gently and threw herself on the bed.

Johnnie heard her muffled sobs and felt the tears wet on his own cheeks. He looked down at the untouched bread and eggs and wanted to swipe the lot on to the floor. Good God! That was the mindless sort of thing his da would do. With a stifled sob he grabbed his coat from the rack and hurried from the house.

Glad that Peggy was babysitting and Harry had gone out, Louise slowly descended the stairs and gazed mutely at the door of her mother's room. Should she offer some comfort? Better not, she decided. Let her mother grieve before her da found out. By then she would have come to terms with the awful news, and whether Nora liked it or not Louise was convinced that her mother would throw her weight behind Johnnie whatever he chose to do. Her father was a different kettle of fish. There would be no soft-soaping him!

3

The next couple of days were comparatively quiet with no mention whatsoever of Mary Gilmore, and it was obvious to Louise that her da had not been told the news that he was to become a grandfather. Indeed, he must have taken his wife's ultimatum to heart, because he was lowering himself to doing menial tasks about the house and keeping a civil tongue in his head. It was a pleasant change for the family. If only he could always be as sociable as this, life would be more pleasant all round. Unfortunately, the state of affairs was all too likely to take a dramatic turnabout once the latest bombshell was dropped.

Nora was very subdued, and when not at work she immersed herself in needless household chores, exhausting herself to the point of near collapse so that she dropped into bed at night too tired even to think about what lay ahead. Watching her black-leading the range in the kitchen, scrubbing and polishing it till it shone, Louise went to her and, taking the brush from her hand, gently admonished her. 'Ma, you're wasting your time. I polished that range on Saturday. Come and sit down and I'll make you a nice cuppa tea.'

74

Listlessly, Nora did as she was bid and silently drank her tea. As soon as she finished she was on her feet again looking round for something else to occupy her. Louise was in despair. If her mother kept on like this she'd have a heart attack or end up in Purdysburn.

They saw little of Johnnie. He joined them for meals but spent his spare time upstairs in his bedroom, saying he was going over the books for Mr McFadden. Tommy was obviously bewildered by all this strange behaviour. Here he was doing his best to be nice to everyone and getting nowhere fast. He gave up in disgust and the rest of the week passed in a far from cordial atmosphere.

Saturday dawned and late in the afternoon Louise reminded the family in a no-nonsense voice that she was going out later and would be in the scullery for some time getting ready, and if anyone needed to use the lavatory they had better do so before she began her preparations to have a bath.

Immediately there was uproar. Johnnie thundered down the stairs in a rush. 'Did I hear you right? What do you mean you'll be in the scullery for some time? I'm going out tonight too, you know. Just how long do you intend being in there?'

'Ma . . . tell him! Didn't I book the scullery last night?'

Nora let out a long exaggerated sigh before admitting, 'Yes, Louise, you did say you were going somewhere special and would be taking a bath.'

'And I booked the scullery!' Louise wanted this made clear. 'Isn't that right, Ma? Remember?'

Nora tut-tutted in exasperation. Now the family had grown up there was always this trouble at weekends if, as was usually the case, two or more of them had plans for a night out. Louise especially was very particular about her appearance, more so than the others, and often went to the public baths down the Falls Road to get a proper bath. At other times, like today, she booked the scullery the night before so she had plenty of time to get ready.

When they were younger, there hadn't been any of this bother. Nora had bathed them all in front of the range in the tin bath every Saturday night. Now she sighed. 'Yes, Louise, you booked the scullery last night, but you were supposed to give everybody plenty of notice.'

'I'm telling them now, aren't I?'

Harry added his plaintive cry. 'What about me, Ma? She never warned me and I'm going to the pictures tonight.'

Nora threw her hands in the air. 'For heaven's sake, give my head peace. Sort it out among yourselves.'

To Louise's surprise, her da sided with her. From his seat by the fire he voiced his opinion. 'Your sister did book the scullery last night. I heard her. So just let her get on with it and maybe I'll get some peace to read this paper.'

Louise turned to him in relief. 'Thanks, Da. Now, did everybody hear that?'

Johnnie crowded close to his sister, and said quietly, 'Please let me go first, Louise. I won't be too long.' He lowered his voice to a whisper. 'I'm meeting Mary.'

'Look, Johnnie, I've the kettle and the big pot heating on the stove. I've the bath rinsed and ready to take in from the yard and I can't let you go first. You'll use all my hot water and I haven't time to wait for it to heat up again.'

'Louise, I promise I'll only use a little water for a quick shave. I'll fill the kettle up again. Please, sis. You know if I'm late Mary will think I'm standing her up. I can't risk that.'

Reluctantly, Louise recognised his plight, and moving away from where she stood blocking the entrance to the scullery she said crossly, 'All right. But you'd better be quick, Johnnie. In ten minutes I'll be knocking on that door and if you don't come out I'll take the hatchet to it.'

'Thanks, sis.'

Before she could change her mind he was inside the scullery and they heard the bolt being shot into place.

Louise busied herself about the kitchen to avoid the angry glare Harry was bestowing on her. She would not let herself be swayed by him. Once she was finished, he wouldn't be too particular and could get ready in no time. This was one date she didn't want to be late for. Nevertheless she felt guilty every time she caught a glimpse of Harry's scowling face.

True to his word, ten minutes later Johnnie was out again. 'I've brought the bath in for you. And thanks, sis. I'm afraid I used your towel but I'll get you a fresh one,' he promised, heading for the vestibule door.

Harry pushed roughly between them, heading for the scullery. 'I need to go to the yard, so I do.'

He made to close the door but Louise pushed him further into the scullery and took a stand in the doorway. 'You'd better be quick, Harry, or I'll lock you out and you can stay in the yard till I've finished,' she warned.

'You wouldn't dare.'

'Don't push your luck. Hurry up for heaven's sake or I'll never be ready in time.' The vestibule door opened and she caught the towel that came sailing through the air towards her. 'Thanks, Johnnie.'

Peggy, just to let them know that she still lived in this house and might – just might – be going out on a date, lifted her head from where it was stuck as usual in a library book. 'God help me if I should ever be lucky enough to be asked out. I'd never be ready in time. I'm always the last into that scullery. You'd think I didn't exist.'

Nora took this opportunity to throw Johnnie a sad, reproachful smile. 'Don't worry, Peggy. When your turn comes there'll be less queuing up to get into the scullery. Isn't that right, Johnnie?'

'We'll just have to wait and see, won't we, Ma? You never know, maybe there'll be an extra one.' With an angry glare in her direction he thumped up the stairs again.

His mother's voice followed him. 'Over my dead body!'

Book forgotten, Peggy was looking at Nora in alarm. Her mother shouting at her blue-eyed boy? Wonders would never cease. 'What's up, Ma?'

'Nothing, love. Nothing you'd understand anyway.'

'I'm not a child, ye know. I'm almost fifteen. Try me.'

'You'll know soon enough.' As was her habit, Nora took refuge in the wee room when faced with questions she was too embarrassed to answer, leaving Peggy looking hopefully at Louise. 'Do you know what's going on?'

Sensing her da was losing interest in his newspaper and starting to pay them more attention, Louise was evasive. 'Sorry, Peggy. I'm not getting involved. As Ma says, you'll know soon enough.' She raised her voice. 'You'd better hurry up, Harry, or I'm bolting the back door.'

Half filling the tin bath, Louise knelt beside it and washed her hair and rinsed it with a jug of clear warm water, until it was squeaky clean. Then carefully pouring the rest of the water into the bath she added a small handful of her precious bath salts, used only on special occasions like this, and stepped gingerly into the hot soapy suds and began washing herself, trying not to knock against the gas stove or the jawbox that took up a lot of space in the confines of the small scullery. It must be the ultimate luxury to have a room with a real bath and hot water on tap, she mused. When they were younger she used to listen, all ears, when her mother talked about one day buying a house with a garden, and when pressed by Louise, Nora agreed that it would certainly have a bathroom. What had gone wrong? Had her mother been living in a dream world? Ah well, at least she had harassed her husband into getting a decent gas stove. That was something to be thankful for. Some of their neighbours had yet to manage this, and still cooked and did everything else on the cast-iron range. Still, it was many a long day since a new house had been mentioned.

Drying herself, she pulled on the old dress she used as a bathrobe to conceal her nudity until she gained the sanctuary of her bedroom. One day, when she managed to save enough money, she would treat herself to a dressing gown and lounge about in comfort. Oh, happy thought! Wrapping the towel around her wet head like a turban, she bailed some of the bath water into the sink with an old saucepan, until the remaining water was shallow enough to let her pull the bath out to the back yard and tip the rest down the drain. Then she dried the bath thoroughly and hung it on a nail on the wall outside the back door where her da had built a canopy to protect things from the rain. It would never do to let it rust.

She was dressed and ready in good time but wasted some minutes fussing with her hair and left the house later than was called for, not wanting to appear too eager. She was nervous as she walked the length of the street, and faltered in dismay when she could see no sign of

Conor. What if he didn't show up? How long should she hang about waiting? Her steps slowed and she felt embarrassed as she passed his house. Had he forgotten their date or, worse still, had his mother put her foot down and forbidden him to see her? Would he do that on her? Well, she would know soon enough. She was perspiring slightly with anxiety when she finally turned the corner and heaved a sigh of relief when she saw him standing there, hands loosely linked behind his back, gazing into the hardware shop window.

His smile was wide and genuine, displaying even white teeth, and eyes as dark as Bournville chocolate appraised her. He must get his good looks from his father, she had often thought. His mother, although very ladylike, was mousy-haired and quite plain. Of course, that didn't stop Cissie O'Rourke from thinking she was a cut above her neighbours.

'Hi! You look lovely,' he said. He was so swarthy he could easily be mistaken for an Italian or some other Latin type, she thought.

Embarrassed at his obvious admiration, she blushed. 'Thank you.'

'Where would you like to go?'

'Surprise me.'

'Well, there's a Charlie Chaplin picture on at the Imperial . . . *The Kid* . . . if you fancy seeing that.'

'Yes, I'd love to. I heard some of the girls talking about it in work. They said it's a smashing film but very sad in parts, and wee Jackie Coogan is brilliant playing the kid.'

That settled, they headed for the nearest tram stop down near the Springfield junction. She felt shy and tongue-tied, flailing about in her mind for something sensible to say; glad when the tram at last arrived and he politely handed her aboard. This was awful. What on earth were they going to talk about? Did they have anything in common?

Crushed beside her on the narrow, hard seat, he gave her a covert sideways glance. She was indeed lovely. Soft curly blonde hair framed a beautiful face, with skin so fine it looked almost transparent. Surely there was another man in her life? 'Are you going out with anyone else at the moment?' he asked hesitantly. Quickly adding, 'I'm not being nosy, mind! I just don't want to tread on anybody else's preserve.'

'No, I'm not. Footloose and fancy free, that's me. And what's more, I don't intend getting serious with anyone until I'm well into my twenties.'

He nodded sagely. 'I agree with you. Marry in haste, repent at leisure. I've seen it happen round our district.'

He sounded so serious her shyness left her and suddenly she was at ease; it was going to be all right. After all, he was just a lad and they were only going out on a date to the cinema. She grinned at him and teased, 'Are you by any chance planning, after a suitable length of time, that is, to ask for my hand in marriage?'

His face stretched with surprise and he leaned away from her, squinting down his nose. 'What?' Then he caught the twinkle in her eye. 'Stranger things have happened, you know,' he retorted, with a nod and a grin. 'So you'd better watch yourself.'

'Not much stranger,' she assured him, thinking chance would be a fine thing. 'I think we're going to get on well together. So let's just enjoy ourselves and not look too far ahead, eh? After all, it's only a date.'

Conor was only too happy to agree. His mother had often said what a nice girl Louise looked, so, expecting her to be pleased, he had confided in her about his date.

To his amazement he discovered that nice though she might be, Louise McGuigan was not good enough for Cissie O'Rourke's only son, and there was no place for her in his life. She had been absolutely distraught when he told her; had tried to put him off seeing Louise, but there was no way he would have stood her up.

It was one of the times he wished he wasn't an only child, so that his mother wouldn't be so wrapped up in him. There were no near relations that he knew of. Just him and his mother. He barely remembered his father, just had a vague recollection of a big bear of a man who had appeared to love them. When they moved to Springview Street he was no longer there. Conor often wondered why he had gone away. His mother would never discuss him with her son. He now lived across the water, somewhere in England, she said, and it hurt too much to talk about him, about his treatment of them.

Conor knew that his father provided for them on a regular basis, so he couldn't be all that bad, surely. Every month money was deposited in his mother's bank account for their welfare and she didn't have to go out to work like most of the women in the street. When he won the scholarship to St Malachy's College, his father had sent over the money to buy his uniform and text-books. There were so many questions he wanted to ask his father. Sometimes he toyed with the idea of seeking him out, longing to know what kind of man he was and why he had deserted them; why he had never sent him cards at Christmas or even on his birthday. But fear of rejection should he ever find him made Conor resist the impulse.

They queued outside the Imperial cinema on Cornmarket for a short while, then filed slowly in. Louise was now completely at ease with Conor and when he reached for her hand during the film she didn't resist. She was very conscious of the warmth of his arm against hers and found it hard to concentrate on the film.

Afterwards they left the cinema in companionable silence. The weather was fine considering it was almost the middle of March, with just a nip in the air and a big pale moon hanging in the sky casting ghostly light. They walked up Grosvenor Road arm in arm discussing the film. She was surprised that she had seen enough of the picture to be able to hold an intelligent conversation about it, or at least he didn't imply otherwise. When they arrived at the corner of Springview Street, Louise stopped. She looked at him through lowered lashes and said, 'Thank you for a lovely evening, Conor. I've enjoyed myself very much, but I think we should say good night here. No need to worry your mother unnecessarily.'

He was surprised at her understanding and reaching for her hand held it clasped between his. 'You're a wonderful girl, Louise. I've really enjoyed your company tonight.' He hesitated then took the plunge. 'Couldn't we just go out now and again, as friends? Surely there would be no harm in that?'

'I don't think your mother would be very happy about that arrangement, if she were to find out,' she said haltingly.

He laughed. 'No problem. I just won't tell her.'

'She'll be livid if she finds out that you've deceived her,' Louise warned.

'I'm willing to risk it if you are. I really like you, Louise, and I'd like to see you again.'

She stood in thought for some moments. That was the problem – she liked him as well. What if their feelings

83

blossomed? Deciding, as he obviously had, that it was a risk worth taking, she nodded. 'OK. Let's meet now and again and see how it pans out.'

'Great! How about Monday night?'

She threw back her head and laughed aloud. 'Is that what you call now and again? Don't be at it, you daft fool. If we date it will have to be once a week, or better still every other week. You know what they're like around here. They can't keep their tongues still for five minutes and your mother will soon get to hear about us. Then you'll be in hot water.'

'Once a week, then. Every Saturday night?'

She nodded her consent, and smiled. 'I'll put it in my diary and . . . I suggest we don't meet here. I'll be at the corner of Grosvenor Road at Dunville Park next Saturday about half six. Is that all right with you?'

'That'll be great.' He felt ashamed because *he* had been about to suggest meeting elsewhere, and she had solved the problem for him. She was a wonderful, perceptive girl. He leaned towards her, taking her unawares, and placed his lips on hers.

Quickly, she backed away from him and wagged a finger in his face. 'There'll be none of that hanky-panky with me, Conor O'Rourke,' she warned. 'We'll be going out as friends, just like you said, and nothing more. Anything else will be out of the question.'

'I'm sorry. It was just an impulse.'

'So long as you understand. You'll have to control your impulses, so you will.'

'I'll behave myself,' he promised.

'You'd better. Good night, Conor. I can see myself up the street.' Her hand involuntarily reached up and gently touched his cheek. And so had *you* better behave, she warned herself.

'Good night, Louise, and thank you.'

There was a warm glow in his heart as he watched her walk away. She was lovely and sweet and he was glad she had agreed to see him again. Then he turned on his heel and walked down Springfield Road. He needed time to get his emotions under control before facing the third degree from his mother. He felt so happy, he knew Cissie would notice and guess the reason why, and then the trouble would start.

As it was, she was sure to question him about his date and he must be nonchalant about it, pretend it meant nothing to him, or she would be watching him like a hawk in future and that was something he could do without. A short brisk walk would give him time to cool off and then he would be able to face anything she threw his way. He had learned over the years to put on an act at times like this; he'd had to. Perhaps if all else failed he could look to the stage for a career.

Johnnie waited impatiently for ten minutes at the corner of Peel Street, then, squaring his shoulders back, was preparing to go to Mary's house when he saw her come out of the door.

She fairly raced up the street, arriving breathless beside him. 'I'm sorry I'm late. I'm supposed to be going round to my Grannie Gilmore's, so I dithered about to put Ma off the scent. Otherwise she would have insisted on you coming down to see her.' She grimaced. 'I think she's getting worried. I suppose she realises that maybe you won't marry me after all.' She looked askance at him but he didn't enlighten her. Let her stew for a while. Maybe then she'd be glad to accept his offer.

'Where do you want to go?' She shrugged indifferently and he continued, 'Our Louise has a date tonight and she took over the scullery, so I hadn't time to wait for tea. Fancy going somewhere for a fish supper?'

Another shrug. 'Why not?'

Some time later, when they were sitting in a booth waiting to be served, Johnnie watched Mary closely. The journey to the chippie had been strained and Mary had appeared to be on the verge of tears. She looked wretched and Johnnie cursed himself for being the cause of this young girl's predicament. The fish and chips arrived and he watched her push the food around the plate. He noted that very little entered her mouth.

He encouraged her. 'Come on now, Mary. Eat up. Remember, you're feeding two now.'

Her head shot up and she glowered at him. 'That's not one bit funny, so it isn't!' she hissed and glanced down at her stomach. 'I'm trying to forget that there's something in there. So don't sit there all smug reminding me.'

He reached across and gripped her hand. 'Mary, we have to face up to this. Decide what we're going to do.'

'What can we do?'

He sighed. She was making it very awkward for him. 'Is marriage out of the question? Don't you want to marry me? Have you met someone else, someone you like better, is that it?'

Her face lengthened in amazement. 'You don't believe me!' He could see the alarm and disbelief written all over her face. 'You think this . . .' Again she shot a look downward, and distaste was apparent on her expression. She shuddered. 'You think someone else is responsible for this. Don't you?'

His shoulders lifted in a dismissive shrug. 'Just what am I supposed to think, eh? You won't talk to me. Tell me . . . if it's mine . . . why won't you marry me?'

'I've no other choice, have I?'

Fed up to the teeth with her stubborn, sullen attitude, he growled, 'Oh, but you do! In fact, you have three options, as I see it. You can rear it on your own, or you can pull yourself together and talk to me about it and see what we come up with.' Her face blanched but he could see she was worried now, and to keep her attention focused he lied. 'I'm willing to walk away and let you pretend another man is involved if that's what you really want. Is it?' When she didn't reply he eyed her closely, adding as an afterthought, 'For all I know, perhaps someone else is in the picture.'

Tears hovering on long lashes lost their hold and trickled down her cheeks and compassion smote him. 'Don't cry, Mary. I didn't mean that! I'm just trying to get you to make up your mind. If you don't marry me . . . what will you do?'

Tears continued to fall and she made no effort to hide them, didn't care who witnessed her plight. Normally she was such a private person that this alone showed him how depressed she was. His own hunger had evaporated and he pushed his plate angrily to one side. 'That was a waste of good money. Come on, let's get out of here. We need to do some serious talking.' He glanced around him. 'Without an audience.'

Arm round her shoulders he held her close to his side as they made their way up the Falls Road. He didn't speak until they reached Peel Street. Then turning her towards him he said, 'Will you marry me?' Her face screwed up and he gave her a gentle shake. 'No more tears. A yes or no will do fine.'

She blinked furiously to stem the flow, and admitted, 'I didn't know anyone could cry so much. There seems to be a bottomless well inside me. What was the third choice?'

'Look . . . we don't want to go down that road. Will you marry me?'

She sniffed and asked tentatively, 'Don't you hate me?'

'Of course I don't hate you. Just say you'll marry me and we'll take it from there.'

'Only if you're sure?' Her eyes implored him for re-assurance.

'I'm sure.' He cupped her face in his hands and kissed her. 'Well then, I'm glad that's settled. Now we can go and face the music.'

She pulled away from him and cowered against the wall. 'Oh, no! Not now. Let's wait awhile.'

'We'll tell your parents now.' He was adamant. 'We've wasted enough time as it is.'

'But you don't understand. Me da still doesn't know about the baby.'

'Well, he has to know sooner or later, so let's get it over with.' She opened her mouth to argue but he fore-stalled her. 'Look . . . the sooner we tell them we're getting married, the better. It'll get your ma off your back and make things less stressful for you at home.'

Mary was silent for some moments. Then, reluctantly prising herself free of the wall, she nodded and straightened her shoulders. 'You're right. Let's go.'

Some of Johnnie's bravado left him at the thought of what lay in store. Would he be able to hold his tongue if Sadie Gilmore gloated, now that the decision was made? But then, to be fair, wouldn't she be justified in doing so? Hadn't he brought shame on her daughter, on her family? With a sigh he stretched to his full height and, gripping Mary's hand in his, marched down the street.

Sadie Gilmore surprised him. She showed only relief at their decision to marry, quietly assuring them that she understood how these things happened and she sympathised with them. No sign of any gloating or I told you so, just relief. Motioning Johnnie to sit down she asked, 'Would you like a cup of tea, son?' At Johnnie's refusal she continued, 'We'll arrange the wedding as soon as possible, and hopefully no one will be any the wiser. Many a woman has a premature birth. Especially with their first child. Mary might be lucky in that respect.'

Mike Gilmore had listened in bewildered silence to all this, looking from one to the other, trying to gauge what they were talking about. He had been pleased to learn that Mary was to marry Johnnie, thinking that perhaps his daughter would start smiling again. He had congratulated them warmly when they had told him the good news. Now he seemed to be struck dumb. Was he hearing right? At last he found his voice, and asked apprehensively, 'What are you all on about? What birth?'

Sadie went to him and, placing a warning hand on his arm, kept his attention focused on her as she explained, 'Mary's expecting a baby, Mike. Our first grandchild. What do you think of that?'

The colour drained from Mike's face and his hands curled into fists. 'What do I think of that?' he ground out through clenched teeth. 'I think she's a bloody wee tart. That's what I think of that. I thought we'd raised her to be a decent young girl and look what's happened. I'm ashamed of her, so I am.' There was contempt in his eyes when they met Johnnie's. 'As for you, young laddie . . . I expected better from you. I thought you were a decent, honest bloke. Couldn't understand why Sadie thought you weren't good enough for our girl. I thought she was safe with you. Looks like I was wrong after all. What a fool I've been.'

'I'm very sorry, Mr Gilmore, but I promise you I'll look after your Mary.'

'Huh! Too late for regrets now that the damage is done. Her name will be mud around here! You do realise that, don't you? And I'll not be able to hold my head high ever again.'

Johnnie frowned. 'Why not? You've done no wrong.'

'She's my daughter!' Mick looked at Mary with sorrow in his eyes. 'You dirty wee slut.' Then, ignoring Johnnie, he headed for the stairs.

'Ah, Da . . . I'm sorry.' Mary started to follow him but her mother held her back.

'Leave him be, Mary. He's in shock but he'll soon come round to our way of thinking. Now, back to business. When do you two intend seeing the priest?'

'I'll have to break the news to my father first, and then we can make plans for the wedding.' Turning to Mary, he said, 'See me out, love, and I'll go home now and get it over with.'

Mary went outside with him, closing the door on her inquisitive mother hovering behind her. 'Would you like me to come with you?' she asked tentatively, and sighed in obvious relief when he declined her offer.

'That won't be necessary. I'll come down tomorrow afternoon and let you know how things went. I'm sorry your da took it so badly, but, as your ma says, he'll get over it.'

Planting a brief kiss on her cheek he strode up the street without a backward glance. He had his own da to worry about now. That was the next phase in this pitiful saga.

Nora sat huddled by the dying embers of the fire darning the heel of a sock. She had looked the picture of misery since Johnnie had told her of Mary's plight, and Johnnie had noticed too that his da must be wondering what on earth was up with her. Tommy was toeing the line all right, taking care not to upset his wife. Now, sitting in the dim light from the gas mantle, she looked even worse. The shadows on her face made her look old and haggard. When Johnnie entered the kitchen he was overcome with such a rush of emotion at the sight of her that he almost broke down. She deserved better than this, he thought. All her life she had worked her fingers to the bone for them and what reward did she get? A drunken husband . . . and he himself not much better, landing in this pickle just when she must have thought that things were beginning to look up. He actually had a right wee pile stashed away. He'd been saving most of his spare cash, planning a surprise holiday for his mother, and now this. His money would have to go towards the wedding.

He stifled a sob. 'Where is everybody?'

'Peggy's in bed and Harry and Louise aren't home yet. As for your da . . . where do you think he'd be on a Saturday night?' Nora glanced at him, suddenly alert. Her brows gathered in a worried frown. 'Why do you ask?'

'I've asked Mary Gilmore to marry me and she's accepted. I want to tell everyone at the same time. Get it over with.' Because of the state he was in the words came out in clipped syllables and he knew he sounded callous and uncaring.

Dropping the sock, Nora slumped forward in the chair, burying her head in her hands. She was completely silent but he knew she was crying because tears trickled from her fingers and fell on the sock lying unheeded on her lap.

Kneeling beside her, Johnnie gently pulled her hands away from her face and wiped her cheeks. 'Don't, Ma. Please don't cry.'

Still blinded by tears she wailed, 'Oh, how could you, Johnnie? I'm surprised at you. Is she so wonderful that you couldn't wait and do things decent? Had you no shame? No respect for the girl?'

The words hurt. Oh yes, he was ashamed all right, to bring this trouble to their door. And hadn't he been blaming himself for not showing Mary the respect she deserved? But it takes two, he lamented inwardly, and he wasn't going to grovel, not to his ma or anyone else. He'd do his duty and give the child a name. What more could be asked of him?

'Listen, Ma, I wish with all my heart this hadn't happened, but it has. I can't turn back the clock so I must face up to the consequences. I intend to marry Mary, and as soon as possible. Please give us your blessing. Please, Ma. I'll try to make it up to you somehow, I promise.'

'Oh, you can have that all right for what it's worth. But you'll need more than my blessing to get you through these next few months. What way's her da taking it? Men always think their daughters can do no wrong. She'll be the innocent party, you can bet your life on it. You'll be the villain.'

'We broke the news to him tonight and to be truthful he turned his back on Mary and insulted me into the bargain. But I don't blame him, her being his only daughter. The apple of his eye as it were. As for Mary, she's heartbroken.'

'I know exactly how she feels.' Nora's voice faltered and she wailed, 'Dear God, I dread to think how your da will take it. He'll be against this wedding, that's for sure! He expects more of you.'

'He won't have any say in the matter, Ma. Tomorrow Mary and me will go and see the priest to find out how

92

quickly he can marry us.' And, he thought, Sadie Gilmore would probably accompany them to make sure he didn't try to wriggle out of his obligations. 'So you see, I'll have to tell me da tonight. It's only fair that he knows.'

He turned, startled, when the vestibule door suddenly opened. Louise looked happy and contented as she breezed into the kitchen, eyes shining. He silently took in the beauty of her glowing countenance and hoped she wasn't making the same mistake as himself. It wasn't worth the risk. Harry was close on her heels.

Louise's glance quickly took in the situation and she guessed what was going on. 'Ah,' she sighed. 'So you're going to get married?'

Rising to his feet Johnnie nodded. 'I've decided to break the news tonight.'

'Well, you'd better prepare yourself. Me da's coming up the street at this very minute.'

'Is he drunk?'

She shrugged. 'No more so than usual. Hush, here he is now,' she said warningly as heavy footsteps scraped past the window. Going to her mother, who had risen shakily to her feet, she took up a protective stance beside her.

Harry was looking at Johnnie in amazement. 'You're getting married?' he gasped. 'Who to?'

'Shut up. You'll hear soon enough.'

They all watched the door. Tommy came in with an affable smile on his face. He had beaten his old mate at darts, something he didn't often do, and was in a happy state of mind for a change. His gaze took in the tableau of his wife and children standing as if petrified and he stopped abruptly.

He looked at each one in turn before asking apprehensively, 'Where's Peggy? Is she ill? Is anything wrong?'

It was Johnnie who answered him. 'Peggy's in bed. As for the other, well, it depends on how you look at it, Da. I've decided to get married.'

'Oh, have you now?' Tommy was silent for some moments, thinking it over in his befuddled mind, then reasoned, 'Aren't you a bit young to be settling down, son? You've all the time in the world, you know. Take my advice and sow a few wild oats first.'

'I'm not all that young, Da. I'm almost nineteen.'

'Wise up, son, you're still wet behind the ears. Wait a few years before you even start thinking about marriage.'

'I can't wait, Da. You see, you're going to be a grandfather and we don't want the child to be born out of wedlock.'

Tommy's shoulders slumped and his body seemed to deflate like a punctured balloon. With measured steps he walked deliberately to his chair and sank down heavily on to it. Cocking his head in Johnnie's direction he said, 'Am I hearing right? Have you got some girl in trouble?'

'That's right. The girl I intend marrying is pregnant.'

Tommy looked gutted. 'Why, you stupid bastard! Have you no sense at all?' He swung round in the chair to glare at his wife. 'Is that why you've been the picture of misery lately? Did you know about this?'

'Not very long.' She sounded defeated.

'Who's the girl, then?'

Johnnie moved closer to get his father's attention. 'Look at me, Da,' he insisted. 'Don't shout at me ma. She's got nothing to do with it.' He thumped his chest with a clenched fist. 'Speak to me! Mary Gilmore is her name and I love her and I'm going to marry her. Whether or not you agree.'

Tommy rose and faced his son, and in a much quieter tone once again tried to reason with him. 'Listen to me,

Johnnie. Be sensible about this. Don't let yourself get trapped by a wee lump of a girl. I advise you to go away for a while. I'll borrow money from somewhere and you can go over to England until the dust settles.'

They were all gawking at Tommy in astonishment. This was a turn-up for the books. They had expected him to rant and rave about the shame Johnnie was bringing on the family. Throw a couple of punches at him. Maybe even turn him out of the house. Instead he was offering him a way out. It was unbelievable.

Nora found her voice. She agreed with her husband that Johnnie was very young to be getting married, but she couldn't let him throw Mary Gilmore to the wolves. 'Are you daft? He can't leave that poor wee girl to take the brunt of this and rear the child on her own while he runs off to England. Remember this is our grandchild you're talking about.'

'Is it?' Tommy held Johnnie's gaze. 'Are you sure of that? How come you've never brought this girl home to meet us, eh, Johnnie, seeing that you're so fond of her? Is she not respectable enough? Are you ashamed of her? Is that it?'

There it was again! The insinuation that he might not be the father. Johnnie was quickly on the defensive. 'She's a very respectable girl, so she is. In fact her mother thinks she's too good for me. And no, I'm not ashamed of her. I intended bringing her here sooner but we had a fall-out before I had the chance.' Johnnie knew immediately that he had put his foot in it, and prayed his father wouldn't ask the obvious.

'You were parted?' At Johnnie's tight-lipped nod, Tommy gasped, 'How can you be so sure it's yours then? Was she seeing anybody else after you broke off with her?'

'No she wasn't! I know it's mine and I'm telling you now that we're going down to see the priest tomorrow and I won't hear another bad word said against Mary.'

'You're a fool, boy! Not a bit of wonder her ma is now welcoming you with open arms. Not good enough, indeed. Take my advice and go away for a while. She'll probably come up with another name if you go. Maybe one her ma likes better. If I get the money will you go across the water?'

'No chance.' With a last sorrowful look at his mother Johnnie crossed the floor and went into the hall. He sounded like an old man as he stumbled his way upstairs.

Louise moved closer still to Nora as her father once again rounded on her.

'Has the cat got your tongue, then? You should have backed me up, woman,' he snarled. 'Do you want to see him tied down at eighteen? He's far too young to get married.'

'I know that! But what's done is done, and he must face up to his responsibilities. There's not a damn thing we can do about it.'

Tommy was so upset he actually resorted to pleading. 'Talk to him, Nora. Make him see sense. He'll listen to you, so he will.'

'I've tried, Tommy, I've talked till I was blue in the face, but he won't listen to reason. Anyway, he's had his pleasure, now he must pay the price.'

Tommy glowered at Louise and Harry. 'You two stay here. I'm going up to have a word with him in private.'

Voices were raised, then fell, as Tommy pleaded with his son to see reason. Nora was weeping softly into a corner of her apron, and putting an arm across her shoulders Louise whispered, 'It'll be all right, Ma. You'll see.'

'Will it? How will they manage?'

'Like everyone else. They're not the first, you know. At least they both have jobs.' She fell silent as Tommy descended the stairs.

He had been gone but ten minutes and he shook his head in defeat. 'He's a fool! Won't listen to a word I say. On his own head be it.' He turned as a sleepy-eyed Peggy followed him into the room.

'What's going on?'

'Nothing to concern you. Get yourself back upstairs again.'

Peggy opened her mouth to protest but when Tommy snarled 'Hop it!' she scuttled back up the stairs. It's a pity I have to breathe around here, she thought.

Johnnie hadn't expected the parish priest to be overjoyed when he heard the reason for their sudden rush, but it had never entered his head that he would, under any circumstances, refuse to marry them. But this he did.

'What do you mean, we have to wait? We've lived here all our lives. I know we should have the banns displayed, but surely it should be easy to prove that neither of us has been married before.'

'Have you forgotten that next Wednesday is the start of Lent? So you can't be married until Easter at the earliest. In fact Easter Saturday and Monday are booked solid and I'll be away for a few days during the Easter week, so I'm afraid it will be the Saturday after that. I haven't time to fit in another wedding before then.'

Johnnie had completely forgotten that Catholics didn't marry during Lent. He stood tongue-tied; how could a thing like that have slipped his mind? Apparently no one else had remembered it either or surely they would have said something.

It was soon obvious, however, that Sadie had given it

some thought. She had insisted on accompanying them to the parochial house, and now she voiced her opinion. 'Father . . . I thought you could get married during Lent if the circumstances were exceptional?' she queried.

Father Riley was a tall man, and drawing himself up to his full height he glared down his long nose at her. 'And just what is so exceptional about this charade?'

Hanging her head in shame Mary wriggled with humiliation and sidled towards the door. With a hand on her arm Sadie stopped her. 'As Johnnie has already explained to you, Father, our Mary is pregnant. And if that is what you call a charade, so be it. Is it a case of no room at the inn? Is that what you're telling us, eh?'

The priest was enraged at her audacity. 'Don't you dare bandy words with me, woman,' he thundered.

As far as Sadie was concerned, a priest was a man just like any other, and, unperturbed, she gestured towards the door. 'Come on, Mary, Johnnie. I'll get in touch with the bishop. If he can't do anything for us, it will have to be a register office job. Good evening, Father. Sorry to have disturbed you.'

'Here, hold your horses a minute. Sit down till I see if there's anything I can come up with. I'll marry you as soon as possible. It's a case of finding a suitable date, that's all. Not because of your threats, mind you. They don't sway me in the slightest,' he said. 'No, it's the child I'm thinking of.' He went over to an old polished oak bureau in the corner of the room and came back to his desk with a notebook and fountain pen. 'Now, sit down and give me all the details.'

It was arranged that the marriage would take place two weeks later in St Peter's Pro-Cathedral Church. Louise was to be bridesmaid and Liam Gilmore the groomsman.

An aunt of Mary's who was the proud owner of a sewing machine, and a dab hand at dressmaking, made the dresses: ankle-length flowing creations of chiffon embossed with small flowers. Louise for one was delighted with hers. A deep blue colour, it darkened the sapphire of her eyes and brightened the natural ash blonde of her hair. She spent a long time preening herself in front of the mirror on the door of the old wardrobe in her bedroom. She had never dreamed that she would ever own such a beautiful gown and she was beside herself with excitement. Mary, on the other hand, seemed indifferent to her gorgeous white wedding gown.

The two girls had gone down to the city centre to choose the white picture hats and matching low-heeled shoes with a bar across the instep that would complement their outfits. As with her dress, Louise was overjoyed with her new possessions and carried them carefully, as if she had a dozen eggs in each bag. In contrast, Mary again seemed quite indifferent, just letting the bags flop about all over the place. Louise dreaded to think what condition the hat would be in when she eventually got home.

After making their purchases they went into a nearby café for tea. It was Louise's treat and as she returned to the table with the tray her heart was smitten with pity at the look of defeat etched on Mary's face. She unloaded the tray in silence, a silence that continued while they sipped their tea. In fact Mary had hardly opened her mouth all morning. It was frustrating and at the same time heartbreaking to watch her. Still, she couldn't go on like this. She would have to pull herself together. After all, it wasn't the end of the world for her. In fact, it was the beginning of a new world. She was lucky that Johnnie was willing to marry her and should be happy about it.

Leaning across the table Louise patted her on the hand and quietly assured her, 'You know, Mary, our Johnnie's a decent bloke. He'll be good to you and the baby. You couldn't ask for any better.'

'I know that. But we hadn't even talked of marriage. I feel he must think I've trapped him into it. That everything's my fault.'

Louise raised a brow. 'And did you?'

'No, of course I didn't! I just don't want to get married so young.'

'Then why did you let him . . . you know . . . ?' Louise's voice trailed off in embarrassment.

'Why did I let him touch me? I was curious, we both were. That's why I feel he must think I knew what I was doing all along and set out to trap him into a marriage that he didn't want.'

'Has he implied that?'

'No, he's been very kind about it all. But that doesn't mean he doesn't think it.'

'You don't know what he's thinking. So be positive. Look on the bright side of things. He's got a good job and he's managed to get Mrs Clarke to rent her two upstairs rooms to him. So you won't have to live with your ma or my ma. Believe you me, it would be a tight squeeze in our house.' She laughed at the idea of it. 'It doesn't bear thinking about.'

Mrs Clarke was their next-door neighbour in Springview Street. After the death of her husband, she had never trusted anyone enough to let the rooms out to them. However, she welcomed Johnnie with open arms, having known him since birth. She was glad of the extra money and it was a happy arrangement for both parties.

Sadie Gilmore, on the other hand, was annoyed at the idea of her daughter living in rented rooms. She had pointed out that it would be better if Johnnie came to live in her house, which had three bedrooms. It would save a lot of problems as she would be able to keep an eye on her daughter during her pregnancy. However, Johnnie was adamant that he wouldn't live under the same roof as his mother-in-law. He had been glad when his mother suggested that he approach Mrs Clarke, and relieved that the widow had agreed to let them have the rooms at an affordable rent.

'You don't understand! I dread living next door to your parents. Your ma can't hide her disappointment and your da won't even look me straight in the eye. He makes me feel so dirty, so he does.' Tears threatened to fall and she valiantly fought to contain them.

Reaching across the table, Louise clasped her hand. 'Listen . . . it won't be for ever. Something better is sure to turn up. Just be patient, Mary.'

'You don't know how miserable I am. Sometimes I feel like ending it all.'

Alarmed at this revelation, Louise shook the hand she held. 'You mustn't even think that. Do you hear me? Promise me you won't do anything stupid.'

'Don't worry, it's all just talk. I'm too big a coward. I have no choice but to grin and bear it.' A harsh laugh escaped her lips at the pun. 'Quite literally!'

Conor listened attentively when, in the strictest confidence, Louise told him the whole sorry tale.

'Do you think they're doing the right thing?'

She shrugged. 'I can't see what else they can do. Can you?'

'Well for one they could wait until the baby is born. See how they feel then.'

Louise looked at him wide-eyed. 'Mary's ma would

101

never hear tell of that. Just think about it, her a single mother. Her name would be mud around here.'

He frowned. 'Is it not already mud?'

'Once the news of the rushed wedding gets out, it will be. She'll be the talk of the district. But with a ring on her finger it will be a nine-day wonder. She might even be lucky and have people think it's a premature birth. Then she can thumb her nose at them, because no one will be any the wiser.'

'Mmm. I suppose you know what you're talking about.'

'Believe me, Conor, in this instance I do.' Feeling self-conscious, she said haltingly, 'Will you come to the church next Saturday morning and see me in my lovely brides-maid dress?'

'Wild horses won't keep me away.' They were walking past the bottom of Leeson Street, and he drew her into the shadows and pulled her gently towards him.

She knew she should push him away but her arms wouldn't obey her brain and she clung to him. His lips trailed her face until they found hers and she willingly submitted to his kiss.

Easing her an arm's length away from him, he said solemnly, 'One day I intend to marry you, Louise McGuigan, and it will be done decent. You mark my words. There'll be none of this hanky-panky business between us.'

She wished she could believe him. 'We've only been out twice, you daft fool!'

'No matter. Some things are destined to be, Louise, and I will marry you. That is, if you'll have me?'

She smiled sadly. If only . . . 'Your ma would never hear tell of us getting married.'

'I mean it, Louise. I'll just have to talk her round, won't I?'

Louise didn't for one minute believe it was ever likely to happen, but she threaded her arm through his and pressed close as they continued their walk home from the pictures. So much for a platonic friendship! But she could dream, couldn't she? Wasn't that what girls did? Dream about the lad who would sweep them off their feet to live happily ever after?

Once the date was set, Johnnie broke the news of his coming marriage to Mr McFadden. Saturday was their busiest day in the shop, but obviously he needed the day off for such a special occasion.

Thinking, for Mary's sake, that the fewer people who knew about the wedding the better, he just asked if he could have the day off as he had some very important business to attend to. He could explain it all to his boss afterwards.

'A Saturday off?' Mr McFadden could hardly believe his ears. 'But surely you know we're rushed off our feet every Saturday? It's our busiest day of the week, lad. Can't you attend to your affairs another day?'

So much for wanting to protect Mary. 'Unfortunately no, Mr McFadden. You see, I'm getting married.'

Matthew McFadden rocked back on his heels in surprise. A scowl on his face, he said, 'This is a bit sudden, lad, isn't it? You never even mentioned you were courting.'

At his tone of voice Johnnie's hump was up right away. It was none of Mr McFadden's business, and he opened his mouth to tell him as much, but managed to curb his temper. He couldn't afford to lose his job, so he had to explain that his future wife was pregnant, hence the big rush.

'Ah, son. Why did you have to go and spoil things, eh? I had such big plans for you.'

Johnnie was bewildered and it showed. 'I don't understand . . . what difference does my getting married make to anything? It was sure to happen sooner or later.'

'All the difference in the world. Those rooms' – Matthew jerked his head towards the ceiling – 'could be turned into a lovely comfortable flat. You see, my wife and I think the world of you, son, and we had hoped that you and our Hannah might eventually hit it off. The two of you would be nice and comfortable up there. The business could have been yours one day. You would have been set for life, son.' He tutted in exasperation. 'I'm just sorry now I didn't speak out sooner.'

Johnnie was speechless. At last he found his tongue. 'Am I hearing you right? You thought that your daughter and me might one day marry?' In spite of himself he laughed at the very idea of it. 'You must be joking.'

Matthew bristled. 'What's so funny about that? My Hannah's a lovely wee girl. She'd make a good obedient wife. You could do a lot worse, you know.'

'Come off it, boss.' Johnnie paused. He had better watch himself here or he might give offence and he *would* end up on the street. 'You know Hannah doesn't think of men in that way. She's very young in her ways.' And never likely to get any older, he thought. He was in a quandary here. Hannah really was lovely to look at, but she was a bit backward and Johnnie couldn't imagine her ever marrying anyone.

'Think, Johnnie. Hannah is capable of doing things about the house and she's learning to cook. Her mother and I have trained her well and she keeps our home lovely. And many a man would be glad to have her in their bed at night. She'd make a grand wee wife. And you needn't be afraid of having bairns. It was a forceps birth that caused her to be a bit on the slow side, nothing else.'

Still flabbergasted, Johnnie flailed about in his mind for something to say. Anything that wouldn't give offence. 'I can't believe you're saying these things, boss. You've always been so protective of Hannah, I thought you wouldn't ever let a man get near her, let alone marry her.'

Matthew motioned towards the office at the rear of the shop. 'Come through here, Johnnie.' He indicated that Johnnie should sit down and from a drawer produced a bottle of Black Bush. He poured some into a glass and held it out to Johnnie.

'Thanks all the same, Mr McFadden, but I don't drink spirits. Just the odd pint is my lot.'

Taking a gulp from the glass, Matthew admitted, 'Aye, you're a good, responsible lad. And . . . you're right. I wouldn't let just any man near my daughter, she's too vulnerable. But you . . . the wife and I are very fond of you. We know you'd treat her decent. We wouldn't mind you as a son-in-law. I think it would work out all right.'

'No, it wouldn't. I think on Hannah as I would a very young sister.'

Bright colour flooded Matthew's face as he continued, 'I'm a bit embarrassed, so I am. Don't know how to phrase what I want to say.' He focused his attention on the whiskey as he swirled it round in the glass. 'You might not be aware of it, but Hannah will be sixteen soon and Liz, my wife, says that she's becoming aware of her body. You know what I mean?'

It was Johnnie's turn to show embarrassment. An ordinary girl would have noticed sooner. His young sister Peggy clearly felt awkward about her burgeoning breasts. He shrugged. 'In the circumstances, that's to be expected, I would imagine.'

'What I'm trying to say, Johnnie, is my daughter would

be safe with you. Do you really have to marry this other girl? Could we not make a bit of a settlement on her? You know, see she wants for nothing?'

Johnnie rose to his feet. He must get out of here before he said something he might later regret. 'I'll have to go now, Mr McFadden. Can I have Saturday week off? I'll work late as usual the night before, getting orders ready for you to do the deliveries. If you like, our Peggy can help you out. She's just left school and is looking for a job. I told her that you might give her some part-time Saturday work.' He was glad he had managed to mention Peggy; she would be waiting anxiously to see if Mr McFadden would take her on. There wasn't much chance of that now, but at least he had asked the question.

Matthew leaned back in his chair and looked up at him. 'Right you are, son. I'm sorry if I spoke out of place. It's just . . . you were the answer to our prayers. My wife will be very disappointed to hear that you're getting married.'

Johnnie was out of the door in a flash. Matthew's voice followed him. 'Tell Peggy she can start next Saturday.'

When Johnnie had gone, Matthew poured himself another large whiskey, and gulped it down in two swallows. Now he must tell Liz about Johnnie's plans. She would be devastated. They had married late in life and were delighted when Hannah was born. Their world revolved around her. But what would become of her when they passed on? he thought in despair.

4

Johnnie walked blindly down Springfield Road, quickly bypassing the bunch of lads gathered at the corner who normally would have invited him over for a chat, and crossed the road to Dunville Park. Usually not one to be abrupt, he was aware that he was causing a bit of speculation by his attitude, but he needed time to think things through. He was in no fit state to talk to anyone at the moment. Mr McFadden had taken all the wind out of his sails. Sinking down on to a bench in a sheltered spot in the park, he clutched his head in his hands and rocked in despair. What was he going to do now? Who was he going to turn to? His mother? Yes, he would ask her what she thought.

That very day, as he'd checked the stock in an upstairs room, he had realised that those rooms above the shop had great potential for a comfortable home. The two big, spacious rooms would serve as a living room and a bedroom, where there would be ample room for a cot, and the two smaller rooms could be converted into a kitchen and a bathroom. Just imagine, if he could offer Mary a home with the prospect of a bathroom in the not too distant future. Surely that would cheer her up?

The more he thought about it, the more excited he had become at the very idea, and he had started roughly working out in his head how much it was likely to cost. He would need a bank loan, that was for sure, but he had a job and getting the boss's backing shouldn't be an obstacle. Once he had broken the news of his forthcoming marriage to Mr McFadden, surely he could persuade him to rent him the rooms?

For the first time since learning of Mary's pregnancy, for that brief spell in those upstairs rooms, he had been happy. He had had something to look forward to; something to plan for. His mind had been rampant with all kinds of ideas; with hope for the future. He had felt that things were beginning to look up and could work out in his favour; that he could make Mary happy. He knew how much she dreaded living next door to his parents. The thought of his mother dropping in unexpectedly whenever she felt like it had filled Mary with dread. So the idea of renting the rooms above the shop had lifted his spirits no end. Lucky for him Mr McFadden had got his oar in first; saved Johnnie from making a complete fool of himself. At least he had been spared that. He shook his head in bewilderment. How could any father of a backward daughter want her married off? She wasn't all that backward if the truth were known, he reminded himself; just a bit slow on the uptake. Still, in his mind it was an unthinkable thing to do. A sin. Especially the way her father doted on her; was forever singing her praises.

But then again, she was very pretty; some lad would be glad to marry her and take care of her. Reluctantly, he even began to see the boss's way of thinking. Mr McFadden knew that soon men would want to pay court to his daughter and he would want her to marry someone he knew and could trust implicitly. Someone who wouldn't be after her for her money alone, or take advantage of her vulnerability. Obviously that's why he'd had Johnnie in mind as a prospective son-in-law. The fact that Johnnie could also manage the business must have seemed like a godsend to him.

It started to rain; a heavy drizzle. He ignored the discomfort for some minutes. Then, tugging his cap down low on his brow and his collar up around his neck, he rose stiffly to his feet and with a forlorn sigh left the park and headed home. If only he could turn the clock back, how different things would be now. But enough of that, he chastised himself. Too late for tears. If he had behaved himself in the first place there would be no need for regrets. Now he must look ahead and face the consequences.

To his surprise his mother was alone in the kitchen. Monday was one of the few nights when all the family normally stayed indoors, usually due to a shortage of funds after spending what little money they had over the weekend.

'Where is everybody?'

'Louise is away to the pictures with Cathie and Jean.'

'I thought she went out with them on a Saturday night.'

'She used to, but I think she's dating somebody now,' Nora confessed. 'Must be someone she really likes. She's being very evasive about it all.'

Recalling Louise's glowing countenance on Saturday night, Johnnie silently agreed with his mother. She must have met someone special to make her look so radiant. He could only hope that his sister would be more responsible than he and Mary had been. She would soon tell him where to get off if he tried to advise her. And rightly so!

'What about Harry?'

Nora smiled. 'Poor Harry. Remember he started work today? Well, he was completely whacked when he got home and went to bed as soon as he got his tea. He said the horses are hard to handle and his arms and legs are killing him.'

'He'll soon get used to it.'

'I know. That's what I told him. He wasn't grumbling, mind you. He's delighted to get a job at last. And his admiration for the horses knew no bounds. He'll be happy working for J.B.'

'And Peggy?'

'She went over to borrow a book from Mrs Duffy and hasn't came back yet. Why all the questions? You aren't usually bothered where they all are.'

'I know, but . . . Mam, could I have a word with you in confidence?'

'What about your tea? You're late. I've saved you some.'

'It can wait. I'd like your opinion on something first.'

She went to the sofa and sitting down patted the space beside her. 'Of course, son. Sit down and I'll lend you an ear.'

He plonked himself wearily down beside her and gazed blindly at his clenched hands where they rested on his muscular thighs. He sat in silent misery and she waited patiently for him to speak. At last he turned a worried face towards her.

At the sight of his sunken cheeks and dark-ringed eyes her heart swelled with pity. Not yet nineteen, this handsome son of hers looked as if he had the worries of the world on his shoulders. She felt bitter, and blamed Mary Gilmore. Life was tough enough without this to worry about. Hadn't the priests and nuns drummed it into them regularly from the pulpit and at school that if there were no bad girls there would be no bad boys? Remembering how she had felt about Bill McCartney, the strong urge that she had longed to submit to, she felt ashamed. Who was she to judge anyone? She was in no position to cast the first stone. Then, recalling how she'd had the strength and sense to send Bill on his merry way, she felt a little justified; Mary should have kept Johnnie at arm's length. If she had been strong enough to resist his advances she wouldn't be pregnant today. After all, men were weak where sex was concerned. It was up to the girl to keep the situation under control.

Perhaps she and the kids could have had a better life away from Springview Street with Bill. Somewhere far from the troubles, when they were at their height. Had she been wrong to spurn his advances? Would the family have been better off had she given in to his pleas and left Tommy? Even Tommy would probably have met someone else eventually and been a happier man today. She sighed. That was something she would never know. She had stuck to her wedding vows. For better, for worse, she had done her duty and stayed with Tommy, and in her opinion Mary should have made Johnnie wait.

With a brief shake of the head to clear away unwelcome thoughts, she gave her son all her attention. 'What is it, Johnnie? What's happened now?'

'I asked Mr McFadden for the day off for the wedding.'

Nora drew back with a look of alarm. 'One day! You've got to be joking!' He shook his head and she continued, 'Can't you get the Monday off at least? Mary will need to get away for a couple of days, Johnnie, before she starts living next door to us. God in heaven, the poor soul must dread the very idea of it.'

Grateful for his mother's understanding Johnnie quickly

agreed. 'She does, Ma, she does. But I'm lucky to get Saturday off. It's our busiest day. Besides, it'll be two days really. I'll be free as usual on Sunday. We could go to Bangor for a couple of days. I wouldn't dare try to get any more time off. You see, it seems the boss is very disappointed in me.'

'What do you mean, disappointed?' Nora was alarmed. 'Is it because you have to marry Mary? It's none of his business what you do in your private life, son.'

'That's where you're wrong, Ma. Him and his wife had big plans for me and I've gone and let them down.'

Nora's blood thundered through her veins. Had Mary Gilmore spoiled her son's chances of a successful future? 'What kind of plans?' Feeling her way, she added, 'Don't tell me he was going to offer you a partnership and because of your having to get married he's changed his mind. Is that it?'

'No, not really. The way he sees it, I could eventually own the business if I fall in with his plans.'

'Oh, Johnnie, that's wonderful news. Just wonderful.' Nora leaned towards him and kissed his cheek. 'Why are you so glum, then? You should be delighted.'

'Ah, but you see, Ma, there were strings attached. More like ropes in fact. He had planned for me to marry Hannah.' He leaned back and watched her in anticipation. He wasn't disappointed.

'Hannah?' Incredulity drained all vestige of life from Nora's face. Her mouth fell wide open and her eyes bulged. '*His* Hannah?'

Johnnie was pleased that his mother was as upset as he was at the news. He nodded. 'The very same.'

'I don't believe you! Is he daft or what?' she gasped.

'Not by any means. The way I see it, if I marry Hannah he would hold the reins until he and his wife died, then

I would inherit the business. My reward for being his son-in-law and looking after his daughter. He even hinted that I should abandon Mary. Imagine that! Just who the hell does he think he is?'

Nora was shaking her head in bewilderment. 'You're right, son. That was very presumptuous of him.' She sat silent for some moments turning his words over in her mind, then asked apprehensively, 'If you don't fall in with his wishes, have you still got a job, or . . . ?'

'For now. But, Ma, how can I work there? I even intended asking him to let me have the rooms above the shop for Mary and me. I'm glad now that I didn't. Seems he had already given some thought as to how the upstairs could be converted into a comfortable flat for his daughter and me. All this was going on in his mind and he never once said a word to me. Ma, it was a nightmare, standing there listening to him.'

'I don't know Hannah all that well; she was never about the shop much. They're very protective of her, and I know she's lovely to look at. Is she very backward?'

'No, not really. Just a bit slow. She's sweet and very pretty and someone will be glad to marry her if that's what you mean, but not me. The boss would like to see her settled with someone he knows he can trust. And I was the chosen one.'

'What are you going to do?'

'Look for another job, I guess. But I'll need a reference from him and the way things stand I can't see him giving me a good one.'

'He will, son.' Nora sounded more assured than she felt. 'He's not an unreasonable man. He's bound to see sense. Besides, you mightn't need to leave. He might keep you on. He couldn't do without you. Why, you practically run that shop yourself.'

'Don't kid yourself, Ma. No one is indispensable. I can only pray that he'll give me a good reference and I'll be able to get another job somewhere.'

Now Nora was really worried. Jobs were hard to come by. What on earth would become of him and Mary with a baby on the way? 'What if he wants you to stay on at the shop? What then? Will you be able to forget his proposition and continue working there as if nothing had happened?'

Seeing her agitation unsettled Johnnie. 'Ah, Ma, don't look so worried. I shouldn't have bothered you with my problems. I only wanted someone to talk to, that's all. I'll manage somehow and I'll continue going to work as long as I can and see how things pan out. He'll still need me until he gets someone to fill my place. Meanwhile I'll look out for another job.' He rose wearily to his feet. 'Don't bother about the tea. I'm not hungry. Besides, I must get out of these wet clothes or I'll catch my death. Good night, Ma.'

'Good night, Johnnie. And I'm here any time you want to talk. Remember that.'

At the door Johnnie paused. 'You won't say anything to me da, sure you won't?'

Nora was hesitant. 'Perhaps *you* should tell him, Johnnie. Working in the depot, he might put a word in for you or know someone who'll know about a job going.'

'That's a gag. When has he ever done anything to help any of us, eh? Tell me that. As a father he's completely useless. He never once encouraged us to better ourselves. Not once that I can remember! All he can do is find fault. I'd rather you didn't mention it to him, Ma. He still thinks I should shirk my responsibilities and take myself off across the water. There's no way I'm going to do that. Look at the way poor Louise was stuck in the mill. She never got a choice.'

114

Nora sighed and said in her husband's defence, 'That was my fault, son. We needed the money then.'

'No, Ma. It wasn't your fault. If me da hadn't been drinking and gambling half his wages week in week out we would probably have been living in that house with a garden you were always on about by now. Far away from the Falls Road. No. It wasn't your fault, far from it! Just don't mention it to him, Ma.'

'OK, son. Whatever you say.'

To Johnnie's surprise, next day, Mr McFadden greeted him with a cheery good morning and treated him as if nothing untoward had happened between them. In fact, he told Johnnie that he could have from Friday night until the following Wednesday morning off, with pay. He also laughingly informed him he'd have to think about giving him a rise in his wages, seeing as he would have two more mouths to feed. Utterly confused, Johnnie stammered when he tried to express his gratitude, but Matthew waved it aside.

'Son, I shouldn't have even mentioned my dreams for you and Hannah once you said you were getting married. It's just I had plans made in my head. I thought everybody, including you, would think it a great idea. So I was very disappointed at the time. I can tell you that Liz was annoyed with me. Very annoyed, in fact. She pointed out, in no uncertain terms, that we just can't arrange other people's lives like that!' He smiled at the memory and continued, 'So don't you worry about your job, son. It's here as long as you want it.'

Johnnie worked in a daze all day, and Nora made the sign of the cross and sent a thank You prayer heavenward when he relayed the news to her. It seemed that all was not lost.

Peggy was delighted when her brother told her that she could start work in the shop on Saturday. Throwing her arms round his neck, she hugged him. 'Thanks, Johnnie. Thanks very much. I dreaded the idea of working in the mill.'

Louise was surprised at the well of sadness that settled on her when she heard the news. She was the only one in the family, besides her mother, who worked in the mill. Apparently no one cared about her or how she felt about working there. Did they think that she was fit for nothing else? No! Her mother had had no choice but to get her started in the mill. At that time nothing else had been available. Hadn't Johnnie been thrown out of the shipyard? Still, if only things had been different and she had been able to get a better job away from the mill, say in one of the big stores down town, she might today stand a good chance of Cissie O'Rourke's accepting her as a girlfriend for her Conor. She sighed and pushed the resentful thoughts from her mind. Too late for regrets now. She should have exerted herself years ago and somehow or other got out of the mill. Still, maybe it wasn't too late? Perhaps if she kept her eyes open when she was out shopping in the city centre, she might just see an opening advertised in one of the big store windows that would be suitable for her. The thought cheered her up some-what.

With a mental shrug she hugged Peggy. She didn't begrudge her little sister her good fortune. 'Good luck, Peg. Work hard and maybe Mr McFadden will take you on full time.'

'Don't count on it,' Johnnie warned. 'But meanwhile keep your eyes and ears open and learn all you can.' He was surprised at how the news transformed his young sister. She absolutely glowed and looked really pretty. He had never seen her so happy.

With Harry's help Johnnie decorated the upstairs rooms in Mrs Clarke's house. He bought a bed, a new one; nothing grand, but it put a big hole in his savings. Still, it had to be done. There was no way he would expect Mary to sleep in a second-hand bed. With Mrs Clarke's permission he painted the scullery a bright yellow and bought a small second-hand gas stove. Mrs Clarke still used the old range for all her cooking needs, but that was something else he couldn't expect Mary to do. Mick Gilmore, like the good husband and father he was, had done away with their big cast-iron range long ago and replaced it with a more modern grate and a new stove in the scullery. It would be too expensive to make those kinds of changes in Mrs Clarke's house; a house he would never own, or indeed want to own. So he made do with buying the stove. He also whitewashed the lavatory walls and renewed and painted the wooden slats that encased the toilet pot. Pleased with the result of his efforts, on the Thursday before they were to be married he brought Mary in to view her new home.

Watched by a beaming Mrs Clarke, who was delighted at how well her house was looking, and an apprehensive Johnnie, Mary managed a smile and feigned pleasure when she saw the scullery and the yard. She was a terrible cook at the best of times; in fact her mother did all the cooking for the family, so how on earth would she manage to produce meals for a working man on this tiny stove? She didn't even know what kind of wages Johnnie earned. Would they be able to cope on his money when she had to give up work to look after their baby?

Upstairs was much better. She didn't have to pretend. After all, she just had to sleep in the front room which Johnnie had looking lovely, or sit in the back room on one of Mrs Clarke's easy chairs and do a spot of reading, or try her hand at knitting matinee coats for the baby, when Johnnie was out at work.

They were alone, Mrs Clarke's rheumatism making it difficult for her to climb the stairs. Sensing that Johnnie was disappointed by her attitude, Mary pressed close to him and muttered, 'Bear with me, Johnnie, please bear with me. There's a lot of things I'll have to get accustomed to from now on.'

'You're disappointed, aren't you?' he accused her glumly.

'No! No, not really.' She lied convincingly, not wanting to antagonise him. 'You've worked so hard to have it all lovely, so you have. It's . . . well, I just wish you would agree to live with my parents. I'd be so much happier.'

He turned away from her. 'No! What you're asking is impossible. What about me? I couldn't live under the same roof as your mother.' A swing of his arm embraced the room. 'Look, I know this isn't much, but it's a beginning. Everything has been done at such short notice and I don't know whether I'm coming or going, but I'm doing my best. This is only a temporary stop-gap. In time I'll find us somewhere decent, you'll see.'

He sat on the bed and patted the patchwork quilt his mother had given him, with new sheets and some almost new blankets to start them off, indicating that she join him. Nora and Louise had spent some time making up the bed and putting the finishing touches to the room, giving it a woman's touch, and he was disappointed that Mary hadn't acknowledged their efforts.

He watched in bewilderment as she slowly backed

away towards the door, a look of horror on her face. Comprehension dawned and he jumped to his feet in a rage. Gripping her roughly by the shoulders he gave her a good hard shake. 'Listen here, Mary. I've no desire to get you into bed. Believe me, no desire whatsoever,' he grated. 'It's the furthest thing from my mind at the moment. I only wanted to talk to you. You'll have to pull your weight too, you know. I can't be expected to do everything on my own.'

She gulped deep in her throat, eyes wide with alarm. 'You're hurting me.'

He became aware of her fear and abruptly released her. 'Come on, let's go.'

They descended the stairs slowly and bidding their new landlady good night went next door where Nora and Louise were eagerly awaiting Mary's verdict. One look at her surly face and they knew that she wasn't too chuffed.

'Sit down, Mary, and I'll make us a pot of tea,' Nora said, and disappeared into the scullery. She hadn't expected the girl to be leaping with joy, but she had hoped she would show some pleasure. Still, it was understandable. Mary was probably used to better. Most men had modernised their homes to a certain extent, unlike Tommy McGuigan, who was content to make do as they were.

Pretending she thought all was well, Louise said cheerfully, 'Well, isn't it lovely? Johnnie has worked his fingers to the bone getting it ready for you.'

Mary smiled and nodded but didn't speak. Johnnie followed his mother into the scullery. Nora glanced at him briefly and whispered, 'So she doesn't like it?'

'Afraid not.' His voice was bitter.

'Are you going to live with her parents, then?'

119

'Catch yourself on, Ma! Do you think I'm not wise or something? She'll live next door whether she likes it or not,' he said grimly. 'If she goes to her ma's, she goes on her own.' He stood brooding for some moments, then confessed, 'Do you know something, Ma? I almost hit her in there.' He jerked his head in the direction of next door, spacing an inch between finger and thumb. 'I came that close. That close. God forgive me.' His head drooped in shame.

Nora's hand gripped his arm. 'Oh, son . . . be careful.'

'Awful, isn't it? I'm at my wits' end. I wish we were married. It'll be all right then.'

Nora turned from him to pour the tea, and hide her expression. In her opinion it would probably be worse, but perhaps she was wrong. 'Here, help me carry this tea in. It's a great cure for all ails.'

Saturday dawned, bright but cold. Louise was very disappointed. She had hoped for a warm morning; didn't want to spoil the look of her lovely new dress by wearing her shabby coat over it on her way down to the church. She knew that St Peter's was a beautiful church, with wonderful altars and statues and colourful lead-light windows depicting scenes from the Bible, but it was also big and cold, unlike her parish church, St Paul's, which was smaller and usually warm. Unfortunately, Peel Street was in St Peter's parish, so the marriage had to take place there.

Mr McFadden had come up trumps. He gave them a very welcome cheque for a wedding present and, arranging for a friend to look after the shop for an hour, offered to run Johnnie, the bridesmaid and his parents down to the church in his car.

When he arrived at the house and heard that Tommy

wasn't going to attend the nuptial Mass he told Harry and Peggy to pile in as well. He warned Peggy that he would expect her to start work at one, adding that if she wanted to earn some extra cash she could help him out while Johnnie was away. Peggy thanked him and told him he would not be disappointed with her.

It was bitterly cold outside the church as they waited for the bride to arrive, and having braved the weather without a coat Louise knew that her goose-bumps were very apparent and her nose glowed red. To her surprise two arms wrapped a warm shawl round her shoulders from behind. She gazed down in surprise at the cobwebby mass of fine wool, then instinctively drew it tightly about her before turning to see who her benefactor was.

'I'm sorry, love. I meant you to have this last night but it was such short notice that I only got it finished this morning,' a voice whispered in her ear.

Louise's eyes glistened with a hint of tears at her grannie's thoughtfulness and she gripped her close. 'Oh, Grannie, thank you. It's beautiful.'

'I knew you'd be cold and your mam said you didn't want to wear your old coat but she couldn't afford to buy you a new one. When I first heard about the wedding I started to crochet like mad and I'm glad I got it finished. It'll still be cold inside, you know. It's always cold in this beautiful church, more's the pity.'

The shawl was white and crocheted in a beautiful shell pattern. Louise realised that her grannie must have burned the midnight oil to finish it in such a short time. It was truly a labour of love, as well as a work of art. She clasped it close to her slim body and could immediately feel the warmth of it. Again she hugged the small woman who had crocheted it. 'Thank you. Thank you very much, Grannie.'

A taxi drew up to the church and all eyes fastened on it. Mary's father assisted her from the cab and she stood gripping a new shawl round her shoulders. It was also white wool but not as pretty as hers, Louise noted. Sadie too had made sure her daughter wouldn't suffer from the cold. She was pale and nervous-looking, Mike grim-faced. Mary flashed a strained smile around her before hurrying into the church porch; Mike ignored everyone completely. For a while it had been touch and go whether or not he would attend his daughter's wedding, but eventually he had bowed to his wife's pleas. Nora, who had been unable to budge her Tommy, wondered how she had managed to persuade him.

Everybody shuffled after them into the church. Sadie was already inside and fussed around her daughter for a few minutes before Mary started slowly down the aisle clutching her father's arm. Liam, who had shared the bride's taxi, fell into step with Louise behind his father and sister. At the altar, Mike, as if leading a lamb to the slaughter, grimly handed his beloved daughter over to a solemn-faced Johnnie.

Louise's heart went out to Johnnie. Her beloved big brother looked lost and bewildered, and she didn't blame him. Mary looked anything but the happy bride. Louise could gladly have strangled her; told her to make an effort to put a brave face on. Still, she admitted inwardly, with a glance around the church, it wasn't very pleasant getting married with all the statues covered with purple wraps for the season of Lent. Even the stations of the cross were covered. There wasn't a flower anywhere to be seen and although the priest had made a concession and wore green vestments instead of the Lenten purple, they were a far cry from the white and gold robes normally worn during a nuptial Mass.

The service seemed to go on for ever, but at last Johnnie and Mary were pronounced man and wife. Sadie Gilmore wept buckets of tears and Nora wasn't far behind her. Louise could appreciate that in their own ways both mothers must be very disappointed, so they were unlikely to be crying tears of joy as they watched the bride and groom, accompanied by the best man and bridesmaid, follow the priest into the sacristy to sign the register. Then everyone gathered outside while a friend of Johnnie's took some photographs. As she hung about Louise saw Conor leave the church. She expected him to acknowledge her with a smile or a nod and pass on, but to her surprise he politely nodded to everyone and drew her to one side.

'You look gorgeous.'

'Thank you.' Louise blushed bright red at the compliment and the admiration in his eyes, but her pleasure quickly faded at his next remark.

'I can't take you to the pictures tonight.'

Hiding her disappointment, she managed to keep the smile fixed on her face and assured him, 'That's all right, Conor. Don't worry about it. No strings attached, remember.'

'It wouldn't be right, Louise. I insist we go somewhere where you can show off that beautiful dress. Will you come to a dance with me?'

Overcome with emotion, she was hesitant as she reminded him, 'Someone will surely see us and start talking.'

He grinned at her. 'Do you know something? I don't give a damn. I'm fed up with all this pussyfooting about. I'd be proud if you'd accompany me, and let me show you off.'

A warm feeling spread through her body and she gave him a tremulous smile. 'I'd love to.'

'See you tonight then.' With a squeeze of his hand he was gone.

Peggy sidled close to her sister, all agog with excitement. 'Was that Conor O'Rourke I saw talking to you?'

Not wanting anything to burst her bubble of happiness, Louise was a bit too abrupt. 'Why ask what you already know?'

'Are you dating him?'

'That's none of your business.'

Peggy sighed dramatically. 'He's so handsome, so he is. All the girls are after him. He—'

Louise cut her short. 'Here's Johnnie and Mary. Let's get a move on.' She didn't want to hear about all the girls who had their eye on Conor. She was already aware how attractive he was to the opposite sex and needed no reminder from her sister.

Sadie Gilmore had arranged for her next door neighbour to prepare a sit-down breakfast for the bride and groom, bridesmaid and best man, her husband, herself, and Nora, at the neighbour's home. The other guests were invited back to Sadie's where a finger buffet and drinks were laid on. The taxi returned for the bride and groom and Mary's mother and father. Johnnie declined to get in, insisting that they take his grannie instead.

It was just a short distance from the church to Peel Street and everybody crossed Albert Street and set out on foot along Raglan Street. Johnnie was flanked by Nora and Peggy and Louise was joined by Liam Gilmore. He had been giving her admiring glances all through the service and she supposed that she should be flattered, but there was something about him that put her off.

'I didn't realise that Johnnie had such a lovely sister.'

'Thank you.'

'Was that your boyfriend I saw you talking to outside the church?' he asked casually.

'None of your business.'

Her abrupt tone should have warned him off, but he wouldn't be deterred. 'I went to primary school with him, you know.'

'Did you indeed? How nice for you.'

He suddenly got the message. 'Look, am I annoying you?'

'I thought you'd never guess.'

He threw a sideways glance at her tight-lipped expression and sneered, 'You know something? You should be glad I'm paying you some attention. After all, you're nothing but a common wee mill worker and we all know what they're like. I don't know what a brainy guy like Conor O'Rourke sees in the likes of you. I'm sure he could do a lot better elsewhere.'

Cut to the bone, Louise managed to retort, 'I'm a better person than you'll ever hope to be, Liam Gilmore.'

'Huh! That's a matter of opinion.' With a snort and a disdainful look he fell behind to walk with the other guests and Louise was momentarily left on her own.

Why do people think that mill workers are less intelligent than others? she lamented inwardly. Her brother chanced to glance over his shoulder and saw she was walking alone. Excusing himself, he immediately dropped behind to join her.

'Are you all right, Louise?'

'Yes, Johnnie, I'm fine, thanks.'

'Well, you don't look it.'

'Thanks! You certainly know how to give a girl a confidence booster.'

'Come on, what's biting you? Who's ruffled your feathers?'

'Nothing. Look, Johnnie, drop it. You've enough on your plate without worrying about me.'

'It's Liam Gilmore, isn't it? What's he been saying to you?'

Louise sighed. He wasn't going to let go until he found out what was bothering her. 'If you must know, he just reminded me that I should be grateful for small mercies. After all, I'm only a common mill worker and shouldn't expect anything better.'

'A very pretty mill worker, if I may say so,' Johnnie chided her.

Her demeanour didn't brighten and he inwardly cursed Liam Gilmore for spoiling his sister's happiness. 'If he bothers you again, let me know and I'll punch his teeth out.'

This brought a smile to her face, albeit a small one. 'If that's a promise, I'll be sure to let you know.'

Eight places were set in the neighbour's house for breakfast for the main characters. Sadie was waiting to usher Nora, Johnnie, Louise, and her son in to join the other two already seated there. When Johnnie discovered there was an extra place set in case his da changed his mind, he left the house and came back with his grannie.

'You've started something, I can tell you. My two grannies will want to know why they weren't invited to the breakfast,' Mary whispered.

Not in the least put out, Johnnie replied, 'Not to worry. Just explain to them that that was my da's place Grannie got. It's lucky my other grannie's dead so there's no competition.'

After the breakfast, an Ulster fry, which was delicious and had been made short shrift of, the groomsman was called upon to make a speech. Liam rose to his feet and took a sheet of notepaper from his pocket. Spreading it on the table in front of him he managed, with frequent glances towards the paper, to get through a passable but pointed speech.

It was apparent to Louise that the message was to the effect that Johnnie had better make his sister happy or he would answer to Liam in no uncertain terms. He was so full of himself that Louise cringed with dismay as she listened to him deride her brother in front of everyone. Johnnie was a better man than this egotist could ever hope to be. She could see that her mother was upset as well, as she sat tight-lipped. Her da should have been here. He would soon have put Liam Gilmore in his place. But that was typical of her da. Never around when he was needed. She would never forgive him for not coming to support his son on his wedding day. Johnnie had shrugged indifferently when she mentioned it to him. 'Why change the habit of a lifetime?'

Next Johnnie was called on to speak. He rose to his feet and, wagging a finger in Liam's direction, laughingly warned him that he had better beware as he would get as good as he gave. Then he thanked all concerned, on behalf of the bride and himself, for putting over the breakfast and buffet and for all the lovely presents they had received. Leaning over Mary, and for all the world as if they were deliriously happy, he took her hand in his and kissing the back of it thanked her for making him the happiest man in the world for agreeing to marry him. Louise was proud of him. No one could fault him or be able to say he was a reluctant groom. She stole a glance at Mary and was surprised to see she was actually smiling. Wonders would never cease. Perhaps now that she had a ring on her finger and the dust had settled a bit, it might all come right after all.

Mike was called on for a speech but with a slight smile he declined. Perhaps he was afraid of what he might say. Tommy was glaringly conspicuous by his absence but no one commented on it, at least not to his family. After the speeches everybody went next door to join the other guests. Glad to get away from all the false gaiety, Peggy and Harry excused themselves and left at half past twelve to walk up to work. Peggy loved working in the shop and was determined to prove she was so good at her job that Mr McFadden would offer her a permanent position. Harry had refused to ask for a whole day off from his new job. Louise wished she could make her excuses and walk home with them, but decided as bridesmaid it was her duty to stay put. Johnnie needed all the support he could get.

After mingling and talking for some time with the other guests, Louise excused herself and went into the scullery. Leaving her empty glass on the draining board she decided to use the lavatory before going home. All that lemonade was taking its effect. About to open the back door, she turned when she heard the scullery door close gently behind her. Liam Gilmore stood with his back to it, his eyes roving insolently over her body.

'I want to apologise for my behaviour earlier on.'

His words were a little slurred and Louise was instantly alert. She decided not to antagonise him and said pleasantly, 'You're forgiven.' To get away from him she opened the door to the yard. 'Now if you'll excuse me.'

In a flash he was beside her and with a push had her outside in the yard and the door closed before she could utter another word. She gaped at him in amazement. 'Just what do you think you're doing?'

He smiled lewdly at her and she backed away until she was against the wall and could go no further. He slowly advanced on her. Leaning a hand on the wall on either side of her, he leered down into her face. 'I've been waiting to get you alone. I think we should take this opportunity to get to know each other a wee bit better, eh? What do you think? After all, we're practically family now.'

She could smell the booze on his breath and warned herself to stay cool. 'I think you're drunk, that's what I think, and I advise you to let me go.' He made no attempt to move. 'I'll scream.'

He actually sniggered. 'Do you honestly think anyone in there will hear you? They're all three sheets to the wind already. It's wonderful how free booze appeals to even the most temperate.' He pressed closer.

'Someone is sure to need the loo,' she snapped.

'Would you be surprised if I told you I barred the scullery door?'

Louise was really becoming frightened now. She didn't want this drunk slobbering all over her. Putting her hands against his chest she pushed with all her might. He didn't budge an inch, but his arms left the wall and closed around her. She struggled fiercely but found herself powerless in his tight embrace.

'You know,' he chided her, 'this could be quite pleasant if you'd only relax. A girl like you will know what it's all about. Isn't that right?'

She raised her head in amazement. 'Just what do you mean, a girl like me?'

He grabbed his opportunity and lowered his flushed face towards hers, his beer-laden breath fanning over her face. She squirmed her head to one side to avoid the foul odour, and his mouth landed on her ear. Gripping her chin he made sure that next time his wet lips found their mark, making her stomach lurch in an attempt to be free of its contents. Someone was banging on the scullery door, distracting him momentarily. She twisted her head free and tried to shout out, but he promptly clamped a sweaty hand over her mouth, stifling her cry for help.

'They'll soon give up and use next door's loo. We've plenty of time to finish our little bit of business,' he assured her.

In a panic she struggled fiercely as his mouth devoured hers and his hands explored her body. She remembered reading about how to defend yourself in this kind of situation: knee the offender where it hurts most. But he was too tall; there was no way she could get her knee up that far. She kicked out at his shins instead, but to no avail. He was far too strong to be hurt by her puny attempts.

Johnnie passed himself, going from guest to guest making polite conversation, all the while covertly watching Mary drown her sorrows. Much as he longed to, he didn't give in to the desire to join her. A taxi was coming at four o'clock to take them to the station to catch a train to Bangor, where he had booked them into a B&B for three days, and he intended to be sober when it came.

He had seen Liam go into the scullery some time ago and to his knowledge he hadn't come back. A smile twitched his lips. Perhaps Liam was ill. Served him right! The way he was swilling the beer back. Johnnie hoped he choked to death on his own vomit. Then he felt ashamed at the pleasure this thought gave him. After all, Liam was nothing but a loud-mouthed lout.

They would be going soon and it was time to say goodbye to his mother, Grannie and Louise. He made his way to where the two older women sat deep in conversation with other guests; there was no sign of Louise.

Perhaps she had left earlier? No, his sister wouldn't

leave without wishing him and Mary well. Where on earth was she? Suddenly, an uneasy feeling swept over him, and he crossed the room in three strides. He tried to open the scullery door. It was barred. He caught Sadie's eye. 'Who's out there?' He banged on the door. No response. Without another word he charged out of the front door.

Sadie shrugged and said to anyone showing interest, 'He must be desperate.'

Watched by startled guests Johnnie stood in the kitchen of the neighbour's house looking anxiously around: no sign of his sister. He quickly crossed the room and surged through the scullery and out into the yard. The lavatory door was closed and he said softly, 'Louise?'

A drunken grunt was his only answer. A glance around the yard showed him an upturned barrel and, rolling it across to the dividing wall between the two back yards, he upended it close to the wall and climbed on top. The wall wasn't high, and as he stood on the barrel peering over into the neighbouring yard the sight that met his eyes made him hoist himself up and quite literally throw himself over the top. He landed awkwardly but was on his feet in an instant behind Liam Gilmore. The thud of his landing brought Liam's head round and at the sight of Johnnie he let go his hold on Louise. Johnnie grabbed him by the shoulder and swinging him round hit him full in the face with his clenched fist. A lot of bad feeling and anger went into the punch and Liam fell heavily, blood pouring from his mouth. Gripping him by the lapels, Johnnie hauled him to his feet, thrust him against the wall and butted him full on the nose, gratified by the sound of breaking bone. He had raised his fist for another punch when Louise grabbed his arm and clung on.

'Don't, Johnnie. He's not worth it. He's had enough.'

Through clenched teeth, her brother grated, 'Did he harm you?'

'No! No he didn't.'

'You know what I mean,' he growled. 'Did he touch you . . . indecently?'

'No. Let him go, Johnnie. Please? I beg of you.'

Slowly Johnnie released his hold on Liam, who moved quickly towards the back door, smearing blood across his face with the back of his hand. Not knowing when he was well off, he paused to sneer over his shoulder, 'So it's all right for you to put my sister up the spout, but wrong for me to touch your precious bitch, eh? And do you know something? I think she was beginning to enjoy it.'

It was his undoing. Fast though he was Johnnie beat him to the door and viciously landed another two punches to his face. All his pent-up frustration was behind the blows and this time Liam made no effort to get up; just curled up defensively on the ground. Glaring down at him Johnnie warned, 'If you ever lay a finger on my sister again I'll kill you. I mean that!'

Louise tugged at his arm, pulling him into the scullery and closing the door. She stood gulping for breath, trying to keep the bile down, but unable to help herself she turned and threw up into the shining white sink. 'Oh, my God, look what I've done!' she cried, on the verge of hysteria. 'What'll I do, Johnnie?'

Johnnie put an arm round her shoulders and reaching across turned on the tap. 'Never mind that. It'll wash away. Now, get a grip of yourself, love. Did he harm you? Tell me the truth, now.'

'No, he just turned my stomach.'

Johnnie moved away from her, but realising his intention Louise got between him and the back door. With great difficulty she urged him towards the scullery door and, unbarring it, pushed him into the kitchen. A stunned silence fell on the room as everyone stopped what they were doing and gazed at them in horror. Straightening his jacket and smoothing down the front of his blood-splattered shirt with damaged hands, a white-faced Johnnie lifted his head high. Going over to his mother, he said, 'Say your goodbyes, Ma. You too, Grannie, and I'll walk you to the corner.'

Uncomprehending, Nora gazed at him wide-eyed, then shaking her head in despair she lifted her purse and nodded for her mother to follow suit. They said subdued farewells to everybody.

Nora went to Mary and, holding her close, whispered in her ear, 'I don't know what on earth has happened to get him in this state, but don't you worry, love, he'll be good to you.' At least she hoped so. By the state he was in she realised that something awful must have happened out in the yard. Johnnie wasn't normally a violent person, yet how did he get all that blood on his new shirt? And his knuckles were raw.

Without another word, Johnnie took Louise, who was still shaking and obviously distressed, by the arm and said to Mary, 'Excuse me, love. I'm just walking our ones to the corner. I won't be long. Be ready when I get back, will you? The taxi should be here soon.'

Mary had risen apprehensively to her feet and was gazing at him, eyes wide with fear. 'What on earth happened, Johnnie? Are you all right?'

He smiled grimly. 'I'm fine. There's nothing for you to worry about on that score. Everything has been taken care of.'

Mike Gilmore observed all this through narrowed lids. When the goodbyes were over and Johnnie had ushered

133

his family outside Mike headed for the scullery where, just as he had expected, he found his son leaning over the sink bathing his swollen, bloody face in cold water.

Glad that his wife had gone upstairs to help Mary prepare to leave for her honeymoon, and had yet to see the state her precious son was in, Mike closed and barred the door. 'What happened?'

Liam turned to him and Mike saw that his lip was split open and his nose appeared to be broken. 'Our Mary's new husband beat me up, that's what!'

'You'll need to go to the hospital to get those injuries seen to,' Mick observed. 'Why did he hit you?'

'For nothing. I never laid a finger on him, and that's the truth.'

'Mmm. I noticed he wasn't marked, except for his knuckles.' Mike's lips twisted and his tone was dry. 'Why didn't you retaliate?'

'I didn't get a chance. He grabbed me from behind.'

'What were you doing? He must have had good reason to attack you. Was his sister out there with you?'

Obviously in pain when he moved his lips, Liam answered, 'Yes, Louise and I were just talking . . .' Blood spouted from his lip and nose as if protesting at the lies he was uttering and he dabbed gently at it before continuing, 'The next thing I knew, he grabbed me and started butting and punching me in the face.'

'I got the impression that he went over the back wall from next door to get at you. Why was that? Did you bar the scullery door? Did he know what you were up to?'

Becoming aware that his father wasn't offering any sympathy, Liam became apprehensive. He stuttered slightly. 'Lou . . . Louise and I were getting to know each other. You know how it is? We wanted a bit of privacy.'

'Really?' Mike advanced until he had his son against the door. 'You lying git! I saw the way that girl was avoiding you. What were you doing that made Johnnie McGuigan so mad? Eh?'

Cowering against the back door, trying to escape his father's scorn, Liam whimpered, 'We were just talking, I tell you.'

'Listen, son, it's not your ma you're talking to now. I know what you're like, and I don't doubt for one minute that you were molesting that young girl. You should be ashamed of yourself. I only hope she doesn't cry rape or you'll really be in big trouble. If the police come knocking on our door, you're on your own. I'll have nothing more to do with you.'

Liam's eyes widened and he gasped, 'No! It didn't get that far.'

'Well, that's a relief. I'm glad to hear it. And a word of warning . . . don't you go getting any brave ideas into your head about arranging for a couple of your mates to help you teach Johnnie a lesson. Whether we like it or not, he's family now and don't you dare touch him. Mary has enough to contend with without you causing more trouble by landing her husband in hospital.' Liam's face became even redder and Mike knew he had hit the nail on the head. 'Understand?'

'You mean you want me to let him away with it?' Liam sounded incredulous.

'You've got it in one. I'm warning you, hands off.'

A loud knock on the scullery door brought both men's eyes to it.

'I hope that's not the police.'

'He . . . he wouldn't dare. Would he?'

Mike could see that his son was frightened and drove home his point. 'Huh! Wouldn't he? You'd better be careful in future. Johnnie McGuigan's no mug. Leave well alone.'

Another loud impatient knock and he drew back the bolt. His wife brushed past him. 'Is he all right?'

'He'll live.'

'Oh, sweet Jesus, just look at the state of him. What has Johnnie McGuigan done to you, son?'

Mike grimaced. He wished his wife could see their son for what he really was: a coward, a bully and a trouble-maker. Where Liam was concerned, Sadie saw through tinted glasses. Mike passed through the kitchen, a silly smile on his face. Everyone avoided eye contact and he quietly left the house. He'd go to the pub till all the guests had left. A wry smile twisted his mouth as he thought how the neighbours would have plenty to gossip about for some time to come. As if a shotgun wedding wasn't bad enough, Liam had to go and make a spectacle of himself. Poor Mary. What an awful start to married life.

Johnnie walked his family to the corner keeping up a running commentary about the wedding and the recep-tion. He refused to answer his mother's questions about what had gone on between him and Liam Gilmore, saying that the least said soonest mended. He also reminded them that Mary was family now and that they must respect his in-laws. At the corner of the street, they wished him well. Before taking his leave he drew Louise to one side.

'Sis, you won't say anything to me da, sure you won't?'

She grunted with scorn. 'As if! He would just love an excuse to go down there and start some more trouble. Don't worry, I won't say a word to anyone. If he does find out, it won't be from me. Thank God our Harry left early. He wouldn't be able to keep his big trap shut.'

Relieved at her understanding, he said, 'Thanks, Louise.

But mind you . . . if that bastard Gilmore should come anywhere near you while I'm away you've my permission to get me da to sort him out. OK?'

'I don't think he will. Besides, he took me unawares. I won't be so easily caught on the hop a second time. Away you go back to your wife. She needs you more than ever now.' She kissed him on the cheek. 'Best of luck, Johnnie.'

With a deep sigh, he admitted, 'I'll need it!'

The honeymoon went from bad to worse. The guest-house where Johnnie had booked them in for bed and breakfast was spacious and clean. The landlady was very friendly and had tea and hot soda farls ready for them in front of an open grate where logs burned brightly.

'Oh, you shouldn't have,' Johnnie admonished her, overcome by the woman's kindness – the first he had been shown all day.

Guessing that money was tight, the landlady was quick to explain. 'Don't worry. It's just a wee friendly gesture. I know you're booked in for bed and breakfast, but it's so cold this evening I thought a nice cup of tea would be welcome.'

'It certainly is, thank you. Thank you very much.' Johnnie nudged Mary.

She came to with a start. 'You're very kind. Thank you,' she said softly.

They hadn't eaten since breakfast that morning and Johnnie was ravenous. He did justice to the freshly baked soda farls, dripping with butter; Mary, dreading the night that lay ahead, listlessly nibbled her way through a single slice.

After tea Johnnie suggested, since it was dry, that they go for a walk along the front before retiring. It was cold and Mary tightened the scarf round her neck and pulled the collar of her coat up to cover her ears. Johnnie trudged glumly beside her, scared to put his arm around her, afraid of rejection.

He was relieved when she moved closer and voluntarily slipped her arm through his. Pressing it tight to his side he bent and brushed her hair with his lips. She stiffened, but then shot him a nervous smile.

'It's going to be all right, you know, Mary.'

'I know. I know it is.'

'I'm glad all that fuss is over. All we need now is a bit of time to get to know each other better.'

Her face lit up at these words and she said in a rush, 'Will you give me time, Johnnie?' He was confused and she elaborated nervously. 'We don't have to do anything right away, do we?'

He turned her words over in his mind and then enlightenment dawned. 'You mean have intercourse? But we can!' She must still think it a sin. He hastened to assure her, 'We're married now. It's not a sin any more, you know.'

She gulped deep in her throat. 'I know that, but can't we just wait for a while longer?' He lifted his cap and scratched his head in bewilderment and she hurried on, 'Remember, we've the baby to consider.'

She was trembling like a leaf against his side and he warned himself to take it easy. After all, what did another few nights matter? 'If that's what you want, we'll take it easy for a while.'

Her relief was obvious as she sank weakly against him, and he was glad he had been able to reassure her. But what about him? Would he be able to control himself, with her lying beside him each night, and him knowing she was his wife?

* * *

138

When Johnnie had taken leave of them, the trio trudged home in silence, each buried in her own private thoughts. Louise refused to betray Johnnie's confidence, to the chagrin of the others. Still shaken from her encounter with Liam Gilmore, she embraced her grannie and thanked her again for the beautiful shawl the minute they entered the house, then excused herself and went straight upstairs to her room. Removing her dress she hung it carefully on a hanger and examined it minutely to see if it had been damaged in any way by the rough wall that Liam Gilmore had forced her against. Finding no damage or obvious stains she hung it in the wardrobe and stretched out on top of the bedclothes, trying to push the whole sordid episode from her mind. She had never been so close to a man before and could still feel his body pressing against hers and see his sweaty leering face looming over her. She squirmed with repugnance, feeling dirty and degraded. The memory made her stomach turn and she shook uncontrollably.

She had been really frightened to discover that Liam had locked the scullery door, and so relieved when Johnnie had come over the yard wall like an avenging angel, she had actually shed some tears. What if Johnnie hadn't come looking for her? Would Liam have dared to . . . her mind shied away from the horrible thought. Yes, she was very much afraid that he would have dared! He had been drunk and beyond reasoning, and who would have believed her word against his? And what other man would have wanted her afterwards? What would Conor have thought of her?

She fell into an uneasy doze and it was the sound of Peggy coming in from work that brought her scrambling off the bed. A glance at the alarm clock told her that she had better get a move on. Quickly stripping, she pulled on her old dress and grabbing her toiletry descended the stairs in a rush. Flashing Peggy an apologetic look, she said, 'I'll only be ten minutes, Peg. I promise. I dozed off.'

'It's well for you. I've been working hard all afternoon. Where's Ma?'

As if on cue the front door opened and Nora came in full of apologies. 'Sorry, girls. I walked home with your grannie and we got talking and I lost all track of time.' Shrugging out of her coat she hung it on the rack. 'I'll start the tea.'

Peggy snorted. 'You'll be lucky.' She threw Louise a look of wrath. 'She's going into the scullery to get ready to go out. Aren't some people lucky?'

'Sorry . . . I'll be quick.' Louise hurried into the scullery and bolted the door. At least she had tonight to look forward to. Conor was taking a chance taking her out in public and she was determined to look her best. Did it mean he really cared?

As she walked down to meet him, Louise wondered which dance hall he would take her to. Perhaps the Gig down Divis Street? She had never been there, but she knew it had a bad name. Still, they were less likely to run into anyone they knew there, so why not? Conor might already regret his impulsive promise and be glad to go somewhere they would not be recognised. She certainly didn't want to upset the apple cart. She had grown very fond of Conor, and really didn't care where they went so long as he wanted her with him. Nevertheless, a visit to a dance hall with him would be nice.

She crossed the Falls Road towards Dunville Park and he came forward to meet her, a happy grin on his face. 'You look a picture.'

Cheeks flushed with pleasure, she curtsied before him. 'Thank you, kind sir.'

'Where would you like to go?'

She shrugged, folded her arms and fixed her gaze sternly on him. Here she was all dolled up, obviously expecting to go to a dance, and he was asking her where she wanted to go? Had he changed his mind about taking her dancing? She eyed him steadily as she waited for him to suggest where they should go. He surprised her.

'Would you be daring enough to go to the dance in Hawthorn Street?'

She was taken aback; couldn't believe it. 'We will know most of the crowd there,' she warned him.

'You're my girl, aren't you? I mean, you're willing for people to know about us, aren't you?' She nodded cautiously in confirmation, and he continued, 'Then let's go.'

They retraced their steps across the Falls Road and made their way along Cavendish Street. Her heart was thumping so hard within her breast she feared he must surely hear it.

Early though it was, quite a few were making their way towards the hall in Hawthorn Street where a dance was held every Saturday night, and Louise was not blind to the sly nudges as several acquaintances greeted them.

'We're creating quite a stir,' Conor whispered. 'Are you sorry you came?'

She shook her head. 'Are you?'

'Not in the slightest. Do you think we'll make the headlines in the morning papers?' he teased. '*Louise and Conor step out*. I can just see it.'

She grinned at him. 'I'm afraid you're getting us confused with the likes of Alice Terry and Ramon Navarro. I was reading that their new film *Scaramouche* was released recently, so it should be over here soon. Maybe you'll take me to see it. Anyway, I don't think we're big celebrities like them. Still, tongues are sure to start wagging.'

She had worn her new shawl for the occasion and went to leave it in the cloakroom. When she returned Conor immediately swung her on to the dance floor and into a quickstep. She stumbled and apologised, 'I'm afraid I'm not a very good dancer.'

'Neither am I, but we'll manage somehow.'

They danced every dance and she soon discovered that he was in fact a very good dancer and in his arms she couldn't put a foot wrong. She was happy enough dancing reels and Gay Gordons and the Pride of Erin with him, but she enjoyed the slow dances the most, when he held her close as they waltzed round the floor. He proudly introduced her to those of his friends they met and she did likewise. She felt as if she was floating on air. Surely he cared for her or he wouldn't have brought her here where he was obviously well known. She hoped so. Life without him now would be very bleak.

Louise was drunk with happiness as they walked home arm in arm. They turned down Crocus Street, and as they passed the entry that led to the backs of the houses he drew her into the shadows it afforded, and gathered her close. The antics of Liam Gilmore that morning surfaced in her mind and she stiffened. Were all men the same, just after the one thing? He released her immediately and straightening to his full height looked askance at her.

'I'm sorry. I had a bad experience today.' She couldn't meet his eyes, she felt so ashamed.

Hand under her chin, he tipped her face up and patiently waited until her eyes met his. 'Tell me about it.'

Reluctantly she related to him all that had taken place at the wedding reception.

His concern was obvious. A frown bunched his brows together and he was so angry he actually spluttered. 'The filthy bastard! Did he harm you?'

'No, he didn't get a chance. Our Johnnie twigged what was happening and leapt over the yard wall from next door.'

Cupping her face in his hands, he whispered, 'You know I'd never take advantage of you, don't you?' She nodded and he continued, 'You're beautiful and I'm afraid I've fallen in love with you. Do you think you could learn to care for me?'

She gazed up at him, eyes filled with trust. 'Yes, I do,' she whispered. He drew her gently against him and this time she went willingly. She discovered it was a different matter entirely being held close by him. They kissed, long warm kisses that thrilled her to the very core, and not once did he cross the line of decency.

Then suddenly he eased her gently from him. 'Come on, I'd better get you home before that damned curfew starts.'

He walked her to the door and planting a quick kiss on her lips he vowed again, 'I'm going to marry you one day.'

'What about your mother? She'll never agree to your seeing me, let alone marrying me.'

'I'll take you home to meet her soon. She can't help but like you. Good night, love.'

Louise watched him stride down the street and her heart was sad. Somehow she didn't think his mother would ever agree to meeting her.

5

Married life was not what Johnnie had expected. Not that he had ever thought much about what it would be like, as he'd had no intention of getting married for some time to come. Then Mary dropped her bombshell and changed his whole way of life. The time after being thrown out of the shipyard had been a miserable one. Until he got the job in McFadden's shop, there had been no money to spend, nothing to do but hang about street corners, sometimes even getting into mischief by pinching apples and the like from stalls outside shops. Then when he and some of his pals had jobs they were able to help those friends less well off and he enjoyed himself going to the pictures, and dances, and football matches with his mates. He hadn't a care in the world and was happy with his lot. Then came the bombshell!

Oh, yes, marriage had been the last thing on his mind then. He certainly didn't mean to be tied down so young. However, he had met Mary and they had dated. As their relationship matured their curiosity had got the better of them and they started experimenting. One thing led to another and the result was Mary's becoming pregnant.

He had been careful, or so he thought, seeking advice from those who knew better than he and following that advice. He didn't think it possible that Mary could become pregnant, but she had. Dismayed at first, he had put his misgivings to one side and, although Mary wasn't exactly enthusiastic either, they got married. There was really no alternative. He had to do the decent thing, after all.

Did he love her? He didn't know any more. She had been his first real girlfriend and had opened up a whole new exciting world to him. Caught up in a wave of passion and delight with all the new sensual feelings she was awakening in him, he had thought her the most wonderful girl in the world, and as far as he was concerned she could do no wrong. Then, out of the blue, she had dumped him. Just like that. No explanation. No tearful goodbyes. She had just refused to go out with him again. He had thought that some other bloke must have caught her eye, and he had been hurt and disappointed for a time, but not heartbroken. No, he would have got over her. That he was sure of. There were plenty more fish in the sea, had been his motto. It was only his pride that had been dented; not his heart.

The message sent through Louise from Sadie Gilmore had changed all that. He had been completely devastated when Louise had delivered Sadie's ultimatum. He'd felt that he had no option but to marry Mary and had convinced himself they could make it work. Now, he just didn't know any more. He had thought that once the knot was tied and the dust had settled, everything would be different and they'd be, if not exactly blissfully happy, at least contented. He'd assumed that they would settle down and make a go of it. Some hope.

The honeymoon, as far as he was concerned, was a total disaster from start to finish. Mary was willing enough to share the big, comfortable double bed, and even liked to snuggle up close to him for warmth and comfort. But that was as far as it went. When he tentatively tried to take things further she gently reproached him. Hadn't he promised to give her more time, she reminded him? His resentment grew as he lay beside her trying to curb his natural instincts. She had no consideration for him at all. Did she think that he had no feelings?

He discovered that they had very little in common. Conversation quickly dried up between them. Even talk of the baby failed to bring them close. He sensed that Mary resented what was in store for her, that she didn't want this child of theirs. Did she think that he was ecstatic at the prospect of being a father? Not a bit of wonder sex had played such a major part during their courtship; it was the only thing of interest between them. Now, with sex being struck off their list of honeymoon activities, there was little else to do. The weather didn't help much either; it rained persistently and the days dragged. He recalled when he was working in the shipyard how the men would jokingly ridicule a newly married mate because of his lack of a suntan, accusing him of never leaving the bridal suite. Well, he would gladly have left their bedroom if the weather had permitted. He was only too glad when, after saying goodbye to their kindly landlady, it was time to leave that room behind and go home. It certainly held no pleasant memories for him.

Back in Belfast he was happy to learn that Mrs Clarke had gone off to visit her daughter in Holywood and would not be returning until after Easter. They would have the house to themselves for a time, get settled in before their landlady returned. His mother had been watching out for them when they arrived on Tuesday night and insisted that they come into her house for a cup of tea and a sandwich before retiring. The family were all there except Harry who was at the pictures, and his da, who was, as usual, down in the pub. For this Johnnie was grateful: his da continued to make no secret of what he thought of Mary, and Johnnie didn't want any snide remarks upsetting his wife. He had enough problems without his da adding to them.

Conversation was a bit strained at first. The girls tried to keep it flowing by plying the couple with questions about Bangor. Mary admitted that they had seen very little of it. Realising how this might be misinterpreted, she blushed to the roots of her hair and quickly explained that they didn't get out much because it had rained almost continuously every day. A slight smile momentarily creased Johnnie's face at the very idea that they might have been actually enjoying themselves. If the truth were known the girls would be horrified.

Nora was puzzled. She could see that Mary appeared reasonably relaxed, but her son was definitely on edge. He was wound up as tight as a spool of cotton. What on earth could be the matter with him? Wasn't he married to the girl he loved? She cornered him as he passed through the scullery on his way to the yard. 'Is anything wrong, son?'

'Ah, Ma, I can't talk about it. From now on everything concerning me and my . . .' his lips twisted on the next word, 'wife is private. Strictly between the two of us.'

Worried now, Nora warned him, 'Don't bottle it all up inside you, son. That's the worst thing you could do. Mary seems contented enough. If you're not happy, clear the air with her. Begin as you mean to go on. Don't let her lay down all the rules of dos and don'ts or you'll soon become her doormat.' Like me, she lamented inwardly. And she wouldn't wish that on her worst enemy.

He shrugged and spread his hands wide in a hopeless gesture. 'I'll try. But it's very complicated.' How could he tell his mother that the activity that had resulted in a shotgun wedding was now forbidden between them? She probably wouldn't believe him.

He dreaded the thought of climbing into bed beside his unresponsive wife, and lingered in Nora's house until bedtime could be put off no longer. 'Come on, Mary. Time we went home.'

Nora rose from her chair. 'It's still quite early. Stay as long as you like. I'll make another pot of tea.'

'That won't be necessary, Ma. We all have to get up for work in the morning, so we need our beauty sleep.' With a sly glance at his wife he added, 'Don't we, love?'

At his sarcastic tone of voice all heads turned sharply in his direction. Mary just pressed her lips together and gave an abrupt nod. Johnnie rose and lifting the cases stood patiently at the door, one in each hand, waiting while she shrugged into her coat.

'Thanks, Mrs McGuigan. You've been very kind to me; I appreciate it. Good night, everybody. See you all tomorrow.'

'Come on, Mary.' As she still dallied, he urged, 'Hurry up! I hear me da coming. Let's get out of here. Good night, everybody.'

He ushered Mary hurriedly through the door just as Tommy arrived on the pavement outside and had to stand back to let them pass. Not a single word was exchanged.

Nora was furious with her husband and rounded on him when he came into the kitchen. 'You could have at least acknowledged them. He's still your son, you know.'

'Did you hear them speak to me?'

'They would have answered if you'd spoken to them.'

'Well now, that's something we'll never know, isn't it? Since they didn't take a blind bit of notice of me.'

'And what do you expect? It was you who were in the wrong. You didn't even go to their wedding for God's sake. You sicken me, Tommy McGuigan. You never make allowances for anything or anybody. It has to be all your way or no way at all.'

Tommy leaned towards her and said slowly and distinctly, 'Listen, Nora, that wee girl is going to ruin our Johnnie's life. I tried to reason with him and he wouldn't listen to me, so I've washed my hands of him. And I've certainly no intention of making her welcome in this house.' Removing his coat he slung it over the back of a chair. 'How's about a cup of tea?'

Nora threw him a look of pure venom. Life was going to be difficult enough for the newly-weds, without him ignoring them.

'Make it yourself. I'm off to bed.' Tight-lipped, she flounced into their bedroom.

Both his daughters, who had been listening to their every word, now stood in stunned silence at their mother's act of bravado, anxiously waiting for their da's reaction.

Tommy surprised them; heading for the scullery he said mildly over his shoulder, 'Anyone else for tea?'

The vestibule door opened and Harry breezed in. He heard his father's offer and quickly accepted. 'I'll have a cup, Da.'

'What about you girls?'

'No, Da, I'm going on up to bed,' Peggy said and Louise followed her lead.

'I'm going to bed now too, thanks anyway. Good night, Da . . . Harry.'

* * *

149

Louise wasn't really surprised that Conor was very quiet when they met on Saturday night. He'd had plenty of time to think things over; time to rue the rash things he'd said in a moment of passion. They queued up outside the Imperial picture house and she found it hard to keep a conversation going. Unable to bear it any longer she moved closer and whispered so others in the queue wouldn't hear.

'Have I offended you in any way, Conor?'

He was immediately attentive. 'No. Why do you ask that?'

'Why do you think? You've hardly opened your mouth since we met.'

He put his arm round her and drew her close. 'I'm sorry. I've a lot on my mind.' The queue started to move and he gave her a hug. 'We'll talk about it on the way home, OK?'

She nodded and tried to smile but she was filled with foreboding. Even the hilarious, impossible antics of the Keystone Cops failed to hold her attention. She had an uneasy feeling that he was going to give her the push.

On the walk up to Castle Street to catch a tram up the Falls Road they talked about everything under the sun . . . everything, that is, except what was really bothering Conor. They got off the tram, and at the corner of Springview Street he stopped abruptly. She grimaced. No proudly walking her to her door tonight. No vows of everlasting love and commitment. Obviously his mother had asserted her influence and changed his mind. Well, better to know now than later; before they got too committed. She decided to make it easy for him.

'Your mother doesn't want you to keep on seeing me, does she?'

He gave an embarrassed shake of the head.

Her heart ached but she successfully fought back the

tears. 'Well then, no harm done.' She held out her hand. 'Let's call it a day, eh, Conor? It was pleasant while it lasted, very nice in fact, but let's part good friends.'

He looked blankly at the hand she offered him, then gripping hold of it pulled her roughly against him and gazed sternly into her eyes. 'What kind of man do you take me for, eh? I told her I loved you, and I intend one day to marry you whether or not she likes it.'

Louise gazed at him wide-eyed. 'Then why . . .' She broke off, bewildered. 'What did your mother say that has you so worried?'

'Oh, she ranted and raved for a while about how young we were. I explained that we wouldn't be rushing into marriage, but that one day I would make you my wife. When she saw how determined I was, she agreed to meet you. I've to bring you in now for a cup of tea. That's why I stopped here, to prepare you for the ordeal.'

Louise was bewildered. If his mother was willing to meet her, what was he brooding over? 'You might think me a bit slow on the uptake, Conor, but I don't understand what you're on about.'

A shrug accompanied his next words. 'To be truthful, neither do I. Suddenly, out of the blue, she wants me to go over and meet my father. Now, my mother would never ever agree to my even corresponding with my father. I've never met him, I've never even seen a photograph of him, she never talks about him . . . so I'm very confused. His name is taboo in our house, and suddenly she wants me to go and meet him? Does she think a stranger will change my mind about marrying you? Surely she can't be that stupid?'

'I should think you are confused,' Louise agreed. 'Where is your da?'

'Over in Birmingham. She wants me to go over at

Easter for a few days, but of course I don't want to go. He's never bothered about me before so I'm sure he won't be overjoyed to see me now. Why would he, just because my mother suddenly decrees it?'

'Doesn't he pay for your upkeep?'

A nod of the head. 'Oh, he does that all right. But he's ignored me all these years, so why should he want to meet me now? He'll probably refuse to see me anyway, so let's wait and see what happens. Ah, to hell with it! Come on, let's get you in to meet my mother and get it over with.'

He took her hand and led her the short distance up the street to his home. She had always thought it the best-looking house in the street, even before she had fallen in with Conor. As she gazed at the door, painted dark green and adorned with a shining brass knocker, she felt somewhat intimidated. Her door didn't have a knocker of any description.

Unlocking the outer door he motioned her into the hall and through the vestibule door into the kitchen. Cissie O'Rourke rose from an armchair by the fireside and came to greet her.

She put on a great show of friendliness, gripping the hand extended to her and commenting on how cold it was. Louise agreed that it was indeed a cold night out. If she had not been forewarned, Louise would have thought that this woman actually liked her.

'I'm very pleased to meet you, Louise. Come over and sit by the fire.'

'I'm pleased to meet you too, Mrs O'Rourke.'

'Conor is a naughty boy not telling me about you sooner.'

'Ah, well, it's only been a few weeks and I'm sure he doesn't tell you every wee detail of his life.'

'Oh.' Cissie's gaze sharpened. 'But he does. We are very close, you know,' she assured Louise. 'You've only been seeing each other a few short weeks and you've already discussed marriage?'

Conor interrupted her. 'Ma, I have talked about marriage. I've yet to convince Louise to marry me.'

His mother latched on to these words and eyed Louise intently. 'So you might not be in agreement with Conor concerning the matrimonial stakes?'

Louise wasn't stupid. She sensed that it would be better if she didn't appear too keen on Conor. 'Well now, Mrs O'Rourke, we are very young, and I for one don't want to be tied down with babies and nappies for some years yet.'

Cissie gave a dramatic sigh and, with a hand to her brow, sank back in her chair as if a great weight had been lifted from her shoulders. 'So there's no urgent need to rush into marriage then, is there?'

Conor was on his feet and, towering over his mother, told her in no uncertain terms, 'No, Mother, there isn't. Louise is not that kind of girl. I want you to apologise to her for your insinuation.'

Cissie looked flabbergasted. 'What? Have I said something to offend her? Louise, if I've offended you in any way, I'm very sorry. I really don't know what Conor is on about.' She put on a good show of being affronted and, excusing herself, headed for the scullery. 'I'll make us a cup of tea.'

When she left the room Conor looked appealingly at Louise. She mouthed the words, 'Don't worry about it. I understand. I can handle it.' And she did understand. Mrs O'Rourke had made it quite plain by her nuances that if she had any say in the matter, her son would never marry Louise McGuigan, but as far as Louise was concerned, if Conor loved her that was all that mattered. She would not be intimidated. Like his mother, she would play it tongue in cheek.

It wasn't a happy time for the McGuigans. Tommy continued to ignore his son and Johnnie avoided going into the house. He only visited his mother when his da was out. Mary refused to go in next door at all and spent more and more time at her own mother's house.

Work was Johnnie's only salvation. He arrived at the shop early in the morning and stayed until eight at night. Nora watched the weight drop off him and was worried stiff. Matthew McFadden was also concerned about him. Calling Johnnie into the office one evening as he was about to leave, he endeavoured to find out what was troubling his assistant.

He thrust a glass with a finger of Black Bush into Johnnie's hand. 'Drink that.' When Johnnie would have demurred, he said, 'Humour me. You look as if you need it.' He watched Johnnie tentatively sip the whiskey and grimace. 'Believe me, it will do you a world of good.'

Johnnie wanted to disagree, but another couple of sips of the whiskey warmed him all the way down to his stomach, making him realise that he had eaten very little all day, and he welcomed the feeling. Wordlessly, he finished the drink, savouring each little drop. However, when Matthew would have poured another he covered the glass with his hand. 'That's enough, thanks, Mr McFadden. That's something I could get a liking for and in my present state that would never do.'

Putting the empty glass to one side Matthew nodded his agreement and sat down facing him across the desk. 'Explain. You're married to the girl you love. You've got rooms near your mother, which is a good thing, since your wife is pregnant. So why are you down in the dumps, when you should be so excited and happy?'

Johnnie jerked to attention, immediately concerned. 'Are people complaining about me?'

'No. No, you always have a friendly smile on your face when serving the customers, and attending to the tradesmen, and that's good for my business. You might fool everybody, but not me. When no one is about you look real miserable, son. I'm not complaining, mind you. It's just that I'm worried about you.'

Johnnie looked embarrassed and Matthew stressed, 'Anything you say here will be treated in the strictest confidence. You have my word.'

Silence engulfed them like an uninvited guest for some moments, until, with a shrug of despair, Johnnie spoke. 'To be truthful, Mr McFadden, I'm at my wits' end. You see, me da won't accept Mary into the family circle. He thinks she trapped me into marriage, but, as I'm sure you realise, it takes two.'

'It does indeed, son, and your father is a very foolish man. The damage is done and he should accept that and bury the hatchet.'

'Not my da. Mary has taken to going to her mother's for her tea every night. It's understandable and I don't really blame her. That's why I work so late. But the result is, we see very little of each other.'

'Can't you find somewhere else to live?'

'Oh, I intend to eventually, but I had no notion of getting married so young, and I wasn't saving all that seriously. The wedding was so unexpected that it ate up a lot of my money.'

Matthew showed his surprise. 'You have a job. You'll be able to rent a house without any bother.'

'I know. But the kind of house we'll be able to afford

will probably need a lot of money spent on it. Money I don't have. Then we'll need furniture and the like. It will all take time. Meanwhile, Mary and I are drifting apart.'

'Well, son, if I can be of any assistance, you let me know.'

'You've been great, Mr McFadden. Just talking about it has lifted me.'

'Any time you want to talk things through, Johnnie, I'm here for you, remember that.'

'Thanks.' He rose to his feet. 'I'd better get away on home now. Mary gets in about eight and she likes me to be there. Good night, Mr McFadden.'

'Good night, son. And try not to worry too much . . . it'll all come right in the end, you'll see.'

Matthew sat for some time after he had gone, deep in thought. It was all such a waste. He would have dearly loved that lad for a son-in-law.

Nora waylaid Johnnie as he passed her doorway. She had seen mother and daughter arrive ten minutes earlier and Sadie had looked so determined that Nora had thought the worst. With a tight grip on his arm she tugged him into the hall. 'Come in a minute, son. I want a quick word with you.'

Reluctantly, he entered the house. 'Ma, Mary will be here soon—'

Nora interrupted him. 'She's in there already, son. Sadie's with her. Now I know I should mind my own business, but I've a feeling Mary is planning to move out and go back to her mother's. I just want to prepare you.'

Johnnie's face tightened into an angry mask. 'Thanks for the warning, Ma.' Quickly turning on his heel, he hurried outside.

Next door, climbing the stairs two at a time, he burst

into the front room. Sadie Gilmore sat on the bed watching her daughter. A suitcase was on the end of the bed and Mary was neatly folding clothes into it.

'Here . . . what's going on? What do you think you're doing?'

Mary froze and Sadie was on her feet, insinuating herself between them. 'Mary has decided to come home until the baby is born.'

'What do you mean, home? This *is* her home.'

'You call these two rooms *home*?' Sadie cried derisively. 'Don't make me laugh. It's little better than a hovel.'

Face flushed with anger Johnnie jerked his head towards the door and snarled, 'Leave us! I want to talk to my wife alone.'

'There's no need for that. She won't change her mind.'

Leaning forward, he glared into his wife's face and cried, 'Have you lost your tongue, Mary? Can't you speak for yourself any more?'

'Mam . . . you go on downstairs. I'll follow you shortly.'

'Mary, don't you let him play on your good nature. Think of the baby,' Sadie urged. 'You shouldn't be under all this stress, not in your condition.'

'Good nature? She doesn't know the meaning of the words. She's a self-centred—'

'Listen, you—' Sadie hissed.

'Please, Mam. Johnnie and I must talk. I owe him that much.'

Nostrils flared in a rage, Sadie headed out the door, throwing over her shoulder, 'If he lays one finger on you, just give a shout and I'll—'

Hastily Mary interrupted her mother. 'Mam . . . he won't. Just go!'

With another angry glare at Johnnie, Sadie descended

the stairs. Silence was like a damp blanket hanging between them until she reached the hall.

Johnnie fixed his gaze on his wife's face. 'Tell me, Mary, just what have you been saying to your ma? Does she actually think I'd hit you?'

'No, of course she doesn't. You know what she's like. She's all talk.'

'Why are you doing this, Mary? I'm doing my best, you know. Not many men in my position would be so accommodating towards their wives. Lay a finger on you? She certainly got that wrong! Good God, you haven't let me touch you since we got married.'

'I know that, Johnnie. I just need time. Once the baby's born things will be different.'

'You asked for time on our honeymoon and I never demanded my rights. What more do you want? I sometimes wonder how you ever got pregnant.' Her face remained mutinous and he changed tack. 'Don't go! I'll do anything you ask, just don't leave me. Let's get through this together. Please, Mary.'

'I can't. I hate it here, Johnnie.' She slammed shut the lid of the case and secured the catches. Tears poured down her face. 'I dread coming here from work every night. I know you're disgusted with me and the way I get on, but I can't help it. I'm sorry, but I'll go round the bend if I stay here any longer.'

His eyes searched her face. She looked absolutely wretched. Resigned, he reached across and lifted the suitcase off the bed. 'If that's how you feel, fair enough. I'll carry this down for you. But don't expect me to hang around for ever.'

'What do you mean?'

'I mean . . . if we can't resolve our differences . . . I'll find someone else who'll be a bit more appreciative.'

'But you can't! We're married.' Her voice was shrill with alarm.

'Take my word for it, Mary. I'll not hang around for ever waiting for you to make up your mind what you want to do. Now come on, your ma's waiting down there.'

Nora walked slowly up the yard to the spinning room deep in thought. She had left the house early because she couldn't bear the misery that Louise tried so hard to hide, but which permeated the air around her like an unseen vapour, wrenching at Nora's heart. Easter was fast approaching and most of her family looked miserable. She had questioned Louise, but in vain. Her daughter insisted that she was fine and that her ma was imagining things. Johnnie – well, she knew what ailed him. Mary Gilmore was a pain in the arse; didn't know when she was well off. It was too late now for regrets. They were married so they must somehow or other make a go of it.

As for Harry . . . his position at Kennedy's was to be reviewed and he was convinced that he would be laid off and he was down in the dumps. Peggy was the only happy one at the moment. Mr McFadden had offered her full time employment starting after Easter and she was walking around on cloud nine. Tommy now . . . well, he was his usual selfish self. That bastard never noticed one way or the other, or cared for that matter, how the rest of them fared so long as he could indulge in his favourite hobbies, drinking and gambling.

'A penny for them?'

Bill McCartney fell into step beside her and slanted his eyes on her face.

Nora gave a start of surprise. 'Do you always creep

up on people like that?' she cried, although a warm glow filled her heart with his presence.

'I didn't creep. You were so lost in thought a bomb could have gone off and you wouldn't have noticed.'

She grimaced. 'You're probably right. I hate holiday times – more expense, less money. The same old story. You know how it is.'

Bill didn't know how it was. Tommy McGuigan had a good job and must earn a fair wage. In Bill's opinion Nora shouldn't have to go out to work at all. They were on regular speaking terms again and at every opportunity he chatted her up, but afraid to frighten her off had managed to keep his distance. 'Is that because you won't see me on Monday?' he teased.

She laughed aloud and nudged him with her elbow. 'Don't kid yourself.'

Delighted to have lightened her mood, when they entered the spinning room he drew her to one side, behind a pile of beams that were stacked ready for the weaving shop. Taken unawares she allowed herself to be manoeuvred and gazed up at him in surprise, not realising that her eyes were full of longing. Without further ado he kissed her, praying all the while that they wouldn't be disturbed. She eagerly returned the kiss and clung fiercely to him, the adrenalin rushing through her blood like electricity. He prolonged the caress until they were forced to come up for air.

His lips trailing her face he muttered, 'I love you, Nora. I love you so much.'

The door opened, and although they could not be seen she pushed him roughly away. 'You've no right to say that!' she whispered furiously. 'You took me by surprise last time. It must never happen again. Do you hear me?'

Before she could take flight, he gripped her by the

elbow. 'It will, Nora. That's a promise. You enjoyed it as much as I did. We must talk. I'll wait at the gate and walk up the yard with you tomorrow morning. OK?'

'No, Bill. There's nothing to talk about. There's no future for us.' She tried to free her elbow from his grip.

He slackened his hold on her but held her eye and repeated, 'I'll see you tomorrow. Don't do anything foolish now . . . like sending in word you're sick, or I'll come and see you at home,' he warned her.

'You wouldn't dare! Besides I can't afford to take a day off.'

'I'll see you tomorrow then.'

Nora went to her spindles, her mind in a whirl. She had enough worries on her plate without Bill McCartney tempting her. And he was right. She had enjoyed it. More than she thought possible. But she would have to be firm with him. Send him packing like she had done all those years ago. But would she be strong enough to do that? She hadn't given any thought to the safe period when she got carried away in the heat of the moment and let him seduce her. A tremor ran through her. What if she got pregnant? What would she do then?

Surely she was too old to conceive. Terrified at the very idea, Nora cast about in her troubled mind for something else to distract her. Johnnie, her next great worry. Should she go down and have a word with Mary? Try to talk some sense into her? No, she had better not. Johnnie was a very independent person. He wouldn't thank her for interfering in his private affairs.

Next morning, as she knelt by her bedside saying her prayers, Nora begged God to forgive her lapse from grace and give her the strength to keep Bill McCartney at arms' length.

After breakfast she dallied, and leaving the house later than usual managed to dodge Bill. She hoped he wouldn't seek her out; then became resentful when he failed to do so. He was like the rest of them, she thought bitterly, after one thing.

Alone in the house that evening she decided to treat herself to a bath. Putting pots of water on the stove and range to heat she brought the tin tub in from the yard and rinsed it before placing it in front of the fire. May as well bathe in comfort, instead of the draughty scullery; she didn't expect anyone home before ten o'clock.

Spreading her nightdress over the arm of the chair near the fire to warm she tested the water. It was hot enough, and she poured it from an assortment of utensils into the bath. Then, stripping, she stuffed her dirty clothes into the bag used for that purpose. She placed her flannel and her coveted bar of perfumed soap – a treat bought for her at Christmas – on the hearth, and knelt by the bath to wash her hair. She was just about to step into the bath, hair wrapped in a towel, when a loud knock on the door caused her to freeze, balanced on one leg. Her mind scooted about. Who on earth could it be? The rent man, the coal man, the milk man – in fact every-body she owed money to – all called at the door on a Friday night. Had one of her family decided to come home early?

Wrapping the bath towel around her she cautiously crept towards the window. Then with an annoyed shake she straightened up, muttering, 'Catch yourself on, girl. Whoever it is can't see through the walls.' Carefully lifting the edge of the blind she peered sideways to see who was at the door. At the sight of the figure outside she dropped the blind as if it was red hot and backed hastily away from the window. In the name of God what was *he* doing here?

Bill McCartney raised his hand and once more knocked on the door. In his other hand he held a neatly folded scarf, the property of his mother. If anyone but Nora answered his knock he intended saying that he had found the scarf near her machine, thought it belonged to Nora and was returning it.

Nora stood in a dither: what to do! In a panic she turned towards the laundry bag to retrieve her clothes, then stopped. What was she thinking of? There was no need to dress. He wasn't getting over the doorstep, that was for sure, she thought angrily.

Cautiously opening the door a crack she hissed, 'What are you doing here?'

For the benefit of anyone else who might be inside, he said, 'I found this scarf near your spindles and thought you might be worried that you'd lost it.' He held the scarf up for her inspection.

At the sheer audacity of him she released her hold on the door and it gaped wide enough for him to see she was covered only by a towel. 'You know damn well it isn't mine! Now take yourself off before my husband comes home.'

Bill quickly calculated that Nora wouldn't be answering the door wrapped in a towel if anyone else was in the house. Thrusting his foot forward to stop the door closing, he said softly, but firmly, 'We've got to talk. I'm coming in, Nora.' His foot edged further in, showing his determination. 'I'll only stay a few minutes.'

'You'll do no such thing. Go away. Tommy will kill me if he finds you here.'

He pushed at the door gently, and, aware that a neighbour might very well be watching, she backed reluctantly into the hall and allowed him to enter. What if Tommy came home early? She trembled at the very idea of it. It happened now and again. Not often, but still . . . tonight might be the very night he felt poorly and decided to come home. He would never believe she was innocent if he found them together like this. Murder would surely be done.

Bill pushed the door closed behind him and made to enter the kitchen.

She gripped his arm. 'Here . . . this is as far as you come.'

He faced her and, pushing the scarf into his pocket, reached for her. Smiling roguishly, he said, 'Here will suit me fine.'

Aghast, clutching the towel which was clinging precariously to her breasts, she backed away from him. 'Bill, please. You've got to go. Tommy will kill us both if he comes home and finds you here.'

'And what will I be doing while Tommy's killing us, eh?' he chided. 'I'm a bigger and stronger man than that selfish husband of yours.'

She gave an exasperated sigh. 'Just go, Bill. You don't understand. I've to live with him.'

He crowded close to her. 'That's just it, Nora. You don't. You're a free woman. Your family are all grown up. You can leave him any time you like and God knows I'm sure nobody would blame you. I'll look after you.'

She looked at him in disbelief. Was he daft? 'Just like that, eh?'

'Why not?' he argued. 'You've done your best for your family. Now you deserve some happiness. And I can make you happy, Nora. You know I can.'

'You know that's impossible, so you do.'

'Is it, Nora? You just have to say the word and I'll take you away from here to a whole new life.'

'Ach, go away. You're talking nonsense.'

'Nora . . . love. Please say you'll at least think about it.'

This time when he reached for her he let him draw her close and nestled against his body. Without thought she slowly raised her face in invitation. The towel slipped down and he placed his hands on her arms to stop her from gathering it up again. It fell to the floor and pooled around her feet like the base of a marble statue from which her slim legs and figure rose. Holding her at arm's length he looked down at the beauty of her. 'You're lovely. Beautiful!' He slowly planted his lips on hers and drew the breath from her body while she stood motionless, her eyelids shut, her head spinning, her toes tingling on the cold linoleum. She felt everything inside her jolt as if she'd grabbed hold of a live wire, and a steady increasing warmth rose into her chest and flooded her whole being. Then she was crushed against him and passion erupted, sending all reason from her mind. Lifted on a great surge of emotion she returned kiss for kiss, caress for caress. This was wonderful. How she wished it would go on for ever.

He urged her towards the stairs. 'Come on . . . let's go upstairs.'

'No! No, we daren't. The kids sleep up there. Come through here.'

He smiled at the idea of three adults being called kids and allowed himself to be drawn across the kitchen to what he guessed to be the room she shared with her husband. He felt no guilt. She was wasted on Tommy McGuigan, and if he had his way she wouldn't be with him much longer.

The next half-hour was the most joyous of Nora's life. She had never experienced anything like it. Not even when first married and in the uncertain throes of first love. At last, rosy and sated from their lovemaking, she reluctantly rose on an elbow and gazed down at this wonderful man who could make her feel so loved and desired. 'You'll have to go, Bill. Any of my family could arrive at any time. Don't spoil it for me by letting it end in a scandal.'

He rose from the bed and she gaped in amazement when she saw he was naked. She must have been indeed out of her mind with passion for that to have gone unnoticed. Suddenly aware of her own nudity she pulled the sheet up over her breasts. 'Please, Bill? I beg of you.' Tears trickled down her cheeks as she realised what she had done and guilt and shame set in.

Concerned, he shrugged into his shirt and started to dress, all the while consoling her. 'All right . . . all right. Don't get upset. I'll be away before anyone comes. But mind you . . . this is only the beginning. We'll have to have that talk, Nora. And soon. OK?'

She quickly nodded her agreement. Anything to get him out of the house. A knock at the door brought her from the bed rigid with fear, unaware of the wonderful picture she was to his eyes with her high breasts, narrow waist and luminous skin.

'Oh, my God. Who can that be? What am I gonna do?' she cried in a panic.

'Shush!' he admonished her. 'Calm down and away and find out who it is. I'll wait here.'

Closing the door on him she hastened to the hall. Grabbing the towel from the floor where she had dropped it earlier she wrapped it tight around her body, glad that Bill had had the wit to shoot the bolt on the front door. 'Who's there?' she asked fearfully.

'It's me, Ma. For goodness' sake let me in.'

Peggy's voice was muffled through the thick wood and

Nora almost fainted. Was her sin about to be discovered? Bill had opened the door and was peering over at her from the wee room. He whispered urgently, 'Let her in. I'll stay in here.'

Nora unbolted the door and Peggy burst through the hall and headed for the scullery. 'Why have you the door barred?' she gasped indignantly. 'I need to go to the loo.' Her eye fell on the bath and she became aware of her mother's apparel. 'Oh, sorry, I disturbed you.' Throwing Nora an apologetic look she continued on out to the yard.

Bill was through the kitchen and in the hall within seconds. Cupping her face in his hands he kissed her fiercely. 'I love you. Bear that in mind.'

She pulled her head away from his grasp. 'Just go away. You got what you came for.'

A frown puckered his brow. 'I don't understand . . .'

'Don't you? Go, just go!'

The water was barely warm but Nora knelt in the bath and was busy scrubbing away the stains of her recent sin when Peggy came back into the kitchen.

'Sorry about that, Ma.'

'No matter. I didn't expect anyone home so early. Well . . . don't stand there gawking. Away up the stairs and give me some privacy to finish here. Then you can make us a cup of tea.'

Peggy headed for the hall. 'Give me a shout when you're finished, Ma, and I'll help you empty the bath before I make the tea.'

'Thanks, love.'

A tear trickled down Nora's cheek. Why had she said that to Bill? Did she really think that was all he was after? No. No, in her heart she didn't, but she had spoiled that wonderful episode with her cutting remark. Perhaps he wouldn't bother about her again. Wouldn't that be all for the best? she lamented. Sadly she admitted to herself that it would. There was no way she could ever leave her family.

Head high, Louise walked quickly past the O'Rourkes' house and continued down the street. She imagined that Cissie must be trying to cast an evil spell on her, as she felt ill at ease every time she passed by her door. She was meeting Cathie and Jean at the Springfield junction. Their usual outing had been postponed because Louise was going out with Conor. Tonight, they were going to the Clonard. She wouldn't see Conor over the Easter holidays. It was going to be a long week. Cissie had managed to convince her son to spend Easter in Birmingham with his father and although not very happy at the prospect, he had confessed that he was intrigued and had agreed to go. He had caught the boat to Liverpool the night before.

Far from not wanting to see him, his father had at once sent the boat fare and some extra money in case he was short. What did that tell you? In Louise's opinion it showed that far from not caring about Conor the man was only too delighted to meet him. So why was his mother keeping them apart? And why all the big mystery?

Cathie and Jean were already waiting at Dunville Park and Louise quickly crossed the road and joined them. She had confided in her friends that she was dating Conor and now Jean asked, tentatively, 'Did Conor get away all right last night?'

Louise sighed deeply. 'Yes.'

'You really like him, don't you?'

'Yes, but I don't think anything can come of it.'

'I've only ever spoken to Mrs O'Rourke once, and that was in the chemist shop one day. She asked my opinion about some face cream. I thought she was very nice,' Cathie admitted.

'I imagine she *is* very nice if you aren't interested in her son,' Louise agreed drily.

Seeing her friend was unhappy Cathie changed the subject. 'You'll never guess what.' She paused dramatically, and waited patiently for Louise to show interest.

'Guess what about what?' Louise exclaimed, exasperated. 'I haven't the foggiest idea what you're on about.'

'Joe McAvoy asked Jean out.'

Louise was interested now. She stopped dead in the middle of the pavement and gaped at Cathie. 'He never did!'

A smug smile was accompanied by a nod. 'He did.'

'Will you two stop talking about me as if I'm not here?' Jean cried indignantly.

Louise swung towards her. 'Did you go out with him?'

'Yes. Why not? There's nothing wrong with Joe McAvoy. In fact he's very nice.'

'Who says there's anything wrong with him?' Louise exclaimed. 'I think this is wonderful news. Where did you go?'

'To the Hippodrome.'

'I'm happy for you, Jean.' She was confused, couldn't take it in. Jean was so shy, and from what Louise had learned about Joe so was he. 'Tell me, when did all this happen? How did he pick up the courage to ask you out?'

'I was walking up Grosvenor Road from work last Wednesday night, and he came charging out of McDonald Street like a tornado and almost knocked me off my feet.' Jean smiled at the memory of it. 'He insisted on walking me home to make sure I was all right and we got on very well. He asked me to go out with him last Friday night and I did.'

169

'How did it go?'

'Very well. Very well indeed.' A pleased smile curved her lips and Louise and Cathie exchanged a knowing look. Could Jean be falling in love? Jean continued triumphantly, 'And furthermore I'm going out with him again on Saturday.'

'Smashing! Good luck to you.' Louise gave her friend an impulsive hug as they entered the foyer of the Clonard and joined the queue.

The film was great: *The Hunchback of Notre Dame*, starring Lon Chaney as Quasimodo and Patsy Ruth Miller as the beautiful Esmeralda. It was the kind of movie that Louise loved and would usually get lost in. Normally she would have been enthralled, but tonight her thoughts centred on Conor. What if he met someone over there and didn't come back? That wouldn't happen, she assured herself. He would never leave his mother. If some girl over there really caught his attention, he would persuade her to come to Belfast. But then, girls just didn't up and leave their family and friends at the drop of a hat. Did they? Perhaps, if they were really interested in a lad, they might. She spent the remainder of the film torturing herself with thoughts of Conor with some other girl.

When they were saying good night at the junction, she apologised to her friends for being such glum company. 'I just can't seem to brighten up. Me ma guesses something's wrong and she's been asking me all sorts of questions and getting nowhere fast. I'm such a misery about the house at the moment.'

'Does she know you and Conor are dating?'

'No, and thank God for that. I can't bear to be pitied. What are you doing on Saturday, Cathie?'

'Going out with you, I hope.'

'Great! That's a relief. I couldn't bear to sit in over Easter with Ma fussing over me like a flustered mother hen. Let's go down town and have a dander around the shops, eh?'

'I'm all for that. It will do for starters.'

'I'll see you here at one o'clock then, and we'll fix something up for Sunday and Monday as well.' Planting a stern eye on Jean she warned, with a laugh, 'You see and behave yourself with Joe. Don't do anything I wouldn't do.'

Highly affronted, Jean retorted, 'Joe's not like that.'

'They're all like that!' Cathie and Louise chorused together and Louise left them in a happier frame of mind, glad she wouldn't be sitting brooding at home all weekend.

Her mother and Peggy sat each side of the fire, cups of tea in their hands, when Louise walked in. 'Mm, this looks cosy. Is there any left in the pot?'

Nora rose to her feet. 'Yes. I'll pour you a cup.'

Hands on her shoulders, Louise gently pressed her down again. 'You stay there. I can pour it myself. I'm not helpless, you know.'

Sitting on the arm of Peggy's chair she eyed her mother over the rim of her cup. Nora was wrapped in her old candlewick dressing gown. Her hair was drying by the heat of the fire and the natural curl was in tresses around her face. She looked much younger than her thirty-eight years. 'You look different tonight, Ma.'

Nora gave a startled laugh. 'What do you mean . . . different?'

'You look . . .' Louise shrugged, a bemused look crossing her face. 'I don't know. Just different.' And she did. Louise couldn't put a finger on the sudden transformation, but her mother didn't have her usual harassed look about her. She actually looked happy. But what had she to be so happy about all of a sudden?

'You're imagining things.'

Remembering how she had used those selfsame words to her mother earlier on, Louise said, 'That makes two of us.'

'Touché!'

Tommy's heavy step passed the window and Nora straightened up in her chair. Shouting good night to someone outside, he came into the kitchen. His eyes fell on Nora and he paused on the threshold, his eyes sweeping over her face and body. 'You look different.'

Nora blushed bright red. 'I must take a bath more often,' she muttered sarcastically, 'if it has this effect on people.'

He continued to look her over, a puzzled expression on his face. She returned his gaze. 'Well?'

He shook his head, bewildered. 'You just don't look your usual self. Perhaps it's your hair down like that.' At last he headed for the wee room and Nora gave a sigh of relief. 'Don't you sit there talking till all hours,' he warned. 'Remember I've to be up early in the morning.'

'I won't be long.'

'Good!'

Nora smiled. She had every intention of waiting until she heard him snoring. As he was well aware, she too had to be up early for work, although he wouldn't worry about that if he were on the late shift. But she had seen *that look* in his eyes and there was no way that she would be able to bear his clumsy attempts at lovemaking. Not tonight. It would be too frustrating. Aware that the girls were covertly watching her and silently taking all this in, Nora tried to change the subject. 'Where have you two been tonight then?'

Louise laughed outright.

'What?' Nora blustered.

'Nothing, Ma. Nothing at all! I think you must have come into some money or something. That's all I can think of, to make such a change in you. Even me da noticed it and that's saying something.'

A chill passed down Nora's spine. If Tommy ever suspected her of carrying on with another man he would torture her until she revealed the truth and then all hell would break out. 'Mm. I should be so lucky. Money goes to money, and where would I get the cash to make more, eh? I ask you?'

Going to her, Louise gave her a hug. 'No matter, Ma. I'm pleased to see you looking so happy, no matter what the reason. Good night, love. I'm away on up to bed.'

Not exactly as perceptive as her sister, Peggy wondered what all the fuss was about. She followed Louise's lead and also rose to her feet. 'Good night, Ma.'

'Good night, girls.'

Nora sat for some time, ears strained. Some minutes passed slowly and then her husband's snores came like sweet music to her ears. With a sigh of relief she got up and rinsed the teacups under the tap, leaving them to drain before quietly opening the door to the wee room.

She'd been had. Tommy's mocking voice reached her from the bed. 'Hurry up, Nora. I've the bed nice and warm for you.'

Stifling the urge to scream, she slipped in beside him, glad that the darkness hid her tears. He gathered her close as she turned to face him. The sooner she got it over with, the sooner she'd get some sleep.

6

Johnnie kept himself busy, working all hours in a bid to blot out the misery of his lonely life and at the same time hang on to his sanity. Lunchtime saw him snatch a bite to eat and continue working right through to eight o'clock every night, watched by a worried but sympathetic Matthew McFadden. Although they were very busy, it being Good Friday and the shop being closed on Easter Monday, when Johnnie approached Matthew at half past twelve his boss was only too happy to grant him permission to take a couple hours off work to see to a bit of business. He guessed what the *bit of business* entailed, and could only hope it would prove fruitful for Johnnie.

Going home to the two loveless rooms he had come to detest, Johnnie had a quick wash and changed into his best clothes and set off again. He was at the end of his tether. After yet another night of tossing and turning he had decided it was time to confront his wife. With long strides he quickly covered Waterford Street and the length of Falls Road to the greengrocer at the corner of Milliken Street where she worked, determined to have it out with her; clear the air once and for all. He had no intention of keeping on paying rent for rooms he didn't need, when he could move back to his mother's, even if it did mean living under the same roof as his da. His da wouldn't mind so long as Mary wasn't there to remind him of his son's fall from grace.

It was coming up one o'clock: Mary's lunch-hour. He dallied outside the pawnbroker's at the corner of Panton Street as he waited for her to leave the greengrocer's. One o'clock came and went and still no sign of her. He was debating whether he should go and investigate when he saw her leave the bank at the corner of Balaclava Street further down the road. Head down, examining a small book in her hand, she failed to notice him as she walked slowly up the road in his direction. She looked happy and contented, and he felt resentment churn up inside him. How come she looked so well and he was so bloody miserable?

Her step faltered when she eventually lifted her head and saw him but she recovered quickly and came on towards him. 'Hi, Johnnie. Don't tell me you're thinking of hocking something in there,' she chided, her eyes sweeping the pawn shop window. There was an embarrassed smile on her face as she tucked the bankbook into her coat pocket, out of sight.

Johnnie watched the book furtively disappear before answering her. 'I might be driven to it yet, the way things are going.'

Her hand reached out and gently touched his face. 'You've lost a lot of weight, so you have.'

'Is it any wonder?'

'Oh . . .' She looked perplexed. 'Is your mother not cooking your meals, then?'

He scowled. 'Do you think I'd let my ma run round after me while I waste my hard-earned money on two rooms for a wife I never see? Eh? She has enough to put up with as it is.'

Mary's face blanched with distress. 'I'm sorry. Truly I am. You know, Johnnie, I never dreamed it would end up like this.'

'Neither did I. Tell me something, Mary. Do you regret ever marrying me?' He gave a dry laugh. 'Mind you, I thought I was doing you a good turn, making an honest woman of you.'

'Johnnie! Don't talk like that!' She sounded scandalised. 'Listen to me. The only regret I have is living next door to your ones.'

He sighed. 'I've realised that and I've been giving it some thought. What if I can find us rooms somewhere else?'

She straightened up, a pleased smile on her face. 'That would be nice, Johnnie. I do miss you, you know.'

This was an unexpected turnabout, and for a moment he was lost for words. 'I never thought I'd hear you say that, Mary.'

Bewilderment clouded her face. 'Why not? I am your wife, and I'm carrying your child. And to be truthful, my ma's taking over my life. She's beginning to get on my nerves.'

He hesitated and she surprised him yet again. 'I know Mr McFadden depends on you on Fridays and Saturdays, especially this week, it being Easter, but how's about us going out somewhere on Sunday? Spend the day together, eh? I've been thinking, and I've come up with some ideas too, you know.'

'That would be wonderful. Shall I come to the house for you, then?'

'No, go to eleven o'clock Mass in St Paul's. I'll meet you outside at about ten to eleven and go in with you.'

176

'This all sounds very promising, so it does. You'll not let anyone put you off meeting me, sure you won't?' His voice was strained, betraying his anxiety.

She stretched up and kissed him on the cheek. 'I'll be there,' she promised. Giving him a slight push, she said, 'Now away back to work. I've a proposition to put to you on Sunday. But for now I'd better get on home. Me ma will have my lunch ready.'

'What kind of proposition?'

'I'll tell you all about it when I see you on Sunday. Goodbye for now, love.'

Before she could move off, Johnnie's arms enveloped her, and pulling her close he planted a kiss on her lips. She stiffened, but only momentarily, then relaxed against him, lips parting and then moving hungrily under his. They stood like that for many moments in broad daylight, lost to the world. Some lads walking on the opposite side of the road brought them to their senses with loud wolf whistles. He released her and the lads gave him the thumbs-up sign. He returned the salute and he and Mary gazed at each other in wonder. He gently touched her face before turning away.

'I'll see you on Sunday then. Bye for now.' He strode off, resisting the urge to look back to see if she was watching. Mary was indeed looking after him, a hand pressing lips that tingled from the pressure of his kiss. He had never affected her like this before. But then, how could he? First they had just been friends curious about each other's body; then the shock of discovering she was pregnant had had her running scared. The whole marriage had been a complete farce. To discover that he could arouse her like that . . . well now, perhaps they could have a happy ending after all.

As he retraced his steps up the Falls Road Johnnie was

in a daze. Mary had certainly surprised him, in more ways than one. What kind of proposition had she in mind? And that kiss had been something else. He should have insisted she meet him tonight, he lamented inwardly. It was going to be a long, long wait until Sunday.

Louise was on her way down to meet Cathie on Saturday to go into town as planned, to look at the Easter displays in the shops and do a bit of browsing.

Hurrying past the O'Rourke house with her usual misgiving, she almost jumped out of her skin when Cissie's hand shot out of the doorway, signalling her to stop.

Reluctantly, she paused and looked inquiringly at Conor's mother. 'Yes?'

'Can you come in for a minute?'

She shook her head. 'Sorry, I'm meeting a friend and I'm late as it is.'

'Oh, I see. Could you call in on your way back, then?' Guessing Louise was about to refuse, Cissie added, 'Please. It's important. I want to talk to you.'

Against her better judgement, Louise nodded. 'I don't know what time I'll be back, mind. I'm going down town to do a bit of shopping.'

'That's all right. I'll leave the front door open so you can just walk in.'

Wow! What a privilege. To Louise's knowledge, the O'Rourke front door was never left open. Cissie didn't chance unwelcome visitors taking her unawares. You had to be invited into her house. 'I'll see you later, then.'

Louise passed on, her thoughts in turmoil. What on earth could Mrs O'Rourke want with her? Probably to warn her off Conor. On the tram going into town, she poured all her worries into her friend's ear. Cathie advised her if she didn't want to talk to the woman just to ignore her request. But having said she would call in, Louise felt she was committed.

It was a beautiful, bright day with just a hint of frost in the air and the town centre was packed with shoppers. Arm in arm the two girls strolled from window to window admiring the Easter displays, watching rosy-cheeked children gaze in wide-eyed awe at the beautiful Easter bunnies and chocolate Easter eggs of all sizes. Louise treated herself to a new skirt and Cathie invested in a pair of shoes. The smell of homemade cakes lured them into a nearby café proudly advertising all cakes and bread 'freshly baked on the premises'. They ordered a pot of tea and hot cross buns, which kept them quiet for a time. With a contented sigh Cathie at last pushed her plate to one side and, licking her fingers, rested her elbows on the table. Fingers entwined under her chin, she eyed her friend intently.

Louise was immediately apprehensive. She could read Cathie like a book and knew she had something on her mind; she would bet on it. 'What are you looking at?'

'Oh, have you to pay now to look at Miss Louise McGuigan? Sorry. I didn't know. Or maybe I should have made an appointment.'

'Come on, I know you only too well. What're you up to?'

Cathie laughed. 'There's no fooling you, is there? I met this very nice lad last Saturday at the dance and he asked me out.'

Louise's mouth dropped open for a moment, then snapping it shut she gasped, 'You never said. Even when we were teasing Jean about Joe McAvoy, you never let on you'd met someone.'

'Hang on a minute. I never said because I hadn't made up my mind what to do about him. In fact, I still haven't.'

'So you haven't been out with him then? Don't you like him?'

'Yes, but you see . . . he's a Protestant.' Cathie leaned back in her chair to watch Louise's reaction to this revelation.

'Oh, I see what you mean. But obviously you do like him.'

'Yes, he seems a smashing lad. He's very well mannered.'

'Where does he live?'

'Blythe Street.'

'And where's that when you're writing home?'

'I think it's somewhere off Sandy Row.'

'What are you going to do?'

'To tell the truth, I was hoping you'd advise me.'

'Me? What do I know about Protestant boys?'

'I suppose it's encouragement I'm looking for. Do you think I should take a chance?'

'I wouldn't dare advise you there. If your da heard tell of it he'd kill you. Is this lad worth all the trouble?'

A sad droop of the head confirmed that Cathie thought he was. 'Surely one date wouldn't do any harm, Louise,' she said forlornly.

'Look . . . it's like this, Cathie. One date could be such a disappointment you'll be glad to see the back of him and that would be the end of it. On the other hand, him being a Protestant might make it seem more exciting and it could lead to another date and another and another. Before you know it, you'll get caught up in a web of deceit. You'll be tripping over yourself with the lies you'll have to tell. And remember, girl, you have to have a very good memory to be a good liar.' She raised a finger warningly. 'Then . . . and you can be sure of it . . . some busybody who thinks they're doing you a good turn will

180

tell your parents and all hell will be let loose. It's not worth all the trouble, Cathie. Take my word for it and steer clear.'

'All right! All right! You don't have to write a book about it.'

'Well, you did ask. I'm just trying to make you see it as it is. Do you still think he's worth it?'

Cathie's lips tightened into a straight line before she said defiantly, 'Yes! As a matter of fact I do. So there.'

'Well then, why ask my advice in the first place?'

Cathie shrugged and smiled wanly. 'I suppose I was hoping you'd encourage me. Say, go for it Cathie. Give it your best shot! Something like that.'

'That kind of encouragement I'm not going to even consider. When do you intend seeing him again?'

Cathie looked embarrassed. 'I said I'd be at the dance tonight and I'd let him know then. I'm hoping you'll come with me.'

'No!' A defiant shake of the head. 'Definitely not.'

'Why not? Jean will be out with Joe and you'll have nothing better to do but sit at home moping over Conor.'

'I thought we'd be going to the pictures. You said you'd come out with me tonight, remember.'

'No. If you recall, I said I hoped I'd be going out with you and you were delighted at the idea.'

Louise stared for some moments at her friend's hopeful expression. 'Oh, all right! But don't expect my blessing. You make up your own mind. Leave me out of it.'

Reaching across the table Cathie gripped her arm. 'Thank you. As you say, I might see Trevor in a different light and that would solve everything.'

'Trevor, eh? Well, on your own head be it.'

*   *   *

It was half past five when Louise tentatively knocked on the vestibule door and quietly entered Mrs O'Rourke's kitchen.

Cissie came from the scullery, a welcoming smile on her face. 'Come in, Louise. Sit down. The kettle has just boiled and I was about to make a pot of tea. Will you join me?'

Louise sat primly, hands joined on her lap, on the edge of the chair to one side of the fireplace. 'No, thank you, Mrs O'Rourke. Ma will have tea ready for the family and she likes us all to be there. You were wanting to talk to me?'

Cissie sat facing her. 'I thought we should have a chat about Conor.'

'What about him?'

'He's doing so well at St Malachy's College, I think it would be a shame if anything should interfere with his studies. He's worked so hard, so he has. Don't you agree with me?'

'Of course I do, but he has to have some leisure time too. You know what they say . . . all work and no play . . .'

'If I could be sure that it's just a platonic friendship between the two of you . . .' She hesitated and eyed Louise questioningly. Louise stared her out, unblinking, and after a long pause Cissie continued, 'Well then, I could relax and make you welcome in my home. I think we could become good friends.'

Louise felt her temper rise. Who did this woman think she was? 'I'm afraid I don't have a crystal ball. I can't see into the future,' she retorted, and rose to her feet. 'Conor and I might get bored with each other; on the other hand we might grow closer, who knows? Now, if you'll excuse me. I don't want to be late for tea. Good day, Mrs O'Rourke.'

Cissie sat gobsmacked at the cheek of the girl and Louise couldn't get out of the house quickly enough. She almost sent Peggy, who happened to be passing by, flying into the road.

'Oops . . . sorry, Peggy!' Gripping her sister by the arms, Louise steadied her. 'You're home early tonight, aren't you?'

Peggy regained her footing and glared at her sister. 'Why the big rush? You nearly knocked me for six there.'

Louise rolled her eyes. 'I was in there speaking to Mrs O'Rourke,' she said as if that explained everything. 'Why are you home so early?'

'Mr McFadden told me I could go. And what do you think? Hannah is coming to the pictures with me tonight.'

Unable to comprehend that the McFaddens were letting their Hannah out of their sight for one minute, let alone a couple of hours, Louise said, 'Do her parents know?'

'Of course they do, silly! That's why her da let me off early. He trusts me to look after her. We're going to the first house in the Clonard, and then I'm going back to her house for something to eat. Her da even give me the money for the tickets.'

As they entered the house Nora overheard the last part of their conversation. 'Who's going to the Clonard?'

'Me and Hannah McFadden.'

Nora looked apprehensive. 'Isn't she a bit . . . soft? You know what I mean.'

Peggy stepped back in anger. 'No, actually I don't know what you mean. I'm surprised at you, Ma. There's nothing wrong with Hannah. She's every bit as clever as I am. Just takes a little longer getting there, that's all.'

Nora managed to stifle a smile, but Louise had diffi-culty straightening her own face and the mirth came across in her voice. 'That's all right, then. We all know how clever you are, don't we?'

Confused at first Peggy dithered, turning the words carefully over in her mind. Then the penny dropped and hands on hips she glared at her sister. 'You think you're so smart, don't you?' she cried scornfully. 'Well I could buy and sell you any day of the week, that's for sure. I'm working in a shop, remember, and you're still in the mill.'

Louise went cold all over and the colour drained from her face. Without another word she flounced from the kitchen and ran up the stairs.

Nora rounded furiously on her younger daughter. 'How could you be so cruel, Peggy? You know our Louise is smarter than the rest of you put together. She shouldn't be in the mill. If your da had been a decent parent, our Louise would have gone on to better things.'

The door opened and Tommy paused on the threshold. 'What have I done now?' he asked, obviously hearing his wife's reprimand.

'Nothing. The tea's almost ready.' Nora practically ran into the scullery. She'd had a lovely afternoon in the company of Bill McCartney and she didn't want it spoilt. They had only gone for a walk up to the Glendalina fields, beyond Falls Park, where they were unlikely to meet anyone they knew, but it had been wonderful just being with him.

Peggy waited impatiently for her father to come in. He seemed stuck to the spot and she said, 'Excuse me, please.' When her father moved to one side she passed him and climbed the stairs, preparing to make her peace with Louise.

Tommy looked after her, then across at Nora in the scullery. His wife avoided eye contact, and muttering

'Women! They'll be the death of me yet,' he sank down into his chair and lifted the newspaper.

Johnnie swelled with pride as he watched Mary approach on Sunday morning. Dressed in a long grey skirt with matching jacket that reached below her hips, hiding her slight bump and making it practically impossible for those not in the know to tell she was pregnant, she looked like the girl he had fallen for when first they met. It saddened him to think that, because of him, she would be the focal point of local gossip when her condition became more noticeable.

Below a white straw Easter bonnet bright chestnut locks fell to her shoulders and wispy curls escaped the confines of the bonnet and curled around her face. Her skin glowed and her eyes sparkled. Gone was the woebegone creature who had driven him to distraction. Heads turned as she passed by and he didn't blame them. In his eyes, she looked absolutely stunning.

Mary blushed at his obvious admiration and when he offered her his arm, she tucked her hand behind his elbow and walked proudly by his side into the church. Louise, seated near the back, straightened to attention and nudged Peggy when she saw the couple make their way up the centre aisle.

Her sister went round-eyed. 'I didn't know they were back together. Did you?' she whispered.

'I know that Johnnie spent last night next door as usual. I heard him moving about, but there was no sound of voices, so I don't think they're actually back together. Still . . . walking right up to the front of the church like that? Well, it looks like a declaration to me.'

'Mary looks lovely, doesn't she?' Peggy said wistfully. 'She has beautiful hair.'

'Indeed she does. She must be one of those women who blossom when they are pregnant.' Louise eyed Peggy's fine ash blonde hair. 'There's nothing wrong with your hair. It's very pretty. We're both lucky to have inherited Ma's natural curl. A lot of girls would give their eye teeth to have hair like yours.'

Peggy's eyes lit up. 'You think so? You're not just saying that?' She fingered her hair. 'It's very fine, you know.'

Louise suddenly realised that her young sister was at that age when she needed reassurance about her appearance and set out to bolster up her confidence. 'Why would I say so if it wasn't true? You're a very attractive wee girl and your hair is lovely.'

'Really?'

'Really.'

The congregation rose as the priest and altar boys came out, putting a stop to further conversation, and Louise turned her mind inwardly to God and her own problems. She had such a lot to talk over with Him. Could she have been more respectful towards Mrs O'Rourke yesterday, she wondered? Well, she hadn't been exactly disrespectful, had she? She had no intention of promising that she and Conor would remain just friends. So what else could she say? Weren't they in love already? It was unreasonable of the woman to put her on the spot like that.

Then, as if she hadn't enough to worry about, Cathie had introduced Trevor to her last night at the dance. He was tall, red-haired and freckle-faced, and he had an infectious grin. It was soon obvious to Louise that Cathie was really attracted to this boy and nothing she said was likely to make any difference. When her friend cornered her in the cloakroom and asked her opinion of him, she'd had to agree that she did find him really nice, but warned that first impressions weren't always the best ones. People tended to be on their best behaviour when first meeting people they wanted to influence.

Bewildered, Cathie said, 'Tell me something. Why would he want to influence you?'

'For the simple reason, he knows you'll be asking my opinion of him.'

'And . . . what do you think of him?'

'He's nice . . . and that's why . . . you shouldn't see him again. However, I think you've already made up your own mind.' She looked askance at Cathie and received an ashamed nod in reply.

Louise sighed, Trevor really was a lovely lad and Louise didn't blame her friend for wanting to get to know him better. In fact his mate George, who danced most of the night with Louise, was also very nice. When he asked her out on a date she might have thought it worth risking her father's wrath and agreed to meet him, but because of her feelings for Conor she wasn't in the least tempted. And she was glad. She didn't often see eye to eye with her da, but in this instance she did. Especially after all that trouble a while back. She had been fifteen when Carson had made that rousing 12 July speech at Finaghy, calling on the loyalists of Ulster to protect their interests by whatever means they deemed necessary, causing them to attack Catholic workers in the Harland & Wolff shipyard and the big engineering works. Wasn't her own brother one of the men to be beaten and thrown out of the yard? The Catholics, in turn, retaliated and attacked Protestant workers. She could remember only too clearly the violence that erupted afterwards, with rioting mobs attacking passing trams and spreading terror throughout the Falls and Springfield road areas. Because of the riots and the fear of going to work in the predominantly Protestant firms, more than half the men in the Catholic districts of Belfast were out of work. No, after that, you were better off staying with your own sort.

'So you're going to see him again?'

'Yes.'

Louise gave her a quick hug. 'Be careful. Won't you?'

Nora had seen Johnnie and Mary file up for Holy Communion and elbowed Tommy. He followed the direction of her glance and his face turned sour. 'Bloody fool. That's what he is! He should have let her stay at her ma's. I bet the kid's not even his.'

'See? Even in the Lord's own house you've no compassion. You disgust me, Tommy McGuigan. I don't know what kind of man you are any more.' She bowed her head and asked God's forgiveness for her husband's transgression, completely forgetful of her own.

Leaving him to follow, Nora left the church before Mass had quite finished, and waited outside for the couple, to find out how the land lay.

'My, you look bonny this mornin', Mary,' she said softly, enveloping her daughter-in-law in a hug. 'Obviously pregnancy agrees with you.'

Grabbing at her hat, which Nora's close embrace had almost dislodged, Mary laughed. 'Hush. No need to let everybody know. But I have to admit I feel much better since I got over that bout of morning sickness,' she whispered for Nora's ears only.

Now aware of straining ears and covert looks, Nora drew her to one side and whispered back, 'Does this mean everything's OK?' Her eyes darted from one to the other. 'You know, between you two?'

'Ma . . . for heaven's sake mind your own business. Mary and I are going to spend the day together, that's all.'

'Oh . . .'

188

Nora looked so downcast, Mary hastened to reassure her. 'We're going to have a good long talk, you know, thrash things out, and I'm very hopeful we'll come to some sort of agreement.'

Nora gripped her hand and squeezed it. 'Now that *is* good news.' She sighed. 'There's Tommy waiting for me. I'll have to go before he has kittens. Would you like to come in for tea tonight?' She looked hopefully at Mary but Johnnie quickly intervened.

'No, Ma. Thanks all the same, but we don't want to be tied down to any particular time. I'll see you tomorrow.' He certainly didn't want his da saying something to send Mary running scared again. Taking his wife by the arm, he led her away. He had noticed his sisters heading in their direction and didn't want her subjected to any more questions. He knew they all meant well but he did wish they would mind their own business.

Trevor and his friend George had walked both girls home on Saturday night. As they approached the Springfield–Grosvenor Road junction, Louise became uneasy. Supposing Conor's mother happened to bump into them, what would she think? She would certainly let her son know of his precious Louise's two-timing antics, that Louise could be sure of. Cissie O'Rourke would make the most of the situation and try to drive a wedge between them. Deciding not to take any unnecessary chances, Louise bade them all good night, waving aside George's offer to see her to her door, and hurried across the road.

Cathie lived in St Peter's parish and went to Mass there every Sunday. Louise was surprised to see her at the corner of Springfield Road next morning, obviously on the lookout for her.

'Is anything wrong?'

'No. I've a favour to ask you.'

'God, you'd me worried there for a minute.' A wary look on her face, Louise invited, 'Fire away.'

'You ran away in such a hurry last night that George didn't get a chance to speak to you. He asked me to see if you would like to make up a foursome to go up the Cave Hill this afternoon. How's about it, Louise?'

'No! Look, Cathie, I've already told you that I don't want to get involved.'

'George has a car and the four of us could go off for the day. Please, Louise. We could have a lovely afternoon. No hassle waiting for trams. Just take off and enjoy ourselves.'

'Listen, Cathie! I don't want to give George the wrong idea. He's a nice lad and all that, but I've no interest in him whatsoever.'

'He knows that. I've already told him you're involved with someone else. Besides, what will you do if you don't come out with us, eh? Sit at home brooding about Conor?'

That was all too true. Her family had different things planned. Even Nora, who rarely went out, was meeting one of her friends from work to go off somewhere for the afternoon, and her da had arranged to go to a darts match in the Beehive pub.

She swiftly changed her mind. 'OK. You've convinced me. What time are you meeting them?'

'Thanks, Louise. The car will be here at the park at one o'clock.'

'Right, that gives me time to go home and change out of all my finery. Especially my shoes.' She glanced down at her bridesmaid's shoes. 'I certainly don't want to be climbing over rocks in these. I'll be here at one. See you then.'

* * *

A small black car was parked at the corner, its engine ticking over, when Louise arrived back at the crossroads. Cathie was already settled in the back seat and George got out to let Louise join her. Cathie turned a radiant face towards her and admitted that she had never been to the Cave Hill before.

Dark clouds had gathered and Louise voiced her doubts. 'Those clouds don't look very promising. Are we wise going up the Cave Hill? There won't be much shelter there, you know.'

Trevor twisted round from his seat in the front and smiled at them. 'Not to worry. That's the beauty of having a car. If it rains we'll find somewhere else to go.'

Louise wasn't too happy about this state of affairs. She had no intention of going off just anywhere in the present climate with these two comparative strangers. One heard of so many unpleasant incidents these days. If it became necessary, she would soon let them know that. She would make them stop the car and let her out, and make her own way home. Cathie could come with her or stay, as she pleased. Louise began to fret; how could she make them stop if they didn't want to? However, she needn't have worried. The clouds dispersed as quickly as they had gathered and as they drove along the Antrim Road the sun broke through.

George seemed to know his way about; he parked the car near the top of Gray's Lane and the four of them tumbled out and stretched cramped limbs. The lads took a holdall and two tartan travelling rugs from the boot.

'We've brought some sandwiches and drinks, so we won't starve,' George jested. Locking the car, he set off, leaving the others to follow. They trailed behind him as they made their way to the foot of the Cave Hill and without much more ado started the uphill trek.

Louise had not been to the Cave Hill since she was a little girl. Before the war her parents had brought them all to a part of the hill called Hazelwood, where they had congregated along with hundreds of other families to roll hard-boiled eggs down the grassy slopes. It was an Easter tradition, upheld religiously by all, regardless of colour or creed. But what with the war and the troubles, she had not felt inclined to stray far from home for some years now. She could, however, still remember the excitement, the shrieking children scrambling down the gentle slopes after their eggs. In the days leading up to Easter Sunday, Nora would boil a half-dozen eggs until she thought they were hard enough for the rigorous task ahead of them. As soon as the eggs had cooled enough to handle, Louise and her brothers and sister would dye them various bright colours and then painstakingly paint unusual designs – which usually started out as a flower or a rabbit or some other childish figure – on them. Their father would give a ha'penny to the one who painted the prettiest egg. She remembered being in tears when at the end of the day the shells were cracked and the eggs wolfed down by her ma, da and brothers. Peggy and she refused to eat theirs because they were too pretty to destroy.

Louise had thought she was reasonably fit until they were halfway up. Unused to climbing, she found the rough going hard and started to stumble and flag, and was glad to receive a helping hand from George. 'Can't remember it being so tough before when I came here with my parents,' she complained. 'And I was only little then.'

'Your parents probably took the easier route. Most folk with kids usually go up by the zoo or the castle.'

'I'm glad to hear that. I was beginning to doubt my memory.'

At last they were resting on a grassy knoll near the first cave. Her legs were aching. They lay there for about fifteen minutes resting their trembling limbs and getting their breath back. As they gazed up at the cliffs towering above them, George pointed out five caves in all and said that he thought they were the reason for the hill's unusual name. Suddenly he jumped to his feet and ordered, 'Right, you lot, back to work. No rest for the wicked.' He pulled a protesting Louise to her feet. 'Let's get the show on the road. We haven't far to go now.'

Soon the four intrepid mountaineers were assaulting the final stage, up the north face of the Eiger, Louise mused, albeit the Sheep's Pad up the east slope of the Cave Hill, on their way to the summit. At last they reached their destination, the top of McArt's Fort, where they threw themselves on the thick heather, gulping deep breaths of fresh mountain air. Reasonably revived, they crawled, still panting from the exertion of the climb, over to the edge of the cliff. A spectacular, panoramic view spread out before them. To their right they could see over Belfast and the shipyard. To their left they could see Carnmoney hills and further away, Carrickfergus and Kilroot. Directly ahead of them lay Belfast Lough and the County Down shoreline stretching as far as Bangor. The view was breathtaking and well worth the strenuous climb. They sat on the rugs and admired the verdant surrounding countryside with relish, pointing out recognised landmarks to each other.

Struck by a thought, Louise said, 'Are we on Napoleon's Nose, by any chance?'

George explained to her that they were sitting on top of McArt's Fort and not Napoleon's Nose, which was further along the ridge to their left. An awful lot of people insisted on calling this Napoleon's Nose. In fact, where it was situated it could be rightly named Napoleon's Hat, he went on to explain. There were quite a few people wandering past or stopping to appreciate the view below. Looking around her, Louise was relieved that she could see no one who was likely to recognise them. Cathie, apparently, couldn't care less who saw them.

Louise sat on the rug with George, arms clasping her legs and chin on her knees, gazing over the lough. Aware that George was eyeing her covertly, she slowly turned her head and looked him full in the face.

His face reddened with embarrassment. 'Sorry. I didn't mean to stare, but I have to admit you're worth looking at.'

Disconcerted by his admiration and honesty, Louise said haltingly, 'George . . . I think you know I'm already interested in someone else?'

He nodded. 'Yes, Cathie told me there was someone else in the picture, but she also said his mother was against the relationship. She didn't seem to hold out much hope for you. But of course that's up to the lad. If I liked a girl I certainly wouldn't let my mother dictate to me whether or not I should date her.'

Louise gave an unladylike snort and angrily tossed her head. 'Some friend she is. She had no right to discuss my private business with you.'

'Ah, now, please don't blame her. I think she felt sorry for me. She knows I fancy you.'

'Well, don't! I'm not interested. Even if there wasn't already someone else, I wouldn't go out with you. This is a one off to please Cathie. I'm only here because of her. She doesn't know when to leave well alone.'

'Ah, come on, Louise. They like each other. What have you got against us, anyway? Is it because we're Prods?'

'Look, I personally haven't got anything against your

religion. I'm not a bigot. I had plenty of good friends who were Protestants from the Shankill but the riots put an end to that. It really is easier to stick with your own kind, and less trouble. My da and brothers would go bonkers if they knew I was here with you today. Believe me, it wouldn't be worth all the hassle. I shouldn't have come in the first place.'

He reached for her hand and held on tightly when she tried to pull it free. 'But you did. So let's enjoy each other's company today, mm?'

She looked into pale grey eyes and found herself nodding. 'So long as you understand.'

He grinned at her. 'You've made it quite clear,' he stressed, using her own words. '*Believe me!*'

His grin was infectious and she smiled in return. He really was a nice lad. But not for her. Definitely not for her.

Conversation flowed pleasantly between them. They exchanged views about how life was on each side of the divide, the girls learning that it wasn't all rosy for the working class Protestants either. It seemed that each side had suffered because of the troubles.

'Mind you,' Louise said, 'I'm not shedding any tears for you. I didn't hear of any Protestants being thrown out of the shipyard.'

Trevor was quick to retaliate. 'Your side were just as bad. They attacked innocent Protestant workers from Mackie's.'

'Here, hold on now.' George held up both hands, palms out, in a placating gesture. 'We didn't come here to slag each other off, did we?'

'Now you can see what I mean by saying you're best sticking with your own kind,' Louise retorted. 'This

195

conversation wouldn't have arisen. But I do agree with George – let's forget all about religion and politics for the day, OK?'

The girls discovered that, working class or not, the lads were much better off than them; especially George, who was able to keep a car, albeit an old banger, on the road, and didn't seem to be short of a bob or two. Despite their best endeavours not to mention politics, they soon found themselves discussing at some length how, in their opinion, things could be changed for the better. But in the end all agreed that none of the powers that be would be likely to listen to them. Soon it was time to eat and the girls were invited to help themselves. The assortment of sandwiches and cakes on offer brought home again to Louise just how different they really were. This spread would have cost enough to feed some poor family – who had been thrown out of the shipyard or engineering works and were still unable to fend for themselves – for a week.

Those families lived from day to day, hand to mouth, not knowing where their next meal was coming from. Feelings of guilt assailed Louise and the food stuck in her throat. Under the watchful eye of George she managed to eat one small currant bun. They washed the food down with lemonade, and afterwards stretched out, lapping up the now strong sunshine.

Then, with a flourish, Trevor produced a deck of cards. 'Do you girls play at all?'

'You think of everything, don't you?' Cathie cried in delight. 'We can play gin rummy,' she added proudly. 'We often play at home, don't we, Louise?'

'Yes, especially with this awful curfew on so we can't stay out too late,' Louise agreed. 'We can play trumps too.'

Engrossed in the card games they didn't notice the

time passing. It was the sight of the parents below them on the grassy slopes, gathering their belongings together and calling their children to heel, that made Louise aware of how late it was. Certainly too late to go to the pictures tonight, she thought with regret. It was with reluctance that she suggested to George that it was time they were getting a move on. He glanced at Trevor and Cathie, who were gazing into each other's eyes.

'Let's give them a little longer together. Come for a walk with me round the back of the hill and then I promise to take you safely home.'

He stressed *safely* and Louise rose at once to accompany him. The other two didn't seem aware of their leaving and Louise admitted to herself that Cathie, the daft girl, was infatuated with Trevor, probably thought she was in love with him.

The back of the hill was new to Louise. It wasn't hilly and rough like the front facing the lough, and it made for easier walking along the well-trodden paths through the heather. It was more private, too, and some couples were taking advantage of the nooks and crannies in the heather to kiss and cuddle. Embarrassed at the antics of some of them, she kept her eyes averted where possible and hoped George didn't get any big ideas. Then from the corner of her eye something familiar caught her attention. Sure that she recognised the shape and posture of the man, she watched as a tall dark fellow rose from a shady nook hidden in the deep heather and helped a blonde-haired woman to her feet.

A smile tugged at her lips when she realised that it was Bill McCartney. Crafty auld bugger, she thought. At work he acted as if butter wouldn't melt in his mouth. Imagine him courting. He was so quiet and shy; who would believe it? Maybe shyness was why he was here, on the side of the hill that was less frequented by the public. Many a doffer and reeler had set their hats at Bill, only to give up in despair. Even some weavers had tried to get him interested, but he didn't give them any encouragement. Just wait until she told her ma this juicy bit of gossip. It would spread through the mill like wildfire. They'd be taking the mick out of him for some time to come. Averting her head so that Bill wouldn't recognise her, she nevertheless managed to get a quick look at his companion. The sight of the face that was gazing lovingly up at him sent shock waves coursing through Louise's body, bringing her to an abrupt standstill.

George bumped into her and had to grab hold to save her from toppling over. He gripped her by the shoulders and as she contrived to hide her face she furtively peered over his shoulder, and saw Bill tenderly pull her mother close and kiss her full on the lips. A kiss that Nora eagerly returned.

Louise silently urged George to keep moving before her mother could catch sight of her. Not that Nora was likely to notice, by the looks of her. She wasn't paying attention to anyone or anything. She was lost in Bill's embrace, unaware of the horror and revulsion her daughter was experiencing as she watched her mother's immoral behaviour. How could she get on like that? What if anyone they knew saw her? She was a married woman, for heaven's sake. Had she no shame at all?

Tottering slightly, George caught Louise by the shoulders and slowed her down. He gazed at her in exasperation. 'Hey . . . hold on. You'll be knocking me over next. What on earth's the matter with you?' he said crossly. However, one glance at her and he was all concern. Putting an arm across her shoulders he gazed anxiously into her face. 'Are you feeling ill?'

She leaned against him, ashamed to discover that she really did need the support of his arm. She was flabbergasted; couldn't take in what she had just seen. Her ma and Bill McCartney in a passionate embrace? It was unbelievable! God, but her ma must really fancy him to get on like that, and in public too. Normally she'd be afraid to be seen even talking to another man. Louise's mind wanted to erase the scene, forget she had ever seen it, but how could she? She had witnessed it with her own two eyes. 'Please, George, can we go back to the car?'

'Of course.' Still concerned, he turned at once, but suddenly she realised that Nora and Bill could very well still be at it, and in a panic decided to feign sickness. Swaying unsteadily against him she whispered, 'I feel faint, George. Perhaps I should sit down for a minute.'

He was leading her towards some rocks when, to her horror, she saw her mother and Bill walking towards them. Arms entwined, they only had eyes for each other. Louise felt as if she was caught up in some slow-moving comedy movie. Desperately afraid of being seen she turned to George, unconsciously looking entreatingly at him, seeking inspiration. Completely in the dark, lost in the vivid blue of her eyes, and seeing sensuous lips so close, he took it as an invitation. Throwing caution to the wind, he promptly claimed them.

In her manoeuvring Louise had managed to guide them off the path, and could only hope that in the shelter of George's arms her mother wouldn't recognise her should she chance to look in their direction. Instinctively, she pressed closer to George's muscular body, unconsciously returning the pressure of his lips. Nora and Bill were long gone and George was becoming aroused when she came to her senses and, with a look of horror, pushed him away.

Pressing her fingers against trembling lips she gazed

at him in dismay. 'I'm sorry. I don't know what came over me.'

He gave a delighted chuckle. 'You can do that any time you like. I won't object.'

'You don't understand. I shouldn't have done it.'

He shrugged. 'Why not? We both enjoyed it, so no harm done. It was only a kiss, after all.'

'I've already told you there's someone else.'

'Well now, maybe you're not as interested in this other lad as you think.' He raised an inquisitive brow. 'Eh?'

'You're wrong. I am. Please, George, take me back to the car.'

'Fair enough.' He put his arm across her shoulders but she shrugged it off. His lips tightened, but he bit back the angry retort that was on the tip of his tongue. What was she playing at? Was she just a tease? No, he couldn't believe that, she was too strait-laced, but he had no intention of letting her off the hook. She wasn't thinking of her boyfriend when she returned his kiss. No, she enjoyed it, he was sure of it. He just had to persuade her to see him again and then it was up to him.

When they returned to the picnic spot the other two were already waiting, whispering and giggling in a huddle. They were all tired and the journey back down to Gray's Lane was somewhat subdued. When they eventually reached the car, Trevor followed Cathie into the back seat, leaving a disgruntled Louise to climb into the front beside George. During the journey home she made polite but erratic conversation to drown out the sounds coming from behind her. George just nodded and grunted in reply. She didn't dare look to see what the couple were getting up to. When she did finally venture to sneak a glance over her shoulder, George reached over and patted her hand. 'Let them get on with it. It's not your problem.' She nearly died of mortification and snatched her hand away.

He flashed her a mischievous grin. 'I'm dead jealous, so I am. Are you not?'

'No I am not!'

'Not even a tiny bit?'

'I think they're disgusting, getting on like that.'

'Wow!' George just smiled. She hadn't been disgusted when he had kissed her. To be fair, they hadn't got as far as the frustrated grunts and pants coming from the back seat.

Angry at her friend's lack of control, at the Springfield junction, with a quick 'Thank you' in George's direction, she was out of the car like a shot and moving over to Dunville Park to wait impatiently for Cathie. Her friend took her time saying good night to Trevor and then had a conversation with George, while Louise seethed silently by the railings. She was just about to give up and leave her friend to stew when the car drew away from the kerb and headed down Grosvenor Road, waved off by a smiling Cathie.

The smile quickly disappeared when she joined Louise. 'What are you waiting here for?' she said with a scowl. 'You should have went on, so you should. Heaven knows you couldn't get out of that car quick enough, so why hang about here? They'd have given me a lift down home if you hadn't decided to stand here like some lost soul.' She tossed her head in disgust.

Hands on hips, Louise leaned forward to glare at her. 'Believe it or not, Cathie Morgan, I thought I was actually doing you a good turn. Do you think I wanted to stand here like an eejit? But what if any of your ones saw you getting out of a car, mm? Who do you know round here who owns a car, eh? And of course they would have wanted to know who the two lads were. How would you have explained that away?'

With hindsight, Cathie had the grace to look ashamed. 'You're right, of course. I wasn't thinking straight.'

'You can say that again! You must have been out of your mind. Why, you behaved like a shameless hussy, so you did.'

Cathie looked bewildered. 'What do you mean?'

'I'm talking about the antics of you in the back of that car coming home.'

'What are you on about? We were only kissing.'

The memory of the kiss shared with George assailed Louise and guilt swamped her. Had they been grunting and gasping like that? She didn't think so, but still . . . she bit back the sarky remarks that were trembling on her lips. Who was she to criticise? Hadn't she been just as shameless? Those kinds of embraces should be saved for someone you really cared for. Was it something in the air on Cave Hill, like the intoxicating fragrance of the heather, that made you lose control? First her ma, then herself and then Cathie. Her friend was looking at her as if she wasn't right in the head and she said abruptly, 'Look, it's getting late. I'll have to run on.'

Cathie gripped her arm. 'Hold on a minute. Will you come for a drive tomorrow afternoon?'

'You've got to be joking!' Cathie's face fell and Louise said, 'Cathie, I warned you I don't want to get involved.'

'George won't come unless you do.'

'Too bad. I would have thought you'd want to be alone with Trevor. If you're so determined to see him again, I'm afraid you'll have to meet him under your own steam. Listen to me, Cathie. Stop this before it goes too far.

You're a fool so you are. No good can come of it. Surely you can see that.'

'A few dates won't do any harm, so they won't. Can't I persuade you to come with us tomorrow? After all, it's Easter Monday. Where else will you go?'

Easter Monday. Louise's one day off work and she had been looking forward to it. But Cathie was right. With Conor away, she had nowhere else to go. Could she bear to be on her own? She brightened up. 'What's Jean doing tomorrow?'

'You can forget about her. I imagine she'll be going out with Joe McAvoy. Those two are as thick as thieves now.'

'Where do you intend going tomorrow, then?'

Sensing success ahead, Cathie perked up. 'Trevor says they'll take us anywhere we like.' She held her breath.

Louise sighed. 'I give up. As you pointed out, where else can I go? I'll come along tomorrow. But this will definitely be the last time. Do you hear me?' Cathie's head bobbed in agreement. 'Will we meet here? Same time, same place?' Struck by a sudden thought her brows gathered in a frown. 'How will they know?' Her head shot up and she glared at Cathie. 'You've already said I'd come. Haven't you?'

'No! Don't be silly. I'm meeting Trevor for an hour or so later on. George intended asking you out but you were so abrupt he was afraid to chance it. He'll be delighted to hear you're coming with us tomorrow.'

'I can't believe you're meeting Trevor tonight. Where will you go? No, forget I asked that. I don't want to know. The less I know about you two the better.'

'Don't worry. We're just going for a walk. Somewhere where nobody knows us.'

Thinking of her mother and Bill, Louise said, 'Don't

count on it. It's a small world. Somebody is sure to see you.'

'I'll risk it. Where do you fancy going tomorrow?'

'I haven't a clue. I'll think about it. Do you have to know now? Can't we decide when we meet them?'

Cathie gave her a quick hug. 'We sure can. Thanks, Louise. See you tomorrow.'

Watching her friend almost skip down Grosvenor Road, Louise sighed. She hoped she didn't live to regret her decision.

Completely absorbed in a tangled web of dark, distracted thoughts, Louise passed the O'Rourke house without so much as a sideways glance. Her father was in the scullery stirring away at something in a saucepan when she arrived. Of her mother there was no sign. Huh! Her ma was taking one hell of a chance if she didn't want to be caught on. But then . . . perhaps she did. Maybe she was deliberately courting disaster. If she was once found out, there would be no alternative. Tommy would throw her out of the house. Not quite physically, perhaps, but he would make it impossible for her to remain. Her life wouldn't be worth living. Oh, for the benefit of outsiders, her da would be careful to keep up the front that he was a caring husband, but he would make life unbearable for Nora. She would have no other choice but to go. Louise cringed inside at the thought that her ma might leave them. Tommy turned when she entered the kitchen and scowled at her.

'Where's your ma?'

'How should I know?'

'You seem to know everything that goes on in this house.'

'Well, you're wrong, I've no idea where she is.' This, in fact, was the truth. For all she knew her mother might have already run off with Bill McCartney. The way they were carrying on, anything was possible. Looking at her da standing there half cut so early in the evening, Louise knew she would find it hard to blame her ma, no matter what the consequences. 'She said last night she was going out with a friend from work, remember?' Nora hadn't told one word of a lie. She just didn't say which sex her friend was and no one had cared enough to ask. It was awful how they all took her for granted. Didn't show her any consideration. 'You were here, Da. You heard her.'

'I didn't think she'd be away all day.'

'Perhaps if you'd asked her, she would have told you she'd be late. Awful, isn't it, that me ma should have a day off.' Mentally she railed at him. You selfish bugger. If you'd pay more attention to her, take her out now and again, she probably wouldn't look twice at Bill McCartney.

Tommy glowered at her. 'What's got into you? She's my wife! It's her place to make my meals.'

'Why? Why is it her place? Me ma has you spoilt rotten. And for why . . . I don't know. You never take her out. You never buy her any wee pressies. As far as you're concerned she's nothing but a skivvy in this house. So good luck to her. She deserves any happiness she can get.'

She stood aghast; her father's attitude had made her condone her mother's wrongdoing. It had also loosened her tongue. Would he twig that his wife was happy, and begin to wonder why?

'What are you on ab—' The smell of scrambled eggs burning in the saucepan wafted across from the scullery, bringing her da's tirade to an end. With a muffled oath Tommy rushed to rescue them. He was too late. 'See what you've made me do, you stupid bitch?'

'Just listen to yourself, Da. Is anything ever *your* fault?'

He lunged towards her and Louise nearly tripped over herself getting out of the house. This was a little sample of what life would be like should her mother ever leave. How would the family bear it?

Johnnie and Mary ended up in Ormeau Park on the south side of the city. They caught a tram down Grosvenor Road, alighting at Shaftesbury Square. As it was such a fine day they decided to walk the rest of the way to the park, ambling along Donegall Pass and on to Ormeau Road at their leisure, stopping now and again to rest on account of Mary's condition. By the time they crossed the bridge on to Ormeau Embankment, which ran alongside the River Lagan, they were completely at peace with each other and Johnnie had high hopes that something good might come out of this outing. They found a vacant bench and sat in silence watching the swans glide gracefully by on the river, each loath to break the spell of tranquillity.

Arm across her shoulders, Johnnie said, 'It's beautiful here, isn't it?' She sighed in agreement. 'I can't believe we're sitting here like this,' he added.

'To tell you the truth, neither can I. I've been driven to distraction, you know. Couldn't see any way out of our predicament. Me miserable living next door to your parents and you not wanting to live with mine.' He opened his mouth to object but with a raised hand she forestalled him. 'I understand, Johnnie. Really! Me ma is even driving *me* crazy.'

'You said you had a proposition?' he said tentatively.

Looking smug, she turned sideways and gazed intently into his face. 'How would you fancy living in Spinner Street?'

His nose wrinkled in distaste. 'Spinner Street?'

She slumped like a deflated balloon. 'You're not impressed. I thought you'd be delighted.'

'But . . . why Spinner Street?'

'Someone me da works with isn't very well and he's retiring and going to live with his daughter down the shore road. Me da says he thinks that if we slip this man a back-hander he'll let us move in and squat, and chances are we'll get to stay, so long as we're willing to pay the rent.'

'Squat?' Johnnie sounded scandalised. 'I wouldn't stoop so low. The neighbours would hate us. Those houses are always earmarked for somebody's son or daughter or other close relative.'

'Forget about the neighbours! But tell me what you've got against Spinner Street? You should have seen the look on your face when I mentioned it. It's the same size and type of house as the one you're in and what you're paying for two rooms would probably cover the rent. The houses are exactly the same. Kitchen, scullery and wee room downstairs, two bedrooms upstairs. And it has its own closed-in yard and lavatory.'

'You've given this a lot of thought, haven't you?'

She nodded and opened her handbag. He recognised the small book she thrust towards him. 'Look at that.' It was the bankbook she had hidden from view when they met on Good Friday.

It was a deposit account and his brows rose when he saw the amount. 'Is this all yours?'

She nodded eagerly. 'Me da has a wee bit salted away that me ma doesn't know about. He knows I'm miserable at home so he opened that account and put the money in for me. I'm not going to throw his generosity back in his face, Johnnie. I thought you'd be pleased, but . . . I'll move in on my own if I have to. Mind you, this man has lived on his own since his wife died and me da says not to be expecting too much. That's why he's giving me this money, so that we can fix it up to suit ourselves.'

Johnnie looked at his wife's happy countenance and nodded his agreement. 'If that's what you want, I'll go along with it. Can we have a look at it first, before we commit ourselves?'

'Me da says if you agree, he'll have a word with Smithy and offer him a few bob. He can't see any problem. We'll go and have a look at it and if we like what we see, Da thinks we could be in within the week.'

'And meanwhile?'

'I think you should give Mrs Clarke notice.'

'She's in for a shock. She's still in Holywood, and won't be home until a week on Wednesday. I think she has plans for the extra money.'

'I'm sure she has, but she'll understand. Besides, you've worked wonders in her house. She's coming out of it all right.' Mary moved closer. 'If we go home early, you can bribe me with some fish and chips and I might even agree to spend the night with you.'

His face lit up with happiness. Standing up he offered her his hand. 'Let's head back now before the rush starts.'

She laughed aloud. 'That's a good idea.'

He took her by the hand and they retraced their steps, Johnnie barely able to take his eyes off his wife's face for a moment, leaving her to laughingly guide him round obstacles along the way. He was ecstatic. It sounded as if their real honeymoon was about to begin. Please God don't let anything – or anyone, for that matter – ruin it.

7

All eyes fastened in stunned surprise on Nora when on Monday morning she said casually, 'Oh, by the way, I'm going away for the day with my friend, and I won't be home till late, so you'll have to make your own teas. OK?' Aware of the sensation she was causing she kept her eyes fixed firmly on her dish of porridge. A nervous smile twitched at her lips but Louise noted that her mother clutched her spoon so tightly that her knuckles almost broke through the skin. So she wasn't as much at ease as she was letting on to be, Louise surmised.

'Where're you going?' Tommy's head jerked up and he sounded disheartened at the very idea of it. 'You were out all day yesterday and I had to make my own tea last night,' he grumbled.

Secure in the knowledge of Bill's love, Nora tried, as she had promised him, to be brave in the face of adversity. 'Well now, that's just too bad, so it is.' A defiant toss of the head accompanied these words. 'Oh, poor deprived you. What a shame. Why, my heart bleeds for you, so it does.'

Tommy couldn't believe his ears. Stabbing a finger in

her direction, he snarled, 'Listen, woman, and you'd better pay heed. I'm warning you, you'd better not make a habit of this.'

Louise sat in stunned silence at her mother's audacity. She couldn't believe what she was hearing either. Her ma, who never went anywhere but to the shops round the corner, or to church, was going out two days on the trot. Why, it was unheard of! And her da hadn't even asked who she was going out with. Didn't he care at all? To make matters easier for her mother, she said, 'Don't you worry about us, Ma. We're all big and ugly enough to look after ourselves. You see and enjoy yourself.'

'I intend to, Louise. Thanks.' Again that defiant flounce. 'In fact I might even stay the night at my friend's house. There's a spare room available.'

Louise gaped at her mother in wide-eyed consternation. Surely she wouldn't dare! Or would she? Bill McCartney certainly seemed to have her under some kind of spell from the way they were carrying on yesterday.

Tommy straightened upright in his chair and glared across the table at her. 'You'll do no such thing! Do you hear me?'

Nora beamed inanely at him. 'Just testing. I thought you wouldn't notice. I will come home tonight all right, but it'll be late, so don't wait up.' She spoke with finality and returned her attention to her porridge. She was so confident that Louise was proud of her, but also fearful of where this might lead.

Suddenly, Tommy showed suspicion. A frown creasing his brow he leaned towards her. 'Who's this woman you're so friendly with all of a sudden, eh? She seems to be leading you astray whoever she is. Anyone I know?'

'No, it's just a friend from work. We enjoy the same things. And you'd better get used to it. I intend having a night out now and again.' She thrust out her chin and glared at him. 'And don't you dare object, Tommy McGuigan! You're out nearly every night of the week flying your kite and I never question who you're with, or where you've been for that matter. I daren't say a word.'

Tommy bristled with indignation and, seeing a slanging match brewing, Louise lifted her breakfast dishes and headed for the scullery. 'You go and get ready, Ma. Me and Peggy will clear up.'

Peggy's head shot up and her mouth opened in protest, but before she could utter a word Louise shot her a warning *don't you dare* look. 'You deserve a break, Ma. Doesn't she, Peggy? Come on, help me clear the table.'

'Why, that's very thoughtful of you, love.' Nora quickly took her up on the offer and, before anyone else could object, disappeared into the wee room.

Grim-faced, Peggy helped her sister clear the table and joined her in the scullery. Harry was working over the Easter holiday and had already gone off to the bakery. His review was due on Tuesday so he was determined to create the best possible impression.

'I'm supposed to be joining the McFaddens on a picnic today,' Peggy grumbled.

'Well, you should have said so earlier. Away you go then and I'll finish up in here.'

'Thanks. But surprising though it may seem to you, I also like a good wash down before going out. Don't want people talking about me, you know.'

Louise smiled at her. Peggy rarely got invited anywhere. 'Sorry, love. I never thought. When me da comes in from the yard use that kettle I've ready for the dishes and take over the scullery for as long as you like. I'm not going out till lunchtime. I'll wash the dishes before I go.'

Before Louise should change her mind, Peggy edged closer. 'Can I ask a big favour of you?'

Apprehensive now, Louise eyed her through narrowed lids. 'What?' Peggy's favours usually meant she was on the scrounge and wanted to borrow one of her sister's few good articles of clothing, and she was so accident prone where clothes were concerned.

'Can I borrow your red jumper? Please?'

Louise opened her mouth to refuse and Peggy's face dropped. She turned away with slumped shoulders. Although Louise had intended wearing that jumper herself, she found herself relenting. Peggy hadn't been earning long enough to build up any kind of wardrobe yet. 'All right. But for heaven's sake be careful with it and don't pluck the wool. You know what you're like with clothes. Borrow my grey skirt while you're at it; they go nice together.'

Her reward was a hug and a kiss on the cheek. 'Thanks, sis. You're the best sister anyone could have. I promise to look after them. I'll be ever so careful. I'll go up now and get them ready.' She added resentfully, 'Me da will probably be out there for a while yet.'

When Nora came out of the wee room, Louise could see that she had taken a lot of trouble with her appearance and she really did look beautiful. Her blonde hair was parted in the centre and twisted into coils around her ears. She wore her best blouse: a pale pink cotton affair which buttoned to the throat with little pearl buttons. The colour heightened the slight touch of rouge that tinted her cheeks. Now, that was a first; her mother had only ever used face powder before, never rouge. She looked real classy. Bill McCartney would be proud to be her escort today.

Glad that her da was out in the yard and wouldn't

see this delightful transformation, Louise eyed her mother from head to toe. 'You look lovely, Ma. Now I know why you were up so early. You were having a bath, weren't you?' Leaning close she added for her mother's ears only, 'You look like you did the other night . . . like a woman in love.'

Colour flooded Nora's face and her eyes widened in alarm. 'Catch yourself on, you silly girl.'

'Ma . . . I was up the Cave Hill yesterday and I saw Bill McCartney with a beautiful blonde . . .'

Nora's lips softly uttered the words 'Oh, sweet Jesus.' Her hand quickly pressed against them as if to smother the ejaculation and instinctively her eyes darted towards the scullery. 'You won't say anything to your da, will you?'

'Don't look so worried, Ma. Of course I won't say a dicky bird. But . . . please be careful. If he ever finds out . . . there'll be hell to pay.' A tremor passed through her at the very idea of the havoc that he would wreak in this house.

Nora had started to tremble. She clutched at Louise's arm. 'I can't let Bill down now, Louise. It wouldn't be fair. I'll have to go and meet him.'

'I wouldn't want you not to, Ma. Away you go before me da comes back. If he sees you looking like this he's sure to guess there's a man involved. Enjoy yourself. But be very careful,' she warned her.

The sound of the lavatory flushing sent Nora scurrying out of the door. 'I'll see you tonight, love. And thanks.'

Louise wished that she could go with her. She was such a poor liar and dreaded the questions that were bound to be thrown at her.

Tommy's glance quickly took in the fact that the wee

213

room was empty. 'Is your ma away already?' Louise nodded. 'She was in a big hurry. She couldn't even bother to wait and say goodbye?'

Louise shot him a look of scorn. 'Like you always say goodbye to her when you go out, eh?'

'Now you listen here, my girl. That's a different matter entirely. She always knows where I am. I've nothing to hide.'

'Is that right? The way I see it, she only knows where you say you'll be. Why don't you take me ma out with you now and again?'

'Your ma wouldn't be caught dead in a pub, and you know that, Louise. She thinks that only bad women go there.'

'And is she right?'

'Believe it or not, very few women go into the bars at all. The odd couple of regulars go in on a Saturday night. That's about it.'

'Well then, why not take her somewhere else? Where she'll enjoy herself. Take her to the pictures or the concert hall some night and buy her a fish supper on the way home. Lord knows she deserves a treat now and again.'

'How many older couples do you know who go out together? Eh?'

'Not many,' Louise admitted and sighed. 'Only the happy ones, I guess.'

'There you are then.'

Louise looked at him in disgust. Was he brainless or what? 'Da, does that not tell you something?'

'Like what?'

'Like it tells me that me ma must be far from being happy.'

'Let me tell *you* something, smart arse. When you're married as long as me and your ma, you go where you want and the other half doesn't object. Understand? That's the way the system works. Always has done. Now, if you don't mind, I don't want to hear another word from you about me and your mother.'

Louise tossed her head. 'Well, it sounded to me very much as if you were objecting earlier on, so it did. Or did I pick you up wrong?' she added slyly.

'Only because I've no intention of starting to make my own meals. So now you know!'

He moved threateningly towards her. Throwing a disgusted look at him Louise retreated to the safety of the stairs before she said something she might regret. Or, worse still, got a slap on the face for her troubles.

The day out with George and Trevor was pleasant enough. The sun managed to break through the clouds, raising a fine mist from the wet pavements and warming the damp city air. The two lads were waiting and Cathie was already sharing the back seat of the car with Trevor when Louise crossed the Falls Road in a rush, full of apologies.

'Sorry. I got caught up at the last minute. Have you decided where we're going yet?'

'No. We're waiting to ask you where you'd like to go,' Cathie said. 'What's your pleasure?'

They eventually decided the Botanic Gardens would be a good venue, and maybe a look around the museum. The run across Belfast was uneventful and the next couple of hours were spent wandering about admiring the beautiful variety of orchids and strange but wonderful exotic flowers and plants and trying to decipher the Latin names exhibited on little nameplates which also indicated their country of origin. After a short rest they had a quick tour round the museum and afterwards set off on a run to Newcastle where Trevor promised to treat them to lunch. On the way there they stopped off at Ballynahinch for ice cream.

It being Easter Monday, Newcastle centre was pretty well crowded and they joined the crowd on a tour of the shops. Eventually hunger set in and they found a café; settling down at a window table they watched the pedestrians strolling by while waiting to be served. When they had eaten they lingered in the café chatting away, until hostile looks from the waitress warned them that they had outstayed their welcome and the table was required for other customers. With apologetic smiles they left the premises, deciding to stretch their legs with a walk along the beach.

Somehow, during their meanderings George managed to separate Louise and himself from their two companions. She hadn't realised his intentions until Cathie and Trevor were suddenly nowhere in sight. She gave him a warning look and he pretended to ward off an invisible blow.

'Have a heart, Louise. Surely you don't really want to play chaperon? Give them some time alone.' She was silent, and leaning into her face he added slyly, 'Or are you perhaps afraid to be alone with me?'

'You should be so lucky,' she retorted. His face was inches from hers and Louise found herself examining his narrow, sensitive mouth, bringing back memories of the pressure of it against her own with a rush of emotion that surprised her. Unconsciously she licked her lips.

George was no stranger to the actions and reactions of the fair sex and he read the signs all too easily. But what to do? Louise McGuigan intrigued him but he didn't want to scare her off. He had gone to the dance in the first instance to please Trevor but had taken a shine to Louise. Perhaps if she had fallen for his charms, as most

216

girls usually did, he would not have been in the least interested in her. But she hadn't, and he was.

'Let's get to know each other a bit better, Louise.' He held up a hand in warning. 'Before you get the wrong idea . . . I mean as friends. OK?'

She smiled. 'I think that's a good idea. I'd like you for a friend.'

'Great!'

After that she relaxed and the afternoon was most enjoyable although all too short. They talked and laughed as they strolled through Tollymore Park and George teased her unmercifully and she enjoyed every minute of it. She even agreed to go to the pictures with him that evening. After all, what harm could it do?

Her da was in one of his foul moods when she arrived home and she went straight upstairs to avoid another row. When Harry came home from work she decided to go down and make him something to eat.

Tommy sat at the table, a plate of bread and cheese and a mug of tea in front of him. Harry sat slumped in the chair by the fireside looking exhausted.

Her da watched her head for the scullery. 'What are you going to do?'

She jerked her head in Harry's direction. 'I'm going to make him something to eat.'

'And it never dawned on you to offer to make something for me when you came in?'

'Harry's been working all day. You . . . I suppose . . . spent your day in the pub.'

Harry's eyes showed his pleasure. 'That's kind of you, sis. We were grooming the horses today and I'm dead beat. I was coaxing myself to make a cup of tea. As usual we got some lunch at the bakery but I'm hungry again.'

'I'll put the pan on then. Streaky bacon and egg all right?'

'Lovely! My mouth's watering already.'

To keep the peace, Louise also made some bacon and egg and another mug of tea for her father. He received it with his usual surly grunt by way of thanks.

'It's all right, Da. Don't mention it. I'm going to the pictures tonight so I'll be taking over the scullery soon to get ready, so consider yourselves warned.'

'As soon as I eat this, sis, I'll have a quick wash. I want to go out for a few hours.'

'What about you, Da? Are you going out again?' she asked slyly.

His head shot up and he looked at her as if she wasn't right in the head. 'Easter Monday? Of course I'm going out.' He drained his mug and she heard the rasp of whiskers as he rubbed a hand up and down his jaw. 'I didn't shave this morning so I'll run the razor over my chin now and get out of your way. 'Thanks for the tea,' he added sheepishly. 'That wee fry sure was tasty.'

Louise's mouth opened in utter astonishment at this sign of appreciation coming from her father. Glad he wasn't looking in her direction she snapped it shut and tongue in cheek said pleasantly, 'You're welcome, Da.'

She felt a bit apprehensive as she walked down to meet George. They were going to the Royal Cinema picture house, just the two of them. Cathie and Trevor had made other plans, and at first Louise had been reluctant to go out alone with George, but he had assured her that he wouldn't do anything that would damage their friendship. He had wanted her to go to the dance with him, but afraid of the attraction she felt towards him she didn't want to be held in his arms on the dance floor. Not that

218

she thought that he could usurp Conor in her affections, no . . . but she loved Conor and didn't want to spoil things between them by sharing any romantic moments, however small or unimportant, with George.

There were two films showing. A Charlie Chaplin comedy, *Pay Day*, left them relaxed and happy, and was followed by a Buster Keaton film, *The Haunted House*. Returning to the car he observed, 'It's quite early. Would you fancy a run out to Helen's Bay or Carrick?'

She gave this some thought, then nodded. 'Why not? I think I'd enjoy that.'

He smiled in that attractive way of his that she had come to like, but she had misgivings. Was she wise going for a run in the car alone with him? Well, she'd find out soon enough.

They settled on Carrickfergus and found that others were also taking advantage of the bank holiday weather to enjoy the historic town. George found a spot to park and they left the car and joined the visitors walking along the front, stopping to admire the castle and the view out over the lough. Buying two cones from an ice cream barrow, they sat on the sea wall to eat them and watch the world go by.

'Ireland really is a beautiful country, you know. Why can we not live in peace and harmony?' George wondered aloud.

'Because there are those who don't want peace at any price. And it's not all one-sided either.'

'But why?'

'Because there's greedy people on both sides of the divide, making money from keeping the troubles alive. Until we stand together and be counted, the troubles will never end.'

'All that aside . . . why can't we all just get on with

our lives, and still be friends? Live together in friendship and work together in harmony?'

'You and me can be friends. But anything else is out of bounds. That's why I think Cathie is a foolish girl. If her da or brothers ever find out she's going out with a Protestant, all hell will break loose.'

'Do you think they're serious about each other?'

'Looks that way to me.'

George was silent for some moments, then said, 'I'll have a quiet word with Trevor, try to talk some sense into him. I wouldn't like Cathie getting into any trouble because of him.'

'It's none of our business, George. Let's forget all about them and enjoy ourselves, hm?'

'That's fine by me.'

Nora, as she had promised, did come home that night. It was late when Louise heard her quietly enter the house. Slipping from under the warm bedcovers she tiptoed across the cold linoleum and stole down the stairs to intercept her.

'Hi, Ma. Would you like a cup of tea?' she whispered, not wanting to risk waking her da, who could be heard loudly snoring in the wee room.

'Louise! You should have been asleep hours ago,' Nora quietly chastised her.

'I noticed the front door key on the sideboard, Ma, and thought that if you were very late getting back we mightn't hear you knock on the door.' She refrained from adding that she didn't want Bill McCartney getting an excuse to whisk her mother away to that spare room that had been hinted at.

'You shouldn't have worried. I got a spare key cut, so I did.'

'Why?'

A finger to her lips, Nora shushed her daughter and whispered even more softly, 'Bill got it cut for me.'

'Oh, I see. But why? What devious plans has he made?'

'Now, now, Louise, don't get on like that. He wants me to feel independent, that's all. There's no harm in that, is there?'

'Mm . . . I see. How did your outing go then? Did you enjoy yourself?'

'It was wonderful, Louise. Just wonderful. We went up to Ballycastle and walked on the beach. We even had a paddle in the water. Then we had high tea in a hotel on the sea front. All very highfalutin, you know. The cakes were scrumptious.' She licked her lips as if at the remembered treat and Louise could have wept. It would take so little to keep her ma happy. Her da was a stupid, self-centred fool! Nora was continuing in a dreamy voice. 'Afterwards we went to a show. It was brilliant. One guy in particular had a beautiful tenor voice. He sang "Danny Boy" and "I'll take you home again, Kathleen" and I confess, I shed some tears. I've never enjoyed myself so much.'

Her mother looked so happy, and was so unconcerned, that Louise felt fear slide like a cold breeze down her spine, causing her to shiver. 'The show must have run late.' She raised an inquiring brow.

A smile wreathed her mother's face and she admitted, 'Well it's like this, love. When the train got into York Road station, we were just in time to catch the last tram in to Castle Junction and we had to walk the rest of the way home.'

'Weren't you afraid being out so late?'

'I was scared, all right. But we kept to the back streets so's not to run into any patrols.' Sensing her daughter's disapproval Nora eyed her resentfully. 'Please don't begrudge me a bit of fun, Louise. He wanted me to go home with him for a while, but I refused.'

'Does he live on his own, then?'

'No, he lives with his mother, but she's getting on a bit and goes to bed early.'

'Ah, Ma, please be careful. Is it worth the risk?'

An abrupt nod confirmed that it was. Still in a whisper, she confided, 'It is. To be truthful, I deliberately wanted to be late so that your da would be asleep by the time I got back. Has he been in bed long?'

'He was home early. About ten o'clock, and went straight to bed.'

'Thank God for that. You get yourself back up to bed now, love. I'll lock up.

Planting a quick kiss on her mother's cheek Louise hugged her close. 'Good night, love. We'll walk to work together in the morning, OK?' And you can tell me all about it, hung unspoken in the air between them.

Not happy at the prospect, Nora nevertheless nodded her agreement. 'Good night, love.'

It was a long time before Louise fell asleep. She lay, her thoughts in turmoil, listening as her mother checked the doors and windows. When Nora quietly entered the wee room, and she heard her father's raised voice, she unashamedly strained to hear what was said. Her da's words were muffled but her mother answered in a shrill tone, 'No! No, I won't. Leave me alone! It's late! Leave me alone, I tell you! I'm too tired.' More terse words from Tommy and then the old bed creaked and groaned in protest for some time and then silence. What an awful end to her mother's beautiful day, Louise thought mournfully, and burying her head in the pillow she cried in sympathy for Nora.

* * *

After a fretful night tossing and turning, Louise awoke with a blinding headache. At breakfast her mother looked as terrible as she herself felt and Louise felt like weeping all over again for her. Such a difference from the night before when she had been so relaxed and happy. Happy, that was, until she had entered the beast's lair. That wee room must seem like a torture chamber to her. It was a shame that she had to live in dread of her husband.

Her da, as usual, was on the late shift. He seemed to be doing a lot of late shifts recently. Knowing that he wasn't an early riser Louise wondered if he was deliberately swapping shifts with someone who liked the day shift, so that he could be with his family in the evenings. Her father didn't put in an appearance at the breakfast table. He was a rough, lazy auld brute. Had he hurt her ma last night? Louise looked for signs of bruising but Nora had the sleeves of her cardigan pulled well down to the wrists, so if there were any marks they were well hidden. She looked cowed; very different from the lovely creature she had been last night. Did her da not realise that his wife was still an attractive woman and his antics could drive her away for good? Someone should have a word in his ear. But who would have the gumption to point out his failings?

As promised mother and daughter left the house together. Anxious to know what her da had had to say the previous night, but not knowing how to broach the subject, Louise walked in a strained silence. She was hoping her mother would confide in her, or at least give her an opening so that she could question her, but Nora remained tight-lipped, locked away in her own unhappy thoughts. They were approaching the gates of the Blackstaff and Nora still hadn't opened her mouth. With a gentle hand on her arm Louise caught her attention. She needed to know just what was going on.

'Ma, what's wrong?' Panic spiked her voice. 'Don't tell me me da knows about you and Bill?'

A harsh laugh escaped pale, pinched lips. 'Do you think I'd still be able to walk if he did? Ah, no. He's just a selfish, unfeeling brute and I hate him. I really do hate him. He treats me like a bit of rubbish. And I deserve better!' She glared at Louise as if daring her to deny it, and repeated defiantly, 'I do, you know. I do deserve better.'

Seeing Bill coming down Springfield Road and worried at her mother's vulnerable state, Louise urged, 'Of course you do. But Ma, promise me you won't do anything foolish. At least talk to me first, won't you?'

Nora gripped her arm. 'Listen, Louise, it depends on what you mean by "anything foolish". Bill, now, he thinks I'm a fool to stay with your da . . . and do you know something? I'm inclined to agree with him.' A hand made a slicing motion across her brow. 'I've had it up to here with him.' As Bill joined them she said to her daughter, 'I'll see you tonight, love. I won't be home at lunchtime.'

Louise glared daggers at Bill. He nodded affably back at her, all the while his eyes questioning Nora. With an abrupt farewell Nora turned on her heel and stepped to his side. They walked up the yard, heads close together, deep in conversation.

Louise watched until they turned into the spinning room. Then, with a sinking heart, she made her way into the weaving shop and started up her looms. Thrusting the shuttles into the boxes with a savage force she went from one loom to the other and clung on to the combs as if by sheer willpower she could make them go faster still. Wallowing in the depths of despair, she hadn't the heart to even acknowledge her fellow workers. They watched in concern for some moments, then just shrugged and mimed at each other to leave her to it. They'd all had bad times themselves, times when they didn't want to talk about their troubles, and preferred to be left alone.

Completely unaware of them, Louise blinked back tears. What would become of the family if her mother left home? God forbid! It didn't bear thinking about. Her da would take his spleen out on the rest of them. There'd be no living with him. She in particular would suffer the most, being her mother's staunch ally, and being the one brave enough to stand up to him. Thank God, she at least had Conor to champion her; she was lucky to have caught his attention at this troubled time in her life.

At lunchtime, Cissie O'Rourke was on the lookout for Louise and hailed her as she passed by her door. With a wave of her hand she motioned Louise inside. 'Louise, come in for a minute, please.'

Louise kept on walking. 'I'm in a terrible hurry, Mrs O'Rourke. I've a lot to do and can't afford the time to stop for a chat. Sorry!'

'I realise that and I won't keep you long. Please?'

Thinking it better not to antagonise Conor's mother, Louise reluctantly retraced her steps and passed through the hall into the kitchen. Cissie motioned her to a chair. When she shook her head and remained standing, Cissie said, 'I just wanted to let you know that Conor will be home as planned, bar any hold-ups with the boat. I received a telegram from his father this morning.'

Louise's expression softened. 'That's good news. I'm looking forward to seeing him tonight.' It would be wonderful to have him to confide her worries to. 'I suppose you know that I'm meeting him at seven?'

'I do. Actually, that's what I want to talk to you about. I was thinking that perhaps you should wait till tomorrow night? I'm sure he'll have been out and about a lot with his father and will be tired from all the travelling. He'll need to rest before he goes back to college.'

Suddenly alert, Louise eyed her closely. 'Has his father said as much?'

'No, not really. I wanted to warn—'

Louise interrupted her. 'Excuse me, Mrs O'Rourke, but I think Conor is old enough to make his own decisions. He's a young healthy man. To say he needs rest after a week away is ludicrous. If he doesn't want to see me tonight, well that's a different matter entirely. But he can come and tell me himself.' Annoyed at the effrontery of the woman, Louise turned on her heel and stamped out of the house. Cissie's voice followed her. 'I'm just trying to soften the blow.'

What blow? What was that silly woman talking about now? Tears blinded Louise; she felt as if her world was falling apart. First her ma causing all this worry with her shenanigans, and now Cissie O'Rourke sticking her oar in. What had she meant? Soften what blow? She was quite sure Conor would be as anxious to see her as she was to see him. Cissie could go sling her hook. Hearing happy whistling behind her she glanced over her shoulder. It was Harry. He fell into step beside her and throwing an arm across her shoulders gave her a wide grin.

She tried to smile back but failed in the effort. However, he was too pleased with himself to notice. 'What has you so cheerful? You look like the Cheshire cat, with that grin plastered all over your face.'

Her voice was strained but in his obviously happy state

Harry didn't notice her distress. 'My job is secure. That's why I can't stop grinning. Better still, I've even been promoted. I am now head lad over the ones who look after the stables. What do you think of that?' His head swung and his teeth nipped his bottom lip in happy bewilderment. 'I can't take it in, so I can't.'

Louise strived to show she was happy for him. 'That's wonderful news, Harry. I'm sure they can see your worth. You're a good worker.' Her brow now puckered in a frown. 'But why are you not at the bakery now?'

'I got the afternoon off, with pay, on account of me working twelve hours on Easter Monday. Kennedy's is a great firm to work for. I sure am lucky I got started there.'

They had reached the door and as he paused to let her enter first, a glance at her face made him aware of the state she was in. He quickly insinuated himself between her and the door. 'What on earth's wrong, sis?'

Big sapphire eyes brimming with tears blinked back at him. 'Nothing's wrong.'

'Come on, sis, you can't expect me to believe that. You're obviously upset about something. What is it?'

'I can't talk about it,' she whispered. 'Please, not now. Maybe later. Please let me past.'

He reluctantly stood to one side and, glad there was no sign of her father, she was through the kitchen and scullery and out into the yard in a flash. In the privacy of the 'wee outhouse', sitting on the lavatory seat she buried her face in her hands and fought for control. Harry was too young to understand. She wished Johnnie still lived at home, then she could confide in him. However, he had enough on his plate at the minute without her adding to his worries. She had seen him and Mary leave the house next door that morning, arm in arm. They had looked happy enough and she hoped that they, at least, had sorted out their own problems at last.

Taking a long deep breath, she made a determined effort to control her emotions and blew her nose, wiped her eyes and rose to her feet. She must strive to put on a brave face for Harry's sake; not spoil his happiness. Perhaps she was jumping the gun and her mother had no intention of running off with Bill McCartney, she thought forlornly. She must wait and see how it all panned out.

The teapot was brewing and Harry was already busy buttering some baps when she at last felt strong enough to face him.

'Got the runs, sis?' he teased. 'Is that what has you in such a state? Surely you're not embarrassed about something as natural as that?'

She grimaced at him and grabbed at the excuse. 'It's not something one wants to broadcast, now is it?'

His grin was back in place. 'Just keep your distance, that's all I can say. I can't afford to be off work or I might lose my new position and that would never do. Sit down and I'll pour you a cup of tea. I've buttered enough baps for the two of us. I hope you gave those hands a good wash.'

Plastering a smile on her face, Louise sat at the table and extended her hands for his inspection. 'Can't you smell that exotic scent of Lifebuoy soap?' He gave a loud guffaw and she was glad she had made the effort. He was so happy prattling on about his new position.

'These aren't Hughes's baps, are they?' she managed to squeeze out through a mouthful of crumbs as she examined the roll.

'No. Actually they're Kennedy's,' he proudly replied. 'The foreman gave me half a dozen before I left work. Why, don't you like them?'

'Oh, I'm not complaining, Harry, they're lovely, so they are.'

Harry's chest was about to burst with pride. 'Didn't I tell you it was a grand place to work?' When he had run out of plaudits for his boss and descriptions of how wonderful it was to work at J. B. Kennedy's bakery there was a lull in the conversation, and it suddenly dawned on him that his mother was not home for lunch as usual.

He turned a puzzled expression towards his sister. 'Where's me ma?'

'She had someone to see at lunchtime.'

He digested these words and apparently put two and two together. 'She's not really seeing Bill McCartney, is she?'

Louise, who was clearing the table, jerked to attention. 'What do you mean?'

'There's talk going around, you know.'

'Talk about what and by who?' Louise asked apprehensively, her pulse racing.

'Well, when I was in the queue for the pictures the other night I overheard these two women talking. The way they were going on I guessed they must work in the Blackstaff. I wanted to give them a piece of my mind, but they hadn't noticed me and I was too embarrassed to say anything. But I didn't believe them, mind. Me ma wouldn't do anything like that, so she wouldn't.' When his sister remained silent and avoided his eyes, he repeated, 'Sure she wouldn't? Sis! Tell me!'

Unwilling to lie to him, Louise left the dishes where they were and lifting her coat muttered, 'How would I know?'

The door slammed shut. Gazing blankly at it, Harry muttered, 'Oh, my God! Wait till me da finds out. He'll kill her.'

All his enthusiasm evaporated as he lifted the dishes and headed for the scullery. Why did this have to happen now?

The afternoon seemed to drag on for ever. Louise couldn't help thinking of her mother and wondered where she had spent her lunch-break. Whereas that morning Louise had hardly noticed her fellow workers, she now imagined they were talking about her family behind her back. But why would they, she argued? They all had their own skeletons to hide. *She* had nothing to be ashamed of. Hell roast Bill McCartney! Why couldn't he leave her mother alone? Did he have a room readily available for their secret trysts? How long had it been going on, she wondered? Bitter resentment rose in her breast at the thought of her mother and him together and doing God knows what. She shuddered at the very idea. How could her ma sink so low?

Catching sight of Nora waiting by the main gates at the end of their working day, Louise dragged her feet as she slowly made her way towards her. Nora threw her an apologetic look and, linking her arm through Louise's, said, 'I'm sorry, love. I shouldn't have left you as I did this morning, but your da really upset me. I just don't know whether I'm coming or going. I know you won't think so, but I'm still a comparatively young woman, and Bill has made me aware just how much I'm missing out on.'

Terrified of what she might hear next, Louise gazed mutely at her in abject horror.

Nora squeezed her arm against her side. 'Don't look so worried. I'm not going to do anything stupid. But . . . I do intend to keep on seeing him. I can't imagine life without him now. So long as your da doesn't catch on and knock me about, everything can go on as normal. Or as normal as life with your da can be. So come on, you can relax. You're all tensed up.'

Louise turned and buried her head against her mother's shoulder. 'I've been so worried, Ma. Mind you, I wouldn't blame you if you did leave me da. But what about us? How would we manage without you? Especially Peggy.' Louise felt guilty. She knew that she was using emotional blackmail but home life without her mother was a terrible prospect to look forward to, and she would use any means at her disposal to get her mother to stay. 'You'll be sorely missed, you know, and me da will make life unbearable for the rest of us.'

Nora breathed a deep sigh. 'I know, love. That's what I said to Bill. I reminded him that I have commitments.' She didn't add that Bill had pointed out that her family were now old enough to fend for themselves.

Sensing her reserve, Louise pleaded, 'Don't let him persuade you to leave us, Ma. Sure you won't? We need you.'

Nora put her key in the lock and opened the door. 'That depends on your da.'

'What depends on her da?' Tommy was sprawled on the sofa, the *Irish News* spread open on his thighs.

Nora stopped dead in her tracks and gazed at him in dismay. She swore he could hear the grass growing. Louise, caught unawares, crashed into her, almost knocking her off her feet. Grasping the door handle for support, Nora muttered, 'What are you doing home at this time of day?'

'I didn't feel too well, so I came home early.' He squinted over at her. 'Is that a problem?'

'No. What was it this time? A tummy ache, headache, piles?' she said sarcastically.

Still eyeing her resentfully, Tommy nodded. 'Oh, very droll indeed. I haven't had anything decent to eat this past couple of days, in case you don't know.'

'And how do you feel now?'

'A bit better.' Pushing himself free of the sofa, he came closer and gazed into her face. 'A light meal and an early night would speed up my recovery.'

Nora now caught the reek of booze on his breath. She recoiled. 'By all means have an early night, but don't expect me to join you. I've made arrangements to go out. And listen . . . if you don't knock off the drink you'll be out of a job and then what'll you do?'

Tommy gripped her tightly by the upper arms and she winced. Louise moved to intervene but a ferocious glare stopped her. He returned his attention to his wife. 'You let me worry about my job . . . and you're not going anywhere tonight, so you're not. You've been out far too often lately. You're getting above your station so you are, and I won't stand for it. You're my wife, and you'll do as I say and stay put tonight. Do you hear me?'

Nora nodded speechlessly. What else could she do? Throwing her from him, he sneered, 'Well, I'm glad that's settled.'

Thrusting her way past her da, Louise warned herself not to interfere. It wouldn't take much to really set him off now, the mood he was in, and send her mother off into Bill McCartney's eagerly waiting arms. That must be avoided at all costs. Shrugging out of her coat she followed her ma into the scullery, where Nora was taking her fury out on the poor old pots as she prepared to make the evening meal.

'Don't let him get to you, Ma. Ignore him!' Louise urged. 'You know he's just a big bully.'

Under cover of the racket she was making with the

pans, Nora muttered, 'That's easier said than done, Louise. No matter what he says, I'm going out tonight. If I don't turn up, Bill has threatened to come here for me and all hell will be let loose. Once your da sees him there'll be no turning back. There'll be no living with him and I'll have to get out.'

'Oh, Ma.' Louise was whimpering in her anxiety.

Peggy's arrival brought a welcome touch of normality to the scene. Tommy, who had remained standing by the door glowering at his wife, slowly returned to the sofa and buried his head in the newspaper. Unaware of the tension that was like a live wire strung between the kitchen and the scullery, Peggy planted herself beside him, feeling important as she blethered on about her job. Setting the paper to one side Tommy gave her his full attention and, not used to such interest from her father, Peggy gushed on, telling him all about her first day in full-time employment.

In the scullery Nora drew an audible sigh of relief. Louise eyed her anxiously. 'Ma, what are you going to do?'

Crowding close, Nora whispered in her daughter's ear, 'What can I do, eh?'

She sounded so distraught that Louise felt panic grip her heart. Eyes stretched wide with fear, she implored, 'Don't leave us, Ma. Please!'

'Ah, Louise, love. What else can I do? If I stay he'll torture me. You know what he's like!'

'What about us? Don't we count for anything?'

'He won't dare touch you.' Remembering the slap her daughter had received, she hurriedly added, 'Not if you keep a civil tongue in your head.'

Tommy had had enough of the conspiratorial whispering going on in the scullery. 'Hey, you two. Cut out all that blabbering and get on with my dinner.'

Nora's shoulders slumped in defeat. With a last appealing look that went unnoticed, Louise smothered a sob and backed out into the yard. She stood wrapped in her own arms and took in the decayed state that the yard was falling into. Nora was as particular about the outside of her home as she was about the inside, especially at this time of the year, when the boys got their orders to whitewash the yard walls and paint and varnish was obtained for the wee house to keep it bright and shiny. The first signs of squalor were beginning to peep through, an indication of how much her mother had been preoccupied with other matters of late.

Lifting her eyes above the dismal sight Louise took heart from the still bright sky. The weather was holding out rightly. She could wear her best clothes and new scarf tonight when she met Conor. It would be a relief to tell him all about her problems. Cry on his shoulder; a problem shared, as it were. See what pearls of wisdom he could come up with.

The meal that was eventually placed, none too lightly, on the table by a sullen-faced, tight-lipped Nora was a slapdash affair, obviously thrown together without much thought or care. Tommy eyed it with disgust, but knowing when not to push his luck he held his tongue. Lifting his knife and fork, with a snort, he got stuck in.

Harry came in just before the meal was served, noted his mother's pallid complexion and, now being cognisant of the reason for the tension between his mother and father, sat down and ate his meal in silence. He kept giving his mother covert glances. Surely she wasn't capable of ruining all their lives by going out with another man. He smiled fleetingly. Wasn't that the whole point? Apparently she wasn't just *going out* with him . . . she was *sleeping* with him. He couldn't imagine a woman of her age doing *that*!

Louise tried to eat her dinner but for the life of her she couldn't force the food down. Rising from the table, with a muttered 'Sorry, Ma, I'm not hungry', she carried the plate out to the yard and scraped the contents into the rubbish bin.

Her mother glared after her. She would be the first to agree that the food was lousy, but Louise should be supporting her, not giving her da an opening to vent his spite. And Tommy did just that. In a loud voice he showed his disapproval. 'I can't say I blame you, Louise. This rubbish is only fit for swill, so it is.' He pushed his plate roughly to one side and leered balefully at his wife.

A strangled oath escaping her lips, Nora rose, pushing her chair away from the table as she did so. With a sarcastic glance at his plate she muttered, 'What does that say about you, then? Only fit for pigs? Isn't that what you meant? How come you didn't leave very much, eh?'

He stood up and bawled into her face, 'Because I'm starving, that's why. I've had nothing to eat since breakfast if ye must know!'

'And why not, you lazy bugger? You're not paralysed. There's food in the cupboard. No need for you to starve. If you don't like my cooking, you know what to do. Because I'm not knocking my arse out of joint in future just to please you. I'm fed up running around after the lot of you and getting no thanks for my trouble.' With a defiant toss of the head, blinded by tears, she headed for the wee room. Tommy was behind her in a flash, and before she could close and bolt the door he pushed her further inside and quickly followed her.

Nora didn't give up without a fight and in the scullery,

as she listened to the muffled sounds coming from the room next door, Louise pressed her forehead against the dividing wall and wept. There was no way her mother would stay here now. She could see that, clear as day.

Peggy in all her innocence was sitting looking bewildered and Harry, who just recently had become aware of his physical feelings regarding the opposite sex, was also bewildered, but for a different reason. Imagine his ma and da still doing *that*! It was disgusting. And by the sound of it his ma wasn't getting any pleasure, and no wonder. She was old. So why was she going out with another man and causing all this upset? He couldn't understand adults.

Louise breathed a sigh of relief. She was glad to see Conor still waiting at Dunville Park when she arrived fifteen minutes late for their date. Too eager to wait for a break in the evening traffic, she dodged between cars to cross the road, apologies falling from her lips.

Gripping her hands tightly between his, he chastised her. 'Hush, it doesn't matter. You shouldn't take chances like that. I wasn't going to run away, you know. You could have been knocked down.'

His tirade released the tension built up inside her and she laughed aloud. 'You sound exactly like my mother.'

'Well, so long as you're here now, that's all that matters. I was beginning to think you'd gone off me while I was away.'

'No . . . I've missed you so much.' Eager lips were raised for his kiss but he gave her a perfunctory peck on the cheek, and pulling her arm through his escorted her towards the tram stop.

'I've missed you too.'

After all his apparent concern his curtness deflated her

fragile bubble of happiness. Disconcerted, she covertly examined what she could see of his face in profile. It looked set in grim lines and her heart seemed to sink right down to her feet. Warning herself not to overreact, she steadied her voice and explained, 'It was hectic in our house tonight. Everyone wanting to use the scullery at the same time.' She gave an abrupt laugh. 'Even Peggy! She's started work full time now and is all full of importance.'

His air of gloom lightened and he showed his pleasure at the news. 'Now that is good news! Where's she working?'

'McFadden's. She starts full time as from today. But tell me . . . did you have a good time?'

'Not bad. Not bad at all. We went to a couple of shows and a football match and they were smashing. The City's a great team to watch.' When they reached the stop there was no one else waiting and he took the opportunity to give her the present he had bought for her. Thrusting his hand into his coat pocket he dramatically fished out a small jeweller's box. 'Here . . . I hope you like it.' He wished with all his heart it was an engagement ring, but he knew now that the chances of ever putting a ring on Louise's finger were slight, to say the least.

Louise's hands shook as she opened the box, and a gasp of delight escaped her. On a bed of black velvet lay a gold crucifix on a fine gold chain. 'Oh . . . it's gorgeous. Thank you, thank you very much, Conor. I'll treasure it always.' She wanted to show her appreciation by throwing her arms round his neck and kissing him; longed to feel the comfort of his strong arms about her, but afraid of another rebuff she made do with, 'But you shouldn't have. It looks so expensive.'

He shrugged. 'I wish it could be more.'

The tram was coming and conversation was put on hold, and taking her by the arm he helped her on board. She felt uneasy, and tried to fathom the cause of his aloofness. All thoughts of confiding her problems in him quickly dispersed as she sensed his unrest. There was something radically wrong. Did his mother know she had been seeing someone else while he was away and hadn't been able to wait to tell him? Would he be influenced to this extent if Cissie had said anything to him? Louise doubted it. He would question her, certainly; ask for an explanation. No, something else was bothering him, but what? Dread was like a vapour seeping through her body, making her feel sick with anxiety. She needed to be able to depend on him to be her rock, but it looked very much as if she was on her own.

She sat in silence on the tram, huddled towards the window, away from him. He made no effort to reassure her; didn't try to bridge the gap between them by so much as a kind word or a touch of his hand. This wasn't the reunion she had anticipated. What was wrong with him? She felt tears well up and fought fiercely against them. Fear squeezed like icy fingers round her heart. Had he met someone else? Was that it? The tears threatened to fall, but pride helped her stem the flow. She'd had enough disappointments in her time to be able to put on a show of indifference, but it was going to be a long, heart-rending evening. The film, which passed in a haze before her eyes, seemed unending, but by the time it was over she had her emotions firmly under control.

Outside the cinema he suggested that they had time to go to the chippie, but she found the idea of sitting facing him in a booth, trying to make conversation, too daunting, and quickly declined. Not wanting to prolong the agony of walking home with this wall of despair between them, she said, 'In fact, I'd like to get home as early as possible, if you don't mind. Can we catch the next tram?'

Whether or not it was her imagination she was too upset to tell, but he seemed relieved at this suggestion. He certainly didn't try to dissuade her.

On the journey home, to avoid dwelling on her strained emotions – time enough for that when she was alone – she made polite conversation. 'How did you get on with your father?'

He drew a deep breath into his lungs and expelled it slowly, bringing her eyes to his face in startled confusion.

'Well, after the initial shock, I got on very well with him. He's a wonderful man. Came across as compassionate and understanding.' Conor sighed; who would sympathise better than his father with the plight Conor himself now faced? 'Very understanding.'

'Did he say why he never kept in touch with you?'

He grimaced. 'It wasn't from choice. My mother wanted it that way.'

Louise was getting more confused by the minute. 'I don't know what you mean, Conor. Can't you be more specific? Did you like him?' He nodded and she continued, 'And why did your mother keep you apart?'

Another sigh. 'She had her reasons. And very good reasons they were, as it turned out.'

'And why—'

He interrupted her. 'Look, I can't talk about it. At least not now. I'm too upset. Maybe one day, but not now. Please forgive me, Louise. I just can't talk about it.' He was so agitated, she drew back in dismay.

The conversation soon floundered and silence once

239

more shrouded them like a cloying blanket. She felt nause-ated and the rocking of the tram didn't help much. What had she done to deserve this cold-shoulder treatment? Blindly, she gazed out of the window. After what seemed like an eternity, the tram shuddered and ground to a halt at their stop. Funny, she had never really noticed how noisy trams were, had always been too busy talking or looking around her to take note, but tonight the clacking of the iron wheels over the joints in the lines and the incessant rocking movement grated at her nerve ends, heightening her sadness, and making her aware of the headache developing behind her eyes.

Eager to be out of his presence she hopped quickly from the platform and walked briskly up Springfield Road. He kept pace with her and at the corner of Springview Street she turned and faced him but avoided eye contact. 'Don't bother coming up with me. I'll see myself home, thank you.'

Before she could move off he reached for her and gath-ering her close buried his face in her hair. 'Louise . . . give me a little time and I'll explain everything to you. Please? I'm too mixed up at the moment and can't think straight. I just don't know where to start.'

Near breaking point, she stood stiff and unyielding in his arms. Then, unable to bear his closeness any longer, she placed her hands on his chest and pushed him roughly away. 'Take all the time in the world.'

Conor watched her walk away and his shoulders slumped in despair. His mother should have told him how things stood sooner, and then he would never have got involved with Louise. He loved her dearly, but how could he expect her to share a life with him now? He had been tempted to confide in her; see how she reacted to his news. He had told her the truth. His father was a wonderful man. After the initial shock, they had got on well together. His new family had made him welcome; he had no complaints there. They were all great. But somehow he couldn't bring himself to tell Louise what he had learned on his visit to Birmingham. It wouldn't be easy to admit to her, or anyone else for that matter, that he was a bastard; the product of an illicit affair. He was still too upset by the ramifications of it all. How could he tell her that he had two half-brothers and a half-sister that he had never heard tell of before? Explain to her what a devious, conniving woman his mother was; tell her that he hadn't even got his own father's name, for God's sake!

Docking at Liverpool, it was with trepidation that Conor had waited at the exit door of Arrivals, where his father had arranged to pick him up. He had been both surprised and apprehensive when his father had suddenly, out of the blue, agreed to meet him. Why, after all this time, was his mother being so conformable? She, who had always scorned the very idea that one day he might meet his father, acting as if he were beneath contempt. He had racked his brains trying to figure out why she felt this way, but was unable to come up with a solution. Now here he was about to meet the man at last. His father.

He hadn't long to wait. Within a few minutes he was approached by a tall man who had been standing nearby. They stared at each other for some moments, then the man came towards him with outstretched hand. 'I don't have to ask if your name is Conor O'Rourke.' A head of tousled black hair exactly like Conor's own shook in amazement. 'It's remarkable. Like looking in the mirror. My name is Donald McAteer and I'm pleased to meet you, son. I think it would be best if you call me Don. Did you have a good crossing?'

Conor was thinking the same thing about their likeness. A bit of an exaggeration to say they were reflections of each other, but they did look very similar. The age difference showed – Don's jowls were a bit slack and grey threaded the dark hair – but their features were alike enough for anyone to guess that they were father and son.

Shaking the hand offered to him, Conor said politely, 'I'm pleased to meet you, too. The crossing was fine, but a bit too long for my liking.' The name McAteer was resounding in his ears. What did it mean?

Unaware that anything was amiss, his father went on, 'I don't know what made Cissie change her mind after all these years, but I'm sure glad she did. I've wanted to meet you for a such long time, son.'

Conor's eyes widened in puzzlement and he looked sceptical. 'Really? Mother led me to believe that you didn't want to know me.'

Bushy eyebrows climbed halfway up a wide brow and Don looked obviously dismayed, 'Just what did your mother tell you about me, son?'

'Not much.'

Don pondered for some time, undecided. 'I think we need to have a good long talk before I take you home to meet the rest of the family. Follow me.'

Conor gazed after him in disbelief. What did he mean, the rest of the family? What family? Lifting his suitcase he followed behind, an uneasy feeling gnawing away at his guts. What other surprises had this man in store for him?

In the cafeteria they sat facing each other over mugs of tea. Don fidgeted and actually dropped his head briefly

242

in embarrassment. 'I can't believe your mother didn't let you know how things stood. I really can't. I know she forbade me to write to you, but didn't she at least explain who the people in the photographs I sent over from time to time were?'

Conor grimaced. He felt a great bitterness gathering in his chest towards his mother. 'What photographs?'

Don slumped back in his chair and, washing his hands over his face, groaned. 'My God . . . I don't understand.' For some moments he sat in thought. Then straightening up he said, 'Something drastic must have happened to make Cissie let you come over here to meet me.' He looked askance at Conor.

Conor was abrupt. 'Could it be because I fell in love?'

Don still looked perplexed. 'But why should that make any difference?' His brow cleared as comprehension dawned. 'Ah . . . now I see. You didn't know you were illegitimate? Is that it?'

'I didn't even know O'Rourke wasn't my mother's married name. I assume it's her maiden name, and she hasn't saddled me with some fictitious title?' He was on the verge of tears as he spoke.

'You've never been to Lisburn to meet your mother's family, then?' Don sounded incredulous. 'All your aunts and uncles . . . your cousins?'

The colour drained from Conor's face as he managed to croak, 'What family? My mother led me to believe that there was just the two of us against the rest of the world; no other relations. She did admit that you still supported us financially, but because you were living life to the full and didn't want to give up the good life you abandoned us, leaving Mother to rear me on her own.'

Don's face was as white as Conor's. 'This is incredible. What on earth was Cissie thinking of? I need time

243

to get my head round this.' He was silent for a few moments, while Conor, gripping the edge of the table, prayed that he wasn't going to faint. Suddenly Don spoke again. 'Is it the girl? You said you'd fallen in love. Is that why Cissie . . . is the girl a snob?'

'You couldn't be further from the truth if you tried. She's a wonderful person, but she works in the mill and my mother doesn't think her good enough for me. Imagine that! Not good enough for a bastard!' The bitterness tasted like bile in his throat.

'Do you think this girl will think any the less of you when she hears that you don't bear your father's name? I mean, it's no great deal, is it?'

'It is where I come from. As for making a difference where Louise is concerned, I don't know. Nothing like that ever cropped up in the course of our conversations – why should it? But no, I'd prefer that she didn't know.'

'You mean you'd keep her in the dark about it?'

'I didn't say that. I don't know what I'll do. It's something I've never given any thought to. As I've already said, there was no reason to discuss anything like illegitimacy.' He relapsed into silence, suddenly recalling the time when, as a young lad at primary school, he had joined in with the other lads poking fingers of ridicule at a boy who had *no father*. Not knowing any better, not even understanding what it meant, he nevertheless had joined in the torture of that poor little lad. Shame consumed him at the memory, and he actually writhed in his seat. 'I'd rather not talk about it, if you don't mind.'

Don waited patiently while Conor weighed things up in his mind, guessing from the succession of expressions passing across his son's face, shadows of alarm and dread, that his thoughts weren't pleasant ones. He made no effort to interrupt. When Conor at last came out of his reverie, Don leaned forward, held his eye, and said, 'Prepare yourself for another shock, son. You have two half-brothers, Andrew and Josh, both older than you, and a half-sister Joan, about the same age as yourself.'

A tear trickled down his cheek. Conor couldn't comprehend what he was hearing. Surely his mother would have told him something as important as this.

'I know how you must feel—'

The anger Conor was trying to curb suddenly exploded. 'No! You can't possibly know how I feel,' he snarled. 'I've been the pivot of my mother's world for as long as I can remember and now you're telling me all this. I'm finding it very hard to understand why she kept me in the dark all these years. As for you . . . you must have been very ashamed of me, to deny me the right to know.'

Don's hands came up in a placating gesture. He cautioned himself to be careful what he said. His son was hurt; he was entitled to be angry and to vent his spleen on him. 'No, you're wrong. It wasn't my idea to keep you in the dark, especially after my wife, Bridget, died. She knew about you . . . indeed it was she who insisted that we leave Ireland and come over here to live when she found out about Cissie and me and that a child was involved. I couldn't bear to be separated from the boys, so I fell in with Bridget's wishes. Sold my share in the business and settled down to a new life here. The times I had to return to Northern Ireland on business I continued to see your mother, to make sure you were both all right.' Don sighed. 'I didn't desert her, you know. I offered to buy her a house. It was she who chose Springview Street to live. I helped her choose furniture and opened a bank account for her.' He shrugged. 'Don't ask me why

245

she chose Springview Street . . . I never could comprehend the way your mother's mind worked half the time. I suppose she wanted to be well away from Lisburn, away from anyone who knew her. My daughter was born and two months later you came along. You were a beautiful baby and it broke my heart to leave you. Eventually I set up on my own over here and I have to admit it was the best move I could have made. I would never have succeeded so well in Northern Ireland. When my wife died some years ago, I jumped at the chance to meet you. I wrote and asked Cissie to bring you over, but she refused.' He shrugged resignedly. 'What could I do? I couldn't force her.'

Conor sat slumped in confusion, his mind spinning. Don's heart bled for him. 'Cissie should have told you the truth years ago.'

'You can say that again.'

'I suppose she was ashamed.'

'Do you know something? I very much doubt that. She doesn't know the meaning of the word.'

'Would you like to meet the family?'

Conor delayed, but only for a few seconds. 'Why not, since I've come all this way? But you must understand if I don't take to them right away. Is that clear?'

Don stood up and smiled. 'Clear as a bell.'

They drove for some time, Don pointing out places he thought might be of some interest to his son. Conor wasn't surprised when they eventually turned into the driveway of a large detached house and came to a halt on the gravel frontage. The car alone must be worth a mint and he had expected a show house as well. He wasn't disappointed. These grounds and this house reeked of money. No wonder this man had been able to keep him and his mother in comfort as well as taking care of his own family. He obviously wasn't short of a bob or two. A tall lad and a girl came out on to the wide steps to welcome them.

'Hello, Conor. I'm Josh and I'm pleased to meet you.'

'And I'm Joan.'

Conor returned the greetings and shook hands. Don looked around and asked, 'Where's Andrew?'

Josh exchanged a guarded look with his sister and answered, 'He had to go out.' He flashed a smile at Conor. 'But asks to be excused, says he'll see you tomorrow. Right, enough said. Come through to the lounge. We've lit the fire so it'll be more comfortable in there than hanging about out here in the cold.'

Josh was quiet but pleasant company. Joan was rather lovely with dark curly hair and a fine figure. He got on well with them, but the worm of resentment against his mother started twisting in his stomach and continued to grow and fester within him. She had done him a terrible injustice by not letting him know about his father and his family.

After dinner on the first night, prepared by Joan – food that Conor had never tasted before, but enjoyed enormously – Joan and Josh started to clear the table. Seizing the opportunity, his father excused them and took Conor to an office set aside solely for his work and told him the story of his conception.

It was just the usual old sob story. Husband working late every night, no time for family life. Wife nagging him and losing interest. New office girl making eyes at him, showing she found him attractive, and eventually they were having an affair. When his wife found out she ordered him out of their house. He refused and she told him she was four months pregnant and if he wanted to stay he must get rid of his floozie. It was that or nothing. He explained to Cissie that he had to stop seeing her for the sake of his family. He was devastated when Cissie confessed that she too was pregnant.

He pulled a face and said ruefully, 'You can imagine how I felt. I was between a rock and a hard place. You understand how it was.'

Disgusted by what he was hearing, Conor said, 'Now, what makes you think I could possibly understand? I think it despicable that you could stoop so low and treat your wife – the mother of your children – like that in the first place. And stringing my mother along as well. I think you're contemptible!'

'Your mother knew I was a married man,' Don retorted sharply. 'I never tried to deceive her or make her any false promises, and she was happy enough to accept a settlement. To be truthful, the affair had already run its course. She was getting bored with me, and I think she was glad to come out of it so well. And you've got to admit that you've never wanted for anything, have you?'

'Only the most important thing a young boy could wish for . . . a father.'

Rising abruptly to his feet, Conor left the room and the house. He trailed around the grounds, but it was a bitter cold night and the idea of the warm lounge lured him back inside again. No one remarked on his absence and the rest of the week passed amicably enough, as his family set about entertaining him. The only rub was the fact that Andrew appeared to be none too keen to get acquainted with him. Conor wasn't too upset by this. You can't please all of the people all of the time, was his adage for his stay in Birmingham.

* * *

At first Conor couldn't see any further than his dismay and disappointment that he was illegitimate, but as time passed he felt enough at ease with his father to confide in him about Louise and how he felt about her. How she was his first and last love.

Don was sceptical when he heard that, but didn't try to put him off. He advised Conor to think long and hard about his future. He assured him that he could set him up in a career in Birmingham. He suggested that once Conor passed his exams he should return to Birmingham for a few weeks and take a good look around, see how the land lay, and take it from there. Conor realised it would be an excuse to put off getting engaged to Louise, as he had planned in spite of his mother; a breathing spell before he made up his mind whether or not to tell her the truth.

He realised that his mother was right. How could he possibly marry Louise now? Indeed, would she even consider marrying him once she knew of his illegitimacy? The district would have a field day if the truth became known. It was such a stigma, being illegitimate; the finger would be pointed. Once it got out, and all the lies his mother had told were exposed, her air of false grandeur would be ridiculed, her better-than-thou attitude sneered upon. Why, she would be the laughing stock of the neighbourhood. She had taken a terrible gamble sending him over to meet his father. Surely telling Louise would have been a better option. Would she live to regret it?

His father's offer to let him stay in Birmingham for a time was the excuse he needed to postpone his engagement. However, he found that he didn't want to leave Louise and all his friends to go and live among a lot of strangers. Even the troubled times they were going through were what he was used to, a part of his everyday life. He was at his wits' end. He didn't want to leave Belfast.

He watched to make sure Louise reached the safety of her own home and was puzzled when she continued on up the street and round the corner. She must be very upset, he decided; didn't feel like facing her family just yet. Lord knows, the evening had been a complete flop from start to finish. He'd have to make sure that she was all right. With that thought in mind he quickened his step and reached the corner in time to see her turn from Waterford Street on to the Falls Road. He continued after her.

The relief of letting the tears flow freely as she walked up the street was unbelievable. They streamed down her face and gushed from her nose, splashing on to the new scarf, carefully chosen and bought especially for their reunion. Harsh sobs tore at her throat, sending great shudders through her body. How could he do this to her? He had convinced her that he loved her; that nothing could come between them. She would have bet her life that he was sincere about it. How gullible she had been. And now this! How could he be so cruel? Would she ever be able to bear this awful pain that seared the spot where her heart should be? But he would never ever know how much he had hurt her. She wouldn't give him that satisfaction. Wiping her face with the end of the soft woollen scarf, she quickened her step. Their house was in darkness, the outer door closed, and she continued on past. It was still quite early: she could take a walk before going home. Why rush into more torture? Her feet carried on to the corner and down Waterford Street.

Home could wait. What would be in store for her there?

More anguish and pain. Would her mother even be there tonight? Louise doubted it. And her da . . . she dreaded to think the state he'd be in. He'd be drowning his sorrows in beer and whiskey and would be full of false bravado when he came in, and Johnnie wasn't there any more to control him. She wished she herself had somewhere else to go to escape from all this misery. Her grannie's? No. Better to face things on the home front first; find out how the land lay. Besides, she owed it to Harry and Peggy to try to provide some kind of stability at home till the dust had settled. Help them through this bad spell. As far as she was concerned things couldn't get any worse.

A car sliding to a halt close to the kerb caught her attention. Her eyes widened and she turned away in panic when she realised who the occupants were. They mustn't see her in this state.

'Louise? What are you doing here?' Cathie shouted. 'Did Conor miss his sailing?' Her friend was climbing out of the car. George left the driver's seat and stood erect, one arm resting on the car roof, watching Louise through narrowed lids. Trevor came round from the back of the car and put an arm round Cathie's waist, pulling her close. They stood on the pavement waiting for Louise to reach them and she felt that they must see by her face how upset she was. However, Trevor and Cathie were too preoccupied with each other to notice anything wrong, and after a quick glance of concern George came to her rescue.

With a flap of his hand he shooed the other two on their way. 'Away you go, Trevor, be a good lad. You can walk Cathie the rest of the way home. It'll give me a chance to talk to Louise. I'll hang about here for a while and pick you up later. OK? But I don't want to be on the road after half ten, mind.'

251

'That'll be great, George. I'll be back. Thanks, mate.'

Cathie had by now noticed that something was amiss. Releasing herself from Trevor's restraining arm she moved close to Louise and scrutinised her face. 'What's wrong?' she asked in concern. 'Do you want me to stay with you? Has something happened? Is Conor ill?'

'Everything's fine.'

'Are you sure you're all right?'

'Yes! I'm fine, I tell you.'

A look and a jerk of the head from George signalled Trevor to be on his way. Needing no second bidding he took Cathie by the arm. 'Come on, love. We're wasting valuable time.'

Cathie reluctantly allowed herself to be hustled away. 'See you tomorrow night, Louise?' she queried over her shoulder. 'I take it we are still going to the pictures?'

'I hope so. If I can't make it, I'll let you know somehow.'

'See you then. Good night, George.'

'Good night, Cathie.'

When the couple were out of earshot, George opened the car door. 'Come on, in you get. It's warmer inside. We'll go for a short run.' He glanced around the quiet road. 'I don't like hanging about here at night.'

Conor had arrived at the corner in time to see George help Louise into the passenger seat. He examined her companion as he got in beside her and started the car. Tall, fair and handsome! Quite the opposite to him. So his mother was right after all. He hadn't believed her, but it appeared she was telling the truth when she said Louise had been seeing someone else while he was away. Looked as if he wouldn't have to explain anything to her after all. His secret was safe. No need now for anyone to know. Face wet with tears he slowly retraced his steps.

He knew that he should be glad that she had met someone else . . . but why hadn't she told him? With hindsight he realised that he hadn't given her much of a chance. He had been too wrapped up in his own thoughts; trying to find a reason, a plausible excuse, for not seeing her any more. Well, apparently that was something he wouldn't have to worry about after all.

George turned the car at the Falls junction, and headed down Grosvenor Road. They passed Cathie and Trevor who were totally unaware of them, even though he tooted the horn as they went by. He eventually drew into a parking spot along Great Victoria Street and, stopping the car, turned to face her.

'If you don't mind my saying so, you look devastated. Did the boyfriend dump you?'

She gave an abrupt laugh. 'You don't believe in pulling any punches, do you? And no . . . he didn't exactly dump me, but mind you, it was close. However, I managed to walk away with my pride intact.'

He reached over and, taking her hand, clasped it between his. 'He'll be back. You mark my words. He's a fool if he isn't.'

Louise longed to feel the comfort of his arms around her – anyone's arms, for that matter – but she didn't want to give him the wrong impression. Gently tugging her hand free, she said, 'I don't think so. Besides, I hardly know him. He's very attached to his mother, so I doubt if it would have come to anything. Please take me home now.'

'Do you not want to talk about it?'

'There's nothing to discuss. Please, I'd like to go home.'

He turned the key in the ignition and fired the engine into life, but before moving off he held her eye. 'Since you're a free woman, how's about coming out with me on Saturday night?'

She turned the offer over in her mind. Why not? No matter how things were going at home she'd be glad to get out of the house. A chance to hang on to her sanity for a while.

'No strings attached?'

'No strings attached.'

'Then I'll be happy to go out with you. Thank you.'

'That's great. Now I'll take you home.'

8

George dropped Louise off at the corner of Waterford Street. She walked home with dragging feet, chastising herself for letting him talk her into seeing him again. After all her preaching to Cathie, was she going down the same road? Hadn't she enough to worry about without courting more disaster? She regretted agreeing to go out with him on Saturday night, but the prospect of sitting at home wallowing in self-pity had outweighed her better judgement and she had agreed to meet him. 'Ach, to hell with it! What's done is done and I may as well go out and enjoy myself,' she muttered to herself with an angry toss of the head. Surely another date wouldn't do any harm. He really was quite charming to be with and a good conversationalist. Seeing him would help salve her pride; take her mind off her problems for a time.

Who knows, in spite of the complications that could arise, she might even start seriously dating George. Cathie seemed to be getting away with seeing Trevor. But then, as yet no one was any the wiser about her new boyfriend. If however it got any way serious, all hell would be let loose when Cathie's brothers found out.

Dating George could lead to a similar fate, Louise reminded herself. Her da and brothers would be up in arms if they ever found out that she was kissing and cuddling a Protestant lad, and God knows she had enough on her plate as it was. Still, she wasn't a coward; she would meet him as planned on Saturday, and then make up her mind what to do from then on. After all, Conor thought she was seeing someone else, so why disillusion him!

First things first, though. Now she must go home and face the music. Her feet faltered at the thought of what lay in store. However, her spirits lifted a little when she noticed the gas mantle casting faint shadows on the blind as she turned the corner and approached her house. Perhaps her mother had had a change of heart. The thought quickened her step. Yes, it could be her mother waiting up for her. Only she would stay up late, worrying in case one of them got caught out during curfew hours.

The outer door was open now. From the small hall she peered through the thick net curtain that covered the glass in the vestibule door. Would her mother be in the kitchen waiting for her? Someone was sitting by the fireside; she sent a prayer heavenward as she eagerly pushed open the door. 'Please, God, let Ma have seen some sense.'

But no. Her prayers were in vain. Of her mother there was no sign. It was Harry who rose from the chair where he had been sitting by the dying embers of the fire to greet her. He had obviously been waiting some time. His body sagged as if weighed down by some invisible weight and his eyes were heavy and red-rimmed for want of sleep. He crossed the floor anxiously to meet her as she came through the door.

Snores could be heard coming from the wee room and Louise breathed a sigh of relief. At least she had managed to avoid a confrontation with her father. She didn't know how she could have coped with that on top of everything else that had happened today. She had enough to deal with at the moment. In a low voice she addressed her brother. 'Where's Peggy?'

'She went on up to bed. She was tired, so she was. So am I, for that matter.' Face screwed in frustration, he said accusingly, '*You're* late!'

'I know, I know.' Louise sounded dispirited and Harry waited for her to continue. 'To tell the truth, Harry, I didn't want to come home at all,' she confessed in a sad voice.

He gripped her arm and panic widened his eyes. 'Don't say that, sis! Don't even think like that. Everything will work out fine. You wait and see.'

Louise grimaced. She didn't agree with him. It had taken a great deal of bravado for her ma to walk out on her family and now that she had taken the plunge Louise couldn't see her coming back in a hurry. Although she already knew the answer, with a nod towards the wee room she asked hopefully, 'Ma's not home, then?'

'No! And me da was in a foul temper when he discovered she'd gone out. That's why I waited up. I wanted to see you safely in bed before I went up. The state he was in he would have taken it out on you, so he would.'

Overcome with gratitude at this admission, she quickly reached out and gave him a hug. 'Thanks, Harry. Thanks for worrying about me. I'm at my wits' end, so I am.'

Embarrassed, he shrugged her off. 'It's my responsibility to look out for you and Peggy now Johnnie's married and left here,' he said gruffly. 'What's going to happen, sis?'

She made a helpless gesture. 'God only knows.'

His expression clouded over. 'Me ma will come back,

won't she? She's just taking a stand, isn't she? She wouldn't be so cruel as to stay away.'

She pondered over his words. 'I don't know, Harry. I don't know what she'll do. Me da treats her like dirt and Bill McCartney thinks the world of her. If she chooses to go off with him . . .' she shrugged in defeat, 'who could blame her? One thing is for sure, there's nothing we can do about it. It'll be up to us three to stick together and face up to me da and his tantrums. And that'll be no easy task. He'll be on his high horse, so he will. He'll be looking for blood. Our blood!' she finished dramatically.

Harry shivered at the words and thrust a concerned face towards her. 'Don't worry. As long as there's breath in my body, I'll look out for you and Peggy,' he vowed.

The snores stopped abruptly, bringing the conversation to an end. Louise stiffened and turned to gaze fearfully at the door of the wee room. Was her da playing possum? Had he been eavesdropping on their talk? Harry sensed her fear and, leaning close, examined her face. She looked as if she'd been crying. God forgive his ma for bringing this trouble to their home, he inwardly lamented. What was she thinking of? They heard the bed creak as their father changed position and stood waiting with bated breath. Then with a final creak of the springs the snores resumed.

Louise relaxed, and with a finger to her lips whispered, 'Will you wait here while I go to the loo, Harry? I won't be long.'

She chastised herself as she hurried through the scullery and out to the yard. Harry had an early start every morning. She should have come home sooner; let him get to his bed for a good night's sleep. For heaven's sake, she told herself, it's not even eleven yet and if there was no curfew Harry would probably stay out much later and still be able to get up for work. He was showing her that he would be there to support her if need be, and for that she was grateful. Not like Conor! Her mind shied away from the memory of his cool behaviour. She felt bewildered and betrayed by his callous attitude; she didn't know what to think. Locking the back door behind her she tiptoed through the scullery and kitchen, ears strained for any change in sound pattern from the wee room, and joined Harry at the vestibule door.

He eyed her closely. 'You all right?' he asked.

She nodded, and, wondering if she would ever be 'all right' again, made to bolt the outer door but paused in thought. 'Do you think there's any chance of me ma coming home at this hour, Harry?'

'I doubt she'd chance it.' He added scornfully, 'She'll not want to be arrested by the police now she's found a new love.' He nodded towards the bar. 'But leave it undone if you want, just in case.'

Louise debated another few seconds and then shot the bar home. 'You're right. She'll hardly come now. If she does she'll just have to knock us up,' she said defiantly. With these words she preceded her brother up the stairs. At the top she thanked him again, and attempted to re-assure him. 'Try not to worry. We'll get through this together.'

'Of course we will, sis. You see and get some sleep. Good night.'

To her ears he sounded as dubious as she felt. 'Good night, Harry.'

She quickly undressed and crawled into bed, pushing Peggy roughly over as she did so. 'How can you sleep through all this?'

A tousled head rose from the pillow and a voice drugged with sleep mumbled, 'What? What did you say?'

'Oh, never mind! Just go back to sleep.'

Peggy needed no second bidding. Louise settled down beside her. She envied her sister; wished she could close her eyes and sleep as soundly as Peggy did every night.

After a lot of tossing and turning Louise was glad when at last the warm arms of sleep began to draw her seductively into their cosy depths. It was a relief to let herself drift away from her problems for a time; to enter a fantasy world where she could be free from worry. She needed all the rest she could get to face the day that lay ahead. Suddenly she jerked upright, eyes staring wide open into the darkness, causing Peggy to grunt and tug the bedcovers back up over her shoulder. All hope of sleep was shattered as she now lay wide awake. She had remembered that her mother wasn't at home to make the breakfast. Afraid now of falling into a deep slumber, with the warmth of the bed coaxing her senses to let go and seek oblivion, she fought to keep her eyes open. Dawn eventually crept into the room through the crack in the blinds and at half past six, afraid to delay any longer, she dragged herself from the warm, cosy bed on to the cold linoleum. Shivering in her flimsy nightdress, she pulled on an old cardigan and descended the stairs to prepare the porridge.

She carefully measured the oatmeal into the pot as she had seen her mother do so many times, and when it was blended to a nice even texture left it to simmer on the back ring of the stove. This was something she would have to do every morning if her mother failed to return. She felt exhausted from lack of sleep but voted against going back to bed for a while, afraid that if she did so she might sleep in. She'd have to make sure the others got up in time for work. Strange, how one took all these things for granted when they were performed by someone else. Her ma had taken on the responsibility of all these chores day after day, week in week out, without any help and without complaint. And me da let her, Louise thought resentfully. With a sigh of regret she muttered, 'And so did I.'

Next she proceeded to clear out the grate and set it with paper and kindling and coals for a fire that evening. Her ma, silly fool that she was, would have lit the fire so the house would be nice and warm for her husband when he got up. Tommy, in fact, regarded this as his due. With hindsight, Louise ruefully realised she should have left this task for him. Now he would expect her to do it every morning. Well, tough. In future he would have to do his share of household chores. However, if she had neglected to do it, she would be willing to bet that it would have been waiting for her to do this evening when she got home from work. At least this way it was over and done with.

With a sigh, she realised that most of the extra work was bound to fall on her young shoulders. Life was going to be just wonderful from now on, one big happy family, she thought sarcastically. Despair filled her heart when she examined the cupboards to see what was in stock for the evening meal. The shelves were almost empty. Her mother had obviously not done any shopping over the holiday weekend. When would she have got the time when she was far too busy with lover boy? Well . . . whether he liked it or not, her da would just have to cough up some money to replenish the food store.

Harry descended the stairs at quarter past seven. At the sight of the grate laid ready, he said, 'You should've shouted on me, sis. I'd have done that. I'll do it in future, OK?'

'No you won't. When me da's on the late shift I'll see that he does it. I just never thought this morning. I've too much on my mind.'

Whilst Harry ate his breakfast, Louise had a quick wash. She then lifted herself a bowl of porridge whilst Harry washed and hurried out to work. At a quarter to eight, Louise shouting from the foot of the stairs failed to waken Peggy and in a temper she thumped up to the bedroom. Gripping her sister by the shoulder she shook her roughly. 'Come on, lazy bones. Time to get up.' Peggy didn't start work until eight thirty. 'I'm off to work now. Don't you dare go back to sleep.' She gave her another shake. 'Do you hear me? Mr McFadden won't be too well pleased if you're late.'

At the mention of her boss's name Peggy swung her feet off the bed and sat up. She peered fearfully at her sister. 'Did me ma come home last night?'

'No she didn't.'

'Oh, Louise, what'll we do? I hardly slept a wink all night worrying about it.'

Louise gawped at her in amazement: how had she the effrontery to think, let alone say, that? 'Believe me, Peggy, you slept like a log . . . as usual.'

Her sister looked shame-faced. 'Nevertheless I did have trouble getting over, so I did,' she insisted.

Louise gasped in exasperation. 'Look, I haven't time to argue with you. Get up. I've made some porridge. Not as tasty as me ma's, mind you, but see and eat some anyway. Whatever you do, don't go to work on an empty stomach.'

Peggy nodded, and seeing she was now wide awake Louise left her sitting on the side of the bed.

Downstairs as she combed her hair the sight of her face looking back at her from the mirror made her cringe. Haggard, with dark rings round her eyes; even her hair hung pale and lifeless about her face. Her father hadn't put in an appearance at breakfast and, determined not to break into her meagre savings, Louise left him a note telling him he would have to leave her some money if he wanted any more food on the table. She added a PS: *When I got there the cupboard was bare.* She managed a smile when she wrote that.

She walked down the street with her head bent in sorrow. Not being a fool, she realised that most of her misery stemmed from her date with Conor. With him behind her to confide in, get advice from, things wouldn't seem half as bad. She would have felt more able to cope had her own situation been happy. Tears at the memory of their last encounter sprang readily to her eyes. She fought them back and vowed that from now on there would be no more self-pity. Her judgement had proved faulty where Conor O'Rourke was concerned, and she had enough on her plate without trying to figure out what had gone wrong between them.

Nearing the O'Rourkes' house she raised her head and held it high as she walked briskly down the street, passing their door without so much as a sideways glance. Still, she felt she could feel Cissie's eyes boring into her back from behind the spotless net curtains and shivered inwardly. She could imagine how satisfied Cissie must feel now that she had finally managed to drive a wedge between her son and Louise.

She had hoped to see her mother waiting by the mill gate, but there was no sign of her. A quick survey showed that neither was she hanging about the yard, so Louise quickly made her way into the weaving shop. Without as much as a glance around her she set about getting her looms in motion, avoiding looking in her workmates' direction. Never had she hung so diligently over her machines. She clung on to the moving comb as if her life depended on somehow making it go faster, sometimes even changing bobbins before they had completely emptied of weft. She would incur the wrath of the foreman should he chance to pass by and notice. But she would resort to anything, take any risk, to avoid a moment when her fellow weavers could catch her eye and mime words across at her. Question her about her mother and Bill McCartney.

She wondered if her mother and Bill was the current topic of conversation among them. Harry seemed to think so. If he had heard talk in the queue for the pictures, how prevalent it must be in the mill. How had she missed the covert looks that must have been abundant? She had probably been too wrapped up in her own budding romance to notice anything. And she had the cheek to talk about her mother's obsession with Bill?

One thing about the weaving shop, the noise from the looms was deafening: to have a proper conversation one had to go to the toilets where the smokers gathered and slanderous gossip was discussed with gusto in full and lurid detail. The juicier the scandal, the longer it would last. Louise, not being a smoker, only used the toilets when absolutely necessary but she could imagine the snide remarks being bandied about; the cruel things being said about Nora. Her mother had always been so virtuous, looking down on those who dared to stray from the straight and narrow. Her workmates would delight now in pulling her apart. To her credit, Nora had never taken part in gossip about another's downfall, had chastised her fellow workers for doing so. But now the boot was on the other foot. *She* had fallen from grace and was on the receiving end of the slanderous tongues. Louise was like her mother in that, although she didn't mind a juicy morsel of gossip, she didn't believe in gathering in the toilets to tear someone's character to pieces. Today she was tortured by the thought that everybody would be talking about her ma and pitying her and the family, and she cringed with shame. Was that why her mother hadn't turned up for work today? Was she too ashamed to face the music?

The morning dragged and when lunchtime eventually came she hung about scanning the workers passing through the mill gates. She carefully avoided eye contact, afraid of seeing the derision there, or soliciting unwanted remarks, but there was still no sign of Nora.

At home she discovered her father had placed some coppers on top of the note she had left. With a vicious swipe she swept the offending pittance off the table on to the floor. Just what did her da think this paltry sum would buy? He was out of touch with reality, so he was. Tonight she would have to have it out with him. That was something else she had to look forward to. She could just imagine his face if she placed some bread and margarine in front of him for his supper when he came home from work that night. Indeed, maybe that was what she should do. Waken him up. It just might bring him to his senses.

Her da had raided the cupboard and taken most of the loaf and what cheese there was left for his sandwiches. Harry and Peggy were lucky to have the option of getting something to eat at work if they felt like it, and for this Louise was thankful. Her lunch consisted of a bit of stale bread and margarine, and she returned to the mill with a heart like lead. A workmate, Kitty Magee, whom she was particularly friendly with, approached her when she was back at her looms.

Leaning close to make herself heard Kitty didn't beat about the bush. 'Now you listen to me, Louise McGuigan. Don't you cut yourself off from the rest of us. What your ma does is none of your doing as far as we're all concerned.'

Louise sighed and turned to face her. 'So there *is* talk?'

'Of course there's talk. But what about it? They've been acting like a couple of teenagers in love. It was obvious to everyone here what was going on. Don't tell me you didn't know?'

'Believe it or not, I just found out on Saturday. I had hoped it wasn't common knowledge.' Tears sprang to Louise's eyes and she rubbed furiously at them with her knuckles.

Kitty admonished her. 'Louise, it has nothing whatsoever to do with you.'

'It hurts, Kitty,' Louise wailed, choking back sobs. 'I never dreamed that anything like this would ever happen in our family. Me ma is such a good person. I don't know what's got into her.'

A comforting arm was slung over her shoulders. 'I know, love. I know how you must feel. But your ma . . . well, I'm about the same age as her, and believe me, there are times when I feel like packing my bags and taking off. And I haven't got a fine man like Bill McCartney fawning all over me, more's the pity, or maybe I would. Your ma's the envy of many of us women and of course that means a lot of jealousy is behind the nasty remarks.' Slowly removing her arm, Kitty gave Louise a slight nudge. 'Speak of the devil,' she whispered, and moved to one side. Confused, Louise turned to see what had attracted Kitty's attention.

Bill McCartney was standing behind one of the looms, gazing intently at them. When he caught Louise's eye he mouthed the words, 'Can I speak to you?'

Louise glared at him but gave a slight nod of consent. She needed to find out what her mother intended to do. Whispering a few words of encouragement in her ear Kitty moved off, and Bill walked slowly round the loom to take her place. Louise flashed a look of contempt at him.

'Ah, now, don't look at me like that, Louise,' he said placatingly. 'These things happen, you know.'

'And just how would you like me to look at you, Bill? With kindness? With understanding? With respect? You deserve none of them. You've taken my mother away from us and our world has bloody well fallen apart. So how the hell do you expect me to greet you, eh?'

'Tell me, Louise, do you really begrudge your mother some happiness?'

'No. I wish her all her heart desires, but not at our expense. We don't deserve to suffer for her misbehaviour, so we don't!'

'Now you're talking nonsense. You're all adults. And if you all pull together your da shouldn't prove too much of a problem for you.'

'Is that what me ma says?' His face screwed up, dismissing the accusation, and she ranted on, 'I thought not. She knows only too well what me da's like. He won't take this lying down, ye know. And who do you think'll suffer? Not her . . . oh no, she'll be tucked away safe and cosy in your little love nest, being waited on hand and foot, no doubt. And what about work, eh? Does she not have to work any more? Will she be a lady of leisure? A kept woman? Or is she afraid to face all the ridicule and scorn she'll get from her workmates if she comes back? Some of whom, by the way, she so sanctimoniously judged for the very same sort of thing she's now involved in?'

Bill could barely contain his anger. 'Believe it or not, and against my wishes, your mother's insisting on coming back to work next week. So if anyone happens to ask, she's off sick. She's afraid of no one. Meanwhile . . .' He thrust his hand into his boiler-suit pocket. 'Here!' A ten shilling note was pushed towards her. Louise gawked at it: a fortune. But to her it represented thirty pieces of silver.

'Don't you dare try to buy me off, Bill McCartney! What do you take me for, eh? Is that what me ma fell for? Your money?'

'Your mother and I happen to love each other,' Bill ground out through clenched teeth. He laughed abruptly. 'Do you know something? Nora was sure that you'd understand. It seems she was wrong. You're like your da. You think your mother should go on taking whatever treatment he chooses to mete out to her. Well, no more. From now on I'm going to treat her the way she deserves to be treated.' He walked to the end of the loom but turned back. He placed the ten shilling note on the shuttle rest and weighed it down with the shuttle. 'Nora will be angry if I bring that money back. She says she forgot to get the groceries in at the weekend. She's worried stiff about youse, so she is. She says there's enough there to tide you over till your da comes to terms with things and starts pulling his weight.' He patted the shuttle. 'So watch it doesn't go astray.'

'I suppose she was too busy in her little love nest to think of something as trivial as feeding her family,' Louise sneered. Lifting the shuttle she swept the money in his direction. 'I don't want your money. Get out of my sight before I hit you with this.' The shuttle was raised threateningly. 'Go on. Get out of my sight before I brain you, and you can take your bribe with you, you lousy bastard.'

Face like thunder he turned on his heel and charged off, leaving the money where it had landed on the aisle that separated the row of looms. During their confrontation the weft had run out and the looms had fallen idle. A broken thread in the warp had made an ugly fault in the sheeting on one of the looms, and she felt like crying. Ignoring the money she ripped the offending fault from the material and put it to rights, then set the looms in motion again. She eyed the money resentfully where it had fallen. Should she take it? God knows she needed it. To her amazement, even as she looked, a hand reached down and the ten shilling note was scooped out of sight. Dumbfounded, she stood stock-still for some seconds. Then with a holler she left the looms and charged after the young lad who had grabbed the note and was now some way down the weaving shop.

She quickly overtook him and gripping him by the shoulder she swung him round. 'Hey, you! Hold on a minute. Just what the hell do you think you're doing? That's my money you've just taken.'

He looked at her in disbelief. 'Is it indeed? Then why was it lying there?'

She held out her hand. 'Come on, hand it over. It's mine.'

He was about to argue when Kitty arrived on the scene. 'Better hand it over, son. It does belong to her.' Still he dithered, and Kitty didn't blame him. After all, it wasn't every day you were lucky enough to find a ten shilling note. 'You're the new apprentice Bill McCartney's training, aren't you?' He nodded and Kitty said, 'Well you can ask him about it. He was the one who gave it to her.'

The lad's eyes widened. He still looked doubtful, but with obvious reluctance he handed the money over.

Louise was so relieved she snatched the ten shilling note from him with only a grunt by way of acknowledgement. As they walked back to their looms she expressed her gratitude to Kitty for intervening. 'Thanks, Kitty. Imagine him thinking he was lucky enough to find ten bob in here!' They both laughed at the idea.

'He's only a kid, Louise,' Kitty chided her gently. 'Probably still believes in fairies.'

'Some fairies.' Louise put the money carefully away in her overall pocket and in a rare show of emotion hugged Kitty before returning to her own looms. She felt shaken. What if she hadn't noticed that lad lifting the money? She wouldn't have known where to start looking for it. It didn't bear thinking about. And to think she had scoffed at the idea of taking it in the first place. God knows how long that money would have to stretch. One thing for sure, she had no intention of telling her da about it. She'd have to milk him for all the housekeeping money she could get; save some of the ten shillings for emergencies.

When the siren blared at teatime she hurried home to prepare the evening meal, and found a surprise in store for her. Conor was waiting at the corner of the street. Her step faltered and she would have passed him by with an abrupt nod but he tentatively put out a hand to stop her.

She slowed down, eyeing him warily. He drew her along the road a little way and into the hallway of one of the shops, all the while his eyes pleading for understanding. 'I want to apologise for my behaviour last night.'

Relief flooded through her. Everything was going to be all right after all. She must have got her wires crossed last night, and now Conor was here to put her right. Unable to hold back the tears of relief she moved close and gazed mutely at him, speechlessly inviting him to hold her. Dismayed at the sight of tears raining down her cheeks, he did put his arms involuntarily around her and she buried her head against his chest.

He pressed his cheek against her hair, savouring the feel of her body against his. If only he had the right to hold her and comfort her the way he wanted to! If he had, he'd fight that other lad tooth and nail to keep her. He whispered gently in her ear, 'Hey, hold on. No need for you to be upset like this. I didn't give you the chance to explain last night. I know now why you were upset. Ma told me you had met another lad but I didn't believe her until I saw you getting into his car.'

Confused, she slowly raised her head, blinking rapidly to clear the tears from her eyes, and looked into his face. What was he going on about? 'What are you talking about?'

'It's all right, Louise. I know the truth. I was a miserable sod last night. Didn't give you a chance to tell me you'd met someone else.'

Withdrawing from the comfort of his arms, she muttered in bewilderment, 'Someone else? But I—'

'You don't have to explain. I saw you get into his car. I understand.'

Still she gazed at him, a puzzled frown on her brow, then comprehension dawned. 'You followed me?' she cried accusingly. 'How dare you spy on me after the way you behaved?'

271

Agitated, he growled, 'I wasn't spying on you. I watched to make sure you reached your door safely and when you walked on past it I was conceited enough to think you must be upset because of me. Naturally after the way I behaved I blamed myself and followed to make sure you were all right.'

'And you expect me to believe that? Just what did your ma tell you?'

'No matter. It was obviously the truth. But I can't understand your attitude.' He reached for her again but she eluded him. 'Hey . . . I'm the one who should be offended,' he chided.

'Come off it. Before you went away you were promising me the world. Did my one date with a bloke change all that? I didn't question what you were up to over there. Did I?'

'Don't be silly. I just want you to know that I understand how these things happen.'

'Why? Did it happen to you?'

'No, not really.'

'But something happened, didn't it? And you're glad to have an excuse to break off with me.'

Because she had hit the nail on the head his face flooded with bright colour. He looked so guilty that she thumped him on the chest with her clenched fist in frustration. He grabbed at her arm but she angrily thrust him away and cried, 'Stay away from me! Do you hear? Just stay away from me. I want nothing more to do with you. Save your promises and sweet talk for whoever else has caught your fancy. I only hope the poor girl lasts longer than I did.'

Conor watched her almost run away from him and his heart ached as he left the doorway and continued on down Springfield Road. He couldn't face his mother at the minute. He had yet to question her about his family.

He wanted to be sure just what he intended to do before he dragged all the unsavoury details out into the open. She, meanwhile, thought everything was hunky-dory and her subdued gloating was getting on his nerves.

He admitted to himself that he had handled his meeting with Louise all wrong. He had waylaid her on the off chance that they could remain friends, but obviously that was out of the question. He'd be afraid to ever approach her again. Couldn't bear another rejection. His best option now would be to do what his father had suggested: get his exams out of the way and then return to England and stay with Don until he decided what to do. It would be a big wrench, but unless he and Louise were at least on speaking terms he couldn't bear to remain in Belfast. Couldn't bear to have her ignore him. He'd have to go. Some things were unavoidable.

First thing Wednesday morning Johnnie sought out Mr McFadden in his office. 'You'll think I've a cheek, but can I have a few hours off this morning, please?' he asked tentatively. 'Mary has taken the day off to go and see a house in Spinner Street and I'd like to be with her.'

Glad that Johnnie and his wife might be about to resolve their differences, Matthew told him to take the whole day off. He reminded him, with a wink and a nod in Peggy's direction where she was stacking shelves at the far end of the shop and had failed to notice her brother, that he had another assistant now. He also told him of a house down in Violet Street he'd heard about through a customer, that would be going on the market to rent. The rent would be higher than Spinner Street, but if they liked it he might see his way to increasing Johnnie's wages to help with the extra expenditure. After all, he was due a rise, and should bear that in mind when they viewed the houses.

Diffidently he offered Johnnie a key. 'I had intended suggesting you have a look at it. I know the lad whose name's on the rent book at the moment. He's moving to Dundonald, and has moved all his stuff out. I hope you don't mind, but I took the liberty of getting the door key so you and your wife could take a look. A coincidence, wouldn't you say, that you're going to view this other house? Now you have two to look at. That is, if the house in Spinner Street doesn't come up to your expectations.'

'That's very kind of you, Mr McFadden. Thanks a bunch.'

Johnnie wasn't too happy about the way Mr McFadden was taking a hand in his private affairs, but he couldn't very well object. Some people would class it as inter-fering. He supposed he should be grateful, but what if Mary loved this other house in Violet Street and they had to turn it down? What then? He could only hope that Spinner Street would be the answer to their prayers and Mary need never know of Matthew's offer. He returned to the rented rooms in Springview Street with mixed feelings to fetch his wife, passing his family home unaware of the drama that was currently unfolding in there. If the house in Spinner Street was any way decent, the rent would suit their pocket better and there would be no need for Mary to know about the other one. He sighed. He could but hope.

He was to be disappointed: the house in Spinner Street was in a sorry state of repair. It had no saving graces whatsoever, and as the present key holder gave them a tour of the premises Mary gazed glumly around her in despair. Her eyes met Johnnie's questioningly. How could they get out without offending this old man?

As if he could read her mind, Johnnie gave her a reassuring smile and faced the man. 'I'm sorry, Mr Smith, but I don't think we can afford to take this house on.'

Mr Smith was obviously affronted. 'It was your da that approached me, ye know,' he shot at Mary. 'I didn't go looking for you.'

Mary drew back in alarm at his tone of voice and Johnnie quickly intervened. 'We know that. And we're sorry if we've put you to any inconvenience. Ordinarily, we would be delighted to take it and do some work on it. But you see' – Johnnie nodded towards Mary – 'my wife's expecting a baby and we haven't enough money, or the time, to put this . . .' for want of the right word to describe it without causing offence, a wide wave of his arm encompassed the ground floor of the house, 'in order and we couldn't move in otherwise.' He took Mary's arm and edged her towards the door. 'We'll just have to stay in those rooms a while longer, love,' he said for the benefit of the old man.

They were almost pushed out on to the street and the door was slammed on them without so much as a good day from their host.

Johnnie couldn't help but laugh at the cheek of him, but Mary grimaced. 'I feel guilty. That poor old man obviously thought he was going to get some money from us as well as from me da.'

Solemn-faced, Johnnie stopped in mid-stride. 'Do you want me go back and give him a quid for his trouble?'

Mary started back in surprise. 'Are you mad or something? You'll do no such thing! Do you think we're made of money?' she gasped. A smile tugged at her mouth when she realised that he was having her on. 'Oh, see you!' She gave him a playful push and they continued on their way, glad to be out of that house without having to commit themselves.

However, Mary was unable to hide her disappointment, and looked so glum that he put an arm round her and drew her close to his side. Against his better judgement he confided, 'I've a bit of good news for a change.' He proceeded to tell her about the house in Violet Street and Matthew's offer of a rise if they decided to take it.

She gazed at him, eyes wide with wonder. 'Violet Street?' He nodded and she said, 'Those are lovely parlour houses. Even if Mr McFadden gives you a rise I doubt if we'd be able to afford one of those. They're quite new. The rent will be huge.'

She rambled on in this vein until Johnnie fished a key from his jacket pocket and dangled it tantalisingly in front of her face. 'Let's have a look at it, eh? Perhaps we won't like it and the problem won't arise.'

'Don't count on it, but let's have a look anyway. It can't do any harm,' she agreed with a smile, her good humour restored. Her step quickened in anticipation as she hurried along by his side.

The house was everything they could ever hope for. It was in good decorative order and Mary's eyes stood in her head as she scurried from room to room, exclaiming in the kitchen, 'There's no way you could refer to this as a scullery.' Johnnie nodded his agreement. The living room had a small grate and the previous owners had left a carpet square in front of it. It was well worn but would do for the time being. The house also had a parlour and three bedrooms, the smallest of which would be ideal for a nursery.

'It's too good to be true. We could never afford a house like this, Johnnie,' Mary lamented. Her eyes nevertheless clung to his like a limpet, and she was obviously hoping he would disagree.

'You're right. The rent's bound to be sky high. Let's see what the yard's like.' He opened a door off the kitchen and stopped in stupefied amazement. Mary couldn't see past the bulk of him and she stared at his back for some seconds, waiting for him to move outside. Then with a rough push she sent him sprawling through the door and took his place, to stand lips pursed in delight at the sight that met her eyes. A bathroom: just the bare essentials, mind. Bath, lavatory pot and small wash-hand basin, but to her it looked like paradise.

'Oh, Johnnie, you never said.'

'I didn't know either,' he confessed. 'Until I opened that door I didn't know a thing about a bathroom. Now listen, love,' he cautioned her. 'The more I see of this house the more I'm inclined to think it will be way beyond our pocket.' He led her back to the hall and, sitting on the stairs, drew her down beside him. Looking at her glowing countenance, he said, 'You like it then?' As if there was any chance that she might not.

'How could anyone in their right mind not like it? Tell me that. It's beautiful, so it is,' she said. 'I can't understand how anyone could leave it. Why do you think the previous tenant left?'

'I believe the man got a better job over at Dundonald and decided to buy a house there. Anybody with a decent wage can afford to buy a house these days. I wish I had a trade. There's a lot of houses lying idle, especially further up the Falls. Nobody can afford to buy them because of the work situation.'

'Is there no way we could possibly afford to rent this one, Johnnie?' Her voice was hopeful.

In spite of his misgivings, Johnnie had already decided

to take the house. The bathroom had been the deciding factor. It was too good a chance to miss. But in case there were any unforeseen snags, he was loath to commit himself. He said cautiously, 'I'll have to talk it over with Mr McFadden before we make a decision. Meanwhile don't mention it to anyone else. We don't want someone beating us to it, do we?' He took her hand and gently pulled her upright. 'I'll see you back over to Springview Street and then go back to the shop for the rest of the day and if I get a chance I'll have a word with Mr McFadden. Is that all right with you?'

'You go on back to work now. I'll go to the butcher's and get something nice for your tea,' she said impulsively. 'You deserve it.'

'You're bribing me, aren't you?' He kissed her soundly. 'Keep your fingers crossed that the rent won't be too high.'

'My toes and all will be crossed,' she vowed laughingly.

At the corner he watched her safely across Springfield Road and into the butcher's. His step was light as he headed for the shop, planning in his mind what he would say to Mr McFadden. He hoped he had meant what he'd said about giving him an increase in wages. It could certainly salvage his marriage if everything went out to plan.

Peggy was on the lookout for him and cornered him the minute he entered the door. He gently put her off. 'I must talk to the boss, Peggy. It's urgent. I'll speak to you later,' he said as he eased his way past her. Then the gist of her words penetrated the happy turmoil of his mind and he stopped abruptly. 'What did you say?'

Glad to have got his attention, Peggy said smugly, 'I said that me ma's left home.'

'What do you mean, left home? Where's she gone?'

'I don't know where she's gone. But I do know who she's gone with.' Delighted to see him so disconcerted, she delivered the final blow to his peace of mind. 'Bill McCartney!'

The colour drained from Johnnie's face and he gripped her arm so tightly she yelped with pain. Easing his hold he said, 'Sorry. When? When did this happen?'

'She went out after tea yesterday and she didn't come home last night.'

A relieved smile relaxed Johnnie's tense features. 'Is that all? She probably got caught by the curfew and stayed with some friend from work. You're worrying about nothing.'

Peggy ridiculed him. 'Oh, yes. And me ma's in the habit of not coming home. Silly us. Why didn't we think of that!' she scoffed.

Inwardly Johnnie belatedly agreed with her that, yes, maybe there was cause for concern. Should he slip out again before the boss saw him? Go to the Blackstaff and ask to talk to Louise? Find out what was going on? Too late; before the thought could be put into action, Matthew's voice hailed him from the office doorway. 'Johnnie. I didn't expect you back today. Is that a good omen? Come in and tell me how you got on.'

A woman had entered the shop and Johnnie said to his sister, 'Serve that customer, Peggy. I'll call into the house and see you later this evening, OK?'

'OK.'

When told about how they had fallen for the house in Violet Street and their misgivings, Matthew was all beams.

'You didn't let on it had a bathroom. Mary is absolutely delighted.'

279

'To be truthful, I didn't know it had a bathroom until I made inquiries about it myself. A nice surprise, eh? I hoped it would be the deciding factor. I know the chap who rented it. It seems he built that bathroom some time ago. He's hoping for a bit of money towards his new house in Dundonald. It was him I got the key from. He hasn't relinquished it to the landlord yet. He's hoping to do a deal with the new tenant over the bathroom.'

'Well now, Mary's father put some money in the bank for her to use, so perhaps we can come to some agreement. It's the rent I'm worried about.'

Matthew smiled. 'I've been doing my homework and made some discreet inquiries, so I have. It's two shillings a week dearer than the one in Spinner Street.'

'Two shillings is an awful lot of money where we're concerned, Mr McFadden. Mary will not be able to work for a while before and after the baby is born, remember.'

'I realise that and that's why I'm going to give you a rise of three shillings a week.' Matthew grinned happily at this young man he would dearly have loved as a son-in-law.

'Three shillings?' Johnnie gasped, completely stupefied.

'I'm not getting any younger, and there will be days when I may not be able to get into the shop, mind you, so I'll expect you to earn the extra cash. A lot more responsibility will fall on your shoulders,' Matthew told him. 'You'll be managing the shop.'

Johnnie was overwhelmed. 'I'll work my fingers to the bone for you, Mr McFadden,' he vowed.

Thrusting his hand towards him Matthew said, 'Let's shake on it. And I think it's about time you started calling me Matthew.'

*　　*　　*

The news about his mother had somewhat dampened Johnnie's happiness and was foremost on his mind when he returned home. Mary met him at the door eager for news. Her face fell at the expression on his. 'We can't afford it,' she said resignedly.

Gripping her by the waist he waltzed her round the kitchen. 'You're wrong, we've got it. Or at least we have to go and see the last tenant and make him an offer for the bathroom. What do you think of that?'

She drew him to a standstill. 'It's wonderful! But why the long face?'

He explained what Peggy had said about his mother and finished with, 'After dinner I'll have to go in next door and find out how things stand. I can't believe me ma would run off with Bill McCartney. They're friends from away back.'

'Well, there you are now,' she chided him gently. 'God knows how long it's been going on.'

'No.' He shook his head. 'You don't know my ma. She wouldn't do anything like that.' Mary looked sceptical but reserved judgement, and to change the subject he sniffed the air. 'What's that lovely smell? Better watch you don't burn it.'

She grinned at him. 'All right, I get the message.' Heading for the scullery she threw over her shoulder, 'First we eat, and I don't want to hear another word about your ma until you tell me everything about our new house.'

It was coming up to quarter to seven and Louise was putting the finishing touches to her hair when Johnnie tentatively put his head round the vestibule door.

'Is it safe to come in?'

'Aye, me da's on lates, if that's what you mean.' She

281

continued working at her hair. 'Peggy says she told you the latest news.'

'So it's true then?'

'Why would she lie, eh?'

'Where is she?'

'She's away over visiting Hannah. Those two are becoming great friends.' Louise laughed softly. 'I suppose it would be unkind to say they're probably on the same wavelength. But Hannah doesn't get out much and she really enjoys Peggy's company.'

Johnnie's face twitched ruefully. 'Hannah's not as slow as some people think. And there's nothing wrong with our Peggy either. I'm inclined to think that Hannah has been pampered too much. It will do her a world of good chumming up with Peggy. Get her away from her parents. Now, tell me. What's happening where me ma's concerned?'

Louise shrugged. 'You're as wise as I am. I suppose Bill McCartney has made her an offer she can't refuse.'

'How long's this been going on?'

'Your guess is as good as mine. But I imagine not very long.' With a final flick of her fringe, Louise reached for her coat.

Johnnie looked scandalised. 'Are you going out?'

'Of course I am. Do you think I'm getting all dolled up to sit and wait for my father coming home from work?' She added scornfully, 'Catch yourself on.'

'What about his tea?'

'What about it? You sound like me ma. Well, I'm beginning as I mean to go on. If he's here at the proper time when I'm cooking for all of us I'll cook for him too, but, mind you, only if he forks out money for the housekeeping every week. Otherwise, he can fend for himself. After all, he's quite capable and I'm certainly not going to be like me ma, and become his skivvy.' She opened the door. 'Are you going to wait and have a word with him?' she asked slyly.

'No. What makes you think that?'

'Then why are you here?'

'I wanted to see if I can be of any help.'

'The way I see it, Johnnie, is that you're well out of it. You've a wife now and I'm sure Mary won't want to get involved in our affairs.'

Johnnie was actually gaping at her. 'What's got into you? It's not like you to act like this.'

'I've had my eyes opened lately, that's what. Everybody seems to be looking out for themselves. I intend to do likewise.'

She pulled the door wider and nodded for him to go out ahead of her. On the footpath he faced her. 'Mary and I are going after a house in Violet Street,' he volunteered.

Brows high, she congratulated him. 'Oh . . . very posh. I'm delighted for you. I hope you'll both be very happy. Bye for now.'

He stood for a long time rubbing his chin and gazing blankly after her. What on earth had changed his lovely sister into this cold, uncaring bitch? The antics of his mother, he presumed.

On the journey down to meet Cathie and Jean, Louise debated what to tell them regarding Conor. She finally decided to be truthful. After all, they knew how much she cared for him, so she may as well put a brave face on and confess that he had broken off with her.

Cathie arrived breathless at the junction as Louise crossed the Falls Road. 'Sorry I'm late.'

Louise nodded in the direction of the hospital clock. 'You're not. You're dead on time.'

'Are we going to the Clonard, as usual?'

Louise shrugged indifferently. 'I suppose so. What about Jean?'

'She's not coming tonight. I think she's in love and hopes Joe will call round.'

'Has it got to that stage, then? Coming to the house when he feels like it?'

'It has. And Mr and Mrs Madden are more than happy to welcome him into their fold. You have to admit, he is a nice lad.'

'He is that and I'm happy for Jean. They seem ideally suited. Who would have thought that they'd have got on so well, so quickly, eh?'

Cathie sighed. 'I wish my love life was as uncomplicated.'

'I take it you still care for Trevor?'

'A lot. In fact I'd go so far as to say I'm in love.'

Louise couldn't hide her concern. 'Oh, Cathie. Take care, love.'

'We do. The more we see of each other the more careful we are. We only go places where we think no one will recognise us, because we don't want anything to spoil it.'

About to turn into the foyer of the Clonard, Louise tightened her hold on Cathie's arm and hurried her on past the cinema. She had spied Conor and one of his mates in the queue.

'What's up?'

'I just saw Conor in the queue. He broke off with me last night.'

Cathie ground to a halt. 'You're having me on. Aren't you?'

'Cross my heart and hope to die.'

Cathie shook her head in disbelief. 'I was about to ask

284

you what was wrong with you last night, but I never dreamed it was anything like this. What on earth did you do or say to offend him? He's daft on you, you know.'

A derisive smile tugged at Louise's lips. 'I thought so too. But whatever his da told him, he came back from Birmingham a different person. Such a changed man. I hardly recognised him.' In spite of all her endeavours a tear spilled over and trickled down her cheek.

Cathie threw a comforting arm round her shoulders. 'Ah, Louise, I'm so sorry. You two seem so well suited.'

Wiping the tear away with the back of her hand, Louise said, 'That's what I thought, but we were both wrong. Can we go to the Diamond instead?'

At the mention of the Diamond cinema further down the Falls Road, Cathie immediately shook her head. 'You know darn well I hate sitting on those wooden benches. The last time we went there my bum was aching for days afterwards. And, if I remember correctly, you were complaining too. You're daft if you go there just to avoid Conor. I think you should face up to reality. Show him you couldn't give a damn. That'll make him sit up and think.'

'That's easier said than done. I do care, you know.' She sighed. 'But I see what you mean. We live in the same street so I'll just have to get used to seeing him about. I can't avoid him for ever.'

'Does that mean we can go to the Clonard, then? In spite of lover boy?'

'All right. I suppose I may as well get used to the idea that I'll be bumping into him now and again,' Louise said bravely. 'Let's go.'

They retraced their steps and Louise was relieved to see the queue was on the move. It had shortened considerably and there was no sign of Conor. They joined the tail end and she was glad to find that the lights had already dimmed when they got inside.

The feature film was a Buster Keaton one and the audience was laughing and cheering throughout, but Louise still felt depressed when it was over. When the curtains closed at the end of the show she hurried Cathie outside, not wanting to bump into Conor. Cathie allowed herself to be hustled and they were halfway up the Falls Road before she said, drily, 'So much for facing up to him.'

Louise coloured with shame. 'I know, but something else happened yesterday that's worrying me. I don't know whether I'm coming or going and I can do without talking to him right now,' she confessed, and immediately regretted her words. Now Cathie would want to know what had upset her so much.

Cathie picked up on it right away, saying with concern, 'I thought there was more to your unhappiness than a fall-out with Conor. What on earth has happened to have you in this state?'

Louise pondered for some moments, then sighed. 'You'll have to promise not to tell anyone else about it,' she warned her. 'Not even your parents or Trevor. Promise?'

Eyeing her through narrowed lids Cathie said, 'If it's about your ma and some fellow she works with, I already know all about it.'

Louise stopped in a state of shock. In a voice that quivered, she wailed, 'You know? How? Who told you? Why didn't you say to me?'

'For a start, I only found out this morning. Winnie McGrath, our next door neighbour, is a spinner in the Blackstaff and she told my ma all about it because she knows I chum around with you.'

Louise was devastated. Looks like her ma was the talk of the district. 'Do you also know Ma has left home?'

'No. Oh, my God! That's awful. It must be serious.'

'Good evening, ladies.' Conor came to a halt beside them and saw at once that something was wrong. He waved his companion on with an abrupt good night and moved closer to Louise. 'What's so awful, girls? I couldn't help overhearing that last remark.'

Amazed at the cheek of him, Louise retaliated angrily. 'It's none of your damn business.'

They had reached the junction and Cathie quickly came to a decision. 'Look, I'll leave you to it. See you at the weekend, Louise. Try not to worry too much. It'll all pan out in the end, so it will. Good night, Conor.' She sincerely hoped she was doing the right thing leaving Louise with Conor. She hoped with a bit of luck her friend and Conor would be able to sort out their differences. She knew Louise doted on him.

Louise gazed after her tight-lipped. She'd have a crow to pick with that one when she next saw her. She turned to Conor. 'Excuse me, Conor, but I'm in a hurry home tonight so I'll leave you.' Quickening her step she checked the road was clear and started to cross.

Step by step he walked beside her until, halfway up Springfield Road, she rounded on him in anger.

'Will you kindly leave me alone,' she snapped. 'I want nothing more to do with you.'

'Can't we be friends, Louise?'

'Why? Your mother would object to that as well, and of course you'd have to do what she says, so why waste time?'

'Look, if it was only my mother I had to worry about, I'd be down on my knees right now begging you to marry me.'

287

'For heaven's sake, Conor, listen to yourself! Stop talking in riddles. I can't take much more of this.'

'Louise, please be my friend. I don't expect you to give up seeing this other lad, but at least talk to me when we meet.'

'And you'll be happy with that? You won't want anything else from me?'

'Look, please understand, it's not that I don't love you. It's just that I can't marry you. And I do love you.'

Utterly confused now, unable to comprehend what he was talking about, and wanting him to go away and leave her alone, Louise said, 'All right. I'll talk to you whenever we meet, but now I have other things to see to at home, so good night.'

'I'll walk you to your door.'

'That won't be necessary, thank you.'

'I want to.'

She stamped up the street in a temper. At the door, anxious to be rid of him, she once again said good night and made to enter the house, already frightened at the thought of what might be lying ahead of her.

A hand on her arm stopped her. Embarrassed colour rising in his cheeks, Conor said, 'I know about your mother, Louise, but I'm sure nothing will come of it. I'm sure she'll see sense and give this guy his marching orders.'

Louise's heart sank. Did everybody know? That is, everybody but her father. Filled with resentment, she decided to shock him. 'I'm afraid it's a bit late for that. You see, she has already moved out, so if you'll excuse me?'

And she shrugged off his hand and pushed open the vestibule door.

*   *   *

288

A glance showed her that the kitchen was empty but her da was in the scullery obviously making a pot of tea. He glared across at her. 'Why was there nothing ready for me to eat when I came home?'

'Two reasons. One, I'm not your wife and I don't intend devoting my life to looking after your needs. The other reason . . . I had no spare money to spend on grub.'

Leaving the scullery he came towards her, a threatening look clouding his face. In spite of her good intentions to stand up to him, she instinctively backed away. 'I left you some money this morning,' he reminded her.

'And what kind of food did you expect me to buy with a few coppers, eh? Me ma has you spoilt rotten, Da. You're living in the past. When was the last time you did any shopping?'

'All right, all right. I'll give you some money. Anyway, where is your ma? When will she be back?'

'I've no idea.'

He thrust his face into hers. 'Who's this woman she's so friendly with all of a sudden?

Louise heard Harry in the hall and felt brave. Pushing roughly past her father, she taunted, 'What makes you think it's a woman she's with?'

Gripping her by the upper arm he pulled her back and snarled into her face, 'What the hell are you implying, girl?'

Harry insinuated himself between them, pushing his father away. 'Away on up to bed, Louise. We'll have this out tomorrow.' Only then did Louise realise that Harry was now as tall as his father, although not quite as strong yet.

'No, Harry. We'll have it out now. If I'm going to stay in this house and look after you all, I'll want money every week from you, Da. And you won't get any of it back for booze, either.' She faced her father. 'And it will have to be more than you gave me ma. We all had to do without because you squandered most of your wages and she let you get away with it. Now we're down Johnnie's and Ma's wages, you'll have to contribute a lot more money to the housekeeping or you can look after the bills and cook for yourself, and I'll look after us three. So there!' she finished defiantly.

'All right! You'll get your money, but what did you mean just now? Who's your ma with?'

'You may as well know, because she's not coming back. She's met another man.'

Tommy visibly paled and his body sagged. 'You're having me on. She wouldn't dare,' he croaked in disbelief.

'Why not? Why would she not dare? She's lucky to have got a younger man to look after her now. Someone who treats her like a lady. She's not afraid of you any more.'

Peggy, awakened by the raised voices, had come downstairs and stood at the vestibule door pale and shaken. 'Away back to bed, Peggy,' Harry advised her. 'You need your sleep, love. We'll deal with this.' Peggy stood undecided and he urged, 'Go on. No need for you to get involved.' His sister backed into the hall, and hurriedly climbed the stairs.

Tommy swung his attention to Harry. 'Is this true?'

'As far as I know it is.'

With a groan, Tommy slumped down in his chair and motioned them to do likewise. They remained standing, and feeling at a disadvantage he rose to his feet again and said, 'Who's this other man? What's his name?'

'Why, so you can come to the mill looking for him?'

Harry gave a gasp and too late Louise realised her slip and hoped her da wouldn't notice.

He did. 'Oh, so he works in the mill, does he?'

'Never mind. Me ma wasn't at work today and I don't suppose she'll need to work any more. This guy can afford to keep her. She'll not have to skimp and make do the way she had to here with you. And she won't have to worry about him coming home drunk and abusing her!'

Tommy stood in thought for some seconds. 'Will you ask her to come and see me, Louise? Please?'

'It's no use, Da. She won't come. And I for one don't blame her. She's terrified of you when you're in one of your tempers.'

'Tell her I won't lay a finger on her. You can stay in the house while she's here. We've been married twenty years, for God's sake! She can't turn her back on me after all we've been through together.'

Wasn't that just like her da – it all came back to him again. 'Are you thick, Da? It's not as if she'll be turning her back on a wonderful marriage here for the sake of a sexual fling! No, she has the chance of a better life with a man who thinks the world of her, so there's no reason for her to come back to you.'

On this righteous note Louise passed him and slowly climbed the stairs followed by an embarrassed Harry. There was more to this sister of his than met the eye. Who would have thought she would know anything about sex? She'd certainly stood up to their da there. He had to admire her for that. But he didn't think that that was the end of it. More like the beginning, he'd say; another episode in the McGuigan saga, if his father had anything to do with it. He couldn't see him just sitting there on his backside and accepting all the humiliation and betrayal.

9

Under duress, Tommy reluctantly parted with his money. When he started in the shop some years ago, Johnnie had taken it on himself to order and deliver his family's groceries, and then when he married Mary his mother had taken over the chore. Thankful that Peggy too now worked in McFadden's, Louise wrote out the list of groceries on Thursday morning and gave it to her sister. Johnnie himself came over to the house at lunchtime with the order in a large cardboard carton.

Examining Louise's dour face, he asked tentatively, 'How're things going?'

Louise shrugged as she glumly unpacked the goods and started putting the food in the cupboard. 'As well as can be expected under the circumstances, I suppose.'

Johnnie nodded towards the cardboard box. 'I hope you're not paying for those with your own money, girl?'

She gave a derisive laugh. 'Do you think it's me ma you're talking to? There's no way I'm going to dip into my wee bit of savings while he wastes his money on booze and horses.'

'So me da's coughing up the housekeeping money, is he?'

'Not all of it. A bit.'

'Well, that's a start.' Louise went on stocking the cupboard in silence, and Johnnie said in exasperation, 'Louise! Will you please stop that for a minute and sit and talk to me. What's happening? I can't understand me ma. Has she come to her senses yet?'

Reluctantly, Louise leaned against the cupboard and gave him her attention. 'Not so far. She won't be back at work till next Monday, so I haven't seen her. But I honestly can't see her changing her mind, now that she's made the break. That took a lot of courage, you know. Bill McCartney did give me ten bob towards the house-keeping, since me ma hadn't left any food in before she took off. I never let on to me da about it. I've it hidden away for emergencies and I'm sure there'll be plenty of those in the future.'

Hastily hiding his surprise at learning that Louise had stooped to take money from Bill McCartney, Johnnie asked, 'How's me da taking it?'

Louise had noted his swift, cleverly controlled expression of displeasure, and upbraided him as if he'd spoken. 'Don't you dare look at me like that, Johnnie McGuigan! I can't afford to be proud where money's concerned. It's too hard to come by these days. Me ma took the money for our keep as usual at the weekend, but obviously in all the excitement of her love affair she forgot to leave in any groceries. As for me da, well, he only found out last night that another man is involved, and needless to say he's far from happy about it.'

'Does he know it's Bill McCartney?'

'Not yet. But it shouldn't be too hard to find out.'

293

'Where's me ma living? Has she moved in somewhere with McCartney?'

'How would I know where she is or what she's doing? I'm not psychic. But really, I was so annoyed I didn't ask any questions and Bill McCartney didn't volunteer any information. He actually expected me to be happy for her . . . and I am, in a way. But who do you think will bear the brunt of all this carry-on?' She thumped her breast with a clenched fist. 'Yours truly, that's who. So it's daft to expect me to be over the moon about it. I imagine she is with Bill McCartney. Where else would she be?'

Johnnie now understood his sister's predicament. 'I'll go and have a word with her, try to talk some sense into her head, and try to persuade her to come home. Do you know where they're shacked up?'

'I've no idea where he lives. Besides, you're as well keeping out of it. Think of Mary and the baby. They're your priority now.' She changed the subject to one that would distract him from further talk about their mother. 'Did you get that house in Violet Street?'

He relaxed and a smile temporarily lifted the worry from his face. 'As good as. We've made arrangements to see the last tenant. He's added a bathroom to the back of the house, you see, and is looking for a back-hander before he'll ask for permission to hand over the key to us. I don't think he'll be unreasonable, but it doesn't do to count one's chickens. I'll refuse to pay if he tries to stick his fist in, and we'll just have to look elsewhere.'

Reaching out, Louise squeezed his arm. 'A bathroom? That's wonderful. I really am pleased for you. You deserve a break. Mary must be absolutely delighted. I hope this guy won't be too greedy. It's not everybody who'd give him money, you know. Most folk would take their chances and go direct to the landlord, bathroom or no bathroom.'

'That's something we want to avoid at all costs. He'd push the rent up for sure, and it's high enough as it is. And that's the deciding factor here. I suppose whoever the owner is could still put it up, but that's a chance we'll have to take. It really is a lovely house, Louise, and worth the extra money.' Johnnie lifted the empty box. 'Anyway, I'd better be getting back to the shop. I'll take this with me out of your way. Let me know how things go, won't you? And if there's anything at all I can do to help out, you've only to ask. And for God's sake don't go hungry. Does Harry get any cheap bread in Kennedy's?'

'With him working outside with the horses he doesn't bother. But the option's there and he will if I ask him. The only one that is likely to go hungry in this house is me da. If he stops giving me money I'll put the food under lock and key, so help me. He'll have to pull his weight or I'll want to know the reason why.' Johnnie dithered trying to find words of comfort and she added, 'Away you go. If I'm really stuck I know where to find you, and don't worry about us. Peggy'll keep you up to date.'

Swamped with worries about her mother and Conor, Louise had completely forgotten to tell Cathie on Wednesday that she was meeting George on Saturday night. Well, she'd certainly know by now. As far as Louise could make out, Cathie was seeing Trevor most nights. She was certainly living on the edge and probably using Louise as her alibi most nights into the bargain.

The women Louise worked with were over-solicitous

in their attitude towards her, making her feel like an invalid who had to be quietly tiptoed around. They were only showing their concern, of course, and didn't ask any embarrassing questions regarding her mother and Bill, and for that Louise was grateful. Nevertheless, she was still mortified. She could imagine just what was being discussed in the toilets, and cringed with shame. To think it had come to this: her mother's affair being bandied about as if she were a common tart. Would she be brave enough to return to the mill next week? Would she have the nerve? Yes. Mentally, Louise answered her own question. Yes, her mother would return. The only person Nora McGuigan feared was her husband. She was a strong character, and would ignore anybody who dared pass any sarky remarks at her.

Seeing Bill going through the weaving shop later that afternoon, she caught his attention and waved him over to tell him about her father's request to see his wife. Bill's lips tightened, but he didn't commit himself, just said that he would give her message to Nora.

'I'll tell her, and I'll try to put her off, you know. I'll let you know in the morning what she says.'

'Thanks. And Bill . . . please don't insist on coming along with her. Da knows she's met someone from the mill, but he doesn't know who. Let's keep it that way as long as possible, eh?' He opened his mouth to protest and Louise forestalled him. 'Look, me ma has obviously made up her mind to leave *us*.' She stressed the word us. 'I know that's not something she'd do on the spur of the moment, so I can't see me da persuading her otherwise. At the same time, Ma won't want him coming here and creating a scene. They've enough to talk about here at the moment without me da adding fuel to the fire.'

296

'She'll only change her mind if you lot gang up on her and persuade her to come home.' He eyed her intently. 'What're the chances of that?'

'I don't know. I certainly won't try to sway her.' Louise crossed her fingers behind her back as she spoke. Bill was a fool if he believed her. She'd stoop to any lengths to get her mother to come home. 'I can appreciate what she's going through, but I can't speak for Harry and Peggy. They're devastated, so they are. They really do miss her.'

He didn't look too happy at this revelation but just said, 'I'll pass the message on to your mother. It'll be up to her what she does.' He strode off down the shop floor, head down, obviously troubled.

Friday morning Bill McCartney was waiting at the mill gates for Louise. Noting the covert looks and elbow-nudging he blatantly stared them out. Taking Louise's elbow and drawing her to one side, away from eaves-droppers, he said quietly, without any preliminaries, 'Your mother says she'll meet your father but not in the family home. She'll be at Dunville Park tonight at seven. If it's not raining they can sit in the park and talk.'

'That won't do!' Louise cried, aghast. 'Ma must have forgotten that me da's on the late shift. He doesn't stop work till ten.'

'Well then, he'll have to make sure he's on day shift on Monday and meet her then. Same time, same place. I've plans made for us this weekend and I've no inten-tion of changing them to suit Tommy McGuigan. Nora has bowed to his whims long enough.'

Louise pictured a weekend with her da working himself up into a right temper. There would be no living with him, so she offered an alternative. 'If he's in the house at lunchtime I'll tell him. If possible, I imagine he'll try to get off work early to meet me ma.'

'Put it to him and see what he says. I'll come through and see you this afternoon, all right?'

'OK.'

Tommy was far from pleased when he received the message. 'I can't meet her tonight. What about tomorrow night? I can't afford to take time off work, especially now that you're expecting more money off me every week.'

'That's your problem.' Bill's name hovered on Louise's lips but she managed to swallow it. Thinking how easy it would be to slip up, she cautioned herself. 'The guy says he's made arrangements to take Ma away at the weekend and has no intention of changing them to accommodate you.'

'Ah, a dirty weekend. Is that so? Well, he'll soon change his tune. I'm coming up to the mill after the lunch break with you and I'm sure someone will be only too happy to tell me the name of this dirty bastard. Not everybody condones adulterous behaviour, you know. Once I know his name, I'll soon put him in his place, one way or the other. I hope he likes hospital food.'

Greatly alarmed, Louise taunted him. 'Have you no shame? Do you want to be a laughing stock? I'm warning you, Da, you cause a scene in front of me ma's work-mates and she'll never speak to you again. Never! Besides, it's you who'd probably end up in the Royal with a busted face.'

Tommy stood, brows drawn, pondering on her words. 'Look, tell the bastard I'll get off work early and meet Nora at Dunville Park tonight.'

Louise nodded her head. 'Now you're talking sense.

And for goodness' sake don't shout and bawl at me ma when you meet her. Show her you can become a changed man, if she'll only just come home. Tell her how much we all miss her. And don't you dare lay a finger on her.'

A grunt was all the reply she got, but Louise thought her words had sunk in. She only hoped he would be able to hold his temper in check when face to face with his estranged wife.

Delighted to hear the news from Trevor that her friend was going out with George on Saturday night, an excited Cathie called up at the house to see her. Louise almost passed out when she opened the door to Cathie's knock and saw that she had brought Trevor along.

Wide-eyed, she beckoned them inside, then rounded on them. 'Are you two mad?'

It was Trevor who answered her. 'It's all right, Louise. Nobody about here knows me.'

'Don't be too sure of that! The way you two are flaunting your friendship, somebody is bound to start nosing around.'

Cathie showed her annoyance. With a light punch on his shoulder, she motioned Trevor to turn round. Mystified, he did so. Pointing to his back Cathie said indignantly, 'See? He hasn't got a big P on his back to let everyone know he's a Prod. You worry too much, Louise. That's the trouble with you. We all look more or less alike, and we talk the same language, as you well know.'

Louise dramatically put a hand over her mouth and, turning aside, said sarcastically, 'Excuse me while I titter. Do you know what's wrong with you, madam? You don't worry enough, that's what's wrong with you. You can't see further than your nose. Look, you can't linger here. Me da got off work early today to meet someone and he could be back any minute now and you'd be in for an interrogation. And believe you me, as soon as you introduced him as Trevor Pollock he'd put two and two together and soon figure out that Trevor is from the other side. So you'd better shove off before he comes back.'

'Oh, all right. It's just that when we heard you were meeting George tomorrow night we wondered if you would like us to make up a foursome?'

'No, thank you. If I decide to see George on a regular basis, I'll start meeting him in town, and leaving him in town. I certainly won't chance bringing him up here. No fear!' She shot Trevor a scornful glance. 'You should have more sense, so you should. Do you want Cathie to get a hiding?'

He actually smiled at the idea. 'And here was I thinking it was me you were so concerned about. But I think you're wrong. Nobody's going to bother themselves about us two.'

'Look, Trevor, not so very long ago they cut off girls' hair, tied them to a lamp post and tarred and feathered them when they dared cross the line.'

He still looked sceptical. 'I'll be more careful in future,' he said placatingly, as if talking to a child. Louise felt like wringing his neck for his complacency. 'Meanwhile, what about tomorrow night?' he continued with a smile.

'You'll have to ask George about that, I'm afraid. After all, it's his car. Now away you go before me da gets back.'

With an abrupt good night they turned to leave, just as Tommy arrived at the door. He had dressed in his best clothes to meet his wife and looked quite handsome and respectable. Cathie eyed him from head to toe before passing him with a nod of acknowledgement, which went unnoticed.

Before entering the house, Tommy stood and watched them through narrowed lids as they walked arms entwined down the street. 'Who was that?'

'Cathie Morgan. Surely you recognised her?'

'Of course I know Cathie!' he snarled. 'Who's the lad?'

'Someone she's dating.'

'He's not from about here, that's for sure. What's his name?'

The dead giveaway. If she said Trevor, her da would guess right away he was a Protestant and she had no intention of starting another argument about sticking to your own sort. 'Oh, Jimmy something or other,' she muttered. 'I didn't catch it.' Abruptly she changed the subject to what was foremost on her mind. 'You weren't away very long, Da. Did me ma not turn up?'

'Oh, she turned up all right. And who do you think was with her?'

He waited expectantly, his eyes fast on her face. Louise's heart sank. Surely, after all she had said, Bill hadn't shown up with her mother. Did her da now know who it was, or was he trying to trick her into exposing Bill McCartney's name? She decided he'd be foaming at the mouth if he knew the truth and put him to the test. 'Ma said she'd come alone and I believed her.'

Tommy acknowledged defeat with a sigh. 'You're right. She was on her own.' He sank down on to his chair and washed both hands over his face. Louise noticed how worried he looked. Utterly wretched, in fact, as he gazed sightlessly into the dead embers in the grate. At that moment she actually felt sorry for him. It suddenly struck her that he must be getting some stick from his workmates. Men in that respect could be like women, enjoying a bit of scandal at someone else's expense. Especially someone as proud as Tommy McGuigan; the all-conquering hero, who thought himself a cut above the rest because he had fought the Germans and had survived the Somme, but couldn't hold on to his wife. That would give some of his mates a lot of pleasure.

He looked so woebegone she felt a sudden urge to go to him and try to console him. After all, he was her father and in this particular instance it was her mother who was at fault. He must feel that the world had gone crazy. It must be incomprehensible to him that the worm had turned. She started towards him, but stopped in time, sternly warning herself to be careful. He was the one who, by his own egotistic, mean, selfish ways, had started all this off in the first place. He should have shown his wife more consideration. Treated her with the respect she deserved. Now he must be prepared to change his ways or put up with the consequences.

By the look of him, his meeting with her mother hadn't accomplished anything. If only he would admit to being in the wrong, eat a bit of humble pie for a change, maybe her mother would listen to reason. Give him another chance. It was up to him now, if any happiness was ever to come out of this sordid mess.

'What did Ma say?' she asked fearfully.

He shrugged. 'She wouldn't listen to reason.'

'So she's not coming back, then?'

'So she says. But I've given her an ultimatum,' he said offhandedly as if he didn't care one way or the other. 'I told her if she's not back here, in this house this weekend, she won't get back at all. Even when lover boy tires of her.'

Shocked to the core at this revelation, Louise sank down on to the chair facing him and leaned forward to glare angrily into his face. 'You said what?' she spluttered. 'Are you raving mad? You were supposed to win her round. Make promises. Beg her to give you another chance. Grovel, for God's sake! Get down on your knees if necessary.'

Tommy's hand automatically rose threateningly but he caught himself on and it dropped back to his thigh. He couldn't afford to have Louise walk out too. 'Listen, you! I'm not going to crawl to any woman. Don't worry, she'll see sense. She's too good a Catholic to live in sin for the rest of her life.' He settled smugly back in the chair and lifted his paper.

Louise had tensed, ready for the blow she saw coming. To her horror she found that she was disappointed that he had held back. Had he struck her, she would have had a good excuse to pack her few belongings and go. No one could expect her to stay. But where would she go? Who could she turn to? She'd have found somewhere. What a relief it would have been to have an excuse to leave someone else to sort out the mess. 'You're a fool, Da. Do you know that? You've pushed Ma too far this time. I bet you she'll take her chance living in sin, and enjoy it, rather than come back here to a life of slavery in this wretched house. I feel sorry for you. You're your own worst enemy so you are, and do you know what? You can't even see it.'

'You can keep your pity to yourself, you cheeky wee bitch. I don't need it.'

Disappointed at the chance her da had wasted, Louise rose abruptly to her feet. 'I made fish cakes for tea. I saved some for you. And that reminds me, it's Friday. I want some more money.'

A grunt was all the answer she got. Without more ado, when she served him his meal she placed a sheet of notepaper alongside it. 'I've made a list of all that has to be paid every Friday night. The rent man, the coal man, the milk man, and what I reckon I'll need for food. I've deducted what Harry, Peggy and myself contribute. If you can't see your way to giving me the rest of the money each week, feel free to pay the bills yourself, do your own shopping and cook your own meals, and I'll look after the rest of us. That's fair enough, isn't it?'

Receiving no reply, she climbed the stairs, intending to stay in her room until he left for the pub. She straightened the beds and dusted and tidied the two bedrooms, all the while listening for any sounds coming from below. It remained quiet and, thinking she must have somehow failed to hear her father leave the house, she descended the stairs. She had plenty to do; needed to get some of the chores out of the way if she was to keep her date with George tomorrow night. As she had foreseen, most of the extra work was falling on her shoulders. Peggy and Harry had got ready and gone out as soon as they had finished their tea, leaving her to clear the table and wash the dishes without so much as an offer of help, but she'd soon put a stop to that. They would all have to pull their weight. She had no intention of becoming the family drudge.

She faltered when she entered the kitchen and saw that her da was still sitting where she had left him. His chin had slumped down until it rested on his chest. He was fast asleep. Or was he . . . alarm sent her quickly to his side.

Apprehensively she tugged gently at his sleeve but to no avail. Gripping him by the arm she gave it a rough shake. He reared up with a loud snort. Head thrown back, nostrils flaring, he glared angrily at her. She drew back, startled and alarmed. At least he was alive. 'It's half eight, Da.' This was awful. She'd be a nervous wreck, just like her mother, if she allowed him to terrify her every time he moved or opened his mouth.

'What about it? Can I not take a nap now, without your interference?'

'Aren't you going down to the pub?'

'No. I'm having a night in. That is if it's all right with you, madam?'

A chance of Friday night down at the pub and he was staying in? This was unheard of, but then he was back on the early shift starting on Monday; there would be plenty of drinking time then, although if Louise had her way he would have less money to spend. She wasn't about to argue with him. 'Suit yourself. Sorry I woke you.'

Tommy McGuigan knew which side his bread was buttered. He'd be depending a lot on his daughter in future, so he tried to appease her. 'The wages weren't made up when I left early today. I've to call up to the depot in the morning for them. I'll give you the money you've asked for tomorrow,' he muttered dourly. 'Now, could you lend me enough for a couple of pints?'

Ah, the real reason he wasn't going out. He was broke. Well, she was starting as she meant to go on. No loans! She quickly reached a decision. Chores or no chores, there was no way Louise was staying in to clean and scrub with her da in a mood. It would be like walking on eggshells. Everything she did would annoy him; bring his wrath down on her head. 'No I couldn't! I'm sorry. I'll clear up in the scullery and then I'm going out for a while.'

'Mean, crabbed wee cow,' he muttered under his breath.

'What?'

'I said "What are you going to do now?"'

She hesitated on her way to the scullery. 'Oh, never mind.'

It was a calm, warm night, a red glow lighting up the western sky above the roof tops, promising good weather tomorrow. Louise headed up Springfield Road briskly enough, but she was tired and dispirited, and before long her body flagged and it was an effort to push one foot in front of the other. Soon she was almost down to a crawling pace. Passing Iris Street she realised she hadn't seen her grannie in a while, and decided that now was as good a time as any to remedy that. Crossing the road she made her way down Iris Street and crossed Cavendish Street into Oakman Street. When Lucy Logan opened the door, and reaching out embraced her granddaughter in a fierce, warm hug of welcome, Louise went hot with shame at her neglect of this wonderful wee woman.

'I've been thinking about you all,' Lucy exclaimed. 'Wondering what on earth I've done to you lot to give offence. It's so long since any of you have bothered to come over to see me. Harry called in on his way from confraternity one evening but getting information out of him was like pulling teeth.' She smiled as she recalled. 'He was full of his promotion. Singing Kennedy's praises. Thank God he got started there. It'll be the making of him. Your mother came over just before Easter but she wasn't a happy woman. I've been worried about her ever since. She seemed to have a lot on her mind, Johnnie in particular. Is young Mary still with her mother?'

Louise was able to smile and say, 'No, her and Johnnie are after a house in Violet Street. Mary has been staying next door this past couple of nights, so things are looking hopeful.'

'That's something else to thank God for. It'll have

cheered your mother up no end. She really was down in the dumps. She stayed here for a hour or so and I'm sure she said she would come back over the Easter break, but she never did. Is she all right? Is anything else wrong at home?' She sighed. 'I've been afraid of going over to your house in case your da was there. You know how he is with me. I can't do right for doing wrong. I'm more of an outlaw than an in-law as far as he's concerned.'

It was two weeks since Louise had last called to see Grannie Logan. She and her grandmother were best friends and she had always been a regular visitor to her house, but she had been so preoccupied with the way things were at the moment that she had failed in her duty. Not that she considered it a duty; she always enjoyed sitting in her kitchen and talking to her. 'Ah, Grannie, I'm sorry. I meant to come over sooner, but I've had a lot on my mind lately.'

'Never worry, love. You're here now and that's all that matters. But remember . . . I need you to stay in touch. I can't come to you, since me and your da never see eye to eye. It always ends up in a slanging match and it upsets your mother.'

'I know that, Grannie, and I really am sorry . . .'

'Enough said. I'll put the teapot on. I was just about to make a cuppa. How's the rest of the family?'

Shock struck Louise dumb as she realised that her grandmother didn't know anything about her mother's affair. Well how could she, she asked herself; no one had bothered to come over and tell her. Lucy Logan didn't hold with idle rumours and slanderous tales, with the result that she quite literally heard no gossip from her friends or neighbours. Besides, no one would dare say a word about her daughter's wrongdoing in her presence.

Lucy bustled into the scullery and half filled the teapot,

returning to join her granddaughter while she waited for it to boil. 'Don't just stand there, love. Anyone would think you were a stranger in this house. I promise not to scold you any more. Take off your coat and sit down. I'm delighted to see you, so I am.' Beginning to feel anxious at the lack of information regarding the rest of the family, she repeated, 'How is everybody?'

Slowly, Louise removed her coat and hung it on the coat rack. 'I've some news but it can wait till the tea's ready. Then I'll bring you up to date on current affairs on the home front.' *Affairs*. Now how on earth did I pick that word from my mind?

Sensing something was amiss, Lucy looked at her from under lowered brows. 'Not all bad, I hope.'

'Well the good news was about Johnnie and Mary. I can truthfully say I think that they have sorted out their differences and that all will be well with them. And you're right, Ma was very worried about them, but that has been resolved. If they get this house in Violet Street, and it looks very promising, I think they will be happy together there.'

'Very nice. Very nice indeed. I'm glad to hear that. Nora will be in a happier frame of mind now. The water's ready – I'll make the tea.'

Louise had to smile inwardly at the idea that her mother would be in a happier frame of mind. She didn't even know the good news about Johnnie and Mary yet. Tea poured, they sat facing each other at the table, and to give herself time to think, and to sort out in her mind just what her grannie needed to know, Louise helped herself to a slice of homemade fruit cake and nibbled her way through it. Popping the last morsel into her mouth, she said, 'I enjoyed that – it was delicious. Thank you.'

Lucy sat watching her in silence, afraid to question

her further. Afraid of what she might hear. What on earth was wrong to have her usually level-headed grand-daughter in such a state of nerves, her hand trembling each time she lifted the cup to her lips? Why, the poor child was wound up as tight as a drum, so she was. 'I baked it in case I'd have some visitors in over Easter, but no one came near me.' She added drily, 'You'd think I had the plague or something.'

Chastened, Louise apologised once again. 'I'm sorry, Grannie. What about Uncle Willie and Uncle Thomas? Didn't they bring their kids to see you?'

'They live too far away now, and the kids as you call them are like yourself, too grown-up to want to waste their time visiting an old woman like me.'

These words made Louise feel worse still. Her grannie had had a lot of problems lately with both her daughters-in-law. Her two sons had left their wives at different times, and landed back home for a while. It had taken a big effort to control her tongue and leave them to sort out their differences in their own way and own good time. Eventually their wives had convinced them to move away from this troubled area and make new starts in Draperstown and Enniskillen. That's why Nora had felt unable to involve her mother in her affairs; Lucy Logan had had too much to worry about this last year or so. Now it was too late. The die was cast and Nora had chosen her corner. Close to tears at her neglect, Louise left her chair and going round the table gathered her grannie close. 'Poor Grannie. You've had a lot to put up with. And you living here on your own. I should have come over to see you sooner.'

Lucy returned the embrace and, rising, moved to the fireside chair. 'That's what I'm here for. To be of help when I can and offer my advice where possible. Come over here and sit down and tell me all the news. Good *and* bad.'

Taking her cup with her, Louise sat on the chair facing her. Clasping the cup with both hands she gazed into its depths as if for inspiration. Lucy was watching her closely, and noting the unhappy droop to her lips, the hooded eyes, the reluctance to speak, felt a great sadness descend on her. All the happiness displayed at Johnnie's wedding was completely gone. That morning her granddaughter had been so carefree and happy – until the Liam Gilmore episode. Lucy had never found out the ins and outs of that carry-on, but Johnnie had apparently put Liam in his place in no uncertain manner. She recalled the tall, dark, handsome lad who had made Louise glow with radiance outside the church and leapt to the obvious conclusion, albeit it the wrong one. So that's what the matter was. She'd had a tiff with the boyfriend.

Unable to contain herself any longer, she blurted out, 'Have you fallen out with your boyfriend?'

Brushing the crumbs from around her lips with the back of her hand, Louise admitted with a wry grimace, 'Yes, but believe me, he's the least of my worries at the minute.'

More alarmed than ever, Lucy said, 'Come on now, tell me what's happened, love. Get it all off your chest. You've got me worried stiff now, so you have.'

Without more ado, Louise confessed bluntly, 'Ma has left home.'

Shocked, Lucy slumped back in her chair. After all these years of putting up with Tommy McGuigan's abusive temper and mean, selfish ways, her daughter had at last seen sense? But she had trouble taking it in. 'Well . . . I can't say I'm surprised,' she admitted. 'But what brought it about? Where is she? I'd have thought

310

I was the obvious one she'd turn to. Her two brothers certainly did.'

Louise bit down hard on her lip before coming to a decision. 'Brace yourself,' she warned her.

Lucy frowned and leaned towards her in fearful anticipation. 'For heaven's sake, Louise. Where is she and what's she done to have you in such a state?'

'She's moved in with another man.'

Lucy smiled slightly. 'Now, that I find hard to believe. My Nora? Never in a million years. You're pulling my leg, aren't you?' She actually giggled at the idea.

'It's true, I'm afraid.'

'Away with ye.' When Louise just kept nodding to show it was indeed true, Lucy focused her attention and asked apprehensively, 'Is he local? Is it anyone I know?'

'Yes. You know him from way back.'

A frown puckered Lucy's brow. She dredged through her memory for some moments but couldn't put a face to the situation. 'Who?'

'Bill McCartney.'

Lucy was once again shaking her head in denial. 'You're wrong. It can't be him. He left Belfast years ago. That I know for a fact.'

'He did indeed, but unfortunately he came back. I think he's been back about three months now and, being the good worker that he is, he got started in the Blackstaff again without any bother, and apparently he's swept Ma off her feet.'

'Bill McCartney . . . he'd have no bother getting his old job back. From what I knew of him, he was a first class fitter.' Lucy was thinking aloud. 'Mind you, I admit, he always did fancy your mother. I warned her against him once.'

'Is he a married man, Grannie?'

311

'Not that I know of. I'm inclined to think he's a bachelor. He was daft about my Nora. I think she spoiled him for anyone else.'

'You knew him well, then?'

'Mm, well enough, I suppose. Surely *you* remember him?'

'Of course I do. He was always very good to us when me da was away at the war. I recognised him when he came back to the mill. He hasn't changed much.'

'Well now . . .' Lucy fell silent. What to do? Would it be right for her to tell Louise her mother's secrets? After a short pause she decided her granddaughter was entitled to an insight into the long trail of injustices that must have driven a woman like Nora to leave home.

Louise waited patiently as she watched her grannie battle with her conscience, then prompted gently, 'You were saying?'

'You'd have been too young to understand at the time, but your mother worked hard during the war. She scrimped and saved, putting every extra penny away towards a new house of her own. In his own way Bill McCartney helped by taking you all out on treats, so she was able to save more money. I remember how excited she was when your father came home. She was bubbling over with happiness that he had been returned safe to her when so many had died. She couldn't wait to tell him that she had managed to save enough money to go after the house of her dreams, and she expected her husband to be pleased with her.'

'I remember,' Louise interrupted. 'She always talked about a house with a garden and a bathroom. I used to love listening to her. She made it my dream too.'

'That's right. You hung on her every word. She could be sure of an appreciative audience whenever you were about. But, you see, your father had never shared that dream. He wasn't all that keen on moving house. He was content to stay in Springview Street, near his mates and his local, so it must have come as a shock to him when my daughter told him that she had saved enough money for a deposit and urged him to go and look at houses with her. It was the right time, after the war. The kind of house she was after was well within their means. She was on cloud nine and still a beautiful young woman in her prime.'

Lucy paused and Louise, not wanting to break the spell her grannie was under, whispered softly, 'What happened?'

'Well now, you'd have been too young to notice, but your da was a changed man when he came home from the war. God knows, he'd every right to be. There's no disputing that. It must have been awful for all those young men in the death trenches as your father called them. Knee deep in mud and dead comrades. Your mother was sympathetic to his needs, and when he discharged himself early from the hospital where he was recovering from the wound to his leg she nursed him for months on end, with loving care and devotion. And mind you, it wasn't easy. Far from it. What with the nightmares and the slow healing of his leg, Tommy was in constant pain and it made him into a crabbed auld bugger and your mother a nervous wreck. But with her nursing and caring, eventually, Tommy was back on his feet and then back to work. Once he was able to get about, in spite of Nora's pleas, all the money she had saved slowly but surely disappeared. You see, she wasn't crafty enough. She foolishly put the money in a joint account and Tommy went through it like a hot knife through butter. She lost heart after that. Never again talked of moving or new houses. She was very unhappy and depressed and I worried about her. I think if Bill McCartney had hung about she could have been easily persuaded to take the four of you and go away with him, because, mind you, when you were young she wouldn't have left you behind. But he had already gone. I tried to talk to your father, tried to make him see how unhappy my Nora was, but he told me in no uncertain manner to keep my nose out of their affairs. Your mother also told me not to interfere, said that it didn't matter any more, she was past caring. My heart bled for her. She was heartbroken and had given up all hope for the future.'

Again she fell silent for some time, her mind delving into the past. Sighing deeply, she continued, 'To get back to Bill McCartney . . . well, when he was taking her and you kids out and about, Nora was still in love with your father, her hero, away fighting the Germans. You've got to believe that. She only looked on Bill as a friend. I knew that for sure, that's why I didn't worry that anything would come of it. Nora was a good woman. However, Bill must have said something or done something to make her realise how much he cared, and she, typical of her, stopped seeing him right away. No half measures where my daughter was concerned. She was very good-living, and she wouldn't take any chances where men were concerned. She wouldn't deliberately lead a good man astray. I remember questioning her about Bill at the time, why he wasn't around any more, but she changed the subject every time it arose. I suppose she thought that I was too old to understand. Shortly afterwards Bill left Belfast. That's the last I heard tell of him, until now. A lot of this is guesswork, mind you, but if you're anxious about someone, you see a lot from the sidelines and I'm pretty sure of my facts.'

Louise ventured to say, 'Do you think she's in love with Bill?'

'Why else would she go off with him? Eh? Risk alienating all of you?'

'To teach me da a lesson?'

'No. No, she wouldn't use Bill like that. If she's gone off with him, then I doubt very much she'll ever come back. And really, you can't blame her. She's had such a hard time of it with your father in one way or another. But she'll not go too far away. I'd bet my life on it. She'll want to be nearby in case she's needed.'

'But we need her now, Grannie! I don't know what we'll do without her.' Louise was so despondent, Lucy reached over and tightly gripped her hand.

'You'll manage.' She was adamant. 'Johnnie's married, and Harry's working. Once Peggy gets a job you'll all be independent young adults ...'

Louise interrupted her. 'Oh, I forgot to tell you, Grannie. Peggy started in McFadden's shop full time on Tuesday.'

'There you are then! When one door closes another door opens. You'll be all right. And I'll be very surprised if your mother doesn't keep in touch and give you all the support you need. Just take it one day at a time, love.'

'I suppose you're right. We'll have to carry on. There'll be nothing else for it. I'm glad I called over to see you, Gran. I feel more positive now.' She glanced at the clock. 'Goodness! Look at the time. I'd better get a move on or you'll be reading about me in tomorrow's paper. "Young girl shot down during curfew hours."'

'It's happened before. But you've plenty of time, love.'

Louise shrugged into her coat and Lucy put her arms round her and hugged her close. 'You make sure that the others pull their weight. Don't let them palm it all off on to you, and remember I'm here, love, if you need me. There'll always be a home for you here if it gets too much for you. And keep in touch, won't you? Let me know what's happening.'

'I will. I promise. Thanks for confiding in me. I've a different slant on things now. Good night, Grannie.'

'Good night, love, and God bless.' Only when her granddaughter was long gone did Lucy remember that she hadn't found out what had happened to Louise's nice boyfriend.

The red sky had disappeared and an inky darkness pressed down on the rooftops when Louise left Oakman Street. The road was now crowded, with people hurrying home before curfew time. Louise pondered on how one could get used to anything. At the beginning, when the curfew was first enforced, she was too young for it to make any difference to her. She was home early each night, but she remembered that there had been lots of trouble in the district. Some folk had rebelled bitterly against it. Defying the authorities. Fighting for their rights. The shooting down of many innocent folk soon put a stop to that. People had no choice but to obey. It was now a way of life to be home before half past ten. Of course, there were those who still risked their lives by staying behind closed doors in the pubs after closing time or in friends' houses and scurrying home well after curfew in the dark. But overall, most folk had adapted to the restrictions.

She was glad to discover that her da and Peggy had already retired when she got home. Harry arrived home close on her heels and insisted on making a pot of tea. She told him about Grannie's missing them and said they should visit her more often. Guilt washed over his face as he agreed with her, recalling the happy times when they were younger and he and Johnnie were never away from their grannie's door when they played football over in the fields. Louise had given him food for thought and they finished their tea in silence, each wrapped in their own private thoughts. As she rinsed the cups Harry said good night and went upstairs to bed. Minutes later she wearily climbed the stairs herself to spend another restless night worrying about what the future had in store for them.

To ensure fair play all round, Louise tried to make sure that everyone did their fair share of housework. On Saturday afternoon, she allocated her da and Harry the chore of taking the mats from the kitchen and bedrooms and shaking them out the back, and then they were to clear up the yard of rubbish and throw buckets of water and disinfectant over the rough concrete and brush it down. She would look after the 'wee house'. Tommy heard her out in silence, all the while looking at her as if she needed her head seeing to. When she had finished dishing out her orders, he shrugged into his coat and informed her in no uncertain terms that he would not, in any circumstances whatsoever, lower himself to do a woman's work, then took himself off to the bookie's.

On the verge of tears, Louise felt her face crumple in frustration. Harry was quick to intervene. He told her not to worry as he would see to the yard himself, wee house and all, and she and Peggy could concentrate on cleaning up inside the house. He said they would be better off without their da grumbling and moaning at having to demean himself doing womanly tasks, and he would probably just get in the way anyhow.

Peggy was allocated the black-leading of the range and

she set about it willingly although she had never done it before. She made a good job of it and stood hands on hips looking at its gleaming surface, a smile of satisfaction on her face.

She also scrubbed the kitchen floor, laid the mats, which Harry had taken out the back and beaten the life out of, back in place, and dusted the mantelpiece and furniture. Louise gave the scullery a thorough going over and cleaned the windows and soon the ground floor of the house was spotless, the smell of bleach permeating the air. The bedrooms would have to wait until another day. She was now free to make the dinner and still have plenty of time to get ready for her date with George.

The black car was there idling away at the kerb near Dunville Park when Louise left Springfield Road and paused to let an oncoming tram pass before crossing over. She glanced idly about as she waited and three lads loitering outside the pub on the corner of McQuillen Street caught her attention. Nothing unusual about that, except that they seemed terribly interested in George's car. Again, she assured herself that wasn't so unusual. Although it was an old banger, George was proud of his car and took good care of it. He had obviously washed and waxed it for the occasion and it looked quite well. It was only natural that the youths would look it over and discuss it; there weren't many cars about these roads.

What disturbed her most was the fact that she didn't recognise any of the lads, not one of them, and that *was* unusual. She knew most of the local crowd, at least by sight. A hand on her arm caught her attention and she swung round, startled, to look up into Conor O'Rourke's concerned eyes. What on earth was he up to? Surely he could see that she was on her way to meet George?

Snatching her arm away, aware that the occupants of the car were probably watching, she hissed furiously, 'What do you think you're doing? Are you trying to make trouble for me?'

He leaned closer and bent down to say quietly in her ear, 'Quite the opposite, as a matter of fact. I'm trying to keep you out of trouble. I've heard rumours that your friend Cathie is under surveillance by some of the lads.' Louise immediately glanced in trepidation over at the strangers, and Conor said, 'Careful now. Don't give them cause to put you in the frame. When we cross over, please take my advice and walk on past the car as if you don't know it. Go on down Grosvenor Road while I keep your date talking. He can pick you up further down the road. OK?'

When she would have objected, he said, 'Please, Louise. This has nothing to do with *us*, I promise. It's for your own good. If you don't do what I say you could be in a lot of trouble.'

George had watched all this, and getting out of the car now stood waiting, a frown on his face. She crossed the road with Conor and gave George a wide-eyed look and an abrupt nod before walking on, while Conor stopped to talk to him.

'Listen, mate, I've heard rumours that a local girl is dating a Protestant lad from Sandy Row and it's come to the attention of the wrong people. Putting two and two together I've come up with the idea that Cathie might be that girl. If I'm right she could be in big trouble.'

He now glanced to where apprehensive eyes were gazing at him from the back seat of the car. 'Don't make it obvious, Cathie, but casually take a look over your shoulder at the three lads outside the pub and see if you recognise any of them.'

319

He gave an audible groan of frustration when, in spite of his warning, Cathie's head jerked round and she gazed directly into the face of one of the young men, who stared back at her with raised brows. 'Yes, I know that one to see. He lives in Gibson Street. Oh, God, he saw me looking at him.' She cowered against Trevor. 'I don't know the other two. Who are they, Conor?'

Conor sighed at the antics of her. She might as well have shouted 'Here I am!' 'I recognise one of the others,' he said. 'He lives near Joe McAvoy in McDonnell Street. So you've been warned. Now it's up to you what you do. Away you go or Louise will be coming back to see what's keeping you and my efforts will have been in vain.' His eyes returned to George. 'You see, it's her I'm trying to protect.' He threw an apologetic look into the back seat. 'No harm meant, Cathie, but you aren't on my list of priorities.' He once more faced George and stressed, 'I'm very fond of Louise, so you see and look after her. And if you care for her at all, don't be so blatant about your friendship or they'll be talking about her next.'

'Thanks for the warning. Nothing will happen to Louise while I'm about, I promise,' George vowed.

'I'm glad to hear that. But it's not as easy as all that if the wrong people are gunning for you. Remember that, and take care. And don't take the word *gunning* too lightly.'

Louise was hovering impatiently at the corner of Sorella Street. Climbing hurriedly into the car when it stopped, she demanded, 'What was all that about?'

Still in a state of shock, Cathie said, 'Did you notice three strangers outside that pub?'

'Yes, as a matter of fact I did. I thought they were acting very suspicious. I was wondering what they were up to when Conor came along and warned me to keep walking on down Grosvenor Road while he had a word with George. Do you think they were planning to rob the post office?'

'I don't know about that. It seems there's gossip about me and Trevor and those boys were probably watching us.'

'Look . . . you're taking this guy Conor's word for all this. It might be all in his head. It could be somebody else they're talking about, you know,' Trevor objected. 'He's letting his imagination run away with him, if you ask me.'

Cathie was not to be pacified. 'It's all right for you. I'm the one they're watching.' She was petrified, ashen-faced and shaking like a leaf; beyond listening to reason. Ignoring Trevor, she wailed, 'You were right. I should have listened to you, Louise.'

'Well, no harm done . . . so far,' Louise soothed her. 'You'll just have to be extra careful in future, or, better still, stop seeing each other altogether.'

At the bottom of Grosvenor Road, George pulled into Durham Street where they sat for some time talking, giving Cathie's nerves a chance to settle down before they debated where to go. It was dry and quite warm so they decided to drive to Bangor and walk along the front; blow the cobwebs away.

It was a lot cooler on the coast with a sea breeze blowing in, and when they left the car George put his arm round Louise's waist and drew her close. Drawing her back behind the other two, he confided, 'Looks like we'll have to meet in the town centre in future. That is, if we're going to continue seeing each other.'

'I've been thinking about that, George, and in my opinion we'd be better not seeing each other at all. It's not worth all the hassle. That was just a taste of it back there. It's too dangerous.'

He smiled wryly. 'I thought you'd say that. Don't you care at all for me?'

'I like you very much, I really do, but I've enough troubles of my own at the moment, without the worry of someone spying on us.'

'Forget about what this Conor fellow is implying. It might be a crafty ruse to come between us. What do you think?'

'Conor's not like that. He must have heard something to worry him or he wouldn't have interfered.'

'OK, so we'll meet in town then and nobody will be any the wiser. We can at least be friends. It's obvious to me that Conor still cares for you,' he added tentatively.

How she wished that were true. 'You're wrong. But it's not Conor I'm worried about. As far as I'm concerned, he's history.' To get away from the topic of her ex-boyfriend, she proceeded to tell George about her problems at home and found him very sympathetic.

'I can see how you're fixed. But it's a family problem and nothing I can say or do will change anything. I can only be here to lend an ear. But please promise me that if you ever change your mind about us, you'll let me know.'

Feeling she could safely say 'Yes' she agreed. After all, she knew nothing about him; had no means of getting in touch with him. So he must be just talking for the sake of talking.

'Good. Now let's enjoy ourselves. Would you fancy an ice cream?'

'That would be lovely, thank you.'

Pushing all worries into the background, they went to an ice cream parlour and then dandered along the sea front, losing a lot of their ice cream as the strong wind buffeted the cones in their hands and moulded their clothes to their bodies. They stopped to watch the yachts bobbing on the swell and Louise did not object when he eased her still further away from the others. She really enjoyed his company as he set about entertaining her. Time passed all too quickly and soon it was time to head back. Before they returned to the car he took a small notebook from his pocket, scribbled something on the top page, tore it out and handed to her.

'That's the telephone number of the engineering firm where I work. If you ever need me for any reason whatsoever, or if by some wonderful chance you discover you can't live without me, just ring and ask for George Carson. OK?'

Maybe she was wrong; perhaps he did care, after all. She folded the slip of paper and tucked it into her purse. 'OK. Thank you.'

He drew her into his arms and she went willingly. His lips were tender and she returned their pressure with passion, getting caught up in the emotions he was arousing in her. Then Conor O'Rourke's face filled her mind and she brought the kiss to an end. She liked George too much to use him to assuage her pride. 'I'm sorry. I shouldn't have done that.'

'That's all right. I understand.' And he did . . . why start something that you can't finish?

Cathie was very subdued when they met up again, and when Louise suggested that the lads drop them off on Great Victoria Street to get the last tram up Grosvenor Road she did not raise any objections. On the tram she confided that she was really worried and had told Trevor they would have to see less of each other.

'I'm glad you're seeing some sense at last,' Louise

agreed. 'Once a week should be safe enough. And for God's sake meet him in town. Don't take any unnecessary chances. And don't let him come up here again.'

'You're not going to date George, then?'

'No. I've enough on my plate without inviting another disaster.'

'This is my stop, Louise. Are we still all right for the pictures on Monday night?'

'I'll have to give it a miss this week, Cathie. You know how things are at the moment. I'll keep in touch.'

'Don't forget, now. Sure you won't?'

'No. I'll be in touch as soon as I can. Good night.'

The tram stopped as Cathie lurched towards the door. 'Good night, Louise.'

Conor's heart was heavy as he retraced his steps across the Falls Road. That George fellow was a handsome devil. He didn't blame Louise for falling for him. He was a bit older than Louise and obviously had a job and could afford to keep a car on the road. He should be happy that Louise had someone like that to turn to now that he couldn't see her any more. He eyed the pub. Not much of a drinker, he didn't fancy going inside, but he wanted a pint. The three lads were still lounging outside the door. Eyeing him closely, they made way for him to enter. He held the eye of the one he recognised and acted as if he knew him. 'Hi, there. How's Joe McAvoy keeping? I don't see much of him nowadays.'

His query was met with a frown and a suspicious look. 'Do I know you?'

'Well, I used to knock about with Joe and I know you by sight. You live in McDonnell Street, don't you?' Maybe the fact that they'd been recognised would be a warning to them.

Slightly mollified, the lad said, 'Yes. Yes, I do. Didn't you know Joe's courting now? A nice wee *Catholic* girl.'

Conor couldn't help but notice the emphasis on the word *Catholic*. 'Of course I do. That's why I hardly ever see him these days.'

The lad's brow cleared and although still dubious, he at least pretended to recognise Conor. 'Joe seems to be getting on all right. Like, you see, McDonnell Street is long, as I'm sure you know. He lives at one end and I live at the other. So I don't know him all that well – we're just on nodding terms, really.'

Conor was tempted to ask him how he knew Joe was courting a wee Catholic girl but curbed the impulse. No need to antagonise them further, if indeed they were up to no good. 'If you do happen to run into Joe, give him my regards.'

'And what name will I tell him?'

'O'Rourke, Conor O'Rourke.'

'I'll do that, Conor.'

Conor nodded towards the pub's interior. 'Aren't you coming in for a drink?' He made it sound like an invitation.

It was the the tallest lad, the one Cathie had recognised, who quickly intervened. 'No, we're not. We're waiting for someone.'

With a scowl at the loss of a free pint, the other lad gave Conor a quick smile and said, 'Thanks all the same, mate. The offer's appreciated.'

'Maybe another time.'

Conor sat for some time over the pint, yarning with some of the local lads while keeping an eye on the door, but the strangers never came in. When he eventually left the pub some time later, there was no sign of them.

* * *

Conor walked home with a measured purposeful stride. He had decided not to delay any longer. He had made up his mind not to tell Louise about his newly acquired family. She would be content enough with this George fellow, so why put her in the position where she had to decide whether or not she'd ever marry an illegitimate lad? But first he would have it out with his mother, and once his exams were over he'd return to live with his father and give Birmingham a try.

Cissie came from the scullery when she heard the key rattling in the lock. 'I thought you were away out for the evening. Is anything wrong?'

'What would be wrong? I saw Louise meeting that other bloke you were telling me about and it's upset me a bit.'

Drying her hands on her apron, Cissie said, 'You'll get over her, son. She's not worth getting upset over. Can I get you anything to eat or drink?'

He shook his head. 'No, thank you. Come and sit down. I want to talk to you.'

Cissie's voice shook as she obeyed him. 'You're too upset to talk, son. Can't we leave it until another time?'

'No, Mother, I've waited too long already. Sit down.'

Cissie sat gazing down at her hands clasped on her lap and waited for all the recriminations that were about to fall on her head. Lord knows she deserved them. If only Louise McGuigan hadn't got him in her clutches he wouldn't have needed to know anything about his father and all it implied . . . at least not for some time. She would have eventually plucked up the courage one day to confess her sins. She sat patiently, waiting for him to speak.

Conor took the chair facing her and gazed at her in sorrow. She was a difficult woman to live with. She expected great things of him and, thinking he was all she had in the world, he had always been afraid of failing her. It had come as a terrible shock to learn that she had family ties in Lisburn. That he had uncles and aunts and cousins that he knew nothing about. That his mother had feet of clay!

Unable to bear the troubled silence any longer, Cissie cast a furtive glance in his direction. He was scowling at her, but when she opened her mouth to speak he lifted a hand that effectively stopped her.

'If you don't mind, I'll ask the questions. First, why did you lead me to believe that my father didn't want anything to do with me?' He saw her tongue flick over her lips as if they had dried up.

'I thought it was all for the best, son.'

'Best for who? You?' he jeered.

'No, you! I came to live here when your father decided to leave us and go off to live in Birmingham so no one would know the truth about us. I didn't want the finger pointed at you.'

'Are you sure it wasn't yourself you were thinking of? What about your family in Lisburn? Surely they would have stood by you. It's not all that far away. Why didn't you at least keep in touch with them?'

'I might have known Don would tell you about them. He just couldn't keep his big mouth shut, could he?'

'My father didn't know he was telling me any secrets. He just couldn't understand how I didn't know about them. Neither can I, for that matter. Why all the secrecy? Are they a bunch of criminals or something?'

'I chose not to tell you about them, because they thought that I was living in sin with your father, over in England. If you'll bear with me I'll bring you up to date on a bit of our family history.'

'Well, what do you know. A bit late for that, but I suppose it's better late than never.'

She scowled, but continued, 'My mother died when I was fifteen. Some years later I fell in love with my boss, your father, Donald, and when my father discovered we were having an affair he threw me out of the house.'

'Did *my* father know about this?'

'No. I was so ashamed at my father's actions that I never mentioned it to Donald. I didn't want to put any pressure on him.'

'Your father was probably worried about you and only put you out to try to bring you to your senses. I'm sure he'd have taken you back once you'd learned your lesson.'

'That's a gag! Your grandfather wasn't worried in the least about me. Oh, no! He was worried about the *other* woman. Accused me of breaking up a marriage. Said I was stealing another woman's husband.'

A grandfather! Not only had she done him out of knowing his father, she had denied him the knowledge of his grandfather, the chance to have a man in his life when he was growing up. Someone he could turn to in times of need, someone to confide in. Conor curbed his rising anger. 'And isn't that just what you *were* doing? Breaking up a family?'

'Donald told me his marriage was over and I believed him. Otherwise I wouldn't have become involved with him in the first place. I certainly wouldn't have got myself pregnant. I didn't think that he and she were . . . you know? I didn't know she was already pregnant with *their* third child. When it came to the crunch, she gave him an ultimatum, and he chose to leave us and all his friends behind and go and live in Birmingham.'

'So I was the means to an end? Is that it?'

She frowned, shaking her head in bewilderment. 'I don't know what you mean.'

'You said you wouldn't have become pregnant if you had known that Don's wife was expecting Joan at the time, so the obvious conclusion is that I was planned by you. The bait in your trap, so that you could have some leverage to hang on to your sugar daddy!'

Her mouth had gaped a bit at all the names rolling off his tongue, but now she sat forward on the edge of her chair, gazing at him entreatingly. 'No! No, son, you mustn't think that. Never ever think that! You're my world. I love you dearly. I couldn't live without you.'

'Well I'm afraid you're gonna have to. Don . . . *my father* has offered to help me start a career in Birmingham once I pass my exams. I suppose, now, you'll be praying that I don't pass them!'

She shuddered, shocked to the core. 'Conor! How can you even think I'd do a thing like that?'

'Why not? You've deprived me of a father, who would have kept in touch if you'd allowed it. The next best thing . . . a grandfather. Is he still alive today? Or don't you even know? There was a family not too far away in Lisburn that I could have visited and got to know and love and you never let on. I thought we were close, but now I don't even know you. Now . . . I think I'll go out again and get drunk. Drown my sorrows.' Taut with fury he left the room, afraid of what might happen if he lost all self-restraint.

Cissie was on her feet. 'But you don't drink,' she called after him.

'Now's as good a time as any to start,' he shouted back. The hall door slammed as he let it swing behind him on the way out.

Cissie huddled back in fear. What on earth had she

done? She would never have imagined that her son could be so enraged, so full of hatred. He had his temper under control at the moment, but she would make sure she was in bed before he came back from the pub.

Nora was waiting by the mill gate on Monday morning. She had never looked lovelier. There was a quiet glow to her that Louise envied. At the sight of her, Louise hastened her step and hugged her. 'It's lovely to see you, Ma.'

Drawing her away from inquisitive eyes and ears Nora said quietly, 'How are you, love? Is your da behaving himself?'

'So far. Oh, Ma, it's awful without you. When are you coming home?'

'I'm sorry, love. I just couldn't take any more. I was at the end of my tether.'

'But you will come home?'

'Ah, Louise, please don't ask me to. Bill is buying a house up the Glen Road, so I'll only be a tram ride away if any of you ever need me. And you'll always be welcome in our home.'

'I suppose it has a garden and a bathroom?'

'We haven't looked at any yet, but I imagine it will have.' Nora smiled wryly and confessed, 'I don't think I'd settle for less.'

'You'd be a fool if you did!' Louise agreed. 'Considering the upheaval it's causing.' The glow faded from her mother's face as Louise watched, and for a moment she felt guilty. Then she hardened her heart. It served her right. Why should she be happy when everybody else was so miserable?

'Don't be like that, Louise. It's not as if I'm leaving the country. Look, I'll have to go in now and face the

330

music. I imagine I've been the talk of the mill this last week. Will you meet me up in the Monastery after tea tonight and we'll have a good long talk? We won't be disturbed there. Will you, love?'

'Do you think Bill will let you out to meet me?'

'He will never interfere in whatever I do where my family is concerned. Trust me, love.'

'All right. But it'll be about eight. I've to see to the evening meal and all now, as you well know. My life's not my own any more.'

Leaving her mother abruptly at the entrance to the weaving shop, Louise hurried inside to her looms. Nora stood for some time looking after her and her doubts returned to haunt her. It was all right Bill saying that she deserved a life of her own, but did she? Wasn't marriage for better or worse?

Louise greeted her fellow workers pleasantly and, setting her looms in motion, laboured industriously over them, discouraging any attention. Even at this early hour she knew the grapevine would be working at full steam and the women would have already heard that her mother was back at work. She knew it was only a matter of time before someone approached her to inquire after her health, and try to prise the latest snippets of gossip from her. Probably Kitty would be elected as chief inquisitor, as she was on friendlier terms with Louise than any of the others. A whole fifteen minutes passed and she was beginning to think that she had misjudged her work-mates – that they were going to leave her in peace – when Kitty sidled over to offer her a sweet. Fifteen minutes was quite a record.

Kitty thrust a paper bag towards Louise. 'Here, love, have a toffee.'

Tongue in cheek, Louise dug into the bag and fished

out a caramel and popped it into her mouth. 'Thanks.' She gave Kitty no help whatsoever, just smiled benignly at her.

Kitty hovered uncertainly for a few seconds, then, getting no encouragement to cause her to dally, she apparently decided to forge ahead anyhow. 'I heard your mother's back at work today?'

'That was quick! I only left her a few minutes ago. But you're right. She's back. She wasn't very well last week. As you can imagine.'

'Is she, you know, back home then?' Colour rose in Kitty's cheeks. She was embarrassed, but determined to find out all she could. The girls were depending on her.

Louise liked Kitty a lot, but she just couldn't talk about her mother to anybody. This was Nora's business and she had no intention of filling Kitty's ear or anyone else's for that matter with something to gossip about. Not where her mother was concerned.

'If you don't mind, Kitty, it's not for me to talk about my mother's business. If you want to know anything, you'll have to ask her yourself.' When the other woman's mouth opened, Louise didn't give her a chance to voice her thoughts. 'I'm sure, being a mother yourself, you understand how it is.'

'Yes. Yes, I do.' A loom fell idle as they talked and Louise grunted with frustration as she let out the tension and changed the shuttle. When a shuttle ran out of weft it was hard to gauge how to get the loom going again without leaving a mark across the material. There was an art to it. Kitty apologised. 'Sorry for disturbing you, love.' She turned away but Louise's voice stayed her.

'Please understand, Kitty. This is my mother we're talking about.'

'Oh, I do, I do. Sorry, love.'

'No hard feelings?'

'None at all, love. I'm a thoughtless fool. I should've known better.'

Peace and tranquillity engulfed Louise as she slipped into a pew in Clonard Monastery that evening. The church was empty and of her mother there was, as yet, no sign. Falling to her knees she prayed feverishly for the Blessed Virgin to intercede for her and make her mother change her mind. She prayed long and earnestly, calling on all the saints that came to mind to put a word in for her. Especially St Jude, patron saint of hopeless cases.

She heard the church door open and glanced over her shoulder. Nora genuflected, and walked down the aisle to kneel beside her. She crossed herself, said a few prayers, and sat up on the pew. Louise rose from her knees and joined her.

Reaching for her daughter's hand, Nora clasped it between her own. 'I've landed us all in an awful mess, haven't I?'

'You did what you had to do, I guess. But you've made your point. Da now knows how you feel. I think he'll be a different man if you'll only come back, Ma.'

'It's too late for that, Louise. I'm thirty-eight years of age. I should be contented with my lot, but I'm not. Far from it! Bill McCartney has opened up a whole new horizon to me. I can't go back to your da. Not now. Not ever.'

Louise wished she could throw caution to the wind; be compassionate and kind and understanding. Assure her mother that it didn't matter, that they'd be able to manage without her. Tell her to grab her chance at happiness while she could, but the words stuck in her throat. It *did* matter! Why should she be the one left to bear the brunt of her mother's sin? To her horror she heard herself hiss angrily, 'And what about us? Eh? You had your chance but we're only starting out in life. We need you at home with us. We need your support. We need your guidance, we need your love. We need *you*.'

'Louise!' Nora was aghast. She had been a fool to ever expect sympathy. Bill was wrong. She owed it to her children to go home and look after them. It was her duty. She used all the excuses that Bill had filled her head with. 'You'll be all right. Johnnie's just next door and Harry and Peggy aren't children any more. You're all young independent adults, your whole life ahead of you.'

That great word. *Independent*. What difference would it make? She would still be left to look after the others; take over the running of the house. With a harsh laugh, she informed her mother, 'You'll be glad to know that Johnnie and Mary have resolved their differences. They're renting a house in Violet Street. A house with a bathroom, you'll be pleased to hear. Something you never managed to achieve in almost twenty years of marriage. What do you think of that?'

'That's below the belt, Louise. I did my best. If I'd had my way, we'd be living in a house with a garden and a bathroom today. Somewhere far from all the troubles. This situation would never have come up. You know that. I tried. I really did try.'

'And failed miserably,' Louise jeered. She warned herself not to be so mean and selfish, but she couldn't stop. 'And now we've got to suffer because you've gone and got yourself a boyfriend.' Louise was ashamed of herself. She couldn't believe she was saying these cruel things to her mother, but the pent-up bitterness would not be stemmed. Why should she suffer because of Nora's sin?

334

They fell silent as a door to one side of the altar opened and a head jutted out; they were looked at with disapproval and then the head was quickly withdrawn.

'Let's go outside, Louise. This is no place for raised voices.'

'It was you who picked it. I suppose you thought I'd be all nice and sweet, being in the house of God. Well you were wrong.' Pushing roughly past Nora, Louise paused for a moment, genuflecting, her eyes on the tabernacle, to ask God's forgiveness before stamping down the aisle, still in a bad temper.

Nora followed her outside. Turning to her, Louise said, 'I'm sorry, Ma. I was out of order in there. But I don't want you to leave us. Will you not give me da another chance? He is missing you. I know he is. He'll be a changed man if you'll only come home. Please, Ma?'

'Ah, Louise. I understand how devastated you must feel, love. But please, don't ask this of me.'

'Leave her alone, Louise.'

Bill McCartney emerged from the shadows where he had been waiting for Nora. 'Yes, I know it's hard for you – it's hard for you all. Do you think we don't know that? But remember, your mother brought you up to be strong and responsible children, and now you're old enough to make your own way in the world. Surely you know how Nora suffered at the hands of your father, but she stuck it out in silence for your sake. After years of torture and misery, aren't you glad she has found happiness at last?'

'You would say that, wouldn't you? You're getting your heart's desire. Tell me, are you leaving a wife and children to set up house with Ma?'

'No! I'm free to look after Nora—'

'That's the difference, Bill. She's not! She never will be free!'

335

Louise practically flew across Clonard Street and down Dunmore Street. She wasn't to know it, but Nora made to follow her, but Bill restrained her. 'Let her go, love. It'll all pan out in the end. Wait and see. Louise is angry and upset now. She's too sensible a girl to really expect you to go back. She's grasping at straws. In her heart she knows you're doing the right thing, and will, in time, understand that you made the right decision.' Realising he was protesting too much, and remembering the old adage – least said – Bill fell silent, but he tightened his hold on her.

'What if it isn't, Bill? Eh? What if my children all hate me? I couldn't live with that.'

'It'll be all right, love.' Bill sounded strong and confident, but he knew that he'd have one hell of a fight on his hands to hold on to her. He loved Nora with all his heart. She was beautiful, sensitive and caring. But he was afraid the very qualities that made her what she was would lay her open to persuasion to return to her old miserable, humdrum existence of a life – the life he would give his very soul to replace with a better one. A life of contentment away from Springview Street. Away from a cruel, uncaring husband.

10

Johnnie popped in on Tuesday evening to let them know that he was now the proud owner of the key to the house in Violet Street. He absolutely swelled with pride as he explained to Louise that he had signed the lease and put down the bond money, and they could move in right away if they so wished. Naturally, he assured her, Mary needed no second bidding and was even at this very moment busy next door packing their bedding, clothes and small bits and pieces into cardboard boxes he'd brought over from the shop. Her father and Joe McGurk the coal man would be here soon with the horse and cart to give them a hand over with the bed and other larger pieces of furniture. The only snag was, he dreaded telling Mrs Clarke the news when she arrived home tomorrow, but he intended giving her a bit extra money to help soften the blow.

He finished his long speech with a fond remark about his wife. 'Mary's in her element. She says to tell you if there's anything she can do to help you, Louise, you've just to let her know. She'll be more than willing. She also said to tell you that you won't have to run down to the

337

baths any more. You can have the use of our bathroom any time you please as long as you give her some warning first.' He smiled benignly. 'I think she wants everybody to be as happy as she is.'

Louise was pleased for him and said so, adding that Mary had enough to do in her new home but to tell her that if she was really stuck, she wouldn't hesitate to call on her. She thanked him for the offer of the bathroom and told him not to worry too much about Mrs Clarke as the old lady was used to having the house to herself and she shouldn't mind all that much. However, although she did her best to share in his excitement, her heart wasn't in it, and she found it hard to show any great enthusiasm. Her sad demeanour didn't go unnoticed by her brother. It was so unlike her, Johnnie's happiness dimmed and he looked at her in concern.

'Is anything wrong, sis?'

'More so than usual, you mean?' she asked sarcastically, then quickly apologised. 'I'm sorry. I'm getting a right nasty tongue in my head of late, so I am. I saw me ma last night,' she conceded by way of explanation.

'Oh, I see.' He rubbed his lips together before continuing. 'That doesn't sound very promising . . .' His voice trailed off and his brows were raised questioningly.

'You're right. It's not. Far from it in fact. She's not coming back here.'

'She'll change her mind. I'm sure of it,' he said with more confidence than he felt. 'As soon as the honeymoon's over she'll start worrying about youse and want to come back.'

Tears, long held in check, poured down Louise's cheeks and she made no effort to stem them; they dripped off her chin on to her pinafore and were all the more heartrending because they fell without a sound being uttered.

Johnnie watched mesmerised, trying to think of something to do, something to say, that wouldn't sound glib.

Drawing in a shuddering breath she said, with finality, 'No, she won't. Bill McCartney has too strong a hold on her. Take it from me, she's not coming back.'

Johnnie was aghast at the state his sister was in. She was normally so strong, so optimistic, so happy-go-lucky. They all looked up to her; depended on her. To see her reduced to this level of despair was unbearable. He didn't know what to say to comfort her. Flailing about in his mind, he came out with, 'Well, then, we'll just have to grin and bear it, get on with our lives without her. We can depend on each other, help each other out, and that counts for a lot.' Turning aside, he muttered as if to himself, 'I don't know how any woman can just up and leave her family like that. Doesn't she realise how it's affecting us all? The hurt and disruption she's causing?'

Louise was contrary and she wasn't having any of that. Wiping her face dry with the corner of her pinny she now fought in her mother's corner. 'Why not?' she demanded harshly. 'She was nothing but a skivvy in this house. I now know exactly how she felt. Just make sure you treat your Mary right. But then,' she gave a slight bark which he supposed was meant to be a laugh, 'you already know Mary's nobody's mug. She left you quickly enough when things weren't going her way. And good luck to her, that's what I say. That's what me ma should have done years ago, before she was tied down with four kids. Then me da would have had to pull his socks up and pay attention to her needs instead of treating her like a doormat. He has a lot to answer for, that man.'

Deciding to ignore the snide remarks about his wife, Johnnie asked, 'Was Bill McCartney with me ma?'

'Not to begin with he wasn't, but he was there at the end all right. Waiting to support her in case I tried to get her to change her mind. Which was exactly what I was trying to do. He soon put his oar in when he heard me pleading with her. She's got herself a good 'un there. He'll not let us play on her sympathy and persuade her to come back here to a life of drudgery. After all, why should she? She's given me da twenty years of her life, most of them miserable bloody years of slavery. She deserves some happiness.'

'Surely you can't mean that! She can't expect to get her happiness at our expense.'

'As has been frequently pointed out to me lately . . . we're all adults now and capable of fending for ourselves.'

'What had Bill McCartney to say about all this? Is he not ashamed of himself?'

'Is he hell! If he is, he hid it well. He told me I was big and ugly enough to look after myself.'

Johnnie was astounded. '*He said that?*'

'Not in those exact words, but that's what he meant.'

'How's me da taking it?'

'Oh, he was his usual charming self. Ma agreed to meet him last Friday night in Dunville Park to talk things over. She didn't have to, mind! And if Bill had had his way she wouldn't have agreed to meet him at all. But to her credit, she did. And Da, big man that he is, gave her an ultimatum. Come home at the weekend or don't come home at all. Strange though it may seem, she elected to stay where she was. Wouldn't you have done the same, under the circumstances?'

'Was McCartney with her? I mean, was Da free to speak without losing face?'

'She was alone, as I insisted that she must be. He had every chance to plead his case, and he blew it.'

'The stupid bastard!' Johnnie spluttered in outrage. 'Has he no sense at all?'

'I said something very like that to his face,' Louise said with a wry smile.

'Is Ma back at work yet?'

'Yes, she came back yesterday.'

Johnnie thought hard for some seconds, then nodded determinedly. 'I'll wait by the mill gates at lunchtime tomorrow, and have a word with her. Talk some sense into her head. Tell her all this nonsense has got to stop.'

'Oh, aye, and she'll come running? Huh! Do you know something? You're your father's son all right. All brawn and no brain. That's exactly what he wanted to do.'

'And why didn't he, eh? Good God, she won't come back if he doesn't make an effort to show that he wants her to.'

Louise glared into his face. 'Because I stopped him, that's why. She'd hate anything like that. A war of words outside the mill with everybody watching and listening? She'd never be able to show her face in the Blackstaff ever again. It would be the very excuse Bill's waiting for. He would waste no time in whisking her off somewhere far away, where we couldn't reach her. Then where would we all be?'

Johnnie considered this and still thought it worth the risk. 'Nevertheless, I'll go there tomorrow. I'm not like me da. I won't make a scene. I'll be quiet and polite and no one else will be any the wiser as to why I'm there.' He nodded vigorously as he saw himself as Sir Galahad, the Peacemaker. 'Yes, I'll do that. I'll be there tomorrow at lunchtime.'

'You don't understand, do you? Haven't you been listening to a word I've said? It won't do any good. It will only make matters worse. It'll keep the tongues wagging. Don't you kid yourself that no one will notice. They'll be watching Ma like a hawk, just waiting for some juicy morsel of gossip to gnaw at. Believe me, Johnnie, it's best to leave things as they are. The sooner all the talk dies down the better it'll be for all of us.'

His hands spread wide in frustration. 'I feel so helpless. Tell me what I can do to help, sis. Should I go up and threaten McCartney? Knock some sense into him?'

'No. We'll just have to play it by ear. Ma told me that Bill is buying a house up the Glen Road, so at least now she'll get the garden and bathroom she's always wanted.'

'Tell me, did she not even suggest that you and Peggy could go and live with them?'

'At the moment I think she's living in his mother's house, over on Stranmillis Road somewhere. Even so . . . I couldn't bear to watch the two of them together. And I certainly wouldn't like Peggy to see them. I got enough of that carry-on on Easter Sunday up on the Cave Hill. Me ma's besotted with him, so she is. It was disgusting to see, so it was. A woman of her age acting like that. They were going at it like two love-struck teenagers.' A slight shudder passed through her body at the memory of it.

'You saw them carrying on in broad daylight up the Cave Hill? I don't believe you!'

A shrug. 'Suit yourself.'

'Did anyone else see them?'

'Talk sense, Johnnie. How would I know? I didn't stick around to find out if anyone else saw the spectacle Ma was making of herself. I was so ashamed. I was terrified she would see me. I certainly didn't want my friend to know she was my mother.'

'Who were you with?'

'Just a friend. Luckily, he doesn't know me ma, thank God.'

About to question her further about this friend, Johnnie paused as he heard a shuffling noise in the hall. Apprehensive, he said in surprised, hushed tones, 'Is that me da?'

Louise flapped her hands in agitation. 'I'm sorry. I forgot to warn you . . . he's back on the day shift.'

Catching sight of his son, Tommy stopped on the threshold and scowled. 'What the hell are you doing here?'

'Can I not visit my sister?'

'Not while I'm about, you can't. If you'd been a better son and kept your trousers buttoned up your mother would be still here. That's what started all this off in the first place, you know. You not being able to behave yourself. She couldn't live with the shame of it. You dirty wee bugger.'

Johnnie's face flooded with colour and he looked fit to burst. 'Hey, you!' he howled. 'Just who the hell do you think you're talking to? It was you and you alone who drove me ma away. Ah, but then, you'd have to twist things round to suit yourself, wouldn't you? Make out you're the innocent victim. Shove the blame on to somebody else. That's what you're good at. That's you all over again. Well let me tell you something, smart arse. Ma wouldn't have looked sideways at another man if you had been even half decent towards her. So don't you dare put the blame on me, you cantankerous auld git.'

Tommy was livid with rage and spluttering flecks of spittle. 'You'd better get the hell out of my house, you cheeky brat, before I throw you out. Go on . . . and don't come back!'

Louise thought they both looked likely candidates for the cardiac ward in the Royal. She was in a quandary, not knowing how to interfere and put a stop to it before

343

it boiled over into a brawl and one or both of them had a heart attack. She heard the clip-clop of a horse's hoofs, and the rattle of wheels over the cobblestones, and from her stand near the window saw the coal cart draw up outside. Thankfully she cried out, 'Joe McGurk's here to move your stuff, Johnnie.' Eyes still locked defiantly with his father's, Johnnie made no effort to move. Giving him a rough push towards the door, Louise insisted, 'Come on. I'll see if I can be of any help.'

For some moments longer he stood, legs spread out and fists clenched, ready for a fight. Then with a last withering glare at his father he swung on his heel and preceded Louise out of the door. How on earth an obnoxious old bugger like his father had ever won a wonderful woman like his mother he'd never be able to comprehend. He'd be a fool to want her to come back to such a miserable old git! Louise was right. Their mother did deserve a lot better than him. Someone who could offer her some happiness. Some love and affection.

Louise stopped abruptly outside when she saw that Liam Gilmore had come along to help his sister flit. He and his father were angling the iron bed frame through the door, whilst Joe McGurk kept a grip on the horse's halter. Catching sight of her and seeing she was in two minds whether or not to come on, Liam flashed her a big false smile and said mockingly, 'Don't worry. I won't bite.'

She heard Mick Gilmore mutter, 'Behave yourself.' Ignoring Liam completely she acknowledged Mick with a nod. She had, however, to pass close to Liam to get into Johnnie's house. When she drew level with him, he said softly, for her ears only, 'Pity about what happened to Conor O'Rourke, eh? But then, he should have known better than to stick his nose in where it wasn't wanted. He'll know better next time.'

She came to an abrupt halt, bringing a startled glance from Mick Gilmore and Johnnie. 'What about Conor O'Rourke?'

'You mean you haven't heard? Ah, then he must have caught himself on and dumped you, is that it?' He grinned smugly at the idea of her getting her comeuppance.

'What happened to him?' Louise ground out through clenched teeth.

'Well, the way I heard it was, he was set upon by some of the boys and landed himself in hospital. I hear he's in a pretty bad way. They say he grassed up some of the lads.'

'I suppose you were one of the thugs?'

Aware that his father and Johnnie had stopped what they were doing and were watching him, Liam blustered, 'No, I wasn't. And don't you dare suggest such a thing. I just heard tell of it in the pub, that's all. I thought everybody knew.'

To ease the mounting tension, Johnnie took Louise by the arm and tried to take her back into her own house. 'I think we have all the help we need, Louise. Away and see what me da's up to.'

Shrugging him off, she rounded on him in fury. 'Leave me alone. I suppose you knew about this too?'

'Yes, but—'

'And you never said a word about it? How could you?'

Johnnie was obviously puzzled. 'I haven't seen you since it happened. Besides, it never crossed my mind that you knew Conor well enough to be so worried about him. What's got into you, sis? Will you stop worrying about everybody, for heaven's sake!'

Only then did Louise realise that Johnnie didn't know about her and Conor. 'I'm sorry, Johnnie, I'll have to go now.'

Without further ado she took off down the street, leaving all four men staring after her in amazement.

Raising her arm to lift the knocker on the O'Rourkes' door, she became aware that she was still in her old pinafore and shabby slippers with holes in the toes. Well, this wasn't a social visit. In fact it was an emergency and no time for niceties. She just wanted to find out what had happened and how Conor was. The door remained stubbornly closed to her loud, urgent knocking, and aware of the interest she was attracting by the twitching of net curtains across the street she abandoned her efforts and, greatly frustrated, retraced her steps.

Johnnie hailed her from where he sat on the back of the cart as it trundled past, the horse going at a steady gait. 'I'll be back over shortly, Louise. Why not keep Mary company?'

She nodded and continued on her way. There was no sign of Liam so she quietly climbed the stairs, ears alert, ready to retreat if she heard his voice. Mary was smiling contentedly when Louise knocked and entered the room, but one look at her sister-in-law's face and she reached for her full of concern. Hugging her and patting her gently on the back, she said, 'Dear me, what's brought this on, Louise?' Pushing her gently down on to a chair, she confided, 'Luckily enough I haven't finished all my packing yet. I'll make a pot of tea. You look as if you could do with a good strong cuppa. I won't be long.' She rummaged about in a cardboard box and, bringing out a teapot and two mugs, disappeared down the stairs to the scullery.

Louise sat trying to work out what could have happened to Conor. She couldn't think why anyone would pick a fight with him. He was one of the good guys. Everybody spoke well of him. Why, he wouldn't even

346

say a bad word about anyone. He believed in live and let live. Then, suddenly, out of the blue it struck her. She knew why he had been beaten up. Those lads he had warned them about on Saturday night must have twigged that Conor was doing just that: was warning Cathie and Trevor that they were being watched. That's what Liam Gilmore meant when he said Conor had grassed up some lads.

Soon Mary returned carefully clutching two mugs of tea. Handing one to Louise, she said, 'Here, drink this. I've put plenty of sugar in it. You've obviously had a bit of a shock. Now tell me, what on earth happened?'

Louise was grateful for the hot sweet tea and sipped at it before answering. 'Thanks, Mary. Conor O'Rourke's in hospital and it's all my fault,' she blurted out.

'What? How come? How do you make that out?'

She took another gulp of the comforting tea before she confided, 'He warned me last Saturday evening that some lads were keeping tabs on Cathie Morgan, and probably me as well.'

Mary was bewildered and showed it. 'Why? Why would anyone keep tabs on you? What business was it of theirs?'

'Because we were keeping company with a couple of Protestants.'

Suddenly, Mary became flustered. She appeared uneasy and couldn't hold Louise's gaze. 'I heard our Liam and one of his mates talking about somebody getting a good hiding,' she confessed. 'But I wasn't interested enough to ask who or why.'

At this revelation, Louise straightened up. 'Think back, Mary. What did they say? Did they mention any names? Do you think that your Liam was in on it?'

Mary was evasive. 'I don't know. I wouldn't think so.

As I say, I wasn't paying much attention to them. But I honestly can't see our Liam beating anybody up.'

Louise thought, Oh, can't you? Well Mary would say that, wouldn't she? After all he was her brother. She changed tack. 'Did they say if Conor was badly hurt?'

They had gloated about it, Mary recalled. Said he deserved all he got, but she wasn't about to drop her brother in it by telling Louise. What good would it do? If Liam was guilty he wasn't about to confess. He knew his da would kill him. Meanwhile, Louise was waiting for an answer. 'No. I just caught the tail end of their conversation, that someone had given some lad a good going over and he's in the Royal. Why are you so interested in him? Do you know him well?'

Great tragic eyes were lifted to Mary's in despair. 'Yes, and I *love* him.'

Mary was completely baffled. 'Then why on earth were you going out with someone else, and a Protestant lad at that?' She gave a bewildered shake of the head. 'Sorry, but you've lost me. You honestly don't strike me as the kind that would play the field.'

'I wasn't . . . I don't . . .' Louise set the cup down and rose to her feet. 'I'm sorry. It would take too long to explain and I must get over to the hospital. Thanks for the tea, Mary, but I'd better get running.' She had a feeling that Mary knew more than she was letting on and Louise didn't want to say anything she might later regret, something that might cause a rift between them. After all, Mary was family now, and she couldn't be held to account for anything that brother of hers did. Louise couldn't afford to take umbrage at her sister-in-law. There was already too much upheaval in the family as it was.

She descended the stairs at full gallop, pushing roughly past Liam Gilmore who was just coming into the hall and tried to obstruct her passage. Wanting to wipe the smug smile from his face with a cutting remark, she managed to curb her tongue. Her best option was to go straight to the Royal and inquire after Conor. Hear from the horse's mouth, as it were, just how badly he was injured and if he had any idea at all who the perpetrators were.

After a hasty wash and a change of clothes, she arrived at the hospital with barely thirty minutes of visiting time left, and by the time she found out which ward Conor was in most of the half-hour had already gone and visitors were beginning to file out. He was sharing a ward with three other patients. A woman still sat by the bed of an elderly man in quiet conversation and the other two beds were empty, their occupants obviously well enough to walk their visitors off the premises. Cissie sat at her son's bedside by a window overlooking the Grosvenor Road. She rose to her feet and glowered when she saw Louise approaching.

Cissie O'Rourke stood belligerent, bottom lip pouting, prepared for battle. 'What are you doing here?' she hissed, bringing the heads of the other two round to gaze at her. Cissie couldn't help herself. She was incensed at the audacity of this girl.

'Ma . . .' Conor warned. He tried to sit up in bed but obviously found it too painful and sank back on the pillows with a gasp.

Ignoring Cissie, Louise examined Conor's face. It was in an awful state. One side was puffed up like a balloon, his left eye so swollen that sight must be impossible, and his bottom lip was a bloody mess held together with stitches. Part of his head had been shaved and a bandage covered what, she imagined, were more stitches. She was devastated at the sight before her. Her breath caught in her throat and her teeth clamped down on her lip as she strangled a gasp of horror. 'I've just heard about it,' she whimpered. 'Are you all right? Oh . . . that was a stupid question to ask. You look awful.'

'Do you think they'd waste a bed on him if he wasn't badly hurt?' Cissie's temper was under control now and she spoke in a low, even voice. 'Now you've seen the trouble you've caused, will you please go and leave us in peace.'

'Give over, Ma. I'm all right, Louise. It looks far worse than it is. And don't listen to her. You mustn't think it was your fault.'

The final bell rang and a nurse came bustling in, warning visitors it was time to go. 'Can I come back tomorrow, Conor?' Louise asked tentatively.

'No need to bother yourself. He's getting out in the morning,' Cissie ground out.

'Ma, if you don't mind, I'd like to speak with Louise alone for a minute.' When his mother would have resisted, Conor sternly insisted, 'Please, Ma.'

'But—'

'Just go. Please.'

He obviously found it painful to talk. Without another word, tight-lipped and seething with resentment, Cissie threw Louise a look of hatred and stamped out of the ward.

Louise moved closer to the bed. 'I'm so sorry. This is all my fault. Did you recognise who did this to you, Conor?'

He shook his head. To save his lip, he gestured that they had attacked him from behind, clubbing him on the back of the head.

'Have the police been informed?'

He nodded and explained slowly, 'I wouldn't have got

350

them involved if I'd known, but I was out of it for a while and woke up in here. The hospital notified them.'

'Do they have any idea at all who did it?'

'No. Leave it, Louise. It'll blow over.'

'I'm so sorry.' The tears, never far from the surface these days, threatened to fall yet again.

Frustrated that he could only lie there looking at her, he tried to ease her guilt. 'Listen to me. It wasn't your fault. And don't you dare think otherwise. I'm a big boy. I make my own decisions.' His lips wobbled with the effort and blood started to dribble from the stitches.

'I'm afraid you'll have to go now, miss.' The young nurse came over to the bed, full of authority.

Conor fixed his good eye on her and begged, 'Two minutes . . . please?'

She wavered, then seeing he was in such a sorry state and that Louise was terribly upset she gave in. 'Oh, all right then. No longer, mind,' she warned them. 'And for heaven's sake watch that lip.' A look of reproof was levelled at Louise before she took herself off across the ward to give them some privacy.

Conor held out a hand and, moving closer, Louise gripped it. 'I feel awful about this.'

His good eye twinkled at her, but he winced when he tried to smile. 'Not as awful as I feel, I hope. In spite of all the tears you've obviously shed, you still look lovely.' He became stern. 'Please be careful, Louise. From what I hear, at the moment they seem to be only targeting Cathie. Don't they know about you and George?'

'Cathie's a nutcase. She thinks everybody's blind and doesn't know what's going on around them. I've only been out with George a few times. And I've already told him I won't be seeing him again.'

'Do you love him?'

351

'That's none of your business, Conor.' She got her dig in. '*I* don't owe you any explanation.'

'Listen, maybe we can put them off the scent. I've been thinking while I've been lying here. What if we see each other, say a couple of times a week, just to give the impression we're courting? Then you could safely see George on the quiet without anyone being any the wiser.'

It saddened Louise, listening to him trying to make it possible for her to date another man. It showed how little he cared. The lengths he would go to salve his conscience over his treatment of her.

'That won't be necessary. I don't want you involved in my affairs. Has this happened because you warned us off on Saturday night? Is that why they did this to you?'

He shrugged. 'For the life of me, I can't think of any other reason why. I haven't done anything untoward that I recall.'

'Here's the nurse. Tell me, quickly. Just how badly hurt are you?'

'I can tell you that. Save him splitting that lip open again.' The nurse fixed a warning eye on him as she stopped by the bedside. 'You're talking too much.' She handed two tablets to Conor. Pouring a glass of water, she watched while he downed the tablets, before turning her attention to Louise and explaining, 'He was hit on the back of the head with something heavy and was badly concussed. So the doctor kept him in for observation and to keep an eye on his kidneys which are badly bruised from the kicking he got. His eye and mouth aren't as bad as they look and will soon heal. They're the type of injuries we get in here every weekend when the pubs close. How's that for starters?' When she heard the ragged gasp that escaped Louise's lips and saw the horrified expression on her face the nurse hurriedly added, 'Bar

352

that, there's not much else wrong with him that a bit of tender loving care won't cure. And I imagine you'll give him plenty of that, when you get him home. But I really must ask you to leave now.'

Still he clung to her hand. 'Will you call in to our house and see me tomorrow, Louise?'

She grimaced. 'Will your mother let me over the door, do you think?'

'I'll make sure she does. OK?'

She leaned over and gently kissed his poor ravaged face. 'All right then, I'll be there. That's a promise!'

Her next port of call was down to Sorella Street to see Cathie. It was Mr Morgan who opened the door. 'Come in, Louise. Cathie's not here. Was she expecting you?' he asked blandly.

'No. No, I just called on the off chance that I'd catch her in. Will she be back soon, do you know?'

Jack Morgan was a tall man and looking down his nose at her he said, 'Now, you'll have to excuse me, Louise, 'cause I'm a bit confused here. As far as I know she's out with you at this very moment. And if I'm not mistaken she'll make it back shortly before half ten like she usually does these nights after being out with you. You seem to go out a lot together these days.'

He was watching her intently and Louise cringed inside. So much for seeing Trevor once a week! Just wait till she next saw Cathie. Guilt brought colour to her face, and realising that she had dropped her friend in it Louise tried to make amends. 'I had to visit a friend in the Royal tonight. I can't think where Cathie could have gone. Perhaps she nipped down to see Jean. Will you tell her I called?'

'I will indeed. Mind you . . . she'll have some explaining to do when I see her.'

In a hurry to get out before she did any more damage, Louise headed for the door. 'Ask her to get in touch with me as soon as she can, Mr Morgan, please.'

Louise couldn't bear the thought of going home. To everyone's surprise, Harry, with Matthew McFadden's blessing, had taken Hannah and Peggy to the Royal Cinema, leaving her da alone in the house. He wasn't good company at the best of times, and was even less so at the minute, sitting brooding by the fireside most of the time. She needed something to take her mind off Conor's injuries so she decided to take Johnnie up on his offer to call and see the new house.

Johnnie was grinning from ear to ear when he opened the door. The smile faltered slightly when he saw her and he looked apprehensive. 'Louise! Is anything wrong?'

'No. I just called in to see the house. I hope it's a convenient time, or I can come back another night?'

'Not at all. Come in. Mary's dying to show it off.'

A voice hailed her from another room which she assumed to be the scullery. 'Come in here and see the kitchen, Louise.'

She removed her coat and handed it to Johnnie. Giving him a wide-eyed stare, she mouthed the word 'Kitchen?'

He laughed aloud and with a wave of the hand motioned her ahead of him into the other room. Mary was waiting for her reaction. She wasn't disappointed.

Louise was mesmerised. The room was twice the size of most sculleries. She touched the beautiful worktops and gleaming, black enamel stove. Tapped her foot on the bright linoleum and peered into deep cupboards and drawers. She had never seen anything like it. 'Oh, Mary, this is absolutely gorgeous. It would be a pleasure to work in this scullery, oops, sorry, I mean *kitchen*!'

Mary bubbled over at all this praise. 'You have to admit it is far removed from any sculleries we know, eh, Louise?'

'It certainly is.'

'And . . . wait for it!' Going to a door to one side of the sink unit Mary dramatically threw it open and Louise was gestured forward. She stood open-mouthed gazing into the bathroom.

'This is beautiful.' She sighed. 'Imagine not having to go outside to the loo on a cold dark winter's night in the rain or worse. You're incredibly lucky to be able to get this kind of house when you're just starting out on married life and I hope you'll both be very happy here.'

Johnnie put an arm round his wife and pulled her close. 'Thanks, sis. We know that . . . and we know how close we came to making a complete mess of our lives. We owe Matthew McFadden an awful lot, don't we, love?'

Mary moved restlessly in his embrace, and he got the hint. Before she could speak he continued, 'And Mary's father was also very generous to us. He gave Mary enough money to pay the bond and there's enough left over to buy some bits and pieces of furniture. So we have indeed been very lucky in one way or another.' He dropped a kiss on his wife's head.

Mary relaxed. She wanted her father's generosity to be known and appreciated. She nodded to another door. 'That door leads out to the yard. A lot of space has been taken up with the bathroom being built, but I can live with that. There's enough room for a clothes line for the baby's nappies and wee clothes and that's all that matters. Have you time for a cuppa? Please say yes, Louise. I'm all newlyfangled in here.'

'I'd love a cup of tea, thank you. And this time I intend

to take time to sit down and enjoy it. I've been down to the Royal Hospital to see Conor O'Rourke and I want to tell you all about him. After the way I've behaved, I'm sure you thought I was going away in the head, so you both deserve a full explanation.'

She told them everything: how she had gone out with Conor on a few dates and had fallen in love with him. How he had professed to love her in return and had asked her to marry him. Then his mother had intervened. Mrs O'Rourke didn't think a mill girl was good enough for her son and insisted on his going over to Birmingham to meet the father he had never known, and Conor had come back a changed man and broken it off with her.

Mary was almost moved to tears at this sad saga. 'Did he not say why he had changed his mind about you?'

Louise shook her head sadly. Then she came to attention, and with a wide spread of the hands to show that this was all of no consequence she said, 'Actually, all that is neither here nor there. The only reason I told you my sad love story is because I want you to know why Conor was beaten up. Cathie Morgan met and fell for a Protestant lad and she wanted my opinion of him. So while Conor was away I made up a foursome with this Trevor and his mate George. I could see that Cathie doted on Trevor and I tried to talk her out of seeing him again, because I didn't think there was any future in it for her. But Cathie is easily carried away. She can't see any further than her own nose and she's been going out with Trevor four or five times a week. Now I know that Conor is not a person to listen to rumours, but I imagine when he heard that Cathie was being discussed in certain circles and was to be kept under observation, he just couldn't ignore the warning signs. As far as Conor was aware I was also seeing a Protestant so he assumed that I was also being watched. As it happened I *was* seeing George last Saturday night and Conor followed me down to warn me off. Sure enough, there were these three lads, strangers, hanging about outside the pub at the corner of McQuillen Street. Even before Conor arrived, I noticed that they did seem to be paying special attention to George's car, which was waiting by Dunville Park to pick me up. Conor crossed the road with me and spoke to George, whilst I continued on down Grosvenor Road as if I didn't know them. They must have twigged that Conor was warning Cathie off, and that's why he's now lying in the Royal with a busted face and damaged kidneys.'

Mary's eyes stood in her head and a hand covered her mouth in anguish. Surely her brother, bad and all as he was, wouldn't take part in anything as contemptible and low down as this, and she opened her mouth to say so. She was saved from any indiscretion by the bell, as it were, only in this instance it was a loud knock on the door heralding the arrival of Mary's parents.

Sadie greeted Louise and Johnnie, then embraced her daughter. 'You certainly kept *me* in the dark about all this, didn't you, girl?' Her eyes rested resentfully on Louise and she added reproachfully, 'Did everybody else know what was going on?'

'No, Ma.' Sensing her mother was deeply hurt, Mary looked to her father for help and he intervened on her behalf. 'Mary wanted everything to be signed and sealed before she said anything about this house. As I've already told you, Sadie, the first I knew of it was when she asked me to get the loan of Joe McGurk's cart to move her furniture.' He lied convincingly and was believed with an 'Oh, I see'.

Taking her mother by the arm, Mary said gently, 'Come and see the kitchen, Ma.'

Sadie glanced around her in bewilderment. 'It's very nice, love.'

Mary went all posh. 'No, Mother, this is our *living* room. The kitchen's in here.'

Listening to all the exclamations of pleasure and delight coming from the kitchen and bathroom, Mick caught Johnnie's eye. 'Thanks, Johnnie. See and keep her happy, now.'

'I will, Mick. That's a promise.'

Embarrassed, Louise quickly drained her cup and set it to one side. 'I'll have to be going now. Good night, Mr Gilmore. Good night, Johnnie. Say good night to Mary and her mother for me.'

'I'll walk you to the corner, sis. I won't be long, Mick. Make yourself at home.'

Louise was sincere in her congratulations. 'That's a beautiful house you've got there, Johnnie. You can be proud of yourself.'

'I feel so ashamed. Everything's going my way and me ma causing you so much grief. And now this business with Conor O'Rourke. It's awful. Who do you think's behind the beating?'

'Who knows? There are some bigoted people about. On the other hand some people can hold a grudge and take their revenge when they get a chance.'

He gave her a sideways glance. 'You don't really think Liam had anything to do with it, do you?'

They had reached the corner. 'You needn't come any further, Johnnie. Go back and entertain your in-laws. As for Liam Gilmore . . . well, I for one think he's capable of anything. And I think you do too. He's as sly as a fox, that one. But there's nothing we can do about it. I suppose he'll get his comeuppance one day. Good night, Johnnie.'

'Good night, Louise.' Johnnie retraced his steps. His sister was right. He *did* think Liam was capable of . . . if not actually doing the deed himself, then organising someone else to do his dirty work. He could only hope that was the end of it. If anyone laid so much as a finger on Louise, he wouldn't rest until he had got *his* revenge and that could ruin a lot of lives and maybe land him in prison.

Louise was about to cross the road when a tram stopped nearby and Harry, Peggy and Hannah tumbled from the platform. Her brother and Hannah were laughing at something they obviously thought very funny but Peggy didn't appear to agree with them. She looked bored.

They greeted Louise, and after engaging her in some small talk Harry said he would see Hannah safely up the Springfield Road to her home. The two sisters walked up the street in silence.

To bring Peggy out of her apparent gloom, Louise asked, 'Was the film any good?'

'Not bad.'

'You sound a bit glum. Is anything wrong?'

'It's our Harry. I think he's taken a shine to Hannah and she's my best friend. I hope that doesn't mean he'll want to come out with us all the time.'

Louise laughed at the very idea of Harry fancying Hannah McFadden. 'I hope not! Her da would never hear tell of it.'

'I wouldn't be too sure of that. He didn't object when Harry asked if he could take her out tonight. Mr McFadden made it clear that I'd have to go along as well, like a blooming chaperon! But still, he agreed. So what do you think of that?'

'Not much. But I'd be inclined to think it's a one off.'

They had arrived home and, pushing open the vestibule door, Peggy said, 'Hi, Da,' bringing the conversation to a close.

Tommy was sitting close to the fire, a long toasting fork in his hand, a thick slice of bread on it thrust close to the bright embers. Peggy's bad mood mellowed. 'That smells lovely, Da. Any chance of toasting a piece for me while you're at it?'

'Why not? Cut some more bread and then add more water to the teapot and get the cups ready.' He was smiling and genial. 'Would you like some toast, Louise?'

The smell coming from the toasting bread assailed Louise's nostrils, making her feel peckish. 'I wouldn't mind a slice, Da, thank you. While Peggy gets the cups ready, I'll give you a hand. I'll just wash my hands first.' She washed her hands at the sink and, fetching the other toasting fork, stuck a slice of bread on the prongs and joined her father at the fire.

'This is nice and cosy, eh, Louise?'

Louise stole a sideways covert glance at her father to see if he was taking the mick. But no, he appeared to be quite serious. Well, if her da thought that sitting together in front of the fire burning a couple of slices of bread made everything all right, he'd another thought coming to him. But it didn't do to kick a gift horse in the face, and with a nod she agreed with him.

At lunchtime next day Louise hurried home. She intended calling in to see Conor during her lunch-break, then she would have an excuse not to delay too long. Not for one minute did she think that Cissie O'Rourke would leave her alone with her son, so if it became unbearable trying to make conversation with Cissie hovering about and glowering at her, she would be able to take her leave without upsetting Conor. She had got up very early that morning and had a thorough wash down and washed her hair before the others came down. Glad that her da was on the early shift and she had the house to herself this lunchtime, she changed out of her work clothes and quickly brushed her hair until it sprang like a halo around her head. It was the only attractive thing about her at the moment. Her face was pale, with dark rings round her eyes and a pronounced droop at the corner of her mouth. She examined her reflection in the mirror and practised smiling at her image, but no matter how hard she tried it looked more like a grimace. She'd have to remember to at least try to soften her features a bit or Conor wouldn't find her very attractive.

Suddenly, she sat down at the table and buried her face in her hands. What was she thinking of? It didn't matter what she looked like. Conor wasn't interested in her any more. Without further ado, she grabbed her coat and left the house in a hurry, before she was tempted to try to enhance her appearance further.

It was Conor who answered her knock and motioned her into the kitchen. It was empty and she darted a furtive glance towards the scullery, but there was no sign of Cissie. Conor answered the question in her eyes. He spoke carefully so as not to put any strain on the stitches in his still swollen lip. 'Ma has gone out for an hour or so to do some shopping. I imagine she thought, as I did, that you would call in tonight. Boy is she in for a surprise.'

Louise's eyes twinkled at the idea of it as she observed, 'And of course she's gone out especially to get something nice for a cup of tea.'

He tried to smile in return but obviously found it too

painful. 'I suppose you could think that, if you didn't know better. Here, give me your coat.' His words were slow and cautious as he favoured his badly bruised mouth.

She was glad that she had taken the trouble to wear her best dress as she shrugged out of her coat and handed it to him. 'I can't stay long. I've to go back to work.'

He hung her coat on the stand and headed for the scullery, signalling with his hands that he would make some tea.

'No. I've already had something,' she lied. 'Come and talk to me.'

He sat down and she observed, 'You don't look quite as bad today, thank God.'

His one good eye looked intently at her and then he reached for a pen and notepad that sat nearby. Quickly he scribbled on the pad and turned it for her to read. *Have been warned not to burst any more stitches or I could be scarred for life, so please bear with me.* When she would have shown her anguish he stopped her with a raised hand and continued to write. *Have you given any thought to what I said about going out a couple of times a week, to keep them off your back?*

'There's no need to do that. I told you so. I've nothing to hide, and I won't be seeing George again. I don't think I'll be of any interest to anyone. Look, I'm not here to talk about George. How are *you*?'

More scribbling. *On the mend. I'll be fine, don't worry about me. I'll be out and about in no time at all.*

She examined his face. Although his eye was not as swollen as it had been, it was now multicoloured with reds and yellows and purples, and his bottom lip still looked like raw liver. 'You still look awful. Not quite as bad as yesterday, but you wouldn't top my list in the beauty stakes.' Her voice broke on a sob. 'Oh, God, I'm so, so sorry, Conor. I've brought you nothing but trouble. You must be sorry you ever asked me out.'

She had chosen to sit on a chair. He was on the sofa. He patted the space beside him and motioned her over.

Tentatively, she left the chair and sat beside him, careful to leave a small gap between them.

He tried to smile and wrote, *Don't worry. I won't bite. Even if I could.*

Liam Gilmore had said those same words to her and she had wanted to hit him, but she hastened to reassure Conor. 'I know you would never deliberately hurt me, Conor.' She sighed. 'But these things happen. If I could just understand why! I feel so much in the dark. I just don't know what's going on, or how I'm expected to react. I'm at my wits' end trying to work out what went wrong between us.'

See me a couple of nights a week and I'll not have to worry about you getting hurt.

'But there's no need for you to go to all that trouble. I've already told you, I won't be seeing George again.' She reached out and gently laid her hand on his cheek. 'Is it very painful?'

He nodded and got busy with the pen. *Two hands might make it feel better. And I can assure you it wouldn't be any trouble at all. I'd be delighted to take you out again.*

She smiled and cupped his face in both her hands and looked into his one good eye. 'I wish I could be of some use to you.'

He abandoned the pen, and said carefully, 'Just meet me now and again, Louise. I've decided there is nothing to keep me here if I can't at least have you as my friend.'

Her hands left his face and she stifled her alarm. 'Where would you go?' She grabbed the pen and thrust it into his hand. 'And for heaven's sake write. I'll get the blame if you're disfigured for life.'

He obeyed her. *My father has offered to help me with my career if I go over to live with him in Birmingham.*

'What about your exams?'

I would have to stay here and take them first. I'll have to study hard and make sure I pass them.

Louise was gobsmacked. Never to see him again, how would she be able to bear it? She endeavoured to hide her dismay and just appear interested. 'What does your mother think of all this?'

She doesn't believe I'll do it. I wish I could kiss you, Louise. Do you think you could give me a little peck?

'It might hurt.' She gently touched his lips with hers. 'Was that very sore?'

Not a bit. Would you like to do it again?

She complied and said, 'It wouldn't work, Conor. There's no way we can be just kissing friends.' She laughed as she added, 'Especially with your mouth in that condition.'

The laughter lit up her face and looking at her now glowing features, the bright sapphire blue eyes sparkling, he came to a decision, and wrote, *When I'm better I'll explain everything to you, what brought about the change in me, and we'll take it from there. See what you think. OK? You mightn't want to know me when you hear what I've got to say.*

She voiced her fears. 'You haven't met someone else, then?'

No I haven't. There has never been anyone but you.

'Oh, thank God!' She kissed his poor mouth again, very gently. He needed no more encouragement, and dropping pen and paper he gathered her close, pressing his cheek to her hair and whispering endearments to her.

So engrossed were they in each other, they didn't hear Cissie at the door. She was in the kitchen before they had time to draw apart.

'And just what do you two think you're doing?'

'What does it look like?' Conor decided to shock her. 'Although not as much as I would like, Mother, but Louise is a good Catholic girl and I love her, so I'll just have to curb my emotions and wait until we're married.' He winced as indignation made him talk too fast.

'You haven't told her about your father, then?'

He spoke carefully. 'No, I haven't. But that is something I intend to put right very soon.'

'Huh! You'll not see her heels for the dust when she hears what you have to tell her,' Cissie said scornfully.

Not wanting Cissie to burst her bubble of euphoria, Louise quickly intervened. 'I'll have to go now, Conor, or I'll be late for work.'

Rising, he got her coat from the rack and held it ready for her. She slipped her arms into the sleeves and all the while she could feel Cissie's eyes burning resentfully into her back. Giving Louise a quick hug Conor led her into the hall. 'I'll pick you up tonight at seven, all right?'

Louise couldn't believe the difference a few words from Conor could make to her troubled mind. Suddenly, all was right with her world. He hadn't met another girl after all and he still loved her, and he was going to explain why he had changed so much. A shadow of doubt crossed her mind. Could he? Could he really put things right between them? She had been devastated by his behaviour. And what did his mother mean when she said Conor wouldn't see her heels for dust when he explained about his father? Was he a murderer? A rapist? Surely not! Still, it had to be something very serious to make his mother keep him and his father apart all those years.

Whatever it was, would it change her feelings for Conor? She doubted it. A fervent prayer was sent heavenward as she hurried home to change back into her work clothes. She would have to be patient and wait to hear what Conor had to say tonight and then see how she felt towards him. It was going to be a very long afternoon.

11

That afternoon Bill McCartney sought Louise out again. She looked so pleased with herself as he squinted down his nose at her that he observed wryly, 'You look like someone who's lost a penny and found a half-crown.'

The knowledge that Conor still loved her was all that Louise could think about and she felt so happy she actually found herself beaming at Bill and asking pleasantly, 'Can I do anything for you, Bill?'

Somewhat taken aback, he said, 'Nora's not feeling very well, so she hasn't come in to work today. She was wondering if—'

Louise's sense of well-being faded slightly as she digested these words. She interrupted him. 'What's wrong with her? Is she very bad?'

'No, nothing to worry about. It's nothing serious,' he quickly assured her. 'She just felt a bit under the weather and I made her stay in bed, take a rest, that's all. She wants to know if you can meet her tonight? She has something she wants to discuss with you.'

The casual way he spoke of her mother in bed brought unwanted thoughts to her mind that filled Louise with revulsion, but when he finished speaking she actually sagged against the loom as relief flooded through her. She felt jubilant. To her, this could mean only one thing: her mother was coming home. Everything would be back to normal soon. What else could she want to discuss with Louise? She must have realised just how disruptive her immoral behaviour was for the rest of the family and decided to come home to them. Overjoyed, she voiced her thoughts. 'Is she coming home, then? Does she want me to break the ice with me da? Is that it?' she asked excitedly.

Bill blinked rapidly, and he drew his head back as if confused at her reckoning. 'No, I don't think that's likely to happen. But look, why not meet her and find out for yourself what she has to say?'

Louise's euphoria dipped somewhat dramatically as she confessed, 'I'm sorry, Bill. I can't possibly meet her tonight. You see, I've a big date on. I can see her here in work tomorrow, if you like. I could slip up to the spinning room for a short while when the boss is on his tea-break, or I could meet her wherever she wants tomorrow night.'

'Definitely not in this place. There's something she wants to discuss with you in private, without her work-mates snooping about trying to hear what's going on. I watched out for you at lunchtime but there was no sign of you. You must have got away right and quick.'

'I did; I was in a mad rush. I had to meet someone urgently. It was important. Look, tonight is also impor-tant to me; will tomorrow night do? Or better still, tomorrow at lunchtime. Me da's on the early shift, so she could come down to the house with me for a bite to eat. There'll be no one else there.'

He shrugged doubtfully. 'I can't see her doing that.

There's bound to be speculation among your neighbours if they see Nora going into the house with you. You know what they're like, they don't miss a trick. She'll want to avoid giving them anything more to talk about. Nora's a very brave woman, but all this has gotten to her. Still, I'll ask her.' He smiled as if at some happy thought. 'She's full of surprises, is your mother. But I must say I'm disappointed in you, Louise. This must be somebody very important you're meeting tonight. I actually thought you'd be falling over yourself to hear what your mother has to say. Anyway, I'll let you know what she intends to do.' With an abrupt nod of farewell he headed off down the weaving shop.

All this was watched avidly by her fellow workers, who immediately busied themselves when Bill moved off, trying to appear not in the least interested in the saga unfolding before them. Realising they would have seen her smiling and having an apparently cosy conversation with Bill, Louise threw them a big grin of delight before devoting all her attention to her looms. Now, *that* would give them something to wonder and fret over. They'd be in a tizzy trying to figure out how they could find out what was happening without appearing to be too nosy. Since their last endeavours to hear what was going on hadn't borne any fruit, she didn't think Kitty would be nominated or even have the cheek to approach her again, and she was right. The afternoon passed uneventfully, and although she was aware of the covert looks and miming going on when her back was turned, she managed to ignore them completely. Convinced that her mother was coming home, she couldn't contain her happiness. First Conor wanting to meet her; now her mother! Everything was going to be all right! Still, to avoid tempting fate she crossed her fingers.

Her looms ran smoothly. There were no breaks in the weft or warp to create any distractions, and as she worked automatically, going from one loom to the other, changing shuttles, watching out for the red dye mark that would herald the end of a cut, she dreamed the rest of the afternoon away, planning what she would wear for her big date with Conor. Cooking the dinner as well as getting ready to go out was going to be a problem, she realised. She would have to make it clear to the others beforehand that she intended to be first into the scullery after dinner, and not to wash dishes either! Harry and Peggy, now that they were both earning a wage, were going out most nights, leaving her to clear up. Nevertheless, they would have to attend to the dishes later. *She* would be preparing to go out on *her* date.

When the matter was put to them, Harry quickly championed her. 'There'll be no problem there, sis. You take as long as you like in the scullery. If necessary, I'll do the washing up on my own when you're finished,' he asserted virtuously.

Peggy's head shot up. 'That's great, Harry, 'cause I'm going out tonight, but I promise I'll do them tomorrow night, honest.'

He turned a frown on her. 'Where are you going?'

His sister smiled sweetly at him. 'I'm going to the Diamond with Hannah.'

Harry scowled. 'Out two nights in a row? And to the Diamond, of all places? Hannah never mentioned it last night.' He sounded resentful.

'And why should she say anything to *you*? It's none of your business. Anyway, I warned her not to. I don't want you hanging around with us every time we go out, and neither does she.'

'Did Hannah say that?'

Peggy shrugged. 'She didn't have to. I know she doesn't want you following us everywhere we go.'

'You know nothing of the kind. Hannah and I get on great together.' He smiled smugly. 'Very well, as a matter of fact.'

'Hah! You're deluding yourself. Dream on.'

It was his turn to shrug. 'I'm for the Diamond tonight anyway. I'll probably see you there.'

Peggy actually gaped at him. Harry didn't like the Diamond picture house. Now she muttered, 'Over my dead body.'

'What's that you said?'

She was all wide-eyed innocence when she replied, 'It'll be a rush for you to get ready. But thanks for offering to do the dishes.'

Whilst making her plans, Louise hadn't considered her father, who never came in at a regular time. Usually he came home when the rest of them had finished eating and she had to keep his dinner warm in the oven, so she assumed that she would be finished in the scullery before he came in. But not today, of course. Oh, no! Today of all days he came in as they were finishing their meal, and with a few words about the weather sat down at the table, waiting to be served. Louise scowled resentfully at the way he was beginning to take her for granted but hadn't time to start a fight with him about it. Quickly she retrieved his plate from the oven and set it none too gently in front of him. With a grunt of thanks, he lifted his knife and fork, and wolfed the lot down in double quick time.

'That was very nice, Louise. At least we won't starve if your mother doesn't come back, eh? You're becoming a fine wee cook, girl.' Then, before she could explain the situation or raise any objections, he lifted his plate and cutlery, something he rarely did, and carried them through to the scullery, announcing as he went, 'I'm going out early tonight and I need to occupy the scullery for about fifteen minutes or so. Is that all right with you?' Not waiting for an answer, he closed and bolted the door after him.

Fuming, Louise noisily stacked all the other dishes at one end of the table, watched by a subdued brother and sister who knew better than to interfere. It wasn't fair! Her da was sure to use the kettle of water she had simmering on the back burner. He had better not use her towel or precious soap, which she had left out ready for her ablutions, or she wouldn't be responsible for her actions. At this rate she'd never be ready when Conor called at seven o'clock and she had no intention of inviting him in to wait.

Unable to bear his sister's obvious distress any longer, Harry tried to pacify her. 'Who're you going out with who's so important, sis? Surely he won't mind waiting for you?' he reasoned.

'He's coming to the house at seven and I want to be ready to walk out when he comes. I don't want to bring him in and give me da an opportunity to grill him.'

Suddenly alert, Peggy exclaimed, 'Is it Conor O'Rourke you're going out with? Do you want me to run down and tell him to wait at the corner, Louise?' She rose, ready for action.

'No! No, I don't. When me da's finished in there, just stay out of my way. OK?'

Harry was gazing at her in awe. 'You're going out with Conor O'Rourke?'

'What about it? Have you any objections?'

'No.' He paused for some seconds, then said tentatively, 'Do you know he was beaten up at the weekend?'

'Yes, I know all about that, thank you.'

The scullery door opened. With an angry glare, Louise hurried past her father, checked that her towel and soap had not been used and that he had put the kettle on to boil again, then bolted the door and started to undress.

Tommy stood open-mouthed looking balefully at the door. 'What's the matter with her?' he growled.

Harry and Peggy knew better than to tell him, so they remained quiet.

Tommy disappeared into the wee room, and keeping his voice low Harry leaned forward in his chair and questioned his sister. 'Did you know Louise was dating Conor O'Rourke, Peggy?'

'I knew she went out with him a few times. She was the envy of all the girls round here, but I thought it was all over between them. And you know what she's like. I didn't dare ask her about it. She'd have told me to mind my own business.'

Her brother looked bemused. He greatly admired Conor. The older lad was all that Harry aspired to. He envied Conor the chance he was getting to make something worthwhile of himself. Wished that he'd been smart enough to win a scholarship to St Malachy's College. But then, would his da have let him go? He was doubtful. There would still have been the uniform and text books to buy. 'Well I never,' he muttered. 'Wonders will never cease. Conor O'Rourke and our Louise. Who'd have thought it?'

Peggy didn't know what he was going on about, nor did she care. She was preoccupied with thoughts of Hannah. Her very best friend ever! One thing she did know. If she had anything to do with it, Harry would never get to know Hannah any better, not if she could help it.

* * *

By cutting corners in her preparations, Louise did manage to be ready in time to walk out of the door when Conor arrived on the dot of seven, for which she was profoundly thankful. With hindsight she realised she should have insisted on meeting him at Dunville Park as usual. Now was not a good time to introduce him to her family. First she needed to know what dreadful news Conor had to tell her about his father; didn't want to jump the gun before she knew how things stood between them and what exactly lay ahead for them.

When she went to answer his knock she was aware that her da, who much to her indignation was still hovering about in spite of taking over the scullery to get away early, moved to the window to peer through the nets to see who was at the door. He'd be surprised to see it was Conor. She didn't doubt for one minute that he had already heard that Conor had been the target of a cruel beating. He would probably also have a fairly good idea who the perpetrators were. It would have been a major topic of conversation over pints in the pub. The local lads would all want to know what Conor had done to deserve such treatment.

Her da would be only too delighted to be the one to put them in the picture, if possible. When he recognised the caller, he turned sharply from the window, a surprised look on his face, but was too late to apprehend Louise. With a brief farewell she was up and out of the door.

Tommy stood for some moments wondering if Conor O'Rourke was dating his daughter. If so, he must make it his business to find out just how O'Rourke had managed to pull the wrath of the wrong people down on his head. If Louise was indeed dating the lad, he needed to know who was gunning for him, and why. He certainly didn't get that kicking for nothing. He debated whether to question Harry and Peggy but decided against it. Even if they knew anything they wouldn't dare tell him for fear of incensing their sister.

As they walked down the street Conor took hold of Louise's hand and tucking it under his elbow pressed it close to his side. 'You look absolutely lovely,' he said carefully through bruised lips.

Louise was relieved to see that it didn't seem to hurt him so much now to talk and gave his arm a sympathetic squeeze. 'Thank you. But I don't feel it. It's awful in our house at the minute. Everything's such a shambles. I don't know how my mother put up with it all those years. I never realised before just how much work is involved in looking after five adults and doing all the housework, and cooking every meal for them. And on top of all that she had to go out to work as well. And not one word of thanks did she ever get for her trouble. My mother was to be admired, and instead we all took her for granted. It's such a shame that we didn't show our appreciation.'

'But then,' Conor reasoned, 'that's a woman's role, isn't it? Looking after the house while the man goes out to work, and . . .' His voice tailed off at the withering look she turned on him.

'It shouldn't be! A lot of women go out to work too, through necessity! I just said that *my* mother goes out to work. A man should do his share of setting up a home and keeping it nice. I would certainly expect my husband to pull his weight round the house.'

Suitably chastened, he tried to change the subject. 'Is there any sign of your mother changing her mind and returning to the fold?'

'I don't know. She wants to meet me, probably

tomorrow night, and I'm hoping that she's planning to come home. She'll want to be sure that me da won't object, since she didn't rush back at the weekend the way he ordered her to. Maybe she wants me to pave the way for her, as it were.'

'What if he gets on his high horse and gives her more ultimatums?'

'Don't you worry. This time we'll all gang up on him. Warn him of the consequences if he doesn't play ball and welcome her back with open arms.'

They were approaching his house and she tried to wiggle her hand free from his hold, but he pressed it closer still to his body. 'My mother will have to get used to seeing us together.' Realising that he was being presumptuous, he paused and glanced down at her. 'That is if you still want to be my girl, when you've heard what I have to say.' They had reached the corner and he drew her to a standstill. Her mouth opened to question him but he forestalled her. 'Later. We'll talk later. My mouth's still quite sore and I'd like to be sitting down before I get stuck in to explanations. It might take some time. I don't want my lip to start bleeding again. Where would you like to go?'

She thought for some seconds. 'Well, it's such a lovely evening, why don't we get a tram up to the Falls Park? It will be more private there.'

His face cleared. 'That sounds good to me. It would be a sin to waste this good weather.'

They walked to the Springfield junction and caught a tram up the Falls Road. Louise was in a daze of happy anticipation, but still apprehensive about what she might hear. She couldn't imagine anything bad enough to stop her wanting to be Conor's girl, but she would feel easier when she knew what was on his mind. And the sooner she knew the better.

They travelled right to the end of the line and entered the park through the top gate, where a stream rippled over age-worn stones in a vale of tranquillity. It was a spot where she had spent many happy childhood afternoons paddling in the water with her sister and brothers. The sun was a fiery orb low in the western sky, bathing the park in a warm glow. The trees, stirred by a slight breeze, were a breathtaking sight silhouetted against a sky awash with pinks and reds from the waning sun.

The park was packed with people taking advantage of the fine weather to meet old friends, and make new ones: mothers pushing prams and fathers with toddlers perched on their shoulders or kicking balls about with them; teenagers covertly eyeing the local talent, some giving each other the come-on signs. Watching the young families, Louise wondered if one day in the not too distant future she and Conor might marry and have children. He caught her eye and smiled. Embarrassed that he might have somehow read her thoughts, she blushed as bright as the evening sky.

They chose a secluded spot close by the river and sat down. Without more ado, Conor reached for her hand and clung on to it, preparing to confess his terrible secret. He hadn't a clue where to start. His mind was churning, unable to find words that would save him from losing too much face should she refuse his offer of marriage. How did one say, 'Oh, by the way, I hope it won't make any difference to you, but you see I've discovered I'm a bastard, but I do love you and want to marry you'? Especially as her answer was so important to him.

Before they had time to settle into conversation, distant music came to their ears, the sounds of a band tuning up. They turned and looked at each other in wonder. Conor laughed. 'You know, for a minute there I thought

I was hearing things. That it was all in my mind because I'm so happy to be here with you.'

Louise blushed yet again, at the magnitude of such a compliment. 'How lovely. I didn't realise the band was playing this evening.' Conor didn't know whether her comment was in answer to his remark, or about the music.

They smiled at each other, then by silent, mutual consent abandoned their selected spot by the river and headed for the centre of the park where the bandstand was, Conor thankful to have been reprieved for a while. They found a comfortable place at the base of an old gnarled oak tree. The branches swept low and gave them a certain amount of privacy. They were still quite close to the bandstand and could see the musicians in their red coats with gold-braided trappings and brass buttons reflecting the dying rays of the sun. Arms wrapped round each other, they settled down to listen to the band, swaying to the rhythm as it started playing a jazz number that set young ones dancing with abandon, then listening in hushed quiet to slow melancholy airs.

The bandsmen played non-stop for about an hour; then, after long, appreciative applause, and shouts of 'Encore! Encore!', they played for another fifteen minutes before packing away their instruments.

With a contented sigh, Louise turned her gaze on Conor and gave him her full attention. 'Now, I don't think you can put it off any longer. Surely it can't be all that bad, Conor?' A dejected shake of the head answered her and she said, 'All right, let me try to guess then . . . did you discover that your father is just out of prison?'

Startled that she could even contemplate such a thing, he cried, 'Good God, no! Whatever made you think of that?'

378

'Well, that's a relief. Here was me thinking he must have served time for murder or rape, or something just as bad, the way you're getting on.'

'No, thank God. Nothing as bad as that.' A slight smile broke the sombre lines of his battered face. 'You're right. I suppose it could be a lot worse.'

A smile of delight wreathed her face as yet another thought struck her. Bigamy! She sat upright and clapped her hands with delight at the thought. 'Don't tell me he married your mother bigamously?' She waited with bated breath at the very idea that such a fate could have befallen haughty Cissie O'Rourke.

His lips twitched. 'You really don't like my mother, do you?' She raised one brow but didn't comment. He continued, 'But no, he didn't. But you're on the right track. As a matter of fact he didn't marry her at all.'

He watched while she turned what he had said over in her mind. He could practically read every word as it sank in. Saw her eyes widen as realisation dawned. Before she could voice her thoughts he said, 'That's right. I'm a bastard.' The very word and the sound of it rolling off his tongue made him cringe inwardly with shame, but his chin rose defiantly. Would she send him packing?

She blinked several times in confusion. 'Forgive me . . .' Her head swayed from side to side as she continued, 'I'm all mixed up. What possible difference does it make to us whether you're illegitimate or not?'

The tense look left his eyes and his features relaxed slightly. Then a slow grin started to spread across his face, until he remembered his stitched lip and quickly straightened his expression. 'You mean you would actually consider marrying a *bastard*? A man without a proper name?'

She gazed at him in befuddled amazement for so long

that he couldn't wait any longer and said, 'Well . . . I'm asking you to marry me, Louise McGuigan. Will you or won't you?'

'Conor O'Rourke, I'm completely astounded at you. How could you have imagined for one single minute that a little thing like that could ever make any difference to me, eh? Come here, you big fool.'

He moved closer but hesitantly confessed, 'I don't even have my father's name, remember. O'Rourke is my mother's family name.'

'O'Rourke sounds good enough to me.'

'There's more.'

She frowned and again flailed about in her mind trying to work out what else he could possibly have to tell her, but drew a blank. 'What else?'

'I've two half-brothers and a half-sister.'

The frown vanished and her face shone with delight. 'Why, that's wonderful! Weren't you happy to learn that?' His face had closed up again and she was apprehensive. 'Are you disappointed? Don't you like them? Have you never wanted to be part of a family, Conor? Is that it?' She realised that she was babbling and pressed her lips together to stem the flow of words and give him a chance to answer.

'To tell you the truth, Louise, I don't know what to think about it all,' he confessed. 'It's not the same as growing up with brothers and sisters, you know. It's strange when they're just suddenly there and you don't recognise them, have no idea what they're like and wonder if you'll like them and what they'll think of you. I nearly died when my father mentioned taking me to meet the rest of the family. You see, my mother had always led me to believe that she and I were alone in the world. That my father had abandoned us and wanted nothing to do with me. That she had no other living relatives. Lies, all lies!' His bitterness at his mother's deception spilled over.

'And what had your father to say about that?' Louise asked gently.

'Well, he said he was between a rock and a hard place and had to go along with what his wife wanted. He was convinced that I knew all about my mother's family. Said from what he had heard about them they seemed like nice, decent people. He was under the impression that I had some kind of family life. He sent photographs over of my brothers and sister and himself, assuming that my mother would show them to me, keep me up to date on how they were all faring over in England. He was very annoyed to learn that she hadn't done so. He also let slip that my mother has family connections in Lisburn.'

'Lisburn? Our Lisburn, as in Lisburn, County Antrim?' she repeated, astonished. He nodded and she continued, 'So close, and she never once told you about them? What on earth was she thinking about?'

'Not a word. Why, I might even have rubbed shoulders with them in town without knowing who they were.'

Sensing his disappointment at all the wasted years, Louise said gently, 'She was probably afraid of losing you. There must have been a very good reason why her family didn't keep in touch.'

'Oh, there was a reason all right. A bloody good one! They've no idea where she is. They don't even know she's still in Belfast. They think she's living it up in sin over in Birmingham with my father. Her mother, my grannie, died when she was young, and when he heard she was carrying on with a married man her father disowned her. That must be why she chose a house in the heart of the Falls. I often wondered why she rarely goes into town.

Because of her lies, her life has been very restricted. Imagine cutting yourself off from your own family and friends because you were too proud to admit that the father of your child had abandoned you.'

Louise's mouth drooped. 'Oh . . . how sad.' And she really did feel sorry for her 'arch enemy'.

'She deprived me not only of a father but of a grandfather as well. I feel so frustrated. It would have been great to have had a man in my life when I was growing up. Someone I could have turned to in times of trouble. Man to man. You know what I mean.'

'She does appear to have a lot to answer for. But remember, Conor, if she had elected to live in Lisburn, I might never have met you. I suppose I've a lot to be thankful for.'

'I never thought of it that way.' He gathered her close and winced when she accidentally bumped against his lip.

'Oh, I'm sorry, love. I'm so sorry.' She gently touched his face as if her fingers could work a miracle and take the pain away.

'I wish this lip would get better. It's such a nuisance. How can you bear to look at my ugly face?' he grumbled.

'With little difficulty.' She blushed fiercely and added shyly, 'I think you're the most handsome man in Belfast.'

'Just Belfast?' he teased.

She couldn't believe that she had just said that, and still blushing furiously at her confession she said, 'That will have to do for the moment. I haven't been much further afield, you know. I suppose when I do, I might change my opinion of you.'

He hugged her closer. 'Don't even joke about anything like that.'

They lost all track of time and the park was quite

empty when they at last made their way down to the tram stop.

Tommy was sitting by the fireside, toasting some bread, when she got home just before curfew time. This could become a habit, she thought. Why couldn't he have been like this when Ma needed some companionship, instead of being a surly auld git all the time? Her sister was in the scullery and by the sound of it was brewing the tea. Strange how Peggy and her father were becoming so close. If this kept up they'd be getting wee hats the same, she joked inwardly.

There was no sign of her brother; no sounds from upstairs. 'Harry's cutting it fine, isn't he?' she said to no one in particular.

Peggy's voice, full of annoyance, reached her from the scullery. 'Oh, wouldn't you know! Although I tried to put him off going to the Clonard tonight by telling him we were going to the Diamond, there he was, big and ugly as life, at the Clonard. He probably checked the queues to make sure that's where we really intended going. Him and that daft Desi McMahon stuck to us like plasters all evening. Now he's walking Hannah home. He shouldn't be much longer.'

Tommy's ears pricked up. 'Is that Hannah McFadden you're talking about?'

'The very same.'

'But isn't she—'

Peggy's head appeared round the scullery door in defence of her friend. 'No she's *not*, Da. There's nothing wrong with Hannah that getting away from her parents once in a while won't cure. Some parents have a lot to answer for,' she added, and shot a sly look directly at him. Louise waited for her da to reprimand Peggy but

383

he just gave her a sad little smile and shook his head. Strange! Wonders will never cease, she thought.

Hanging her coat on the rack, Louise silently acknowledged and welcomed the growing camaraderie between her sister and her father. It was nice to see. It would make things a lot easier all round should the unthinkable happen and her mother not come back. She pulled the stool close to the fire and sat down.

Her father wagged the toasting fork towards a plate of bread already toasted and keeping warm on the range. 'Would you like some toast, Louise?'

'Yes, I would. I am feeling a bit peckish. I'll have a couple of slices, if you don't mind.'

Looking pleased with himself, he said, 'Get another cup ready, Peggy.'

The vestibule door opened and Harry took in the situation at a glance. 'Will you make that another two cups, Peggy, please?' he shouted cheerfully.

Louise carried the plate of warm toast into the scullery and buttered it. She smiled as Peggy quietly ranted on about the cheek of her brother, finishing her tirade with, 'And the worst part of it is . . . in my heart I think that Hannah really likes him.'

Louise smothered a smile and said solemnly, 'I don't think you need worry too much. I think it will soon peter out. I'm sure Mr McFadden will have other plans for his daughter. And I can't see them including our Harry. Can you?'

Peggy still looked doubtful. 'You reckon?'

'I reckon. So stop sulking and let's go in and enjoy our tea in comfort. It isn't every night that me da's in such a good mood. Besides, what's wrong with Desi McMahon? He seems a fine young lad to me. Don't you fancy him?'

A grunt and a grimace was all the answer she received, but Louise smiled inwardly when she noticed a tinge of pink creep up her young sister's cheeks. As she sat savouring the hot buttered toast and tea, she debated whether or not to pass on the good news that she thought her mother would be coming home soon. She ran the pros and cons over in her mind but, not wanting to tempt fate, decided against it. Better to be sure before she said anything. She eyed her father. 'You're up late, Da. Considering you're on the early shift.'

'I wanted to have a word with you.'

'Me?'

'Yes, you. How long have you been seeing Conor O'Rourke?'

Louise objected to his tone of voice and straightened to attention. 'Why do you want to know?' she parried.

'Because he's rubbing the wrong people up the wrong way, if you must know, and I don't want you getting caught up in anything stupid and bringing trouble to this house.'

'Well now, that's where you're mistaken, Da. Conor hasn't done any wrong.'

'Not according to what I hear. To be on the safe side, I'd prefer you didn't have anything to do with him, Louise. So pay heed.' At her angry tilt of the head, he added, 'It's for your own good, girl.'

'I don't believe this! You're warning me off a perfectly good, kind man because three cowardly thugs – hiding behind balaclavas, mind you – couldn't even get their facts straight and knocked the stuffing out of an innocent man? Where's your sense of fair play, eh, Da?'

'You watch your language, girl. He must be guilty of something. Those boys don't go round beating someone up for the fun of it. They always have had a very good reason. That much I do know.'

'You don't know what you're talking about. They got their wires crossed, so they did. I just hope they have the decency to admit it. Conor was looking out for me. That's how he came to get beaten up. His poor face is in a right mess and his kidneys are badly bruised. And all because he was trying to protect *me*.' Her fist thumped her chest and she repeated, '*Me!*'

Tommy looked at her in open-mouthed amazement. 'You? What on earth have you done that's so bad it warranted them 'uns to take notice?'

'Nothing, as it turns out. It was Cathie Morgan they intended making an example of. Not that she was doing anything so terrible. Just dating a Protestant. Conor happened to get in the way and all because he cares for me. You see, I had been out a couple of times with a Protestant and Conor thought that I was still seeing him. When he heard the rumours that we were being watched, he assumed it was me they were talking about. In spite of the trouble he knew he'd get into if they found out he was the one blowing the whistle on them, he followed me on Saturday night to tell me what was going on. And he had heard right. There were three lads, strangers, hanging about outside the pub watching Cathie getting picked up. I would've been in the car too if Conor hadn't turned up when he did and warned me off. The thugs must have twigged why Conor was talking to us. If he hadn't intervened God knows what would have happened. They might have followed us and maybe torched the car or something worse. Instead poor Conor fell foul of the cowardly bastards.'

'He should have known better than to interfere where those boys are concerned. That was only a warning he got. Next time it'll be much worse. Just stay away from him.'

'So you'd rather it had been me who got beat up? Is that what you mean?'

'I mean nothing of the sort. You've just said it wasn't you they were after. I do have to say, though, I thought that guy who was with Cathie the other night looked a bit shifty to me. Was he the Prod she was dating?'

'For heaven's sake, Da, catch yourself on. You're off your rocker, so you are. Brainwashed! Trevor doesn't look in the least bit shifty. Believe me, he's a really nice lad who'll make some girl a good husband one day. He just happens to be a Protestant but that's not his fault. You're too easily influenced if you listen to what amounts to slander. And you can't really mean that you don't mind if a young girl like Cathie gets beaten up. Besides, I would have been there too. We could have been seriously injured, if Conor hadn't intervened when he did.'

'Shifty or not, he's the one that's brought Conor O'Rourke under surveillance. And that's your fault for having anything to do with him in the first place. This Trevor fella shouldn't be up here sniffing around our girls. He should stick to his own kind. I advise you to stop seeing Conor O'Rourke. Do you hear me? In fact, if you're wise, you'll stay away from Cathie Morgan as well, seeing how she's risking her neck. She must have a death wish, that girl. That's my opinion. Keep well away from them!'

'I'm sorry, Da, but that's not possible. You see, Cathie happens to be my best friend, and no ignorant thugs are going to tell me who I can be friends with and who I can't. As for Conor O'Rourke, well he has, just this very evening, made me the happiest girl in Ireland by asking me to marry him and I've accepted his proposal.'

In her excitement at hearing this news, Peggy shot out of her chair like a rocket going off and with a squeal of delight threw herself at her sister, almost knocking her off the stool. Peggy grabbed hold of her to keep her from falling and clasped her close. 'That's wonderful news, sis. He's gorgeous, so he is. Oh, you don't know how lucky you are. You'll be the envy of every girl in the district. Can I be bridesmaid?'

Harry also rose to his feet and, roughly pushing Peggy aside, hugged Louise. 'Congratulations, Louise. I admire Conor. You couldn't do better. He's a smashing bloke.'

'Thanks, Peggy, Harry.' Louise eyed her father.

He returned the look, his own eyes filled with a great sadness. 'Ah, daughter, they've branded him an informer. You know what that means, don't you? They'll be watching him like a hawk. If he makes one wrong move they'll be on to him in a flash, so they will. Just you tell him to watch his back.'

Louise felt fear grip her at these words. 'But they're wrong, Da. Someone should point out to them how wrong they are,' she pleaded. 'Conor's the finest person I know. He doesn't deserve to be persecuted like this.'

'Just tell him to watch his back. That's all I'm saying.'

The meeting with her mother wasn't what Louise had hoped for. Nora was surprised to see her companion was Conor O'Rourke, but after a quick scrutiny of his battered face she squeezed his hand in a sympathetic gesture, nodded and smiled in acknowledgement of his greeting, and introduced Bill McCartney. Bill warmly shook the hand offered, and suggested that he and Conor should give the women some privacy to have a chat. When Louise, with a slight nod, gave her consent, Conor walked some distance away with him.

Mother and daughter eyed each other warily, and Louise felt her spirits plummet. Nora was pale and haggard and looked far older than her thirty-eight years. She guessed, by the defiant tilt to her mother's head and the glint in her eye, that she wasn't here to ask Louise to prepare the way for a homecoming. Louise prepared herself for battle.

Hoping she was wrong in her assumptions she trod cautiously. 'You don't look too good, Ma. I trust you're on the mend?'

'Yes, I'm fine now.'

'It appears to have taken a lot out of you, whatever it was. What was wrong with you?'

Nora squirmed as if in discomfort. 'I'm not quite sure.'

Daisy Hill was a popular meeting place for the youth of the district and the fine weather had brought them out in force.

'Let's walk, Louise. Find somewhere a bit more private.'

They fell into step and for the life of her Louise didn't know what to say. She covertly watched her mother from the corner of her eye and could see that she was also at a loss for words. Something was definitely troubling her.

Eventually, Nora broke the silence. 'How's things at home?'

'Why? Do you care?'

'Of course I do. You know I do. I worry particularly about Peggy. This must be having an awful effect on her. Her being the youngest. I dread to think what she must be thinking of me.'

Louise gave a harsh laugh. So, no how are *you* coping, Louise? Are you managing all right, love, without me? Did her mother ever give a thought to her older daughter's needs? Sadly Louise had to admit that her mother never had put her first. She was the one thrust into the mill. True, it had been a bad time with very little else available. But still, her mother hadn't considered the mill good enough for any of the others. Had refused to let them go there. So why her? Why sacrifice her?

To cover her hurt feelings, she rushed into conversation. 'You'll be glad to hear Peggy is doing well. She loves her job and she and Hannah McFadden are as thick as thieves now.'

Nora relaxed. She was smiling widely. 'Now that is good news. And Harry? What about him?'

'He's also coping all right. According to Peggy, he's taken a shine to Hannah and apparently Hannah likes him as well. Peggy's not too happy about it though, but I don't think she need worry. I'm inclined to think that Mr McFadden won't be over the moon about it either. I imagine he'll soon nip any romance in the bud, before it has a chance to blossom.'

This brought a light laugh from Nora. 'You can't imagine how relieved I am to hear all this. That everything's going on as normal. I don't feel so guilty about it now.'

Slanting a sideways glance at her, Louise said casually, 'How about *me*, Ma? Don't I count for anything?'

Nora rounded on her in astonishment. 'What makes you say that? Of course you count and you always have. I do realise, you know, that without you the others would be lost. I depend on you to look after them and keep the house going.'

'But what about *me personally*! Am I supposed to step into your shoes, take over the running of the house? Give up my personal life to look after the family you've walked out on? Is that what you mean? Is that the future you've mapped out for me, eh?'

'Ah, come on, Louise, love. You're more than capable of looking after the house. I wouldn't have left otherwise.'

'Just like I was tough enough for the mill? Is that it?'

Nora frowned. 'What's that got to do with it? I don't understand what you mean.'

'Forget it, Ma. I don't expect you to understand. But, you see, I'm afraid I can't take over your job as housekeeper and foster-mother. Conor O'Rourke has asked me to marry him, and I've said yes. So now that you've had your fling, it's your duty to come home and take over where you left off, caring for your family again.'

Nora stopped abruptly. Gripping Louise's arm, she swung her round and gazed entreatingly at her. 'I can't, Louise. I really can't.'

'You have to, Ma. There's no two ways about it. We can't carry on like this. We need you to take your proper place at home. And me da really has mellowed, honestly.' Louise didn't think for one moment that a smile and toasting a bit of bread really made a new man of her father, but he was trying and she was desperate to persuade her mother to come back.

Nora was looking at her with tears in her eyes. 'You don't understand. I really *can't* come home.' Her head dropped as if in shame and she said in a hushed voice, 'I'm expecting a baby.'

Louise felt her mouth gape open and snapped it shut. So that's the reason why she had been ill. Morning sickness! Huh! Didn't know what was wrong with her, indeed! She felt devastated; couldn't take it in. This was something that in her wildest dreams she'd never even contemplated. 'You can't be! You're too old,' she spluttered.

'That's what I thought . . . but I *am* pregnant.' At the

391

look of revulsion on her daughter's face Nora cried, 'Please be happy for me, love.'

'Happy? *Happy?*' She almost screamed the word. 'Do you think I'm daft or something? I'm ashamed, so I am. So ashamed of you. How can you do this to us?' All the scorn that Louise could muster was in those few words, and she turned on her heel and left her mother gazing after her in despair.

As she blundered down the hill, Louise's world came tumbling down round her. *A baby!* she kept repeating to herself. Who'd have thought it? This certainly changed everything. There was no way that her da would take her back now. No way under the sun. And she wouldn't blame him. His mates would have a field day. He'd never be able to face them again if he took his wife back and her carrying another man's child. Not that she thought for one minute that Bill McCartney would let her mother return. This secured his future with Nora. He must be in his glory! Had probably planned it this way, so that there would be no going back. The sly bastard!

A hand on her arm slowed her down, bringing her back to reality. Conor swung her into his arms and held her close. She buried her face against his chest and deep, raw sobs tore raggedly from her throat. He kept hold of her, letting her get rid of all the pent-up emotions, until she sagged exhausted against him. Thrusting a handkerchief at her, he gently questioned her. 'Hush, love. Calm down. Take a deep breath and tell me what happened that has you in such a state.'

She wiped her face and blew her nose on the handkerchief, and muttered bitterly, 'She's not coming back. She's *never* coming back.'

'Ah, now, we don't know that, love. Never's a long,

long time.' He was rocking her gently in his arms, as he would a child, offering consolation.

She thrust back from him and gazed up in despair. 'Oh, but we do know. Da will never take her back now. Not in a million years. She's expecting a baby!'

He felt as if all the wind had been knocked out of him. That certainly changed things. Surely Nora was too old? He voiced his thoughts. 'Isn't she too old to get pregnant?'

'Apparently not. And do you know what? She expects me to take over her place in the house. A glorified bloody housekeeper! That's me! Make sure Peggy and Harry don't suffer too much because of her selfishness and she won't have to feel so guilty.' Her voice became shrill. 'Did you ever hear anything like it, for God's sake?'

'She can't expect you to do that! You're only young yourself. You have your whole life ahead of you.'

'Nevertheless, she does. She says I'm quite capable of it. It was as if she was bestowing a great honour on me.' All the hurt at her mother's apparent callousness came across in these words.

'Ah, love. Ah, love, don't worry. We'll figure something out.' Conor hugged her close. He could barely control his anger. As far as he was concerned, this was the final straw. His mind was made up. Come what may, if he got good grades, in fact so long as he passed his exams, he'd marry Louise as soon as possible and take her across the water to Birmingham. To a better life. His father would be able to help him get a job and settle down over there. Look after Peggy and Harry, indeed! He couldn't get over it. As far as he was concerned the rest of the McGuigans could fend for themselves. As for his mother, well now, she was the fly in the ointment. What would he do about her?

* * *

Conor walked Louise to her house, and as they stood quietly talking outside the door opened and Tommy waved them in. Louise groaned and reluctantly preceded Conor into the hall. She was in no fit state for another confrontation tonight.

'Put the teapot on, Louise. I want a quiet word with this lad of yours.'

Louise shot Conor a warning glance. But then, he wasn't stupid. He'd know better than to mention anything to do with her mother. She went into the scullery and closed the door. Let them get on with it. Conor was one of the best. Let her da try to find fault with him. She would soon tell him where to get off.

She brewed the tea and loaded the tray, opened the door, and glanced into the kitchen.

They sat on either side of the range, Conor sitting upright listening intently, brow furrowed in concentration, her father leaning towards him arms on thighs, talking earnestly. Catching sight of her, Conor excused himself and came to her assistance. Carrying the tray into the kitchen, he placed it on the table.

'Your father has some good news, Louise. Tell her, Mr McGuigan, go on.'

Tommy unconsciously preened himself at Conor's obvious excitement and straightened in his chair. 'Down in the pub tonight I've been putting out some feelers, and those in the know have assured me it wasn't any of "the boys" who ordered that Conor be given a *warning*, as they put it. In fact, they're doing all in their power to find out who's putting it about that they're the culprits. Who's using their name as a cover for their own foul deeds. I wouldn't like to be in their shoes when they're found out. And believe me, they will be found out!'

'Oh, I think that's wonderful news, Da.' Going to

Conor, Louise put her arms round him. 'At least *they* know the truth now and won't be watching you any more, love.' She turned to her father and said humbly, 'Thanks, Da. You can't know how relieved I am to hear that. Have they any idea who's behind it?'

He shook his head. 'This guy I was talking to just knows that none of the lads were involved. I've been asking Conor if he knows of anybody who has a grudge against him, but he can't think of anyone.'

Liam Gilmore immediately leapt to Louise's mind and her eyes locked with Conor's. She realised that he also had Liam in mind, but she managed to curb her tongue. She didn't want her father to upbraid Mary the next chance he got. It had nothing to do with her. But to Louise's way of thinking, if it was Liam, he mustn't get away with it or he might be tempted to try it again. Maybe herself next time. She shuddered as she recalled just what Liam Gilmore was capable of and vowed to have a quiet word with Johnnie.

At the sounds of Harry and Peggy outside the door, Tommy put a finger to his lips. 'Mum's the word,' he warned them. 'This guy was talking to me in confidence. You know what I mean.'

Louise went to work next morning with a heavy heart. She was bitter and angry at her mother for putting her through this latest trauma. Still, Conor was in the clear and that's what mattered most. It was her da she had to thank for that.

At lunchtime Johnnie had obviously been on the lookout for her, and crossing over from the shop when he saw her coming down Springfield Road he said, 'I called over last night about nine, to avoid me da, but no one was home. How are things?'

'The house was empty because Conor and I were out on a mission and the other two were up at Hannah's as usual. We met Ma and his lordship, Bill McCartney, over on Daisy Hill last night.'

Running these words across his mind, Johnnie asked tentatively, 'You and Conor O'Rourke?'

Louise smiled. 'Yes, me and Conor. Ah, Johnnie, I could write a book on the state of our sorry affairs. But I haven't time to explain it all now. Suffice to say Ma is definitely not coming back. She's pregnant.'

She watched his face as this information sank in, saw him turn a little paler and his eyes widen before he gasped, 'She can't be!'

'She says she is, and somehow or other I don't think she was joking.'

Johnnie was gobsmacked. His mother and wife expecting babies at the same time? An uncle or aunt younger than his child? It was preposterous.

'Look, Johnnie, I've things to do during my break. We'll talk about this some other time. OK?'

'Come over tonight and bring Conor with you. Seems he's back in your good books again, eh?' An eyebrow was raised in query.

'He is, thank God! And we'd love to come over, thank you. Is around eight o'clock all right with you?'

He nodded in agreement and she hurried off. He watched her out of sight before retracing his steps, his mind in a whirl. He was glad that Conor was back in the picture. Louise would be a lot happier now. His mind baulked at the news that his mother was pregnant. Wait until Mary heard about it tonight. He couldn't take in the enormity of it. A new wee half-brother or sister?

*　*　*

Mary was at the sink straining the potatoes when he came home at teatime. She received his news in silence. 'Well, aren't you going to say anything? Like "I don't believe you"?'

She shrugged. 'Why should I doubt you? It does happen, you know. What's done is done. It won't really make any difference to us, but your Louise must be in an awful state over it.'

'She is . . . and what do you think? Conor O'Rourke and her are friends again. That'll help soften the blow. I've asked them over tonight.'

Mary turned a stricken face towards him. 'You've what?'

'I've asked . . .' His voice trailed off. 'What's wrong now, for heaven's sake?'

'Our Liam's upstairs. Him and his two mates were attacked on their way home from work. He's in a bad way so he is, but refuses to go to the hospital. And he's afraid to go home. He fears me da more than the ones that beat him up. I told him he could stay here for a night or two, give me da a chance to come to terms with it before he sees him.'

Johnnie sagged against the worktop. 'Who did it?'

She tutted in exasperation. 'Use your brains, Johnnie. Who do you think?'

His mind had blanked out at her revelation. Now it surged back to life. 'It was him, wasn't it? He was one of those three brave fellas that beat up Conor O'Rourke.' His face twisted with fury. 'Well, he deserves everything he got! I hope he's even worse than Conor is. And by God he's not staying in my house hiding away from your father, the cowardly brute. He'll face the music like everybody else has to. It just might make a man of him.'

He was in the hall, one foot on the stair, when her

raised voice stopped him. 'Unfortunately, he is my brother and this is *my* house too, remember.'

'He's not staying here, Mary. I can't possibly allow him to stay under my roof after all he's done. He's one troublemaker, that one. You don't know the half of it.'

'Our roof, Johnnie. Remember it's *our* roof. Don't ask me to take sides. I just can't throw him out.' She was on the verge of tears. 'He's my brother, for goodness' sake!'

Johnnie realised her predicament and, going to her, took her in his arms. 'It's all right. It's all right, love. I'll go over and tell Louise not to come tonight. But . . . I want him out of here as soon as possible. OK?'

'All right. And thanks, Johnnie. What about your dinner? It's almost ready.'

'Put it in the oven. I won't be too long.'

Crossing the road Johnnie walked slowly down Springview Street. He approached his father's house with trepidation. He realised he should have waited until later when he could be sure that his father would be out. However, he couldn't come to terms with the idea of Liam Gilmore upstairs in his bed and he had to get away from the house. He wanted to drag his brother-in-law down the stairs by the scruff of the neck and throw him out on the street, maybe even add a punch or two of his own for good measure, but he *was* Mary's brother and he didn't want her upset any more than was necessary. There was the baby to think about.

Facing his da had seemed the lesser of two evils. Now he wasn't so sure. He didn't want to set his da off, but he needed to talk to Louise; put her off bringing Conor over to his house. That would be adding insult to injury. In the hall he paused. He could hear voices and recognised his father's among them. Wanting to get it over with before he could renege, he tapped on the vestibule door and, drawing a deep breath, thrust it open.

They were all there. Tommy and Harry still sat at the table. His sisters were on their way to the scullery carrying the dirty dishes. All heads turned in his direction, different expressions on each face.

Unable to believe his eyes, Tommy rose to his feet, outraged at the cheek of his elder son. 'I thought I told you never to come back here,' he growled.

'Hold your horses, Da. I need to speak to Louise.' Not wanting to get into an argument with him, Johnnie retreated outside again.

Seeing the state he was in, Louise set the dishes down on the table. 'Look after those, Peggy. I won't be long.' Reaching for her coat she followed her brother out of the door.

Johnnie was leaning against the window sill looking dejected when she joined him.

'What's the matter, Johnnie?'

'Liam Gilmore was beaten up today and he's in *my* house. Lying in *my* bed.' He shook his head as if to clear it. 'I can't believe that I didn't throw the bastard out.'

Louise gave a snort of delight. 'Ah ha, so they found out who did it. I can't tell you how happy that makes me.'

'What do you mean?'

'Me da heard that the boys were trying to find out who had attacked Conor, and were letting them take the blame for something they didn't do. Since it wasn't them, there was no way they were going to sit on their backsides and do nothing about it. Liam and his mates got what was coming to them. They'll think twice before doing anything like that again.'

'I guessed that was the reason, the attack on Conor. I feel awful for not throwing him out . . . but he's afraid to go home and Mary couldn't turn her own brother away, bad and all as he is.'

'He can't be all that badly injured or he'd be in hospital.'

'I haven't seen him yet, but Mary says he's in a bad way. He wouldn't go to the hospital and he's terrified of his da.' He smiled wryly. 'I suppose he's afraid his da will give him another good hiding. Mr Gilmore doesn't say much, but I think he knows that his son is one bad apple.'

'Well, you go on home to your wife and reassure her that there are no hard feelings on my part. Not now that Liam's got his just deserts.'

'You won't come over tonight, then?'

'No, I don't think that would be a good idea. Some other time when this has blown over.'

'Thanks, sis. I'll be in touch.'

Johnnie didn't feel ready to face his wife yet. It was going to be an ordeal, watching Liam Gilmore making himself at home in their house, and he needed to get into the right frame of mind to handle the situation. His steps led him aimlessly up Springfield Road and he calmed down a bit when he left the houses behind and hedgerows took their place. It was cool and peaceful and he was surprised when he found himself at the foot of the mountain loney. He continued on for some distance, but before long the sight of the young courting couples interested in no one but themselves was making him regretful. This is how Mary and he should have been enjoying a courtship, with marriage ahead of them. Instead they'd let curiosity get the better of them and fumbled about until she had become pregnant. At least they were getting a second chance to make a go of it, and for that he was grateful.

Resolutely, he retraced his steps and headed for home.

Still some distance up Springfield Road he saw Mr and Mrs Gilmore approach and turn down Violet Street. That could mean only one thing: they had heard about Liam and where he was hiding and had come to take him home. His step quickened. He must be there to support his wife and make sure there were no ructions in his house. He'd be glad to get rid of Liam, but quietly. After all, it was a respectable street and they planned to live here. They'd just moved in and he didn't want to upset their neighbours with an out and out slanging match for all to hear. He speeded up still more and reached the house on his in-laws' heels. Greeting them quietly, he unlocked the door and motioned them inside.

Liam was at the table, trying to eat through lips that were swollen and split. He rose in a panic when he saw his parents. With a whimper of pity, Sadie hastened to him and gathered him close.

Johnnie saw that he was indeed in worse shape than Conor had been. One arm was clasped to his body as if his ribs were broken and both eyes were discoloured and beginning to swell. Mike was grim-faced. 'If you weren't such a sorry sight I'd give you another hiding myself. You've brought shame on us, and by God, one way or another you'll pay for it. Now get your coat till we get you home.' He turned to Johnnie and shrugged. 'I'm sorry about this, Johnnie. What else can I say?'

'It's all right, Mike. You've just said it all. But I think you'd be as well taking him to the hospital. He doesn't look too good to me.'

'Aye, you're right. We'll take him straight to the Royal and get him checked over.'

Mary and her mother placed Liam's jacket loosely round his shoulders, and with a shamefaced nod at Johnnie he allowed himself to be led away.

401

'I'll try to make this up to you,' Mike vowed. 'I convinced myself he wasn't capable of such a cowardly act. How mistaken can one be.'

'Don't worry about it. You did no wrong. Come back soon.'

Farewells over, they took their leave, and Mary looked sheepishly at her husband. 'I'm sorry, but I had to take him in.'

'Of course you did. He is your brother, after all. Now let's forget all about it. And do you know something, love? I'm starving.'

'I love you, Johnnie McGuigan. More than you'll ever know. Sit yourself down and I'll lift your dinner.'

Louise couldn't hide her delight and everybody paused in what they were doing when she came back into the house.

It was Harry who spoke. 'What are you looking so pleased about, sis?'

Ignoring him, Louise went to her father and laid a hand on his shoulder. 'You were right, Da. They found out who attacked Conor. Johnny just told me.'

'I'm relieved to hear it. That *is* good news. Did he say who they were?'

Pulling a stool over close to his chair, Louise sat down and placed a hand on his arm. 'Da, I know you and Johnnie are at loggerheads at the moment, but I ask you to be patient and hear me out.'

Tommy was puzzled. 'What're you talking about? What has Johnnie got to do with it?'

'Liam Gilmore was one of those involved in the attack on Conor.' Her hold on his arm tightened when she felt him tense and she held his eye, silently pleading with him to be understanding before adding, 'Don't take it out on Mary. Sure you won't? She really is a decent, kind girl and her and Johnnie are now in a position to make a good life together with your grandchild. Don't drive him further away because of something that he has no control over.'

She had heard Harry and Peggy both gasp at her revelation, but now, as she paused to let it sink in, so profound was the silence that if a pin had dropped it would have made a clatter.

Tommy slumped in his chair. 'Louise, I was just trying to help Johnnie, ye know. I thought he was too young to be tied down in married life. I wanted to give him a way out if he wanted to take it, but he spurned my efforts and I admit I was annoyed at the time. Then before I could do anything about it, it had all spiralled out of control.'

'You should have swallowed your pride and come to the wedding, you know,' she gently chastised him. 'That would've been the Christian thing to do. Support Ma, even if you weren't on speaking terms with Johnnie.'

'I know that now. But at the time I felt too ashamed. I felt that I must show my true feelings. Stand up for what I thought was the right thing to do. I wanted to stop the wedding but Nora gave *her* consent.'

Surprised that her father was agreeing with her, Louise controlled her emotions. With a bit of care here, perhaps she could mend some bridges. Her da was going to need them all behind him when he heard that his wife was pregnant by another man. The scandal was going to be horrendous. The family would have to join forces and weather the storm.

She glanced at the other two. 'Could you two make yourselves scarce? I want to talk to me da in private.'

Peggy opened her mouth to protest, but Harry, grabbing her coat off the rack, thrust it at her and bundled her towards the door. 'When you're finished here, you go ahead and get ready to meet Conor, Louise. We'll do the dishes when we get back.' He stifled another protest from Peggy with an angry glare and, opening the door, pushed her outside.

Louise flashed him a look of gratitude. This young brother of hers was growing up into a fine, compassionate, understanding young man. Maybe there was hope for him and Hannah. Surely Mr McFadden couldn't fail to see the good qualities in him, if, as Peggy intimated, Hannah also liked him. 'Thanks, Harry.'

When the door closed on them, she shut her eyes and tried to work out the kindest way to tell her father the bad news. She delayed so long, he prompted her. 'You wanted to have a word with me about something?'

Still the words wouldn't come and he unwittingly opened an avenue for her. Sounding apprehensive, he said, 'Are you trying to tell me you're pregnant? Is that it?'

She was offended and showed it. 'No! No, indeed I am not! Conor has vowed that he will never lay a wrong finger on me. We will wait till we're married, so we will, and not be living in sin like some. There'll be no shotguns on display at our wedding, you can bet your life on that.'

He smiled at the vehemence in her voice. 'Well, I'm sure glad to hear it. So what are you finding so hard to tell me?'

Her fingers tightened on his arm, and she quietly confessed, 'I'm not the one who's pregnant.'

She watched closely and could almost read his thoughts. Surely not Peggy? Then the penny dropped. '*Nora's* expecting a baby?' The horror came across in his voice.

Louise nodded and waited for the explosion. She hadn't

long to wait. Tommy shot up from his chair and stamped back and forth across the restricted width of the kitchen, ranting and raving and swearing like a trooper, threatening all kinds of revenge on Bill McCartney. Poor Louise sat looking on with horror. She couldn't believe the expletives spewing from her father's mouth. She trembled with trepidation as she readied herself to make a dash to the door in case he vented his spleen on her. However, her fear was unfounded and her father's anger subsided after what seemed like hours of cursing Bill McCartney, when just as quickly as the tirade had started he suddenly went very quiet and slumped down on his chair, his chin resting on his heaving chest. Once again he surprised her. 'I must say I'm devastated,' he mumbled in a muted voice. 'I had hoped that if I made a bigger effort, showed willing, Nora would come back. I've even been saving up to take her on a holiday, make a fresh start, when she came home.' He lifted his head and gave Louise a wry smile. 'I can just picture what she'd say if she knew. "Too little, too late, Tommy boy," and I can't say I blame her. I've only myself to point the finger at. You know, I've been doing some hard thinking this past few days, and I realise what a blind fool I've been. It's all been my fault, all of it. And I'm going to show you all I'm sorry.'

Louise was overwhelmed with bitterness. Why hadn't he told his wife how he felt, then; made a bigger effort at a reconciliation? A tear rolled down his cheek and she was aghast, her bitterness washed away by his grief. Hard man Tommy McGuigan actually crying? As if reading her thoughts he brushed it roughly away and said abruptly, 'We'll manage without her. Won't we? You won't leave me, Louise, will you? I promise to be a different man and pull my weight in this house.'

Overcome with pity, Louise found herself agreeing with

him. 'Of course we'll manage. I won't be able to afford to get married for a couple of years, so I'll be here for a while. Conor won't mind helping out so long as you prove willing and agreeable. All right?'

His hand covered hers. 'Thanks, and I'll be behind you every step of the way, Louise. I'll do all I can to give you the best wedding ever. That's a promise.'

Louise wanted to weep at the misery she felt radiating from him, but she smiled brightly and threatened him, 'It's a promise you'd better keep.'

She closed her eyes to hide the pity she knew he wouldn't want. Perhaps life in Springview Street wouldn't be so bad after all.

Other bestselling titles available by mail:

☐ For Better, For Worse	Mary A. Larkin	£6.99
☐ Ties of Love and Hate	Mary A. Larkin	£7.99
☐ Best Laid Plans	Mary A. Larkin	£5.99
☐ Sworn to Secrecy	Mary A. Larkin	£6.99

──────────── sphere ────────────

Please allow for postage and packing: **Free UK delivery.**
Europe; add 25% of retail price; Rest of World; 45% of retail price.

To order any of the above or any other Sphere titles, please call our credit card orderline or fill in this coupon and send/fax it to:

Sphere, P.O. Box 121, Kettering, Northants NN14 4ZQ
Fax: 01832 733076   Tel: 01832 737526
Email: aspenhouse@FSBDial.co.uk

☐ I enclose a UK bank cheque made payable to Sphere for £ . . . .
☐ Please charge £ . . . . . . to my Visa, Delta, Maestro.

Expiry Date ☐☐☐☐   Maestro Issue No. ☐☐

NAME (BLOCK LETTERS please) . . . .

ADDRESS . . . .

. . . .

. . . .

Postcode . . . . Telephone . . . .

Signature . . . .

Please allow 28 days for delivery within the UK. Offer subject to price and availability.